Praise for

The Riven Country of Senga Munro

and The Riven Country Series

"A riveting debut. . . In Carrier's debut novel, the first in **The Riven Country Series***, the old folks of rural Wyoming and magical realism color a tale of family tragedy, regret, resilience, and long-lasting friendships. Carrier deftly uses the protagonist's backstory to heighten the drama, and her prose is both crisp and engrossing. She juggles the shifts from the backstory to present-day time period and vice versa with the surety of an experienced author. Her characterization is top-notch: Senga's resilience and strong will make her readers' favorite immediately, and the touch of magical realism add to the intrigue of the story. The intriguing finale leaves the reader eager for the next installment. A thoroughly enjoyable literary tale!"*
~Prairies Book Review

"What a lovely book. I was looking for something to help pass some cold winter evenings. Happily, I found this one. I thoroughly enjoyed it and recommend it to anyone looking for a good read. I'm always on the look-out for a worthy book series, so it's auspicious that these characters and story line will continue in the author's next novel." ~Linda Hughes, Nebraska

"An Excellent Beginning to an Excellent Story! I first curled up with The Riven Country of Senga Munro *knowing I had only a few minutes of reading time, but I was curious. I found it easy to return to Senga's story, hard to lose my place with her characters because author Renée Carrier shares characters she knows very, very well. I love a book with this quality!" ~A.M. Hummel, Wyoming*

"The Riven Country of Senga Munro *is an excellent read. Carrier is a Michelangelo of words as she paints a vivid picture of the land and characters. Having read descriptions of the characters, one has the feeling of being there and identifying with the characters' personalities. I was* mesmerized by the main character, Senga Munro, an absolutely extraordinary woman. She is a healer and knows about medicinal herbs and tinctures, and has a good sense of sizing up people. The book makes you want to have coffee in Caro's kitchen, help neighbors with chores, and have long conversations with a monk. Senga goes through a lot of good and bad and shows so much moxie. She indeed has a Ph.D. in life. It will be exciting to read the next book in the series."

~Laura Jones, South Carolina

"Renée is truly a gifted storyteller, and in The Riven County of Senga Munro she brings you along on a tale that becomes personal to each reader in ways hard to explain. The characters are like old friends and relations, and you find yourself wondering what they are doing while you read about someone else. Renée writes easily of emotions and frailties, guilt and forgiveness, happiness and grief.

And oh yes, there is quite a story going on at the same time. A wonderful read, one you're sorry to come to the end, but . . . it's a series!"

~Kevin Sweeney, Pinehurst, NC.

"Renée Carrier's novel, The Riven Country of Senga Munro, draws upon elements found in both the rough magic of North Carolina's mountainous back-of-beyond and Wyoming's tough and tender landscapes. Carrier has created a character who can stand her ground among some of literature's iconic women. The novel is to be treasured in so many ways, all of them well worth getting to know better."

~Morgan Callan Rogers, Red Ruby Heart in a Cold Blue Sea. Maine

"Renée Carrier's writing creates a rumble in the heart. It's not like any style of writing I've seen. The phrasing is totally unique. It's like poetry. . . A considerable accomplishment and a gift. A story peopled with whole souls; big lives lived small, made big by attention to detail. Sensual, intimate and wise...a meditation on spiritual magic and so much kindness, matter-of-fact kindness, fully expressed. In fact, all the relationships feel intensely connected...the way we are."

~Linda Spears, Georgia, Television and Film Production Sound Recorder

"Captivating read. I loved this book and look forward to the next one in the series! This story speaks to me on so many levels: from the simplicity *of the lifestyle in the hills of Carolina or Wyoming, the lovable quirkiness of the characters, the herbal remedies, and the mysticism laced throughout while dealing with a heart-rendering tragedy. Love strong women, and caring, strong yet gentle men!" ~Cindy,*

"5.0 out of 5 stars. An absolute triumph and must read!!"

"Renée Carrier's debut novel, The Riven Country of Senga Munro, *graced me with a new heroine in my life: Senga, the herbalist whose experiences in tragedy fuel her survival and independence. What results is an emotional and thoroughly enjoyable, heartfelt story of independence, friendship, loyalty, loss and love.*

Making her home in the rural Black Hills of Wyoming, Senga's intuition, healing talent, compassion, and loyalty earned my avid trust almost immediately; I couldn't get enough of her ability to find strength in her unfortunate suffering. Carrier masterfully weaves the poignant events in the lives of Senga's close friends and family; a talent crafted in such a way to garner my heartfelt respect and admiration - both for author and characters.

Senga became a trusted and loved friend through Carrier's tale. The more complicated foes in the area - individuals carrying the heart-wrenching burden of hate for all those who would be different - successfully drummed-up my ire, contempt and anguish. My emotions truly ran the gamut while experiencing Senga's life story. I recall silently cheering while riding the emotional wave as Senga reconnected with Sebastian, a first-person witness to her tragedy. A truly magnificent debut, this spellbinding story is absolutely wonderful, and left me immediately hungry for a sequel!!!"

~Joe G., Washington

STARWALLOW

Renée Carrier

Cover image by Candace Christofferson

Braeburn Croft
Hulett, Wyoming

For AdriAnne and John

STARWALLOW

PART ONE

A s can happen when tides turn, life had changed appreciably. At least for the duration, she reasoned. The night before, as her lover traversed her own peaks and chasms, she considered her human topography. He was a Danish photographer who had named her "the riven country of Senga."

In one photo of his new photograph series, she will stretch across a stately sideboard to wind an old clock. *Tick-tock,* it will greet her evenly, even playfully, as she adjusts her studied stance to instruction. A Yin-Yang pendulum—a disequilibrium of two legs in motion. Or, when negotiating stilts—as privileged view from above demands. And after, swaying her hips in quick rhythm to the mechanism, she will turn only her face to him.

"Senga, no-o-o!" he will beg. "You must be still, my dear, and look not at me! Look at the face of the clock—" And so she shall, her expression intent on her objective of pleasing him; of intently twisting the smooth metal key clockwise in a round aperture, of which there are two: one for the chime, another for the timing gear. Her interest in the workings of the old timepiece (with French, silk-thread escapement, he'll explain) will distract from the singular intelligence that she wears nothing.

The lovers will make their photos for another two hours, until winter sunlight fails to provide. And then, they will make love.

Her first lover—and father of her child (not to be parenthesized)—composed a song for her. A singer, he'd traveled through time in her mind, by conveyance of unheard (as yet) lyrics and melody. Music is nothing if not a journey, she believed. Still trapped inside a cellophane-wrapped package in her two-room cabin near the Wyoming border, the piece awaited

1

attention and ears. She'd noted the title: "Nothing's Lost, Nothing's Wasted; For Emily and Senga."

Had she been a writer of songs, her own lyrics might have read:

When I was seventeen and pregnant,
I ran away to sea,
With the father of my baby,
I ran away to sea.
With no notion, Wyoming's ocean
(I ran away to sea)
Had long been high and dry, and . . .
  I'm still away at sea.

Without my baby . . . she tagged on. It was, in most respects, the One Thing underscoring her existence. Her Soil. Like the Very Earth.

It was the Very Earth . . .

. . . Three bright tings! and I woke. The clock on the sideboard. I tip-toed from the bedroom loft, where Sebastian slept, to the chair that belonged to his late Aunt Karen. Feminine contours and silk fabric play grace-notes to enliven such an hour. The fire beside me (and within) smolders in the blue-and-white ceramic stove. Having been banked for the night, I hear its soft shushing and pitch-spitting noises through the glass. Wakeful, welcome company on a cold night.

Aunt Karen's silk dressing gown felt inadequate against the seeping chill of the tall windows, however curtained-off from the winter storm. I've borrowed the magenta mohair throw from the sofa. It warms my shoulders.

On a far shore, this unexpected landfall of me (minus the salty detritus and noise of life) feels lovingly gathered up, sorted and drawn into a protected cove. I am found; I am salvaged; I, Senga Munro, am made useful once again, in the remedial vocabulary of my grandmother.

A life of the spirit demands spirit, dearie, and not only bread and water.
She'd have paraphrased her own savior.

As driftage, I survived on bread and water for too long . . .

CHAPTER 1
FIRST, DO NO HARM

Northern Black Hills, Late October

S enga Munro pulled into the last parking space on the busy Spearfish block. None were available near the health food store, where she was to lead the herbal workshop. She sat a moment to collect herself and asked Grannie to help her be clear. Then, she opened the door, stepped out and walked to the passenger side for two sacks of materials. Two more remained. She lifted her face to the source of heat.

The sun shone brightly over the Northern Hills, as it did most days. Patches of snow still lay on north slopes and drifting in ravines, like melting ice cream. Damaged from the recent blizzard, crowns of trees resembled jagged palisades, or worse: broken teeth.

"Good morning, Senga," the petite, older woman called when she entered the store. "Roads good? And your hair! It must grow quickly. Guess I haven't seen you in a while," she said. "Whatever herbs you've been taking—they're working. You look radiant! As fit as when we first met. . . How long's it been?"

Senga made a rapid appraisal of her own appearance, which rarely changed, save the length of her hair and its shade at the crown.

"Hi, Marie . . . and thanks. . . You're sweet. Um, it's been about twenty-five years; the roads are fine and, yes, it's been too

3

long . . ." she replied, as she held the door open to slide in another bag. "And, you're never in when I come."

"Have more to bring in?"

"Yes. Let me put these on the table. Can you help?" She smelled something baking—and cinnamon hot apple cider. Coffee. All competing for her senses.

"Of course—here, let me take that," Marie replied. "We're expecting a good turn-out, with two more coming at 11:00."

"Well, good. I'm looking forward to this. And, I have a friend stopping by later. He's not attending the workshop . . . just wanted to have a peek, I think."

"Sebastian Hansen."

"Ah—yes. . . You know him?" Senga asked, eyebrows arched.

"Betty, at the gallery, has pretty much canonized the man," Marie said, while lifting one of Senga's canvas bags onto the table.

"Careful!" warned Senga. "There's a bottle of vodka in there, and jars. . ."

"Yes, I hear them. *Mm* . . . I heard what happened at the gallery—I mean, about the photograph and all." Marie paused and turned to Senga, her warm brown eyes wide with concern. "How *are* you? That must have been hard."

"Oh, Betty. . . No, it's all right, Marie. She worries, you know. I wasn't prepared is all. . . And Sebastian? *Sainthood?* Betty's a stark raving romantic. But it's good he's coming by—to see what I'm, um, about." *I'm the raving romantic*, she realized.

Ignoring Marie's questioning look, she asked instead, "Have you . . . seen the photographs? The falls isn't hanging anymore. He took it down. For me. It's under my bed for now."

"Yes, I saw them. They're astonishing. And, so is *he*, by the way." With this last word, Marie grinned and stepped to the door and waited for Senga, who smiled shyly. *Yes. He is.* . . She pictured his naked back as he'd shaved this morning; the lighting, the curve of his backbone as he leaned into the mirror to reach the side of his face; his sheepish grin when he caught her watching.

The women walked down the block to Senga's old Honda hatchback.

She was a simpler. An herbalist who mainly uses one herb (a *simple*) at a time to make remedies. In her late Grannie Cowry's fashion, Senga spoke to plants and listened for their preferences: when to harvest, what part to harvest and, to note where they grew. She experimented with how much to use. The plants offered solace, beauty and healing. In Senga's case, friendship.

Her daughter Emily had died nineteen years ago. Having slipped on wet stones beside a high waterfall, hidden deep in Spearfish Canyon, she'd fallen off the earth. She was nine years old. Senga had watched helplessly.

Born forty-seven years ago, she was raised in the highlands of North Carolina. Named after two grandmothers, Agnes and Maria Teresa, she changed her name to "Senga," reversing the letters, after her Grannie died. Senga, and Emily's father, Rob McGhee, a musician, moved to rural Sara's Springs, Wyoming, in the Black Hills. Rob eventually left, not finding enough work in the sparsely populated area.

They never married. Senga managed.

She found work in the local library and accepted several herbal clients. Workshops and regional weed-walks augmented her small income. While his daughter still lived, Rob sent money from the road. After Emily's death, Senga moved to the country. She was frugal.

Sebastian Hansen and his father were on holiday from Denmark when they witnessed Emily's fall. The younger man was holding the child's lifeless body when Senga reached the bottom of the cliff. He had made photographs of the falls and canyon stream before returning to Copenhagen, and every day since, Sebastian had told her, he'd pondered the tragedy. These were the images Senga happened to see when she visited the gallery two weeks ago. He had only recently returned to the area.

Through time and space, suffering expressed and grieving received, they had met again. Sebastian could hold it. As a crucible might. And allow it to burn. Now, this burning was reserved for Senga. She would tolerate interest from Marie or Betty for being sure of Sebastian's love and, more important, the certainty of her own.

Focus! Senga reminded herself as she unpacked the sacks. Marie brought over an easel and a large tablet of newsprint. She placed four color markers on the table.

Senga arranged a stack of herbals, some recently published and several old stand-bys: *Common Herbs for Natural Health*, by Juliette de Bairacli Levy; *Healing Wise*, by Susun Weed; *The Healing Herbs*, by Michael Castleman among others. Also, baby food jars, dropper bottles, masking tape and several Sharpies; a bottle of cider vinegar, one of olive oil and the vodka—100 proof for tincturing. And finally, two-quart jars of linden flower infusion to share. Her materials in order, she took a deep breath and let it out slowly.

"There's time for a *cuppa* tea if you'd like," Marie offered.

"Coffee?" She and Sebastian had talked late into the night at his home, and she felt less alert than she wished to be.

He lived on the outskirts of town, in his aunt and uncle's extraordinary hand-made home, now his. Uncle Harold had died years ago; Aunt Karen in mid-summer of this year. Sebastian had resolved to spend part of his year at work in the Hills and the balance in Copenhagen, his home and where his daughter, granddaughter and son-in-law lived. He needed to return to Denmark soon to attend to matters, professional and personal. His family planned to return with him in time to observe the twin feasts of Winter Solstice and Yule. Senga would then meet them. She felt strangely at peace with the prospect. Sebastian's wife, Elsa, had died the year before Emily.

"Come to the break room—that's where we've set up for lunch," Marie broke into her day dream. "There's cream and sugar beside the carafe."

The store offered the meal with the cost of the workshop.

"Oh, thank you. . ." Senga followed the woman to the counter where she unscrewed the carafe's lid to pour the proffered cup. "I think I'm ready. So, how many do you think?" she asked.

The store would be open for business as usual, and a few customers would likely be drawn to the talk and demonstration. The workshop's fee included handouts and samples of remedies.

Senga lived sixty-some miles away, in the Wyoming Black Hills. In a hunting cabin built for one. With a *near*-ample-for-two double bed. Her walnut table could accommodate four chairs, two of which were normally placed elsewhere. If three were meant for society, then four invited revelry, she reasoned. Six? It'd be tight.

Of late, Senga had learned the singular delight of cooking for friends. She'd lived a solitary simpler.

Marie answered with a scrunched-up face. "Hard to say, but seventeen signed up. . . That's good for around here."

Senga brought her attention back, the coffee assisting her concentration. "All right. I'm going to sit a bit, Marie."

"Tony made some honey flaxseed cookies for later . . . want one?" She held out the plate.

"Yes!" The cookie was still warm and, settling into a chair, she savored the unexpected treat and the cup of good coffee. *Ah, the simple joys.*

Scanning the seated attendees, she recognized a young woman who'd attended a foraging walk. Senga's smile was returned.

"Good morning, everyone, and thank you for coming. My name is Senga Munro. I'm an herbalist. A simpler—meaning one herb at a time. I'm sorry to repeat myself to those of you who've attended previous workshops. Bear with me, please.

"I was taught by my Grannie in western North Carolina. She was a midwife and healer, used the old remedies, but she conferred with the clinics on a regular basis. They could do that then, there in the mountains. . .

"My great-great grandmother was Cherokee. Our knowledge—or *notions*, as Grannie called them—was passed down for generations. Except for my own mother, we have all been healers, though she healed herself before she died." *Hmm, I've never thought of that . . . but of course she did. . .* Senga paused and considered: *Lily of the Valley—for happiness. Yes.* Senga remembered, and gave her head a single nod to the left.

"I hope to pass on some plant wisdom as well, so I am especially grateful you're here. Marie sells many of the herbs, dried, that I'll discuss, though I prefer to gather them fresh, when possible. I do make herbal infusions with dried material, and I've brought one for you to try. I'll describe wildcrafting, or foraging, as it's popularly called. People have always foraged, you know . . . so this is 'People's Medicine'—what many contemporary herbalists consider the age-old practice, and so do I, yet I'm required to spell out caveats and disclaimers so's not to offend the, um, authorities."

Here Senga looked at her audience to gauge their response, to see if they apprehended properly.

"Practicing medicine without a license is against the law. For good reason. Think about it. Use your common sense here, people. But I do have a question for you to consider; don't answer yet. . . Is pregnancy a disease? This is one instance where I differ with the law."

The women had thoughtful looks on their faces. The three men in attendance sported blank expressions. Senga's usual piece of advice, her disclaimer, guided clients or students to seek the best medical resources available. She suggested that health is a continuum, and there exist myriad possible remedies between doing nothing, "sometimes the best solution" and, draconian measures, which include surgery; in cases of trauma, it is often the best, and only, option.

"These workshops are meant to be educational and informative, and I always begin an herbal teaching with the familiar phrase, 'First, do no harm,' adding, '*and* ask permission.'" Senga wrote this on the tablet in large letters.

"The first is self-evident; then seek permission from the plant you're taking from the Earth. Even if it's from a garden you've planted. It's only polite. . . And third?" She wrote, "*We are already whole. Always,*" repeating it. "Fourth, the practice of herbal medicine is about *relationship,*" printing the word in large letters, ". . . which we'll discuss later. These I'd have you remember if you forgot everything else."

The attendees exchanged glances and some shifted in their chairs. Several took notes.

"Important, too: Know where an herb might be contraindicated with certain drugs, especially those you might be prescribed or, perhaps your family members. This point in itself shows how powerful an herb can be. For example, if you take medication for low thyroid, you'll want to limit lemon balm because it can interfere with the absorption of your thyroid hormone. So read your tea labels carefully. Ask yourself if a benefit outweighs the cost. Now, lemon balm smells lovely and tossed into a hot bath as a sachet, or infused in a facial steam are good ways to enjoy its benefits, as a calmative."

Someone raised their hand.

"Yes?"

"I've heard you shouldn't take St. John's Wort if you're on anti-depressants."

"What's your name, please?"

"Jenny."

"Thanks for the question, Jenny, and please, if anyone has a question or comment, jump in. It's simplest. And yes, Jenny, St. John's Wort—or *Hypericum perforatum*—is contraindicated with some MAO inhibitors and SSRIs, mainly because it may increase that action.

"I, quote, *take* St. John's Wort tincture alone—against mild depression. Have for years. I gather it near here, actually. We 'take' our herbs, just as we 'take' exercise, or 'take' the waters or the air, as they used to say. It's a prescriptive term. . . Here—" Senga reached for a small amber bottle. "I brought some of my tincture and the oil, to show you the wonderful color it turns when you add whichever menstruum, or solvent."

Senga squeezed a few drops into a small bowl. She passed it to the nearest person, who marveled at the deep red color, then handed it to her neighbor. The oil exacted the same response.

"The oil is good or, 'indicated,' as we say, against skin irritations, especially sunburn, hives—even shingles, though I hope I never have to find out. . ." Laughter.

"In Germany, the herb's been a respected, *prescribed* remedy for decades. There's quite a strong herbal tradition in Europe, but 'Hope springs eternal,' as they say. In some states in the U.S., this either/or attitude regarding western medicine and traditional remedies is being replaced with an integrated approach. *Integrative* or *Complementary Medicine,* it's called. 'Alternative' is misleading. I expect future medical clinics will house a practicing herbalist, as well as physicians and other body-work practitioners. In some states, New York for one, this is already the case."

A hand flew up in the rear. "Yes?" called Senga.

"I was told I shouldn't use *Echinacea* because I've got an auto-immune disease. I thought it strengthened immunity. What's that about?" the heavy woman asked.

"Ah yes. It's a bit confusing, I know, and a common misperception. But it's true you need to avoid it. Okay. In a nutshell, your immune system is already on override. It doesn't need strengthening, but rather, modulating." After registering the thoughtful expression on the woman's face and her nod, Senga demonstrated how to chop Oregon grape root. She gathered the pieces and placed them in one of the jars. Because the roots were still fresh and wouldn't absorb to swell, she told her students to fill the jar, then fill it again with the vodka. Preferring hands-on teaching, she invited the class to come make their own small jars of tincture to take home. *Chicks' peeping* was how she heard their enthusiasm.

Out of the corner of her eye, she noticed Sebastian leaning against one of the long shelving units at the rear of the store. He was bundled against the weather, but now raised his hands to untie his muffler, his eyes never leaving hers. He smiled and nodded, not wishing to disturb her. He disturbed her. Down to toes that had only begun to warm up. Marie kept her store cool, and the high ceiling didn't help, but Senga felt heat course through her veins and, nodding back to him, she resumed, wondering how long he'd been watching.

When teaching, she inhabited a zone of concentration, now broken.

She stole another quick glance in his direction, an unconscious gesture, as if her soul needed reassurance the man wasn't a figment; wasn't like the recent flash appearance of the American Indian hunter she'd glimpsed behind her cabin. No; she'd made love to *this* man. Sebastian was more real than . . . well . . . *stone*, she concluded.

Her eyes fell to the markers, grateful for the anchor. Choosing the green one, she quickly drew the holly-like leaves of Oregon grape, adding yellow berries. Senga preferred drawings to photographs, as there might be an individual difference in the latter. Drawings proved more universal.

How many of you have seen this plant?"

Several hands went up.

"Where did you find it?"

A stately young woman spoke up, "It grows behind our house on a hillside, low to the ground. Lots of reddish-purple berries this year."

"That's it. Makes good jam, too." Senga printed the plant's names on the paper. "One of its active constituents, or ingredients, is berberine. Oregon grape, or *Mahonia aquifolium*, is antibiotic, but don't separate active ingredients from the whole plant—as when ingesting a root tincture or, berries. In powdered capsules, the, *quote,* 'active ingredient' has been isolated; in other words, it's not whole. Oregon grape also stimulates the immune system; it can reduce blood pressure, is anti-inflammatory and has been known to shrink tumors. Oh, and don't worry about writing all this down. . . It's on the hand-out, unless, like me, you learn better by taking notes . . ."

She asked, "How do plants communicate? How do they process information? Charles Darwin proposed they were 'upside-down animals,' with the brain on the bottom—located in the roots, and their sexual organs on top, in the flowering aspects."

Silence.

"*They communicate?*" a young man whispered to his neighbor.

"Through their nervous system. Or, something very much like one. They eavesdrop on one another. It's thought to behave like a network of sorts, among a population. A field of *Echinacea*, for example; or, a stand of aspens. *Yes!*" she addressed a woman's incredulity. "It's led to a new field: plant neurobiology. Remember that study, where they found that eighty-percent of human communication is non-verbal? So, body-language; but couldn't you say, 'through our nervous system,' as well? And what fires that?"

Someone in the back muttered, "Nerves?" to soft laughter.

Another participant mentioned neurotransmitters.

"Neurotransmitter-*like* chemicals, and when released, these alert the neighbors, mostly in warning. Humans share several neurological behaviors with plants, such as response to stress. Sagebrush will release these defensive proteins, called trypsin proteinase inhibitors, or TPIs, that actually interfere with an insect's ability to digest protein. Sibling plants sense these and, in turn, ready themselves against the hungry worm, or the like. Are you duly impressed?"

Senga continued for another forty-five minutes. She showed them how to infuse fresh herbs in vinegar and dried ones in oil. The class remained curious and enthusiastic, a gratifying combination. She reminded them to watch and listen for rattlesnakes when foraging.

After, an organic lunch was served, effectively grounding the teaching: a hearty vegetable soup, muffins and various cheeses, paired with a glass of local organic wine, coffee or tea and the cookies. Marie invited Sebastian to join them. He agreed cheerfully and gave Senga a kiss on both cheeks before sitting down. She noted Marie's wistful expression.

Senga passed on the wine, but took the opportunity to mention how medieval monks perfected medicinal wines and liqueurs by adding various herbs. *Benedictine*, for example. Someone asked for a recipe for medicinal wine, whereupon everyone laughed, and she offered to send them an email with a recipe for mulled wine—infused with calmative herbs, raisins and almonds.

Sebastian leaned in to Senga's ear and whispered, "I bow to your feet in admiration, my dear." She coughed to cover his speech, but not before catching a few looks of rapt female awareness.

"Um, thanks. . . " she squeaked, lifting her glass of water to cool her insides. Were her cheeks as red as they felt? *Damn nuisance, this so-called 'change of life.'*

CHAPTER 1
SEAGULLS AND JAMBALAYA

Halloween

Rufus Strickland had suffered an attack by an angry buck, the sheep variety, when he'd tried to coax the animal into another pen. His pelvis was badly bruised and the recovery proved just as painful. And, he was tired.

What they needed, he decided, was a vacation. His wife was right. Both in their late seventies, he and Caroline had never had a real one, he realized. Some things you just put out of your head. Running a ranch allowed for little time off. *But now that we've got good help, and with Jake coming for the summer. . . well, might be possible,* he speculated. *And this damn hip should be healed by then. . .*

Jake was their grandson. Whom they hadn't seen in six long years. He'd graduate high school in May.

Maybe he's grown a mind of his own by now, he hoped. *We could take off for a couple weeks . . . maybe even three . . . Gabe could handle things with the kid's help, I think.*

He continued to lie in bed and pretend he was stretched out on a warm, sandy beach, blue sky overhead, listening to crashing waves. *Listening* to them—not merely hearing them. He wanted to take Caroline to the ocean. Neither had ever seen it.

"Rufus? You all right?" he heard his wife ask.

"Yeah. I'm listening to waves, Caro. Can you hear them?"

"You ain't all right. . . *What* waves? Radio waves?"

"No, hon. The ocean. I'm lying on the beach listening to sea gulls and waves. Kids laughing too."

"You been around Senga too much, old man. Come on, get up. I need some help. Folks are coming around 2:00. Gabe's moved the press next to the porch."

"He's too happy these days. Engaged, my ass. Hell, he's liable to do something stupid now. Won't have his mind where it's supposed to be."

"He ain't your personal slave, hon . . . Now come on—breakfast is about ready."

Rufus took a deep breath, allowed his vision of waves to fade, threw off the covers and turned carefully to his side. He swung his legs to the floor and pushed himself up to a sitting position. The hip was sore. He deplored complainers, so tried not to be one. *But there's a difference between complaining and making an observation, Caro*—he'd once told her. She'd rolled her eyes, he remembered. Then, she'd kissed his pale forehead.

He reached for the undershirt on the back of a chair, where Caroline had put it for him. He'd slept in his long john bottoms. Painfully, he pulled on the jeans. He'd take his socks to his wife, as leaning over proved difficult. He stood, winced, grabbed his cane off the back of the chair and padded to the bathroom.

The face in the mirror appeared rougher than usual. *They say, whoever "they" are, to accentuate the positive,* he reflected dryly, but how to do that in his case? Rufus ignored the left side of his face as he splashed water on it, patted on shaving cream and placed the edge of the razor to his neck. The task took less time for not having to shave half his face. *The 'positive,'* he conceded. His shock of white hair had recently been trimmed, and his white, beetled brows gave him a wild terrier look. Caroline had always told him he had beautiful eyes, though the left's lower lid was now distended by the taut skin of the graft. His eyes were hazel. And shone like just-washed marbles.

A massive, burning truss had fallen on him when he was nineteen. Several weeks in a burn unit, several grafts later, and his once "Hollywood handsome" face would be unrecognizable from the one side. The family barn had burned down one night during a dry storm after the annual barn dance. Violent lightning could, and did, cause fires. He'd run in to save the doomed horses.

He and Caroline were married shortly after his release from the hospital. Rufus insisted she always sit or stand to his right. It came natural to her now, he'd noticed, like realizing you always tied a right shoe before the left.

He finished shaving, pulled a brush through his thick hair, brushed his teeth, grinned and was given to see himself at nineteen before the accident—how Caroline still saw him, she once let slip. She'd felt badly about that, he recalled, but it didn't matter. They were sweethearts still, after sixty-some years of marriage. That's what mattered.

You're a lucky son-of-a-bitch—he sent the face staring back.

Rufus pulled on his good Pendleton wool shirt, a past Christmas gift from one of his daughters, then his wool vest. Still barefoot, he stepped into the warm kitchen. It smelled like fried sausage.

Gabe was seated in his usual place.

Gabe Belizaire, thirty-nine and recently retired (he claimed) as a bull rider, was born and raised in Louisiana on a ranch. An MFA from Tulane, he'd given up a teaching position to concentrate on writing. He'd just submitted a collection of short stories. But he still wanted, what he called, a "day job," so he continued to work for the Stricklands, who now considered him family.

In 2006, one of his rides was ignored by the arena clown and pick-up men in a case of abject discrimination. The bull mauled him in a horrifying spectacle. Rufus remembered the bright red blood drenching the yellow shirt of the Louisiana man, whose skin gleamed as black as a no-moon night.

And what color was that bull? A brindle, maybe, Rufus recollected.

The Stricklands had invited Gabe to recover at their ranch, offered in the guise of a job, and the man accepted their hospitality.

After he had been treated for his injuries at the rodeo, Caroline and Senga continued his care. Senga Munro, their nearest neighbor, provided salves, tinctures, compresses and an ear.

Gabe explained he'd traveled to the Black Hills in search of his sister, who'd disappeared after Katrina's destruction in New Orleans. A truck driver contacted his parents to say he'd driven the girls—Allie and her friend—to western South Dakota, where they had waiting jobs at a guest ranch in the Wyoming Black Hills.

"Mornin', *patron*," said Gabe. "How's the hip? Or should I just shut up?" he grinned after Rufus threw him a look.

"Mornin', Gabe. And how's the recently engaged man?" He smirked. Distractions were gifts from God. *Maybe they* are *God.* He lowered himself gingerly onto the chair, placing the cane on the back. "Caro?" he held up his socks.

"Doin' well, boss, doin' well," and Gabe picked up his mug of coffee.

"Be there in a sec, hon," Caroline said, as she moved the skillet off the heat and covered the eggs with the lid. She stepped over to Rufus, knelt down and pulled on each sock. Then she reached for the slippers he kept beside the stove. "There," and she looked up at him.

Caroline was heavier than she liked to be, and rising to her feet took some effort.

"Thank you, wife," he said, meaning it, then to Gabe, "You'll like it, being married; they're handy to have around. Like pliers, you know?" He winked at her.

Narrowing her eyes at him, Caroline poured a cup of black coffee and set it before him.

They ate in silence this morning.

When they finished, Caroline cleared the table and set about washing the dishes. She refilled their mugs and refilled the creamer for Gabe. Rufus rolled his first cigarette of the day and they both sat back a moment before Rufus spoke:

"How much longer is Francesca here?"

Gabe's olive-skinned, Italian fiancée worked as an interpreter at the Blue Wood Guest Ranch. She was returning home to Italy, as usual, after the season. She'd asked Gabe to meet her family, and this he'd do after helping Stricklands with their hunters.

"Next week. . . She was able to find a good fare out of Rapid. Senga and I need to apply for our passports this week."

Eleven days before, Francesca discovered she was acquainted with Senga's grandmother in Italy. The woman had returned to her native country thirty-eight years ago, and lived down the street from Francesca's family in Lucca, Italy. "Truth's weirder than fiction," Rufus had declared when told. Gabe and Senga planned to travel to Italy together to spend ten days in early December.

"Now that's just a miracle, ain't it, Rufus?" Caroline spoke up. "Talk about a small world. . . I still can't believe it," she added, "And now Jake's coming this summer. Almost too good to be true. Makes me nervous, somehow."

"Yep, well, and here's something else—" Rufus spoke in Gabe's direction, after exhaling a long plume of smoke. "I don't know if we could do it yet or not, but I'm thinking about taking Caroline to California, to the ocean. This summer, after docking. Maybe I've still got some gas left in my tank." He looked at his wife to gauge her response, then winked again. He liked to keep her, if not off-balance, then at least capable of being upended.

"You been talking with Senga, old man?" she asked him, eyes round in disbelief.

"No . . . *Why?* And what's the woman got to do with *everything* this morning?"

"Oh, we just had a talk about that—seeing the ocean. She told me I need to see it, that's all." Then, she gave him a sidelong glance, questioning his assertion.

"No, *I swear*, Caro. I haven't talked to anyone—'til now. So, you up for it?" he asked, in a tone he reserved for persuasion. The kind of sweet-talk he used with young horses. Worked every time.

Gabe chuckled, recognizing it.

"Well, hell yeah, I'm up for it. After docking? So, maybe July?"

"Yep," Rufus smiled his crooked grin. "For maybe two-three weeks, I figure." Then, he looked at Gabe. "I should have talked with you first, I know; I just thought of it this morning." He stubbed out his flattened, hand-rolled cigarette and reached into his pocket for the tin of tobacco to make another.

"I mean, you and Francesca aren't going off to get married then, are you? And the boy'll be here to help—well, I'm counting on that a bit, I know. Haven't seen the kid in a while. Don't know what he's like. Oh hell, might've spoke too soon."

"Boss, we'll be *fine*. You and Miss Caroline go see the ocean. I think it's great. And I'll let Francesca know right away. To tell the truth, I've no idea where this thing's going to happen—here, or in Italy. She's the only daughter, you know. Could get tricky."

Caroline stood at the sink, drying her hands. "Well, I'd love to sit and make plans and all, but we've got an apple pressin' to get on with, you two," and she shot them each a hard look.

He knew she couldn't accept it, but he loved her strong and, substantial *confirmation*—how he thought of it. That of a Belgian mare.

"What do you want me to do first, ma'am?" Gabe inquired, as he pushed his chair back with accompanying screech on the linoleum and stood. He assisted her as much as he helped Rufus. It came easily, Rufus realized, his hired man's natural grace, and Rufus loved him for it.

So, he sat and watched and smoked as Caroline and Gabe prepared the ingredients for the late afternoon meal. Gabe's mother having cooked for the southwestern Louisiana ranch where he grew up, he'd learned a few things in the kitchen, he told them: Cajun cooking and some good 'ole Southern cooking too. He'd promised to make jambalaya today. Sounded good to Rufus. He knew Gabe was doing it for Caroline's sake, mostly.

They were expecting Francesca of course, Senga with Sebastian, and Lee and Mary Rogers—the owners of the guest ranch where Francesca worked. Rufus would have preferred a smaller number. He didn't like to disturb others by his appearance. Not self-conscious as much as *hyper*-conscious.

What the fire had seared into him.

So, they didn't entertain as a rule. But, for some reason (a complete and utter mystery to him), Caroline had wanted this shindig.

CHAPTER 3
PRESSING FUNNY BUSINESS

W hat are their names again, Mary?" her husband, Lee, asked, as they prepared to leave their home at the Blue Wood, for the Strickland's apple pressing. Francesca had forwarded the invitation to the Rogers from Caroline, who wished to include the employers of their hired man's fiancée. As this was a recent development, Mary didn't know if Francesca would continue to work at the Blue Wood, but she also knew that Gabe didn't earn much as a hired man, so Francesca would probably remain—she hoped. *Unless his book of short stories does exceptionally well.* He was a writer; "a good one," Francesca had assured her, but he believed he'd need another job for a *long* time.

What Mary hadn't asked about was their living arrangements after the wedding. Gabe's tack room bunkhouse digs wouldn't pass muster with Francesca. *Absolutely not,* Mary decided. And they needed Francesca during tourist season. It was a long drive from Strickland's.

"Rufus and Caroline," Mary said.

"Pardon?" Lee asked.

"Rufus and Caroline are their names, darling. The Stricklands. And remember Francesca mentioning the man's face? Burned in a fire long time ago? She warned it's shocking at first but, after a while, you don't notice so much." She saw her husband wince behind her in the mirror.

"She says he's *bello.* Seems the one side of his face is quite attractive, but she means his heart, I expect."

She finished dusting her face with blusher, knocked residue off the brush and placed it back in the drawer with the rest of her perfectly organized products.

"Yeah. . . Now I remember. . . Are you ready?"

Mary Rogers enjoyed dressing for the occasional occasion. Raised in "proper" Florida, she'd practiced the art of the *toilette,* fashionable wardrobe enhancement and her *Charleston manners* since preadolescence. At late middle age, she was still striking, with bright red hair clipped short and attractive features, if aided by plastic surgery. Today, she wore dress jeans, which meant sapphires on the back pockets, and a pink wool sweater. Turquoise boots completed the outfit.

"As ready as I'll ever be. Have you ever been to an apple pressing? Is it messy?"

"I've never been, but, no, it's not like stomping grapes, *Lucy,*" Lee told her in his best Ricky Ricardo voice.

"Oh, Lee—you are *so* funny."

"In this business, it's essential," he said dryly, then leaned over his wife, planted a kiss on her pout and smiled.

While not newlyweds, they had preserved light-heartedness.

In Caroline's kitchen, Gabe had sautéed the chicken in butter; next, shrimp, sausage and chunks of ham. He'd chopped onions, celery and green peppers and placed these and the tomatoes into Caroline's roasting pan. After adding broth, he'd sprinkled rice over the top, stirred it, then covered the pan and put it in the oven. The kitchen smelled of onions and Cajun seasoning, and his mouth watered in anticipation. Caroline had never tasted jambalaya and he envied her the first-time pleasure. Rufus believed he'd had it sometime, but couldn't remember where.

"Must not have been too good if you can't recall the circumstances," Gabe told him. "This is my Mama's recipe. *Talk about good!* As we say down there. . ."

He sprinkled his speech with Cajun expressions more from nostalgia than habit, he knew. *Verbal lagniappe,* he coined it, the word meaning, "a little something extra," usually associated with leaving behind a surprise gift.

Would he and Francesca ever return to Louisiana? His sister cooked for the ranch now—his mother's job until she died. His father still worked for the rancher, who raised rodeo stock—how Gabe began riding bulls.

Nah, you can't go home again, like the man says. But he did want Francesca to meet his family. When?

Rufus called from outside. "Somebody's here! Can you come on out?"

From the kitchen window, Gabe saw the van with *The Blue Wood Guest Ranch, Wyoming Black Hills* lettered on a front door panel as it rolled over the car gate. He ran his hands under running water and dried them on the tea towel. The vehicle had just pulled up when Gabe opened the front door and stepped out, Caroline behind him.

"What's that you're wearing, Gabe? Cologne? You smell like orange juice and Christmas trees."

"Yes, Miss Caroline—something Francesca brought me from Italy. Have I got too much on?" he asked quickly as they descended the porch steps.

"Nah . . . I just never figured you for it, that's all. You smell real *purty,* Gabe," she whispered, then gave him a wide smile. Caroline liked to tease.

The Rogers and Francesca climbed out of the vehicle, wishing everyone a Happy Halloween, and Gabe introduced Lee and Mary. Francesca kissed Caroline and Rufus on both cheeks—Rufus showing confusion about which cheek to turn. Gabe's fiancée was impeccable in her appearance, as usual, and he gave her a bear hug. As usual. She would make Caroline and Rufus at ease with the Rogers, and Gabe felt his pride swell in proportion to his fiancée's natural charms. Two of which were her social decorum and her glorious bust.

Rufus arranged six bottles of hard cider in an ice chest. "Next year we might have our own batch to try," he said. "Senga and I are going to start some in the next couple days." And, as though summoned by name, Gabe noticed her arrival as he added more ice to the cooler.

"Caroline," said Mary, who held a Saran Wrap-covered pan, "It's so good to finally meet you. Francesca thinks the world of you and Rufus. We brought some of Lupita's brownies for dessert. Aren't they cute?" They were decorated with candy corn. "Where would you like them?" Gabe heard Mary's practiced manners and expected Caroline might feel *a mite* overwhelmed.

"Oh, thank you, hon. Let's just put 'em inside for now," she said, then, "Here's Senga and Sebastian. How's that saying go? Twice in as many weeks? I learned that from Gabe. He's real good with fancy talk. You know he's a writer? I suppose Francesca's told you. And now they're getting married. . . *Whoee,* but when it rains around here, it *floods.*"

Guess she can hold her own, thought Gabe, as Caroline reached for the pan of cute brownies. She turned toward the porch steps, then asked if she needed to stir "whatever" was in the pan. Mary and Lee exchanged glances.

"Uh, no, Miss Caroline. It's fine for now, but, thank you," and he walked into the open garage to bring back two lawn chairs, setting them beside the press. Then, he carried the two new Adirondack chairs down from the porch. Francesca followed with the small table. They'd eat indoors after the pressing.

Rufus opened the passenger door for Senga and, when she stepped out, she gave him a hug. An unusual gesture for her, Gabe thought. *Must be the lovin'.* Sebastian reached into the back seat to retrieve a basket. Senga had offered to bring a salad, and another bag held two loaves of French bread, their smooth noses peeking out.

"Sebastian, good to see you, man," said Gabe, as they shook hands. "Here, let me take that. Looks good. Thank you!"

Seeing the man thus freed of his burdens, Rufus hobbled over and held out his hand.

Caroline squeezed in beside her husband to search the Dane's face, in appraisal.

"Rufus. Caroline. Gabe . . . and the lovely bride-to-be, Francesca," Sebastian greeted. And these must be your friends," offering his hand first to Lee, then to Mary. Lee and Sebastian stood roughly the same tall height, Gabe noted. Moreover, both resembled literary seamen, with Lee, the elder of the two, wearing the more heavily-lined face. He took notice of their handshake, how firmly each grasped the other, as if to signal a code.

Notice what you notice, a writing professor had once told the class. *And why am I noticing this?*

Senga stood by absorbing all. He read her cues like a book, he realized, surprised at this small epiphany. Stepping over with a smile, Gabe kissed her cheek, equally unusual for him. She appeared nonplussed and stepped back.

"Gabe," she said, "I hear you're cooking us some jambalaya. Can't wait. Grannie used to make it once in a while. Usually with leftovers. Sebastian, have you ever had it?"

At his name, the Dane turned, his eyes questioning her.

"Jambalaya. Have you ever eaten this?" she repeated. "It's a Louisiana thing."

"Ah, no. But I know the dish. My wife, ah, my *late* wife—Elsa—once attended a dinner party at some friend's home, and she reported it was marvelous. So I am eager to try it, Gabe. And to press apples. . ."

With this prompt, the party moved to the press. Senga began hauling over her baskets of apples with Sebastian's help. After a short introduction to the contraption by Rufus, an assembly line formed; pocket knives cut out bad spots before the apples were tossed into the wide maw to be chewed up by the rotating grinder. When the mash bucket was filled, a stout wooden stick was used to crank the spiraling press gear, with leftover pulp placed into a large bag to be frozen for the deer. Hunting season began in the morning, but Rufus would reserve the treat until their hunters left, as small consolation toward the animals.

Amber liquid soon flowed from the mashed fruit, a foaming layer on top, and when the five-gallon pail filled, Senga poured the cider through a funnel into bottles. A bushel of apples produced a gallon of cider, depending on the freshness of the fruit.

The blizzard hadn't discouraged the wasps, attracted by the sweet fragrance. Gabe returned to the kitchen for a fly swatter and to stir his recipe. He saw Caroline at the liquor cabinet, her back turned to him. She looked over her shoulder and grinned, then cackled.

Back outside, he watched her pass everyone samples of the new cider to taste in paper cups, some "virgin," apparently, and some with a splash of Jim Beam, unbeknownst.

"Trick or Treat!" she called.

"This is some amazing stuff, Caroline. I thought it had to ferment to get hard," gasped Lee.

From Mary, who had sampled the plain sample. "Of course it has to set a while, Lee."

Senga caught on after she tasted a just-poured dip from the bucket, then tried Sebastian's, whose features betrayed the ruse. She kept mum. Meanwhile, Rufus handed out the bottled hard cider. Everyone took turns at the handle, grinding apples, and by late afternoon, they'd pressed nearly four gallons. Caroline transferred it to plastic jugs for the guests to take home. Rufus and Senga would have plenty to run their fermentation experiment.

Caroline was behaving giddier than usual and Senga followed her into the house.

"Hey, what can I do to help, Caroline?"

"Oh, I'm good. Gabe's about got it all done . . . no, I guess you could put those—" And here, Caroline staggered a bit and steadied herself against a chair.

"You okay?" Senga asked her friend, who then sank into the sofa.

"I ain't used to having people over, Senga. It's nerve-wracking. Guess I had too much . . . uh, *cider*. . ."

"Mm-hmm. Coffee. You have some made? I could do it."

"No, there's some—there in the thermos. Yeah, pour me a cup, would ya, hon? And thanks. *Sorry.*" She sparkled her eyes in supplication.

After Caroline drank a glass of water, then coffee, Senga asked, "You want to lie down for a few minutes? We're not ready to eat yet, and I don't have to say anything, Caroline. How about it?"

"That's probably a good idea. . . Help me up, hon? Guess the trick was on me, *ha.*"

Senga supported Caroline into her bedroom. "I'll come back in about fifteen minutes," she said, then returned to the kitchen where she placed the bread on the table. Gabe entered the kitchen.

"I think we're ready. Where's Caroline?" he said, looking around.

Senga gestured with her head toward the hallway, saying quietly, "We need about fifteen minutes. . . Maybe go ahead and clean up the press. Oh, and later, I want to go see Sadie. Is she still in sick bay?"

Caroline's chestnut mare that Senga rode on occasion had stepped into the car gate during the latest storm, narrowly escaping a tragedy.

"She's doing well and I'm sure she'd love to see you," he said as he checked the table. "She can be turned out with the others next week, but we put them up while the hunters are here. Might get confused for elk; you never know. . ." He winked at her. "Tabasco," he remembered, then stepped to the cabinet and took down the McIlhenny's.

"So how's everyone getting on?" she asked as she brought down plates from the cabinet.

"Oh fine. Mary says Lee's son, Pete, and their cook, Lupita, are seeing each other. Guess that was inevitable. . . And Jim and that Deputy Carter are both interested in the Russian woman . . . Larissa?"

"Sounds like a gossip fest, Gabe. Have you decided on dates for Italy? And where we go for passports?"

"Hunting season's over on the thirtieth, so we could leave the next day if you want, or wait a couple days. I guess it'll depend on when we get the passports back. Let's do that on Monday—and we'll need photos too."

Senga was still reeling from a recent revelation. She'd inherited the proceeds from the sale of her grandparents' property in North Carolina. Never having had money in her life, save for bare essentials on which to live, her needs were few, and she was simple—as well as a simpler. But now she'd be able to do this thing called travel. She felt like Alice peering down the rabbit hole. But this seemed more like a wormhole. Probably the same thing, she'd reasoned, wormholes having yet to be imagined when the tale was written.

"Francesca's going home next week—found a decent airfare," Gabe interrupted her ponder: "We'd better do that soon too. She suggested we go through Amsterdam. Then transfer to an Italian line to Florence and she'll pick us up. It's what she does, anyway. Always wanted to see Amsterdam . . . Anne Frank's house . . . but probably won't have time."

Senga hadn't told Gabe about her windfall. *May as well now.* She carried the salad to the table, then returned to the refrigerator for three bottles of dressing.

"Um, I had this thing happen recently, besides, uh, Sebastian and finding out my *nonna* lives near Francesca. . . I still don't exactly know what to do with it all. . ." She paused, seemingly waiting for the resolution. "My grandparents' property in North Carolina . . . it's been sold and I'm the beneficiary. So, it seems I'll have some money."

Gabe's eyes opened widely, then he grinned. A wide Buddha smile.

"Out*standing, chère!* But your grandmother. . . Didn't she die a long time ago?"

Just then the front door opened and they heard Francesca call for Gabe.

"In the kitchen, love," he answered.

"Grannie did, yes . . . Papa too, but my cousins lived in the house for a while," Senga explained.

"We are hungry, *cara mio* . . . Is your goose almost cooked?" she asked, using a recently acquired idiom. She looked from one to the other. "And, why do you both look like—like rats that ate the cheese?"

Gabe laughed and drew Francesca to him. He looked to Senga, asking with his eyes if he could say.

She spoke up. "I've inherited some money from the sale of my grandparents' property, so the trip will be sweeter for not having to pay for it after I return."

"Ah, *sì!* This is true, Senga. *Assolutamente.*" Absolutely. "So much to . . . ah, *celebrate!*" Her friend gathered her and Gabe into an embrace.

From the bedroom, Caroline called out, "Now, that's as good a reason to get drunk as any I've heard. You could have told me, Senga! Bring me a cold wash cloth, will ya, hon?"

"Coming, Caroline," Senga replied as she smiled at her friends, adding, "I think we're about ready. . . Serve it up, would you? And call them in?"

CHAPTER 4
TO THE DOGS

Jacob noticed Dale's silence on the way back to Belle Fourche after their run-in with the black cowboy and his white girlfriend at the bar in Montana. She'd thrown a glass of wine into the kid's face and spewed a load of something afterwards in some language that wasn't English. It sounded Italian. Sure, the kid had been upset at seeing the two of them together and he'd made some crude remarks, but whatever she said to him, well, Dale hadn't taken it well. The kid moped. And didn't eat much, Jacob noticed. Or drink, which was unusual.

That was almost two weeks ago. He'd had them gather their gear when he and Dale returned to the motel and they'd driven on to Rapid City. Jacob thought they'd be less noticeable in the city and, they had buyers there. They needed to unload the meth. *And quick.*

The old man complained. George wanted to return to the house up in the Bear Lodge Mountains. "I'm comfortable there, Jacob," he'd told him. Jacob thought his second cousin once removed, *or whatever*, was growing feeble-minded. *But hell, we need some of that cash.* It'd been stupid to leave it up on the mountain. The place was being watched, he figured, against their return. *How would they do that?* he wondered. *Camp out in the fucking snow?* The higher elevations had gotten several more inches in the last week. He wasn't even sure they could drive in.

Jacob Brady and George Canton had a lab up in the hilly backcountry, and had imprisoned (for *all* their intents and purposes) a permanent hostage, *slash*, sex worker, *slash*, cook, and her child. Jacob's child too, as it happened, but he felt nothing for the girl, and less for the woman who was called Larissa. She was a Russian who'd been lured to the country by a proposal of marriage. In Idaho, thrown in with other trafficked victims, she was later sold to him. He shared her with George. (Since he was family.)

Dale arranged the drug deliveries. Dale's little brother Joey procured wild game on a regular basis, legally or not. He enjoyed playing mountain man.

They lived at the old Berry place in Wyoming's northeast corner, not far from the Blue Wood Guest Ranch, but far enough to have avoided contact. Until the woman and her kid ran off one evening before the heavy snow came. If they lived through it, she'd have talked, and the place, *no doubt,* would have been searched.

After the weather cleared, he'd looked for Larissa and the girl, and met a guy on the logging road. Asked him if he'd seen anyone. The man answered *no,* as though he'd been crazy to ask, Jacob remembered now. The man was busy plowing the road in a fancy new tractor and Jacob asked him to help them out, adding their rig was down. Not entirely true, but the guy's tractor would make faster work of it. As it happened, Dale cleared their road with listing blade, because Jacob decided they'd better get the hell out.

They left after clearing out the trailer and setting fire to what could bust them, taking the two watch dogs with them. But they were quickly running through the cash he had on him. The meth they'd brought would sell, but Jacob suspected they were high on some cops' lists by now. They needed to get farther away. How to get Dale back to the place, to get the money and his truck, so they could split up? That was the question.

Joey wanted to bail. He was fed up and wanted out. At seventeen, he'd lived among his older brother Dale's friends (*Some friends!* he'd decided a while back) for going on two years. He'd begged to join them in Wyoming when they'd first moved to the old Berry place, a dilapidated sawmill, hidden in deep timber.

Dale had raved about the deer, elk and coyote hunting, but being no hunter himself, he thought Joey would take the bait. So, he arranged for the boy to ride a bus from Idaho, where he was a city kid.

"You got enough schooling!" Dale declared to his little brother. "Hell, I left school at sixteen. Didn't hurt me none," he'd added. Their mother was raising three younger siblings; and their father, last heard, was a member of an OMG, or, outlaw motorcycle gang, somewhere.

"Dale," Joey asked him now, "can I go with you when you go get the truck? And then can we just . . . you know, like, leave? *Alone?*"

They were walking back to the motel from a convenience store. The late afternoon sky was clear, the temperature not too cold. But Indian summer had passed, and the recent blizzard signaled coming winter. Joey's mind flew to the spot on a trail he'd discovered two-hundred feet from the house, where deer passed regularly. Before all this business started, he'd planned his next hunt down to the first recipe. He wasn't excited about eating raw liver, but that's what they did, the mountain men. Gave them strength, he'd read.

"You mean leave with the money? Are you *fuckin'* nuts? And we don't know how to go *get* the truck, moron." Dale said, throwing him an exasperated look.

"Don't call me that. . . Well, you wanna get caught? Cause all of us together like this, well—"

"I know, I know. Been thinking the same thing. I just don't know how we'd do it, Joey. We gotta be taken up there, and they're probably watching for us. . . Suppose we went at night, but no, we'd need headlights to *see* anything. It's a pisser."

They headed for a motel door that a sucker punch could splinter. Joey knew his brother was *between a rock and hard places*, one of the only phrases he recalled their father ever using, referring to their mother and them. But it was Dale who knew the meth buyers and where they lived. And they trusted him.

Things were half-way decent until the woman took off with the kid, Joey thought with a long sigh. *No. No, they weren't,* he corrected. Sometimes he felt sorry for the woman and the girl. They were treated badly. And worse, the woman was expected to help cook the meth and sleep in the back of that smelly trailer. But while he'd never tried the crap—because he'd heard it was pretty-much instantly addictive—he'd also pretty-much closed his ears and heart to everything else. Except his brother's affections. When those were available. This wasn't often. Dale

29

was too busy vying for Jacob's attention and Joey wanted to puke.

He knew his brother used. "My teeth are bad, but yours look *really* gross," he once told him, and he was acting weirder than usual, he also told him—getting the side of his head knocked in for the observation.

Yeah, they needed to blow this scene, Joey decided. He'd figure it out. Somehow. And he stuck another pinch of chew between his cheek and his own deteriorating gums.

George Canton lay on his bed, alone in the dark motel room. It smelled like a cross between a bean fart and rotting potatoes. Dale and Joey had wanted something from the Quik-Mart across the street, and Jacob was off somewhere; *oh, yeah, taking the dogs for a walk.* George had blamed the odor on them, but he'd had the three burritos for lunch. He started to raise his head off the pillow and felt a sharp *ping!* in his brain.

He felt like his head exploded.

And then, he felt nothing much at all . . . maybe a vague sense he was drooling. The spittle tickled his chin. When he tried to reach up to wipe his mouth, he found he couldn't move his arm. The television was on but George couldn't focus on the image. *George?* he heard from inside his head. He thought he heard voices outside the door as well, but when he tried to speak nothing came out. Then came nothing . . . at . . . all.

Dale couldn't remember where he'd put the key to the room and he slapped his back pockets for it. Joey reached into his brother's inside jacket pocket and lifted it out, dangled it in front of his face, inserted it into the lock, all the while shaking his head.

Dale felt stupid and uneasy again—like he had after that woman's rant. A tugging inside, as if someone were trying to pull the bathtub plug on him and his insides were leaking out. He'd rather be beaten bare knuckles to the ground than undergo another chewing-out like that . . . if that's what it was. *Hell,* he had no idea. But he did know, in his very bowels. He'd been cursed. She was a witch and he'd been cursed. Why else would she be out with a . . . a . . . *Fuck!* He couldn't even *think* it

anymore. What had she *done* to him? But the niggling awareness
dawned: *This all started with that woman in the store—that root-digger
and her goddamn knife; not the other one.* He muttered something
aloud.

"Huh?"

"Oh, nada—*Jesus*, the stench!"

The smell was revolting. Joey groaned and opened the door
again. The lights were still off, except for what shone from the
television. The sound was turned down. George was asleep,
Dale guessed. He put the six-pack of coke in the fridge, then
turned on the desk lamp. Still nothing from George. Not a peep.
He turned to the lamp between the beds, switched it on and,
drawing a quick breath, nearly fell over Joey who was sitting
behind him on the other bed, removing his boots.

"What the fuck, Dale!"

George was staring up at him, bug-eyes wide open, but still,
dull and vacant. Something like a white caterpillar chrysalis sat
on his half-open lips.

"Oh shit, oh *shit* . . . Joey? I—I think George is gone.
George? George! You awake?"

Joey shut the door and walked over. He tentatively reached
out then shook the man's shoulder. Nothing. "Look at that
coming out of his mouth, Dale. . . Some kind of foam or
something. Ever see anything like that? I think . . . I think he
purged . . . I think he's dead, Dale. What do we do?"

"No shit, *Sherlock*, he's dead. . . Oh this ain't good, Joey.
Where's Jacob?"

It was hard to find grass in cities anymore, thought Jacob, as he
tugged on the nylon ropes to control the dogs. Daisy and Duke
were half Rottweiler, half Pit Bull, from the same litter. *A
ridiculous combination*, he'd thought, when George first introduced
him to the beasts. But they minded, which was something. They
were George's sole family, except for him, and Jacob knew
where he came in line.

The fresh air felt good. After the dogs did their rather large
business on someone's front lawn, he turned back toward the
motel. Nothing occurred to him about retrieving the money

from their place. The dogs were eating better than they were, but George had insisted they *wanted* to keep feeding the dogs. . .

Daisy and Duke finally relaxed on their leads and Jacob felt a moment of pride and yes, power, at accompanying such animals. Maybe it's what George needed.

At the next block, they began to pull once more, and it took all Jacob's strength to not have to break into a run.

"*Heel!*" he commanded, but they were having none of it. He tried cajoling them. "Knock it off, you two—" He figured they just wanted to return to George, so Jacob broke into a jog and they soon reached the motel. *Good thing we're with the traffic light . . . might have got run over.*

When the dogs began whining and scratching the excuse for a door, Jacob wondered if something was wrong. He knocked, having no key. Dale answered, his face pastier than usual, Jacob noticed.

"He's dead, Jacob. George is fuckin' dead. What do—"

The dogs charged in before Dale concluded, pulling Jacob with them. They set up a racket and Duke let out a howl. Daisy jumped on the bed and began to lick George's face, including the foam around his lips.

"Get off, dog!" Jacob pulled on the rope. "Dale! *Christ.* What *happened?* I leave you for a half-hour and—" he yanked harder on Daisy's leash, but she swung her head in his direction, as a deep, low growl issued from the back of her throat.

He dropped the line and backed away.

Duke stood between the beds, looking from his deceased master to Dale, Joey and Jacob, as if to ask, "What did you *do* to him?"

"We didn't do *nothin'*, Jacob, I *swear*. . ." Dale said, as if having read the dog's mind. "He was like that when we got back from the Quik-Mart a few minutes ago—wasn't he, Joey?"

"Dale's right. We just got here. But he purged, so, that's good."

"*What?* What are you talking about?" Jacob turned from Joey to George. "At least close his eyes. Christ."

Daisy growled again when Joey reached. He pulled his hand back.

"Don't *do* that! Quickest way to draw back a nub, pulling your hand back like that from a growling dog. . . What do you mean, *purged?* And this—this is too damn much. *Damn* it!" Jacob sat down on the second bed and held his head in his hands.

"We better lower our voices or the manager'll be coming over," Joey said now in a low, controlled tone. He'd sat down at the desk and looked to be the picture of reason in an otherwise crazy scene.

Jacob thought a moment. Then, he stood and walked to the bathroom, returning with a white face towel. He reached out with both hands and carefully tossed it onto the man's staring face. The dogs looked at him, then at George's now disappeared visage, then back to Jacob. Daisy craned her neck and, gripping a corner of the towel in her teeth, she pulled it away. George's surprised look all the more apparent.

"Shit. Okay. . . What's *purging*, Joey? What you said—"

"Grandma said that about grandpa at his funeral. It means he'd got rid of whatever was on his chest before he died. His sins were *purged*—something like that."

"Were you there, Dale?" Jacob looked at him, even as he was trying to decide what to do next.

"Nah, I was in the pen," he stated casually; he could've easily meant a *play* pen. "I never heard of that before. Sounds possible though, don't it?"

"Aw shit, Dale. Both of you. *Idiots.*"

"Well, now, no cause to get all superior, Jacob," Dale said. "Nobody knows this stuff, exceptin' those who've passed on, right?"

The dogs finally settled, each guarding their master's corpse, forgiven or not. Jacob went into the bathroom again, closed the door and thought. After several minutes, he reappeared, holding his few toiletries, and these he stuffed into the duffle that held his and George's gear.

"We're leaving them here," he announced, to the wide-eyed disbelief of Jacob and Dale. "I'll leave a note on the outside of the door. Come on—what else can we do? They'll deal with it. Happens all the time."

"What about the dogs, Jacob? They won't let just anybody go near George. . . You know that," said Dale as he began to gather his gear. He was glad to be leaving.

"Well, that's their problem, I figure. They'll come up with something. Hell, a steak would do it," and the corners of his mouth turned up for a second, then relaxed again into their usual grim lines.

"But he's your *family!* How can you *do* this?" asked Joey now, appalled.

Dale threw his brother a look in warning. The kid looked back with concern, knitted brows and disgust. Joey grabbed his hunting magazines from the desk, his toothbrush and toothpaste, deodorant, razor and shaving cream, and began stuffing his backpack.

"*Unfuckingbelievable*," he muttered, just before the back of Jacob's right hand landed hard against his still-smooth right cheek.

Dale didn't appreciate Jacob's treatment of his little brother, but he ignored it. He visited the ice machine before they drove off, wrapping some in a towel for Joey, who said nothing, whose eyes said it all.

Dale felt confused at George's death. He couldn't say he'd liked the man, much less loved him, but they'd shared a home for the past year and a half, and he wondered what he *should* be feeling. He hadn't a clue. Feelings were a mixed-up ball of mud to him. He confused them all the time. Was he angry?—or frustrated? Depressed?—or angry? Horny?—or in love? Pissed?—or afraid?

He loved his brother Joey. This he knew . . . he guessed. The sensation held a protective sort of quality, but maybe a *feeling sorry for*, too. The kid hadn't had the greatest childhood. But, at least Joey hadn't been in the clink—yet. Now why'd he think that? *Yet?* No, if he did nothing else in his sorry-ass life, he'd figure out a way to keep Joey out of prison.

Dale stole a quick look at Jacob, whose eyes were riveted on the road ahead. *Damn. There's a fucking tear rolling down his cheek.* He wanted to say something but decided against it. Turning to Joey in the back seat, he saw he was holding ice to his face and looking at his magazine.

Dale turned back and stared out the window, to see early trick-or-treaters being herded by their mothers. *Hell,* he realized blankly, *it's Halloween. Figures.* Jacob had told them they were returning to the house, to get there after dark. "In and out fast, no lollygagging," he'd said, and they'd go from there. Where, he didn't yet know.

"I'm taking the truck, Jacob," Dale informed him.

"Why? They'll be looking for it. It's more visible than this one."

"Me and Joey, we just need to go on alone."

"Well, let's get rid of this shit first—since you're *the man*," he said, with sarcasm.

"Yeah, well, it won't do for all of us to show up... Let's drop Joey off at the mall and we'll pick him up after. Got that, Joey?" he said over his shoulder.

"Yeah. What time'll you be back?"

"We need a couple hours. So be standing out in front, around 8:00." Dale looked at him, for emphasis.

"Yeah. Do you have a couple dollars?"

Dale reached into his pocket for his wallet.

By 10:00 p.m., they were driving onto the logging road that led to the old Berry place. Joey opened his eyes at the familiar turn-off and checked his watch. At the higher elevation, snow still covered the ground, but the tires rolled easily over it. He settled back against the seat.

Jacob pulled up and told Dale to check if anyone was staked out and waiting for their return. Joey heard his brother mutter as he buttoned up his coat and pulled on his hat and gloves. After stepping out of the old Bronco, Dale rolled the window down two inches to quietly close the door.

"If there *is* anybody there, won't they have heard us?" he asked Jacob.

Feigning sleep, Joey didn't mention that recent tracks, in or out of the place, would be clearly visible. *Yeah, I could've been a mountain man . . . in another life.*

CHAPTER 5
PETRIFIED

Sebastian drove to Senga's cabin after the party in silence and waning, sickle-moon darkness, save the light beam ahead. His appetite fully sated with food and drink, he groaned at the wheel.

"Eat too well?" Senga asked.

"How did you know? That was quite possibly the best meal I've eaten in America."

"Helped along by Caroline's aperitif, I expect. . . What a hoot—*watch out!*"

In reaction, he slammed on the brakes as a great horned owl winged low before the windshield from the west, to veer off to their right into the wash of light. It rotated its large round head in their direction, small beak and wide eyes meeting their startled gaze.

"Senga—hoot? Please stop *calling* them," he said under his breath. Owls were portents of doom in his culture.

"*I heard the owl call my name . . .*" she said quietly.

"Pardon?" He'd heard and didn't know if he wanted to pursue the subject. Slowly accelerating, he continued through the darkened landscape. Watchful.

"It's a Northwest Indian tradition . . . not sure if Plains as well. Owls are about something dying, but they don't always represent physical death. Like the hanged man in the Tarot, it can just mean the end of something. That's all." She was watching him, then—

"Here's the turn-off; it can be hard to see at night. See the glow?"

He could, in the near distance. The shrine to her daughter. A year-round Christmas tree near her cabin, illuminated every evening. If away after dark (she'd explained), it served as a "candle in the window," for her homecoming.

Sebastian dismissed the owl and negotiated the drive onto her property.

Indoors, Senga leaned down to light a ready-laid fire. *The night is young*, he recalled the idiom. His English had improved in the three months he had lived in this country. He put away his and Senga's outer garments, then turned to wash out the salad bowl she'd set on the counter. Her hand gently pulled his away from the task. A whisper—"Mine to do." Then, she indicated the woodstove, ". . . but that could be watched and fed. Please."

"As you wish," he replied in courtly manner. He chose a length of split pine from the tub to add to licking flames. After closing the windowed woodstove door, he moved to his chair.

"Who splits your wood for you, my dear?"

"I do it . . . though I dreaded it this year. I have enough for this winter, but next winter I may hire it done. My neighbor fells a dead for me about every other year and saws it into logs." She wiped the wooden bowl dry as he watched her.

Observing Senga had become ritual for him. Her actions proved economical; her intentions, astute. He watched her as if she were a poem; *louder than words* went the saying, yes? But she was quiet. Did everything quietly. *Except in bed. . .* He felt his face flush. The three joys of travel occurred to him: anticipating the travel, the trip itself and, soon after, reviewing it with pleasure. *If all went well*, he amended.

He pushed the thought away and resumed his exercise. She did not seem to mind his scrutiny. Some women might. Some women were self-conscious, he knew. He loved to watch Senga at her toilette, often made in the nude. He did not know if it was her usual practice, or if she did so for his sake.

The crackling fire lulled him. He turned his head sleepily as she spoke from the bedroom.

"There are a couple guys in town who have a wood splitter. That would be great. Mm. Thank you, Papa and Grannie," she said as she returned to the room and began filling the electric kettle with water for tea. She had changed into her robe; she needed a new one, he noticed. Hers was clean but worn. *Aunt's bright silk one suits her better.*

"Indeed," Sebastian said as he stood, then stepped, to one of the candles on the sill to light it. Then another, and another, until the cabin glowed like the votive stands in cathedrals he'd visited. He enjoyed candlelight at dawn and dusk, a practice in his country. The glow from the juniper shone beyond the periphery of the large window; no other light was necessary for their purposes.

While the water heated, Senga sat in her chair and closed her eyes for a moment. She opened them and smiled, eyes resting on an object on the table. "I've left it where you put it. . ." she told him, "as you can see, but what *is* it, please? It looks petrified."

"Ah. Well. This is one of those moments when I wish Uncle Harold were still alive. It is old. Prehistoric, I believe. I found it when I was walking along the creek bed that day," and he inclined his head toward the west. "Do you know the place where dark gray soil slopes to the creek? A very steep bank?"

She nodded.

"I stood, wondering whether to descend, when sunlight fell on this. It was partially hidden in soil." Sebastian picked up the object, still covered with powdery silt. He moved to the sink and turned on the tap.

"Do you have a cleaning brush, my dear?"

"Under the sink to the left. . . So what do you think it is?"

"I'll photograph it and make some inquiries, Senga. See how the bone has, *hmm*—"

Senga rose and stepped to the sink. She reached for the light switch and turned it on. "Better?" Then, "May I?" as she reached for the piece.

Cleaned of its debris, it measured four or five inches across, the same in length. A rounded cavity marked the middle, with sides like small wings. Sebastian recognized *lacunae* or, pock-marks of time on bone. Senga hefted the piece for its weight then brought it closer to better examine it.

"It's a vertebra," she declared.

Sebastian looked at it, then to Senga and back to the bone. His face broke into a wide grin. "Yes! I think so, too. Of course it is—I can see it now. But you astound me." He reached over and kissed her temple.

"One of my studies was paleontology . . ." she explained, "But a vertebra to what? You didn't see others? Seems the whole beast should be there."

"Parts could have washed down the creek—or river—if it ever was, eons ago. But yes, it could still be intact. Or, it could have been left as a kill by another animal and simply dropped there."

"Hadn't thought of that. Good point. Nice find, Sebastian. You'll have to show me the spot."

The kettle whistled and she took down two mugs for their usual tisane.

"Chamomile or linden tonight?"

"Linden, please," he said as he scanned the room for a place to put the bone. "Where do you want this?"

"Oh, take it with you—to photograph, right?" She set the timer to brew the tea.

"I have my camera; I'll do it tomorrow. Here—is this a good place?" he asked as he lifted the bone to a spot on the shelf above the window.

"Perfect." When the timer beeped, she turned it off and stirred milk and honey into hers, while he preferred his plain. After sweeping the dirt off the table with a hand, she brought the mugs and set them down, then arranged her only upholstered chair, an old blue wingback, to face the fire. They were settled.

"Did you enjoy the party?" she asked, facing the flames.

"I did. . . Lee is an interesting chap."

She smiled at his use of the noun.

"You mock my language skills, wicked girl. If you persist, I will begin to use some particularly annoying American expressions . . . like, you know. . ."

"Please, no!" she begged. "I'm sorry. And I was not mocking. I love how you speak, Sebastian. You are too defensive . . . or insecure, my Pooh Bear."

His teacher of English in Denmark was enamored of *Winnie the Pooh* and had taught by using the classic.

"Senga." He turned to her after setting his mug on the table and, drawing her image into his cells, he said, "I am afraid of leaving you—so, yes, I am insecure." His return flight loomed on the horizon, four days away. "I would have you come with me and not travel to Italy. Do you see how selfish I am?" He paused, staring into his lap. "Travel invites a certain kind of chaos, you see. One is at the mercy of the weather, the airlines. . . Strangers. . ."

"And Providence," she added, searching his face and finding his eyes, "I've never truly traveled, Sebastian, and I expect it *can* be uncertain—part of the attraction, I suppose. I have read travel essays though. Next best thing. . . A diary I found in a second-hand shop from the mid1800s recounted a grand tour of Europe, including Greece and, *not* allowing for contingencies permitted the element of surprise—or, adventure. What do you think?"

"Now I am more nervous, my dear. . . Have you contacted your grandmother?"

"No. Francesca will visit her when she gets back. Somewhere around the eighth, I think she said. It will give Nonna only four days before I arrive, but enough time to digest the thought of me, I hope."

"The thought of you, Senga . . ." Sebastian muttered, then stood. Stepping to the east window, he inhaled deeply, exhaled into the receding darkness past the tree light. Shifting his attention to her walking stick tucked into the corner, his eyes ranged up and down its two-toned length, with diamond-shaped clefts and a carved ball, two-and-a-half inches in diameter, adhered to the top. *Remarkable.* Eyes wide, he looked at her.

"Diamond willow. A client's uncle carved it. Fungus creates the patterns. As the branch grows away from the cankers, the diamond shapes are formed. The creamy color is the sap and the red wood is actually the heartwood. Beautiful, eh? I take it hiking. . . See the antler bit and sharp tip on the bottom? And you never know when you'll need a head-knocker around here—" she ran on, stopping abruptly when she saw his expression.

"How *strange* have been these last two weeks. . ." he said, his face twisting now in misery, his eyes both glistening and burning, the sound of his voice unfamiliar, even to him.

He looked at her again, locking eyes. Neither moved for several moments.

Senga asked, "What's your definition of 'strange'? O *Sebastian*. . ." As he sat once more, she touched his face.

He smiled as tension left his body.

Rather than replying (some questions demanded reflection, but he thought he meant "strangely wonderful"), he bent to the stove, opened the door and added a log. Closing the door, he rose, stepped to the window sills and moved the candles to the table, placing them in a tight collection of light. Then, he turned back to draw the drapes, first raising his eyebrows to Senga for permission. This granted, the space felt immediately warmer and he wondered why she hadn't closed them earlier—*To be inwardly warmed by the tree lights, likely.*

"Do you celebrate Halloween in Denmark?" she asked as she retrieved the water kettle to add more water to their teas. Then she stepped to her silverware drawer, and, from the back, pulled out a bar of chocolate, without even looking. Placing this on the table, she opened the wrapper and broke off a few squares, her actions reminiscent of a ballerina knowing her steps, though Senga had never studied dance.

"Have you heard of carving faces on turnips? This is done in Denmark. Not as easy as it sounds. Your method is simpler. Pumpkins. New World species—you fortunate Colonists. Where is yours?" he asked, glancing about.

"I've never had a single trick-or-treat-er here, do you know? Em and I—" He watched her take a breath and release it slowly, as if uttering the name aloud might unintentionally summon her, and now she needed to prepare her consciousness for her daughter's memory. *Surely it is ever present.* He waited.

"Em and I would both dress up and walk all over Sara's Spring, from the time she could walk. . . Some years it snowed, hard, and we only—ha! begged for maybe twenty minutes or less, but it was a big deal—for both of us. All that free candy! Or homemade cookies. You don't worry about razor blades in stuff—at least we didn't. We'd go to the annual breakfast supper at the hall, the one put on for the hunters. The season starts tomorrow, you know," she added. "Yes, Halloween was a highlight of our year. We enjoyed dressing each other up. . ." She turned away from him.

"It is the natural time of year for such remembrance," he said. "But thoughts are not ghosts," he countered and watched for the characteristic shake of her head, the nod to the left, once, to dispel a bothersome one. Emily did not *bother*. Nor did Elsa. They blessed.

The newly placed log popped with pitch and grew brighter. Both quietly watched. Faintly, through the walls, they heard an owl call and turned to gauge the other's response. Senga smiled and said, "I'm going outside for a moment. . . Um, would you like to come?" Her nightly habit of stepping outdoors every evening to unplug the tree, to inspect the skies, to remember her place in the universe.

"No, I'll stay," he spoke in a tone both sad and loving, how he felt in this moment. He watched her wrap in a shawl, lift the door latch, step onto the porch and gently pull the door closed.

Poignancy ruled the emotions, he believed. Its opposite occurred to him for some reason. *Ahh, I long for this night's sleep: to calm, to reassure, to simply restore.* Thinking in his first language relaxed him; the mental travail of conversing in another tongue neared an end for another day. One's own language was sweet to hear—like a mother's voice. *Mama. Yes, of course it is you who would come. And yes, I am in love again—with Senga. You would love her as well. I love you. Good night, Mama. Papa. And goodnight, my Elsa. I'll always love you—so very much. Rest well now. And our Emily. All of you. . .*

His prayer was interrupted by Senga's return. She draped the shawl over the chair back, then added one more log to the fire for the night. Taking her mug to the sink and rinsing it out, she glanced over her shoulder to him in question, or so he thought.

"Yes, I am ready, my dear. It has been a long, but good day. Rufus and Caroline are treasures, and the ocean will be such . . . such—" He struggled to find the word.

"Fun? Speaking of which . . . let's have some," and she unbelted her fleecy robe and let it fall in her wake as he followed her into the bedroom, picking up the garment as he passed. It was a small bedroom, *but adequate*, he noted, with her clothing hanging from various hooks. The large print of Waterhouse's *Mermaid* hanging by the bathroom door evoked—*what?* he wondered.

"I need to visit the ladies'," and Senga disappeared into the tiny room, pulling the door closed behind her. After a moment, he heard a flush and she opened the door.

From where he sat on the end of her bed, he could see her
at the sink, naked, and cleaning her teeth. Smiling with her eyes,
she gave him a side-long glance as she brushed. Then she leaned
over and rinsed her mouth.

His Senga, but *her* body.

No longer young, it retained a firmness due to exercise and
a mostly healthy diet, he decided. Her limbs were free of
dimpling and loose skin that can characterize the middle ages.
She did not bother with shaving; unusual in America. She had
never seen any reason to, she had told him. She wore jeans all of
the time, and if she did have to wear one of the two skirts she
owned, to a funeral or, a wedding, they were both long. In any
case, it did not matter. Her body felt feral when they made love.

He sensed the familiar tug upon seeing her as she turned to
him. . . Like an extraordinary nest it was—he had thought the
first time he saw it: thick, dark, soft, with no razor stubble; silky
and scented.

A thin stream of water *whished* in the sink. Senga stood with
one foot on a blue bath mat, the other perched on the closed
toilet seat. She was washing and seemingly enjoying the
experience, he thought. Judging from the contented look on her
face. Taking a face towel, she patted herself dry, then placed it
in the basket behind her.

Scents of violets and hyacinth mingled in the perfumed soap
he had brought her from his aunt's collection. Senga poured oil
from a glass bottle to anoint her face, breasts and vulva. *O Gud.*
He trembled but said nothing. She progressed to her feet, then
rinsed her hands and dried them.

Turning to him, she asked, "Loosed or braided?"

"Loosed," and with the word his loosed senses seized him.
He leaned over and hurriedly pulled off his socks (the boots left
at the door), then he rose, stripping off his teal wool sweater and
Henley. He unbuttoned his jeans, pulled them off and then his
underwear—his cock quite prepared ahead of him.

She stood before him, and he thought he could not wait
another second, when she whispered, *"Your turn,"* with a smile
and cutting her eyes toward the bathroom. And reaching down,
her hair falling over her shoulder, she touched him, and caressed
the tender underside. *"Mmmm,"* Then, she glided to the head of
the bed, pulled back the covers, cracked the window an inch and

slipped between cool sheets. He made a sound and moved toward the bathroom, leaving the door open. *Hoohoo—hoo!* called the owl, to be answered in the distance

CHAPTER 6
NATURAL HISTORY

The Black Hills, circa 1820

High Wolf returned to the camp disgruntled, having missed his quarry. The large deer, a drop tine on his right antler, had acknowledged him and blithely bounded off to live another day. *Inconceivable* that he had missed, he thought, and he should have searched for the arrow. *No time;* the sun was setting, and so he marked the area in his mind: beneath the horned escarpment, about ten paces from an old juniper.

His wife would have liked to have watched him stroll into camp carrying the beast across his broad shoulders. Alas, not this evening. He was glad She Who Bathes Her Knees was even-tempered and not prone to sarcasm, as were some wives of his friends. No, this wife was affectionate. They had as yet no children, but hoped to soon.

She would offer to return with him to search for his arrow. He knew this about her.

Her sister, called Lona (meaning "beautiful" in the *Tsitsistas* language), was causing a stir among the elders and talk among the rest. She had met a Little Eagle man and they had professed their love. This would have been accepted by her band, were she not promised to another *Tsitsistas*. Her betrothed had challenged the Little Eagle man, who would surely lose—given his size and lack of experience. Lona had wept as she related the circumstances to her sister and brother-in-law. Their mother took a hard stance and refused to back down, clearly preferring the *Tsitsistas*.

If only Father were here, She Who Bathes Her Knees lamented. A sickness took him in the cold time. Their mother was only being pragmatic; the tribesman would provide better for her daughter, hence, for her.

To distract Lona from the situation, Bathes Her Knees asked her along to help them find the arrow. They set off in the morning—a chill forecasting the coming season. High Wolf explained the distance. Bathes Her Knees carried a small bag of leftover meat from last night's meal.

"Will you keep your eyes open for that drop tine buck, or *any* game? And no chatter. The leaves are crisp as it is," he said. He wanted to take an animal before the moon was full, another eight days. It was his responsibility now to provide for his wife's family, as well as his own mother and a child she had adopted. He would surely welcome another hunter. *Pray it be soon.* But he kept his thoughts to himself regarding his wife's sister's affairs. The tribesman was a hard man, he knew. Not kind. Not gentle. Not a friend.

After trekking over hills and valleys for nearly two hand widths of time, High Wolf spotted the sheer rock face of the cliff to the east. It formed the curved end of a wide crescent of rim rock. Across the valley to the west, a similar abutment stood, but not as remarkable in appearance. Below, a dry creek bed meandered through the narrow valley. Here High Wolf turned to look at his wife and her sister.

"Do you see that dark soil rising from the creek bed?" High Wolf asked quietly, almost whispering. "The charcoal shade that reaches the shrubs?" He pointed with his lips. "When I was young, my father and I discovered a large bone there, like a gift sticking out of the earth. From the backbone of some ancient beast, he told me. I wanted to continue digging, but he said we would never be finished. That it was a task for those who came after us, and to leave it to them. But he allowed me to carry home the one bone. I still have it, do you know?"

"Yes, I do know. It is heavy," his wife smiled at him as she too whispered. She understood the bone as touchstone, in memory of his father, so she did not complain more than this simple assertion. He admired her patience. And now, he'd revealed where he had found it with his father. This was important.

Lona raised her eyes to the rim above the smooth wall and shuddered.

"What is it? Did you see something?" Bathes Her Knees asked the girl in a low tone.

"No, Sister. But I felt . . . I *feel* a coming fear."

High Wolf looked at his wife, but said nothing. He frowned as he turned east, toward the hillside from where he had aimed at the unusual buck. The women followed deftly to avoid the dry leaves.

In late fall, the pungent smell of sagebrush mixed with tang of deer or elk. They had passed several beds where dry grasses lay matted down near scattered, brown pellets. High Wolf tried to concentrate on their purpose, but presentiments unnerved him. When he turned to look at Lona, her eyes were lifted once more to the top of the rock face.

"Look where you step," he warned her.

CHAPTER 7
NO ONE'S HOME

The woods surrounding the old Berry place retreated into the black void. A light shining from the window aggravated his night vision, at least where seeing how to place a pair of pliers was concerned.

"Joey, *come 'ere!*" Dale needed help to remove the plow blade from the front bumper of his truck. In the headlights, he saw the lanky teen finally step around the corner of the house with several bags of gear. He set these down and grabbed the other end of the heavy implement. After Dale unbolted the last screw, they let it drop and he climbed into the cab.

The truck started; he'd been afraid it wouldn't. Dale leaned over and pushed open the passenger door. Joey stowed two of the duffels behind the seat and placed a third sack at his feet. Then he pulled two bungee cords from his jacket pocket and laid them on the flat bed. The boy walked back to the house, returned with a cooler and fastened it to the bed against the cab.

"What the fuck's all that?" asked Dale.

"Provisions, smart-ass. . . I'm not going to starve—or freeze."

Dale had seldom heard his little brother use bad language. It tugged somewhere.

"Oh. Well . . . good for you." He was feeling circumspect, for other reasons, having moved the money, wrapped in an old rag, from the truck's tailpipe, to a new home between the seat and seat cover. He'd told Jacob it was gone—that the cops must've discovered it. Jacob had peered at him without an ounce of faith, he thought. *So, what's new?*

Dale watched as Jacob turned toward the house. Joey twisted in his seat and looked through the back window. *He ain't gonna wave bye-bye,* Dale thought, but didn't repeat it aloud, and then he nearly drove through a pile of snow he'd pushed aside with the plow after the storm. Finally turning onto the logging road, he headed for the highway.

After several hundred feet, Joey startled him: "Stop! Dale, back up a bit, will ya?"

"What is it?"

"I thought I saw something. Just stop. No, back up—I'll need the light."

Dale shifted into reverse. "Here?" and when Joey nodded, Dale put the truck in park. Joey stepped out and headed toward a pine tree just off the road. He reached up for something and carried it back to his brother's side of the truck, smelling the smoke as it escaped a crack at the top of the window.

"I thought you'd quit—geez, Dale. . . Look; it's a game camera, or something like it. *I* didn't put it there, so *some*body's keeping tabs."

"What do you mean?" Dale asked, taking a long drag from the cigarette and blowing the smoke in Joey's face.

"C' mon, Dale! Knock it off!" He waved away the smoke. "There's a computer chip in here. See?" He slid back a small panel and pulled out a one-inch square chip.

"Hunh," Dale grunted. "So the cops were here, you think?"

"Well, I doubt it's hunters. Though I guess it could be . . ." Joey put the piece in his pocket then returned the camera to the tree. He walked back to the truck, opened the door and slid in.

Dale finished his smoke and pitched the butt. "There's that campground—you know? The one we stayed at when we first moved up here?"

"You want to go there? All right. I'm tired. Won't be comfortable though."

"Well, no shit, but at least it's close."

They turned off the road at the National Forest campground entrance and dug out their sleeping bags, then fixed peanut butter sandwiches and drank a coke between them. Dale stuffed his jacket behind his head. Joey did the same.

They lay in opposite directions and finally fell asleep. The windows' condensation at his head, cramped quarters and dropping temperatures made for bizarre dreams. The hideous image of a large, white worm crawling from George's mouth woke Dale, causing him to hit his forehead on the steering wheel—The dead man's eyes, open, were white as well; no pupils. "*Jesus*," he muttered under his breath.

In the old Berry house, Jacob cranked up the heat on the propane stove, hoping the tank outside held enough gas to last a while. He wandered from room to room, carefully checking for signs of entry. The place looked much as it had when they left. A pigsty. It would be hard to tell if anyone had trespassed.

He didn't know what to do. His skin crawled, as though he'd sat too long in the sun, and he felt as if he were shrinking inside. Something was sucking the air and juice right out of him.

It was only a matter of time before the cops would return and find him. *What the hell?* he thought, as he stood before the open refrigerator and considered the meager possibilities: a package of American cheese, mayo and soured milk (after smelling it). He returned it to the shelf mindlessly. A carton of orange juice and a package of ham. And mustard, he was gratified to see.

From a cabinet, he pulled down a loaf of multi-grain bread to make a sandwich. Joey had removed half the slices. The kid had taken the peanut butter too. Jacob noted this with no judgment. He was running out of judgment. It was leaking out of him like dry space in a scuttled boat.

He gathered the items and carried them to the old kitchen table. It was like one he'd grown up with in Idaho: curved chrome legs and a Formica top. He sat on the hard, plastic-covered chair, then rose again for a knife and paper towel.

Opening the jar of mayo, his mind acknowledged the same gesture, of his mother showing him how to prepare his lunch for school. The clock on the stove read 11:45. He was dog-tired, but hungry. *No wonder.* He'd hated to fall asleep on an empty stomach. Two tablespoons of peanut butter usually quelled the pangs.

"Hope you enjoy that Jiffy, kid," he said aloud to no one. *No one.* He turned the phrase over in his mind. *No one. No one. No one's home*. And it wasn't a home, he realized, catching the two meanings. It was a hide-out. Nothing more.

Less than nothing, he added.

Jacob spread the mayonnaise on the bread, both mindlessly and hyper-focusing at once, if that were possible. He watched the creamy substance smear in swirls and dips as he tried to cover every centimeter of the grainy slice. He remembered it made all the difference in taste and satisfaction. *'And no one to praise your paltry efforts. . .' Now where'd that bullshit come from?*

"What the hell?" he asked again, while glancing around the shabby room; the naked light bulb dangling from the ceiling, shining on a filthy collection of dirty dishes—if it'd been summertime, the mold would be thick; stacks of cans, trash and garbage. The lack of anything resembling pride of place. And yet George had felt at home here. Wanted to return. *Maybe he's here now.* Jacob swallowed the suggestion and returned to building his ham and cheese. *Nah, I don't feel him—not at all. He's gone, I guess.*
. .

He dismissed the memory of George.

Larissa had kept the place up, but now she was gone. And the kid too.

He wondered if they'd been found, after running off two weeks ago before the blizzard hit. She would've pretty much told the cops everything. If so, he was screwed. Then where *were* they, the bastards? And Larissa and the girl?

He'd check the burn pit and trailer in the morning for signs. *Signs of what?*

Anything.

Life? came the thought.

No one's home, the reply.

But it sure felt like someone, or something, was in the room with him. Funneling thoughts into his ear as it siphoned his nerves.

On the other hand, he reasoned, *maybe they froze to death during the blizzard and are out there somewhere, food for mountain lions and coyotes.*

He shuddered, then took a large bite of his sandwich, followed by a swig of orange juice from the carton. It was Dale's voice, disembodied, that interrupted his feeding frenzy.

How the fuck can you sit there and eat anything after thinking something like that?

"Yeah, leave it to you to grow a conscience . . . must be Joey's doing. . ."

He finished the sandwich, drank up the juice, then stood. The room had warmed. He'd be able to sleep, he thought, but first, he took a screwdriver from a drawer and stooped to a wall socket beside the chair where George always sat. He unscrewed the plate and pulled out a tight roll of bills, a rubber band encircling it. What good was it going to do him now? he wondered then shoved it down his front jeans pocket.

Larissa.

Jacob pulled on his jacket, grabbed the flashlight and walked out the door. His feet sank into the new-fallen snow as he headed for the trailer.

They'd left the door open to allow air to circulate and remove any residual odor. But that's why he was here; that's why he was stepping up into the trashed space, moving to the back where Larissa and the girl had slept.

He stood before the open closet and recognized the gray wool sweater she wore on most days. He lifted it off the hanger and brought the heavy garment to his face and inhaled. *Yeah.* A memory synapse fired and she was there. Not enough though. He pulled open a drawer. A couple of tee shirts and a pair of the girl's leggings. Under a pillow on the bed he found what he wanted. Bundling up the sweater and nightshirt, he returned to the house, where he crawled into bed, clutching the clothing tightly against his chest with one hand, while the other released his particular demons for the night.

CHAPTER 8
SAINTS COME MARCHIN'

hat? Senga asked the inky darkness. The phone rang again. Her back and bum fit snug as a puzzle piece into the hollow of Sebastian's groin. After climbing over his sleeping form, she reached for her robe and stumbled into the other room to snatch the phone from its cradle. A dim, orange glow shone from the woodstove glass.

"Hello?" she answered quietly, after reading *Joe Rafaela* on the caller I.D. She drew the robe around her shoulders with one hand.

"Senga? I'm so sorry. Did I wake you?"

"Joe, what's the matter? Anything wrong? What time is it?"

"Eleven. I'm sorry."

"No, it's all right," she sighed and sank into her wingchair. Then, rising in one fluid motion, phone to her ear, she opened the woodstove door, picked up the poker and spread the coals for another log. After it caught, she closed the door.

Seated once again, she asked groggily, "How are you?" for form's sake.

"We're doing well, Senga." (His adopted Cheyenne family—the Two Bears—and his assistant, Sister Joan.)

"I know this is late notice, but we're driving down in the morning to visit the Tower. . . Leaving right after 6:00 a.m. Mass; it's the feast of All Saints. Anyhow . . . just wondering if you'd like to meet for lunch, either near the Tower, or, ah, at your place?"

She caught the hesitancy behind his words, much as a brother might sound if he were planning to drop in with three extra guests.

She thought a moment.

"Senga? You there?"

"Yes, yes, I'm here, Joe. Just thinking. . . Hang on a second, will you?" She put the phone down and returned to the bedroom, where Sebastian was likely awake.

"Yes?" he asked.

"That's Joe—the Franciscan I've told you about? He and his adopted parents and assistant are coming tomorrow and want to have lunch. Can you stay to meet them? They're, ah, like family to me."

Sebastian rolled over, firmly planting the side of his face into the pillow and grunting another yes, added, "You have a large family, my dear," his voice trailing off, "for being orphaned . . ."

She returned to the phone, smiling.

"Sure, Joe," she said into the receiver, ". . . that'd be great. What time? And we can have soup here, as usual." Then, "I may or may not go to the Tower with you—I, um, have company."

"Yeah? Oh Senga, I'm *sorry*. Let's do this another time. I didn't—"

"Quit saying you're sorry—and no," she interrupted, "It's not like that. Besides, I want you to meet him." She waited for the surprised response. A moment passed.

"I cannot wait, Senga."

They said goodbye after agreeing on a time.

After replacing the phone on its cradle, she shuffled back to bed, where she fell back to sleep easily, her left leg draped over Sebastian's thigh.

"They are here, Senga." In mid-morning light, Sebastian stood at the small window over the sink. He was filling a glass with water and glanced at his watch. Ten-forty-five. The sky was cloudy and ponderosa tree tops across the valley swayed. It looked cold.

His mind raced as he conjured various tasks on his imminent trip list. Giving up, he shoved the matter away. He'd wanted to return to Spearfish early to begin packing, but this meeting apparently meant much to Senga, so he postponed his leave-taking. Sebastian reviewed their breakfast discussion as the beige sedan rounded the last curve in the drive. Senga had described the Franciscan monk, now a priest, as the man who had counseled her when she couldn't find her way through the months after Emily's death.

If anyone deserved the first-class, return-trip ticket from the underworld . . . it was she, Sebastian silently declared, honoring the hard-won wisdom that often accompanied such descents and, more importantly, the resurrections. *But, at what cost?*

Her imagery of the Franciscan's counsel bounced in the air. The *telling* was cursory, Sebastian expected; a quick précis. *Red and yellow hot air balloons? Ropes? A large and hirsute monk?* And the man's adoptive parents; the quiet and good-humored Cheyenne rancher named Milo, who called Senga "Missy"; his wife, Moona'e, who had taught Senga about Cheyenne medicinal herbs—their regional names and uses. She acted still as a mentor of sorts, it seemed—this Moona'e.

No, he decided he wanted to meet Joe, and his family, adopted or no. Something more than simple curiosity fueled the wish. His lover enjoyed regular correspondence with a priest and he needed to understand *why*.

He drank the water, rinsed the glass, dried it and returned it to the shelf. Senga was removing a pot of soup from the fridge; "ham and beans," she announced. It was her wont, she'd told him during their first encounter, to make a pot of soup a week, sometimes two pots.

This had been a two-pot week.

She placed it on the stove and set the heat to medium. Then, she lifted away the lid and stirred the contents. It would soon release its aroma into the air.

"Enough for six, you think?" she asked.

"With your bread, certainly," he said as he pulled her to him, embracing her before her attentions necessarily diverted to her guests.

He needed her. Seemingly more than she needed him; *feeling*, rather than hearing the desperate thought. When she raised her face to his to say, "I need you, Sebastian. *Like air*," he swallowed, wondering how she managed it. He cupped her face in his large hands and kissed her. She tasted of berry jam and coffee.

The sound of stomping on the porch steps drew them apart and each took a deep breath. Of air. Sebastian watched Senga smooth her hair as she opened the door.

"Hello! Come in, come in . . ." she greeted first Joe, then the Two Bears. Sister Joan was just reaching the steps, carrying a canvas grocery bag. *The cabin just might burst*, Sebastian feared, calculating the displacement of various weights and measures.

"Aw, you didn't have to bring anything, Sister Joan," Senga said. "There's enough, I think—" The last spoken in Joe's direction. The big man clearly enjoyed his meals.

The brown-robe guffawed with merry eyes sparkling from under thick brows, and above a full, round beard, betraying his age by its turning shades: white, auburn and flaxen. Hair in its usual unkempt style (according to Senga), *longish*, Sebastian noted, the length pulled back with a rawhide tie.

When everyone was inside, coats removed and hung, the sack taken from the no-nonsense looking nun—*no*, Senga had corrected him; Sister Joan was a Franciscan *sister*, not a "nun." *What was the difference again?* Senga exchanged hugs with her guests. Joe stole glances in his direction, Sebastian also noted. The guests settled into the four chairs, including the blue wingchair (for Moona'e) and the captain's chair, to which Senga directed Milo. Ladder backs for the priest and sister.

Senga fetched the teak wood shower stool for herself and a round, wide log from the wood pile, placing a pillow on it and indicating it for Sebastian with a flourish. He smiled at her and took his place. His height made up for the lower seating. After coffee mugs were filled, and spoons provided for sugar and Caroline's good cream, Senga introduced him. *Yet again.*

They had only met a little over two weeks ago; *a fortnight?* Yet it seemed, of a sudden, the woman's entire social network (such as it was) had conspired to inspect her choice. *Her choice?* No. *Incorrect again; it is comfortably mutual,* he decided, as he allowed himself to be swept along this new round of introductions.

Senga noted Sebastian's rising at each name. She watched Sister Joan betray slight awe at his courteous manner. *When did men stop rising when women entered rooms?* came the left-field thought. Perhaps it wasn't chivalry, as much as his sheer presence. Senga was certain Joe treated his assistant well, as politely as he treated herself.

Eighteen years ago, she'd roused the brown-robed, disheveled monk before dawn by persistent knocking, believing she was losing her mind. A spirit stronger than mere belief had led her to his home on the Northern Cheyenne Reservation, his small church's bell tower on that night illuminated by no moon's light. He gently coaxed back her ravaged senses, by inviting her to imagine faith, small "f," as a hot air balloon. Facile perhaps, but weren't simplest solutions best? She revisited the ritual on occasion, as a touchstone.

"Now, Senga, please tell us where you saw your Indian," Joe looked at her.

Oh, boy . . . she thought, looking down at the table, her consciousness struggling with itself.

"What's this, my dear?" asked Sebastian.

She raised her eyebrows, inhaled and blew out. Milo was scrutinizing her, she felt. *Of course he is. This*—other—*tall Indian*, she suspected, would have brought sage to smudge her home and the site where she'd seen the hunter, *just in case*. . .

"That red scrap over there in the tree," she addressed Sebastian, ". . . You asked me about it last week. I haven't mentioned it, because—"

"You do not *trust* me, Senga?" he whispered, a frown creasing his forehead.

She sensed his shame at having to admit this before near strangers.

"No—not that . . . well, not exactly." She turned to him and placed the palm of her right hand on his cheek. He raised a hand and pulled hers from his face. *Oh no,* she thought. *No, no, no* . . .

Joe spoke. "Forgive me for entering where I may not be welcome. . . Sebastian, you and Senga have only recently met, I believe? She didn't want to give a crazy impression. Is this close, Senga?"

"Sebastian was there when Emily died, Joe," she said, first looking at the Dane, then back to the Franciscan, ". . . and well, yes, it does sound nuts. . . Let me tell it, please?" She looked into Sebastian's face, which had blushed pink in confusion, in humiliation; she couldn't know. Not yet.

He gazed at her a moment as a sad smile turned the corners of his mouth. "So, tell me . . . tell *us*, please."

She leaned over and kissed his cheek and he lifted her hand to his lips and kissed her knuckles.

"*Aw,*" Moona'e and Sister Joan quietly spoke in unison.

"This won't take long, but it's still a story. Milo, do I need a prologue or something?" Senga asked.

"Missy, you only need to tell it *true*. Don't add stuff, don't leave out stuff. But I wouldn't mind a refill—" he said, lifting his mug. "I see you still have some on the stove." He lip-pointed to the French press steaming in a pan of heated water.

She rose and refilled their mugs. "Anything else before I begin?"

"Got any chocolate, Senga?" Moona'e asked, aware of her friend's penchant.

With a grin, Senga walked to the drawer and pulled out the bar. Just enough remained, she saw, and she placed it wordlessly on the table. Closer to Moona'e.

"Well, it *is* a feast day, after all," said Sister Joan, dryly, as she reached for a piece. Moona'e playfully pretended to slap her hand back and took a square.

"Wait," Milo said. He stood and stepped to the clothing pegs near the door. He uncovered his jacket hanging beneath another and, reaching into an inside pocket, he drew out a small paper sack. He set this on the table and returned to his seat.

From the bag, he withdrew a bundle of dried sage and an abalone shell. The expression on his face remained neutral, his features dignified and calm as he retrieved a lighter from a front shirt pocket. Sister Joan slipped a dark brown square of chocolate into her mouth.

"Moona'e?" Milo addressed his wife. She reached into her purse at her feet and lifted something wrapped in a length of blue cloth. She passed it to her husband. Milo uncovered the brownish-black and white feather of a bald eagle, closed his eyes for a moment, opened them and began.

"We ask you, Grandfather, to help us today, and to help Senga here tell her tale true and well. We thank you, Creator Spirit, for helping us."

Joe crossed himself.

Senga had never heard Milo call her by name. That he even knew it surprised her. She felt a tickle in her heart toward the man and paid attention. *The sweet sound of one's own name.* She reached for Sebastian's hand. She wanted him to be with her in the telling.

Milo lifted the light-green sage stick and lit the end, holding the flame to it until it burned well. He lowered it toward the bowl and gently blew it out, sending the plume of heavy, gray smoke into the air. The scent filled her nostrils—a clean, ancient smell.

After setting the smoldering end of the stick into the mother-of-pearl shell, Milo solemnly lifted this and the eagle feather in the direction of each one seated, to waft cleansing smoke in their direction and to ask help from the Seven Directions: North, South, East, West, Above, Below and Within.

"Receive this story into your hearts with the spirit it is given," he said after setting down the bowl. Smoke continued to drift up.

"Please begin, Senga."

Giving Sebastian's hand a squeeze, she said as she met each one's eyes, "Thank you all for being here. . ." She paused. "I was sitting here waxing the table. About three weeks ago. It was evening, just dusk. . ."

His reason felt assaulted. Sebastian said nothing; rather, he looked to the others for their responses. It did not help. They sat quietly absorbing the story. Its possible import. Its impossible premise. He knew why she had not told him. She apparently knew him well enough to guess what his reaction might be. And he proved her right.

He would say nothing; he would simply feign interest. And his being from the land of the fantastical Hans Christian Anderson . . . *But it does not compute*, his reason complained.

Milo wanted to hike over to the red marker, he heard the man say, as though from the end of a long tunnel, as if he were already on the other side of the ravine. Then, he actually heard him say he wanted to search for the point, the arrowhead, the projectile supposedly sent flying toward a large buck. According to Senga, the deer had looked at the vanishing hunter before bounding away; the large-antlered one, a "drop tine," she'd called it, later spotting it below the pond. Sebastian wrestled with—*yes, the "point"*—of all this.

Did his Senga hallucinate? Did she use psychoactive herbs among others?

Was there something he did not wish to accept about her? *Is she unstable?*

They pulled on their coats. Milo asked *Missy* (once more calling Senga her pet name, he noticed) for a piece of foil in which to wrap the sage. He wanted to smudge the area, he explained. Sebastian did not know if it was similar to the use of incense in church, or for another purpose. She handed him a scrap from a drawer after he made sure the stick was extinguished.

He noticed Senga glancing at him from time to time. *She knows I struggle with this.* He forced a smile, but she frowned in recognition.

"Don't do that," she said in a hushed tone of sad contempt.

"I am sorry, my dear. It *is*—"

The Franciscan spoke. "George Catlin painted a portrait of the Cheyenne chief named High Wolf in 1832. The book's in the car. We know something about the man by Catlin's written descriptions, and through oral history. Senga's drawing bears remarkable resemblance." Then Joe quoted: "*There are more things in Heaven and Earth, Horatio. . .*" nodding once in Sebastian's direction.

Well, at least he picked the appropriate play, thought the Dane. *Ghosts, indeed.*

Nothing else was said as they carefully picked their way down the ravine behind her cabin. Sister Joan and Moona'e reached for ponderosa saplings to aid their uncertain descent. They crossed the narrow, snow-covered bottom and slowly ascended the other side, avoiding the still-slippery mud.

At last they gained the sloping, pine-needled ground under the thin strip of red cloth. Torn from a bandana, Senga explained. She'd hung it from a broken-off twig at approximately the same height as was the top of the hunter's head. Milo stood a close second. She watched him gaze across the ravine toward the cabin, then turn to her with a guarded expression.

"I hung it as close to the hunter's height as I could. He was tall," she told them.

Sebastian reached for Senga's hand and drew her several feet away from the others. Joe occupied himself with examining the ground for signs. Moona'e and Sister Joan quietly conversed, looking in the direction of the now-visible bank of the nearly dry pond where Senga had seen the buck. Milo simply stood and stared toward the cabin, lost in thought.

"I must leave, Senga," Sebastian told her. "Will I see you tomorrow or Sunday? Please?"

He felt her scrutiny for a tell-tale sign. *A withdrawal of his affections?* Not finding one, happily, she answered, "Yes, of course. Sebastian—"

He didn't allow her to finish, but leaned down to kiss her forehead. Turning to face the others he said, "It was a pleasure to meet you. Forgive my leaving now—before the end of your, ah—ceremony. I may not be the right man to have along," he added.

"I don't believe that, Sebastian," he heard Senga say as antidote, ". . . but you have a lot to do before Monday. I wanted you to meet everyone, and now you have," she said as she turned to them, smiling. They stood by quietly, not wishing to intrude.

Joe looked at Milo, then turned to Sebastian. "My family and I, and Sister Joan, are honored to have met you, Sebastian, and I pray for another opportunity to become better acquainted. Safe travels back to Denmark, and may God be with you." Then he turned to Milo and nodded. Removing the sage stick from the foil, the old Cheyenne set about smudging the area around the tree.

"I'll walk you to your car," Senga said.

"No, I can find my way, my dear. I'll be fine. Stay here." He started for the edge of the ravine, turned back and reached for her, brushing her forehead again with his lips, and then left. He saw her squat down and touch the ground with her palm, to ground herself, she had once explained.

CHAPTER 9
REAL OR IMAGINED

Her guests finished the pot of ham and beans, each lost in their own thoughts, while sopping up the last savory bits with Senga's bread. She had no appetite, however. The two Franciscans and the Cheyenne couple then left for the Tower, having much to pray about, consider and ponder.

Senga stayed behind, feeling at loose ends. Travel details to Italy needed to be sorted, as well as pressing decisions regarding her inheritance, and, if truth be known, this developing relationship with Sebastian. All these jockeyed for position with regard to her emotions. Never mind the discovery of an old arrowhead buried in soft earth, very near the site of the buck's appearance. Twice in as many days, a thing, unearthed, lay on her table. Like a question, or, a riddle.

First things first usually served her well. She walked into her bedroom and opened her top dresser drawer. A collection of colorful ribbons, each cut to twelve-inch lengths, lay neatly in rows. She chose one at random, closed the drawer and made her way to the old juniper tree behind the cabin.

"Tall Juniper" was the name given her Cherokee ancestor, her great-great grandmother. This living tree, where she remembered her daughter Emily, had become a prayer for Senga. It was decorated with lights and notions, prayer cloths and baubles, trolls and fairies, dolls and tiny mirrors. She closed her eyes.

"Be with me. Let me *see* where I'm going." And, "I love you, Emily, always." She stood a moment longer in silence.

Opening her eyes and reaching for a green spray, she tied the glossy blue ribbon to its end, loosely. Stepping back, she nodded once and turned back to the cabin.

Recent events pulled like four head-strong horses, and she was riding each pair Roman-style, where the rider stood on, rather than sat astride, her mount—a circus trick, one she and her young cohorts once practiced in the army base stables' arena, much to Sgt. Brown's abject disapproval. She now found herself having to leap, figuratively, from one demanding priority to the next, while maintaining a semblance of balance.

Dynamic disequilibrium, eh, E.O.?

And then she snorted. *Easier said than done,* she addressed the eminent biologist, E. O. Wilson and his theory.

She cleared the table and filled the sink with hot, sudsy water to wash the dishes.

Senga subscribed to his hypothesis—at least in theory—that life, in absolute balance, cannot exist; that absolute balance signifies death. Rather, a kind of "dynamic *dis*equilibrium" prevailed. A verb. A back and forth. Perpetual motion. Tides.

It countermanded ambivalence, or equal value given to two opposing notions, not the culture's popular definition of *uncertainty* or *indifference.* This is where her disequilibrium had abided most of the time. In a watery limbo.

Until recently.

Now, she considered (like the pair of horses) the American Indian notion of harmony. Senga invited it to bring her peace.

Two voices, or more (it is to be desired), singing in harmony, signify the Christ's 'life abundant': a soul at peace with herself, couples, children, siblings, neighbors, towns within counties, countries simply living in peace— ever the challenge; the struggle; the work—she had written in her journal long ago.

She shook her head to refocus. There was much to do, and she'd promised Sebastian she'd see him tomorrow. She *wanted* to see him, and looked forward to sharing the arrowhead's discovery, despite his skepticism. Was there room for both doubt and love in a relationship? She heard Grannie's reply, "*Of course, dearie!*"

She rinsed the last glass and set it in the rack to dry with the rest of the dishes.

No need to stoke the fire; the cabin felt warm. Her gaze fell to the flinty point on the table. She picked it up, stepped to the sink and ran cold water over it. It measured an inch across by one-and-a-half in length. She dried it carefully with a dish towel and set it back on the table, then glanced at Grannie's small cedar box, the one containing letters from her mother. The postmark on the first envelope read October 8, 1960. Six years before she was born.

What would be gained by reading them? Would they help her understand, or at least explain her mother's mental illness? How crucial was that knowledge? Or, she could simply burn them and be done with it. Be none the wiser. *Be none the more disturbed.*

Senga grabbed the canvas bag in which she carried necessities when pockets wouldn't do. She'd have lunch at the café and treat herself. From the top of her dresser, she took her journal and wallet. From a shelf in the sitting room, she lifted the letter from Colin, and the envelope containing the check, placing all in the bag.

Before latching the door behind her, she stepped back inside to check the calendar. Sebastian would leave for Denmark on Monday, three days from now, not to return until December 20 or 21. "Francesca to Italy" was noted for Thursday, with herself and Gabe to follow on December 2, rendered simply, "To Italy!" Only four weeks in which to prepare and sort through her increasingly complicated life.

She backed out of her garage and carefully drove to the highway, concentrating on previous tire tracks. After replacing the mail carrier's bag in the box, she turned south toward town. The sky gleamed, like milky-white abalone, and she noticed the road-side grasses bending with the wind. From the north-west. *Something blowing in,* she guessed. A muffled *boom!* resounded outside the car and she remembered it was the first day of deer season. Another blast and another, and she decided the animal had escaped the hunter's aim. Lone shots usually signaled a kill.

When Senga reached town, she stopped for the resident peacock to cross the road—its crest a raised hand, urging everyone to "wait!" A semi pulled up opposite her, also giving the road to the bird. She wondered if the peacock had been conferred a name.

Cocky Bastard came to mind.

The exotic creature had joined the resident flock of turkeys, possibly believing itself a member of that species. And what did *they* think of the interloper and his screech? Senga watched the bird stride imperiously between her and the trucker, and she smiled up to him in his cab. He lifted both hands, palms up, as she'd often seen *Nonna* do, in the universal gesture. The trucker grinned when they proceeded, bird now safely on the other side. *And so why did you cross?* She chortled and continued into town, where she parked at the library and entered.

"Hi, Muriel," she greeted the librarian, who wore the same navy blue cardigan every day. In warmer months, she switched to a lightweight cotton style, still navy blue. The woman once admitted she'd attended parochial school when young and the habit stuck. "No nun-pun intended," she'd added, laughing. Senga occasionally envied her sanguine heart. She worked with Muriel, contentedly, on Tuesdays and Thursdays, sorting books, creating seasonal bulletin boards and displays and performing other tasks as needed.

"Hi, you. . . What are you doing here today?"

"I need to use the computer, please, ma'am," Senga answered, heading to the bank of machines. They were alone.

"Charlie tells me those yahoos haven't been caught yet." The old Berry place folks, Senga guessed. Muriel dated Charlie, the chief of police, and while he might not discuss ongoing investigations with his girlfriend, he couldn't help the occasional slip, especially where public safety was concerned.

"No?" Senga replied. Changing the subject, she asked, "Will you want some *Echinacea* tincture for the winter? I just made some. It'll be ready in another month or so. And I've got some elderberry syrup, too." She signed her name on the computer use sheet, then sat down at a terminal and keyed up the State Department website.

"Yeah, I do, Senga; both please. Oh, and a jar of that salve. Charlie likes it. Same prices as last year?" she asked.

"Sure, and thanks."

Muriel was an herbal client, as well as her supervisor. Senga didn't like the idea of selling remedies to her clients, preferring they make their own or find other sources. But given where she chose to live, she wouldn't scruple a conflict of interest that selling her remedies might create. As a solution, she tallied the simple cost of materials and left it at that. Her charge for consultation was kept to the minimum as well. She preferred to barter for services when possible.

Gabe had once told her something: In 2006, after she had applied a poultice to his injured collarbone, she refused payment when offered. He'd looked at her long, grimacing through the pain and said, "You know, the *traiteurs* in Louisiana don't charge money for their healing work either. Believe the remedies won't work if they do. So . . . is that right?"

"Hmm," she'd replied, "Can't answer that. I wouldn't know," and she'd given him a sidelong glance. "I do know you need to keep movement to a minimum. Give it time, Gabe."

She knew what a *traiteur* was; it described her Grannie Cowry. French for "healer," or someone who renders treatment. Gabe Belizaire had repaid her in friendship and called her *chère*.

She'd never spotted the connection between *cherished* and *chère*. Dear. Sebastian also called her *my dear*. Grannie had called her "dearie." *Hunh.*

In a short time, she'd printed off the necessary pages, paid for them and jotted down what Muriel wanted on a page in her journal, reserved for such notes.

"So, where are you off to now?" asked her colleague.

"Oh, the bank. Then I'm having a late lunch, ah, *treating* myself—a unique idea, huh?" Senga smiled, turned and headed for the exit. "Enjoy your day, Muriel," she called from the door and, "See you next week. . . Oh, I forgot," she stopped and turned. "I'm going to need to take some time off in December. A couple weeks."

"Oh?" Muriel waited for details. Then accepting they weren't forthcoming, she said, "All right. I'll put it down. See you Tuesday, Senga," and she turned back to her monitor.

"Bye," Senga said, as the door closed behind her.

The Cottonwood Café was bustling. Remodeled in Old West motif, nearly every square inch of wall space sung with memorabilia and examples of western art, thanks to a collector who fancied himself aficionado of "all things cowboy." Maybe he'd earned a lifetime of complimentary meals. Western décor and biker kitsch spilled into the bar. The ambience clearly succeeded—the town richer for it.

Senga spotted a quiet table in the back of the snug room. She hung her jacket near the door and settled into a chair facing out. Something she'd picked up from Gabe. "See 'em coming," he'd once explained. *And why is he on my mind today?* she wondered. *Circumstances?*

Answering her own question, *Yes*, Senga smiled at the server as she approached. The woman did a double-take, having recognized her. Senga rarely came for an actual meal. A cup of coffee to accompany an herbal consultation comprised the formal extent of her patronage.

Across the room, also seated alone, a familiar face nodded. She nodded back. Tom Robinson. She hadn't seen him since the incident in the grocery store. *Figures I'd run into him,* she sighed. Tom tucked back into his meal. She remembered he'd checked on her after. Called Caroline. She owed Tom Robinson a debt of kindness—and, for saving her from herself that day.

"What can I getcha, Senga?" the server asked, holding up her pad and pen, "Same?"

She couldn't remember the server's name and felt badly. "Uh, no . . . Is there a special?"

The woman handed her a menu, adding, "Yep. . . A bowl of lobster bisque and a Portobello mushroom *panini* with provolone. A small side salad too, with Caesar dressing. A small brownie for dessert. Coffee if you want it."

"That—" and she tried to think of an appropriate response to being presented with such an unusual prospect for her—well, *lunch*. "That will be fine, thanks, and just water, please." The woman smiled, turned and strode toward the sound of clatter in the noisy kitchen. From where Senga heard the forgotten name.

"Hey, Annie! Order up!" from the affable owner-chef.

Annie, Annie, Annie, Senga repeated to herself.

Judging from the lunch crowd, it might take a while, there being *only* Annie working, so Senga pulled from the bag her journal, the letter from Colin and the passport application. The check was safely deposited in her savings account, having substantially increased its earlier balance of $243.56. She cringed, recalling the teller's expression at seeing the check, and felt that knee-jerk, guilty reaction one occasionally experiences when presented with an impossible scenario in one's favor.

Senga shook her head in her fashion, then used the time before her meal arrived to record the morning's spine-tingling discovery in her careful handwriting:

All Saints Day.

This is important—the way the Aurora Borealis is important, the way water is important, the way, oh, orgasm is important. . .

CHAPTER 10
IN THE SHADOW OF THE BEAR

A sweet apple smell filled Joe's car as they reached the Tower. He handed the ranger his yearly pass to enter the nation's first national monument and proceeded at the snail's pace speed limit, over the Belle Fourche River and past the prairie dog village, to finally arrive at the visitor center nestled beneath the monolith. He eased into a parking space, turned off the engine and became still. As did his passengers. The Kiowa, N. Scott Momaday, once wrote, "There are things that engender an awful quiet in the heart of man; Devils Tower is one of them."

It loomed, a colossal ship's smoke stack; or, a giant stump of a tree, 867 feet in the air. Six-sided columns of stone ranged the entire height in some places, with many broken off and fallen round the base. Here is where bears had once made their dens in the huge rip-rap of stone shelters. But no more. An asphalt path circled the rock, with benches placed for viewing climbers, falcons, eagles and any other species aspiring to great heights. Also, for simple contemplation and rest.

"Here we are, *Nakovehe*," announced Moona'e, speaking the Cheyenne name.

"*Aho*," grunted Milo, signaling their exit from the car—in greeting, respect, readiness. They would hike clock-wise on the path and pause to offer prayers, their usual practice when visiting the place, set apart as sacred.

Joe wished to discuss Senga's vision, and trembled with questions and awe. There would be a proper time for this, he knew, so he took yet another deep breath and carried on, panting, as the path inclined for several yards. Milo, Moona'e and Sister Joan regulated their pace to his slower one. In the silence, Joe reviewed the morning's discovery. Perhaps they all did.

After Senga's friend left (with Joe's sympathy), Milo finished smudging the area around the ponderosa where the sad strip of bandana still clung. Senga pointed to where the buck had stood. The hunter had loosed his arrow directly after the animal had acknowledged the man's presence. She had seen the deer turn and bound away. When she looked back, the man had gone. "Vanished."

The group hiked to the spot where the buck had stood—marked with a stick. The elder Cheyenne examined the area then gestured to them. Not excitedly. Like someone casting a line into a stream. With easy grace. They saw four double, comma-shaped footprints, indicating a large buck, its hock marks pressed firmly into the soil behind each, and the telltale scoring. These lines followed each track in the soft clay at water's edge, by the buck's hind legs having slid along the bank. Milo pointed out more tracks, spaced in a large deer's stride, heading in the direction Senga had mentioned.

He cautioned them, too, against treading on the area; they might press the arrowhead farther into the earth. Milo asked them to stand aside and he'd search for it. But first, he re-lit the sage stick and wafted smoke in a circle. Moona'e and Sister Joan stood by patiently and, as the wind came up, they pulled their jackets closed. Joe realized none wore bright orange on this first day of deer season. He searched the woods with his eyes and uttered a quick prayer.

Milo handed the abalone shell and sage to his wife, returned his lighter to his shirt pocket and faced Senga's torn bandana marker, back to the hoof prints and again to the marker in the tree. Joe then watched his adopted father lower his gaze three feet and back to Senga's stick.

Of course, the man knelt to shoot, Joe remembered. In air charged with expectancy, he prayed *Thy will be done.*

Milo, with blank expression, had stepped to a spot about five feet behind the stick marker, squatted down and carefully pulled away tufts of grass that anchored the soil of the bank. He used his pocket knife to scratch. Then, he rocked back on his heels, turned to them and grinned.

(Joe lived for the moments when this man grinned.)

Milo said nothing. It was unnecessary. They crept up beside him, and there, on the earth—rather, un-earthed—lay a perfectly-made point. Only a point, Joe noticed—no sinew; no shaft. Both would have been long gone. They looked at one another and Joe shivered, even in his long brown robe.

"Well," he said. Then he crossed himself.

"Well, *I'm* impressed," said Sister Joan, wryly. Moona'e giggled. Senga whooped and they all laughed, in sheer stupefaction.

Milo addressed Senga. "Go on, Missy—it's your medicine. You gonna take it or leave it alone? I don't think it matters, taboo-wise," he added.

She glanced up to the red cloth on the tree, then back to the point and slowly reached for it. . .

There are more things in heaven and earth . . . Joe repeated silently as they continued their way around the great rock. Wind soughed in the tree tops and the sky shone a luminescent pearl gray—like nacre of abalone.

They met a young couple coming toward them. Joe wondered why people preferred to walk counter-clockwise around the Tower. Senga once told him she wanted to leave a suggestion that hikers be asked to walk sun-wise, *with* the energy, instead of against it. Joe understood. The Cheyenne held similar ideas regarding ceremonial protocol. Especially in dances. Ring around the rosy. *It probably has more to do with logistics—fewer run-ins, if all go one direction,* he'd parried. She'd snorted.

A *large* rosy then, the Tower.

In a monthly letter, Senga discussed how rose petals grow in a clock-wise spiral, citing but one example of nature's repeating patterns. She also proposed the Tower exuded some massive, *massive*, magnetism, and the closer you were, the stronger the vortex of earthen energy, and the crazier or, more "enlightened," you might grow. *Six of one* . . . he remembered thinking. "Probably a little of both," he'd responded. It was how he viewed her.

Joe started at Moona'e's unexpected voice, and looked up to see "their" tree twenty-five feet below the trail, an evergreen. Ever-greening. *Viriditas*—a favorite word coined by the twelfth

71

century nun, Hildegard of Bingen. Colorful prayer bundles and cloths hung here and there.

No one intruded because no one passed above on the trail. Crows called. He heard a far-off turkey gobble. The chattering of squirrels, several peeps from an unseen bird and four doe passing farther below reminded Joe he was in, or on, a preserve. Milo and Moona'e sat down beside each other on a log; Sister Joan and Joe moved toward their usual boulders. Joe spoke after a period of silence.

"So, how do we speak of this thing?"

"It is Missy's, Joe. We do not need to speak of it," Milo said, gazing straight ahead.

"Joan? What do you think?" asked Joe.

"I really haven't had time to digest it. But I remember thinking—as Senga was telling it—that we'd try to come up with an explanation, where there might not be one."

Milo grunted. *In agreement.* Joe knew the man's habits.

Moona'e sighed. "You white folks always need answers. . . I have read one of your poets. The German man, Rilke. He said learn to live the questions. Seems like this is enough to do in a day. They're crowded as it is."

Sister Joan chuckled. "Moona'e, you are so right. Still, aren't you the least bit curious?" Her friend remained quiet.

Milo finally spoke up. "I think it is not something we are so amazed at, as you seem to be. Even as a holy man and woman, you are both surprised sometimes, by what you say are your stories. I mean the Scriptures. There is wonder in them. Why should it ever stop? And isn't it *always* so?"

Milo had him, but not in a one-over way, he knew. It was a simple teaching. Effortlessly delivered. *If only we could live the wonder moment to moment.* He groaned. *Live the questions, indeed; and accept mystery.*

"All right," Joe stood and arched his back. He could already feel his calves stiffening. "But science and wonder don't have to be enemies," he said now, more as an aside. He didn't expect a discussion.

"This sighting or, *vision*—if you like," his assistant suggested, "was, ah, *unusual,* yes, but I see wonders daily . . . and so do you. Why should this be any more special? I mean, consider water, or light, or . . . rainbows, or . . . birth—any number of everyday miracles. Let's put this in perspective, shall we?" and she peered at Joe through horned-rim glasses that had served her for forty-five years.

"I repeat," said Joe, "science and wonder don't have to be enemies," then he smiled at Sister Joan while extending his hand to help her stand; next, Moona'e. Milo took a deep breath and rose.

"This is still Missy's," the Cheyenne man said, ". . . and only she will know what to do with it when the time comes. We have our own purposes here; let us not forget," reminding them of their intentions: prayers for their young, their old and their families. The Cheyenne Nation. They resumed the circumnavigation of the Bear's Lodge—the Tower—in procession and entreaty. A walking meditation for each.

CHAPTER 11
PANDORAS

At home, after reviewing the arrowhead's discovery in her journal, Senga rose from the table, her eyes still examining the finely-worked point. '*Tidy cupping, stippled in stone,*' she leaned over to scribble on the page's margin. The arrowhead lay beside the brass candle stick, its tip pointing due south, signifying something on a Medicine Wheel, but she couldn't recall what. *Rebirth?* No, that's east.

Night had fallen. As the soup was no more, she boiled two eggs for her supper and ate these with toast. An apple with Swiss cheese, for dessert. After clearing her few dishes, she lit a candle, as was her habit when writing. The flame borrowed a property of company—or possibly, conscience. She settled into her chair to draft a letter to her cousin, to be revised in the morning; she wrote what came to mind, not censoring herself. The practice also served to sort her emotions, their being untidy at present.

"Dear Colin," she began. "I received the box and news regarding the sale of Papa and Grannie's home. I remain in a mild state of shock, mind you, owing to this—and other events. But I want to thank you for sending those precious items. And, the check. It came in the mail shortly after the box, and the sum now rests in the bank. The contents of the box would have been treasure aplenty, but you've heaped more upon them. Thank you, again, and for all your trouble on my behalf. The prospect of having money, however, is strange to me.

"I live simply, as a simpler (like Grannie), apple grower and part-time library assistant. And, I live missing my Emily. Rob may have told you about our daughter's death in 1994. But, now I'm with someone—only recently; I hadn't realized how lonesome I'd been. The heart's a muscle after all; it can and, does, atrophy.

"With some of the money, I am traveling to Italy next month with a friend, to see my grandmother, Maria Teresa. Most strangely, an Italian friend here happens to know her in Lucca—located in Tuscany. Nonna and I lost touch after Emily died. I lost touch with life as well, save the perfunctory bits. Existing is not the same as living. . ."

Senga reviewed her thoughts. They sounded too personal. She slipped the letter into the table's slim drawer. The words, like an herbal infusion, needed to steep overnight.

The clock on the stove read 8:10. She stoked the fire in the woodstove, then fancied a hot cup of milk with nutmeg and cardamom sprinkled in it. Honey too. Caroline's cow gave enough for a cottage industry of products.

Had my heart atrophied, Grannie?

Not entirely, dearie. You were saved by the bell—ha! The one in the pretty pictures store. The gallery in Spearfish, after Sebastian entered.

Senga smiled, lifted a pan from a hook and set it on the woodstove. There was the conventional stove, but this one was already hot. She poured milk from the jar, and stirred it with a whisk until small bubbles formed around the edge. After adding spices and honey, she filled the mug, rinsed the pan and set it in the dish rack to dry.

While the milk cooled, she crossed to her bookshelves for Grannie's cedar box, included in Colin's package.

When Senga had opened it two weeks ago, a familiar scent had wafted from the long-closed container. Cedar, to be sure, but something else. She had lifted the box to her nose. It was, quite simply, Grannie; specifically, a soap she liked. *Lifebuoy.* Her grandmother wouldn't have placed it in the box for mere aesthetic reasons. No; it must ward off insects, or mildew, or both. Senga had rooted beneath the papers and letters until her hand touched the smooth coral shape.

Curiosity trumped an earlier notion to wait until winter to inspect the contents. She set aside the soap and lifted out the top sheet of paper, this folded into thirds.

December, 1976

> *My dearie,*
>
> *I am writing this in the days after your sweet mama's dying. I have some things I want to say, and if I don't say them now, I'm liable to never, so whether you read this one day or not, this is my testament to you, and to your mama—my baby girl.*
>
> *You stand on either side of me. I write this to Lucy's too-short life, and I write it to yours, which I pray will be long, and it is also my wish that you understand how strong you are, and how loved.*
>
> *But I also want you to know that sometimes these things don't matter a lick. I remind you that my remedies don't always work. Things happen that I, or we, can't control. Strength and love can sometimes cover us like a warm blanket, yet the cold seeps in—is what I mean to say. But a blanket is a blanket, you might say, and you'd be right.*

Senga laid her forehead on the table. On the letter. She turned her cheek to the cool paper, drifting her gaze to the burning flame, dancing on the wick, alive and bright.

A blanket is a blanket is a blanket . . . she repeated silently.

Raising her head, she took a sip of the milk, and another. It tasted like peace smelled, of nutmeg and cardamom. Scents of Christmas. Grannie's *Glory Robe* came to mind—the old healer's method of arranging all her senses into "a one *big* one."

The letter included several more paragraphs, then a signature. No closing; simply "Grannie."

Senga's mother was killed in a car accident, only a few weeks after she'd begun to regain her sensibilities. She'd passed long months in a state hospital, being treated for mental breakdown. Agnes, as Senga was then known, was ten years old. *Emily was nine when she—*

She returned to the letter:

> *. . . Your mama was a lot like you when she was your age now. She gloried in everything. Like a newborn foal. Her eyes were bright as stars then, all the time, do you know? And how she loved to lie on the front hill on summer nights to watch for the falling ones!*

*Between them and the lightning bugs, we lived in magic.
That's what she called it "livin' in magic," I remember.*

*Law, she was a 'nervous Nellie'—like one of those
race horses. But how she could make your Papa laugh!
Oh my, yes, she surely could, and talk monkeys out of
trees, he'd say...*

Now, something happened. I expect you wonder.

*I left to go to nursing school that fall of 1960. Your
mama was thirteen, so I thought she and your Papa
could get on without me for a spell.*

Seems Old Scratch himself paid a visit...

Old Scratch? A mountain name for the Devil. Did she want to
continue? Senga's hand trembled as she lifted the mug. She set it
down again, and rose for the motherwort tincture, against anxiety,
squirted several drops into her mug and drank. In a few moments,
she would repeat the dose, and again, if her nerves—and heart—
required it.

Setting her grandmother's letter aside, Senga removed the
separate packet, carefully tied in a light pink ribbon. Flipping
through the postmarks, she noted their order, date-wise, and they
included both Grannie's *and* her mother's correspondence. Sitting
back down, she placed the beribboned parcel on the table, leaned
back into her wing chair and thought. *Is this a good time to do this?*
Life hinged on timing, she believed. More so, as the years seemed
to gather speed. She closed her eyes...

An image of school-yard jump rope appeared and Senga was
thrown back years—the top of the rope looping endlessly around,
daring her to jump in. She considered this for several moments.
Not unlike Joe's imagery of the balloon, she mulled. *And yet I hang on to
that tether ... for dear life.*

"*Now, let go!*" she heard and did, backward—past stars, through
a firefly darkness, the silent pulsating gaps between these notes
of—

Time.

But, from a distance, she remembered, *there is no Time.* (Vaguely;
inaccurately.) *It's only when we're steeping in it, day by day, moment to
moment, that Time exerts its will, its purpose. I open a box—like curious
Pandora—and, what? I'm Instantly flung to the far reaches of known physics?
And, from a distance, isn't space and time synonymous?*

A star explodes into being hundreds of thousands of years ago, and I only witness its light tonight. What price then, Time? What worth, value or significance? Pandora's frail Hope, this humble virtue dangled ever before us, depends solely on the future. And faith? Love? Are they related to Time? Love as the past? Faith as the present? And hope . . . faith in what's to come? Hope—in love's capacities?

It may all be a revolving door of infinite ingress, endlessly spinning around and around, like the jump rope . . . while I orbit the Sun, this star of finite magnitude. . .

Larissa Ivanovna lay awake in the double bed beside her daughter, Tanya. She stroked the child's back, humming as she did so. It comforted Larissa to do this, though the child was asleep, her breaths slow and even. Larissa was thinking of her mother in Russia, from whom she had not heard in all these many years. *Five, now.* The woman had not known she had a granddaughter.

And now she did.

The sheriff had made some calls.

The question put to Larissa: did she wish to return home, or stay—at least for the present—in the United States? There had been no marriage—the pretext for her immigration. Sheriff Miller had gently told her that her testimony would be needed, even valuable; that these human traffickers must be stopped. *What finally moved her to escape?* she had been asked. Overhearing Jacob and George discussing the sale—*the sale!*—of her child, Tanya.

She would do whatever was necessary, she told the sheriff. Meanwhile, she waited for her brother Sasha to arrive in the coming days.

Five long years. . .

Her left arm was still in a cast. It had required surgery to be reset properly. She had suffered beatings at the hands of her captors, little Tanya as well, though not as severely. For now, she accepted this shelter's hospitality, and while *gratitude* did not occur to her yet, she felt less trepidation and fear. A county psychologist paid visits.

She learned she could actually take a complete breath and release it slowly, and take another. With less fear of impending doom. With less anxiety.

Aren't the wolves simply hiding in wait?

78

The counselor had told her she might believe this for a long time; that it was natural, if not true. *Not "necessarily" true*, he'd said. *He has warm eyes*, she had observed, and he was kind. They had managed the language barrier by nothing more than his feeling tone, and by employing a child's vocabulary and a doll.

Tanya's breaths sounded peaceful. Larissa sighed and timed hers to her daughter's; then, with her right hand, she reached over and turned off the lamp. Out the window, she watched stars twinkle brightly in the cold air.

On the mountain, the expanse of sky had been hidden by trees, though she and Tanya could just make out three constellations through the trailer's small window. Scorpio's question mark and the tea kettle of Sagittarius ranged to the south in summer and, overhead, Polaris.

She looked forward to seeing her older brother. How angry he had been when she announced to the family that she had met someone online in America and was marrying him! *Dúra*, he'd called her. Fool. Larissa had had time to regret her actions (*never* her Tanya), and what help was there for it anyway? She'd opened that box herself, she lamented. No one had forced her hand. . . *Well. Until they had . . .*

But where could Sasha stay? The couple who owned the shelter were good people, but she did not want to further intrude. The guest ranch? She would ask Jim.

So many stars. . . She fell asleep while gazing out the window.

A dream: a wash of yellow and green coalesces into a field of waving daffodils against a blue sky. Jim, their erstwhile savior, stands beside her, and Deputy Carter, the knight in brown uniform, on her right. Tanya, her red curls bouncing as she skips among the flowers, gathers a bouquet. Larissa knows they are meant for her. God is in this child, *she hears, in English.*

Senga allowed for pure sensation. Air rushed up from below—no; not from below. *From all sides.* It felt too as if she were suspended in space. *But there's no air here*, reason interjected. She inhaled; there was. Never having experienced zero gravity, she could only imagine. *But is it imagination when something works its way with you?*

A tingling amusement pressed from outside. Senga swallowed it, letting it out again as full-throated laughter.

Oh!

It was not unlike rolling fast in a car over a "tickle-hill," as Papa had called them. Her tummy lurched, giving a small thrill. An inkling of *That Exquisite Pleasure.* . . And then, the phone rang.

It showed a Spearfish number. *But of course.* She picked up and answered, "Hello?"

"Do I call too late?"

"No, no, Sebastian. How's the packing coming?"

"I am finished. Now I look to housekeeping affairs. What time can you come tomorrow? To lunch? I am thinking of making another *quiche.* . . Senga—"

She interrupted, "We found the arrowhead. Or, Milo did. Right where the deer stood, or just behind."

Silence.

"Are you there?"

"Yes, yes. I see. How marvelous! Will you bring it? I should like to see such a remarkable thing. Senga—"

"Sebastian," she broke in again, immediately regretful. "Sorry . . . go ahead."

"No, no, my dear. What is it?"

"Um, I can be there for lunch . . . and stay the night, or two. I could take you to the airport on Monday, if that would be useful." She didn't know why she chose the word. It fell out of her mouth. Sebastian quietly chuckled.

"Are you sure, my dear? I had thought to ask, but. . . And yes, please stay, as long as you like, Senga . . . Senga?"

"I'm here. Things are just . . . a little (laughter), *crazy* right now (more laughter)."

"What time may I expect you?" he asked. She heard the smile behind his words.

"I can be there—Creeks don't rise—around eleven."

"Creeks don't rise? I do not understand."

"Oh, sorry; just a saying. The first part is 'God willing,' and some believe *Creeks* mean a stream, but it refers to an Indian tribe, the *Creeks*, and whether they would, um, attack, you see. It was coined around the Revolutionary War . . . but it's become a cliché. Except, I *do* like to, ah, 'knock wood' when I state an intention. Do you know this expression?"

"Yes. We say this in Denmark as well. Some call it superstition, but I believe it denotes respect. Perhaps—humility?"

After Senga hung up the telephone, she unplugged the juniper's fairy lights, walked into the bedroom, stripped off her clothing, lay down on her unmade bed and for the next quarter hour endeavored to recreate the tickle-belly sensation, only lower. It was an activity she'd seldom engaged in, pleasuring herself, and she wondered why. It was, after all, much like letting go. Perhaps she'd held on for *far* too long; the Franciscan had called the hot-air balloon "faith," from which hung a saving rope—frayed and slippery after all these years. . .

My hands have veritable rope burns, she decided.

She arched her back and moved her hand until she felt the rise in heat and sensation. Small animal sounds arose and she understood that she *was* an animal. Little by little, her fiery turn came and she let go into the morning's blind mystery, and then into Sebastian's stark blue eyes, even now, like the sea, filling the recesses of her mind and her body, where time and space indeed converged.

We hang on. We let go. And then Senga slept, and did not dream.

CHAPTER 12
THE HUNT

Since autumn of 2007, Rufus had offered hunts on the ranch. Caroline had nudged him to consider it to augment their income. He'd taken long to warm to the idea, but came to view the practical side. The extra income paid the taxes, yearly motor vehicle registrations, supplemental health insurance and more. During the forties and fifties, while he was growing up on this very property, his parents had invited family and friends to take a deer or turkey, but the area was being increasingly touted as, "The Whitetail Capital of the World," and, exaggeration or not, the annual season—which coincided with fall turkey—brought a yearly migration of camouflage and orange vests to the county.

Their first advertised hunt drew interest, "and it must've *took*," as Caroline said; three groups returned, year after year, as a kind of ritual and, perhaps, tribute. Rufus knew his wife respected tradition. Learning the hunters' preferences and habits made it easier for her. More comfortable. Spread out through November, each group claimed a week, unless they filled early and packed up. The month, per force, was a busy one. Some years a group had only two members, sometimes four. *Never more than four at once*—another condition.

Rufus also knew that Caroline anticipated the hunters' arrival. She enjoyed the masculine atmosphere. (So far, a huntress hadn't breached the bastion. *God forbid*, he'd silently pled. He wouldn't know whom to feel sorrier for: the woman, or his wife.)

This year, Rufus' injury presented a problem, but he'd shown Gabe a few things; rattling antlers to call a buck, for instance, or staying up-wind from their quarry, if it could be helped. His hired man was no hunter. *No heart for it*, Gabe had once admitted, but he'd assured Rufus he'd help out where needed, and Gabe appreciated the principles of game management—

"Whatever—" Rufus had interrupted a looming professorial treatise on the subject.

Familiar with the trails and usual watering holes, the hunters could be left on their own for the most part. Caroline fed them breakfast, a mid-day meal and leftovers for supper, and provided showers and snacks. They knew where to park their campers. This was another stipulation: their own sleeping quarters. But meals and showers made up for it.

Twice in the past, the present group had set up a canvas wall tent, this coinciding with blizzards that had dumped two feet or more of wet snow on them, and wind that threatened to blow their housing back to Minnesota.

Caroline attributed their solution to mere superstition. The men rented a camper, and the weather behaved. But occasional light snow was a good thing. It dampened sound in the woods.

The sheep were moved to fenced pasture near the barn, with Gus, the Great Pyrenees watch dog, settled in among them.

The alarm clock buzzed, jarring Gabe awake. The darkness was complete, and for a moment he forgot why he needed to wake so damn early. The clock read 4:30.

Hunters.

He groaned, stood up, stretched, farted and stumbled to the corner bathroom.

Gabe had worked late into the night, adding edits to a short story. His editor wanted him to tie up loose ends before leaving for Italy in December. He had time, he hoped.

Caroline set the breakfast casserole in the oven. A favorite through the years, she always served it on "First Day." The recipe called for slices of buttered bread, ground sausage, eggs, half-and-half, much cheese and seasoning. She knew it was rich, but it held everybody until they returned, whenever that was, depending on their luck. She'd bake another one toward the end of the week, substituting ham for the sausage. The usual hunting breakfast was oatmeal, toast and coffee—a lot of coffee.

Rufus took his seat at the table, on the heating pad turned to low, radiating warmth into his hip bone. He'd passed a restless night.

"Must be something coming in," he said, after a sip of coffee, meaning weather.

The hunters and Gabe hadn't yet joined them. Caroline enjoyed these early mornings with her husband, before the day's purpose hijacked their own sensibilities.

"Yeah. I felt it last night. You could smell it," she replied, then, "Rufus?" staring at him squarely, hand on hip. Caroline was dressed in her usual winter attire: jeans over long johns and a flannel shirt over a Henley. She alternated among three shirts in the winter. This morning it was the red Stewart plaid. She looked at ease.

He raised his face, then his white beetled brows.

"You really want to go to California this summer? I mean, what with Jake comin', I thought you'd want to spend all your time with him, you know?"

Rufus lifted the mug of coffee, took another sip, and set it down.

"You'd think so, wouldn't you?" he said, still searching her face. More than searching it, she guessed, *reading* it and ciphering her intent. He lowered his own to the coffee mug, then, "Nah. I want him to spend some time here on his own . . . well, with Gabe. I got my reasons, Caro. Might not be able to say them plain, but, well . . . I got my reasons." Then he stood with difficulty, lifted the crooked cane off the back of the chair, and padded from the kitchen toward the bathroom.

With a sigh, Caroline turned back to the coffee pot and filled a thermos, then readied another pot for a second container. A third pot would be reserved for breakfast.

As she set the table for five (she'd eat after), her mind paged back to that week in 2007. Mid-August. Their daughter, Leigh, and son-in-law, Mike, had brought Jake to spend two weeks on the ranch. Leigh and Mike visited for two days and drove on to Denver and Estes Park. Upon their return, they learned that Rufus had taught the boy the rudiments of shooting a .22 rifle. Jake, then twelve and as excited as Christmas morning, couldn't wait to tell his parents.

What transpired next, Rufus and Caroline had yet to comprehend.

All they knew for sure was their grandson had been ripped, for all intents and purposes, from their affections, their influence and their presence.

"How dare you put a gun in my son's hand?!" Mike had shouted. *"He could have been killed!"* And perhaps his more absurd claim, Caroline had decided: *"It could have exploded!"* Their daughter couldn't meet their eyes for mortification, for feeling squeezed in the middle.

Rufus had quietly and repeatedly tried to assure his son-in-law that he would never, *ever,* put his grandson in danger. Caroline felt nauseated by the insinuation, she remembered. Rufus teaching Jake a healthy respect for fire arms and gun safety was simply a *good idea* to their way of thinking. *Country wisdom.* Rufus hadn't gone on to ask Mike where the hell did he think his fancy elk meat came from, what he bragged was stored in his freezer back home. He did ask Caroline, however, later, when they were trying to understand what had happened.

The rant still burned Caroline's ears, even now, six long years later. Leigh had paid visits, alone, showing photographs and sorrow. The more Caroline tried to analyze Mike's reaction and his upset, the more her heart ached and her blood pressure rose. So they'd learned to ignore it, in the interest of self-preservation. A sore subject. Not to be discussed.

But what had it done to Rufus? *Well. . . He ain't a bitter man,* Caroline marveled. Not even after fire destroyed half his face.

Maybe that worked as a kind of cauterization against future infection. Maybe God works in mysterious ways.

Maybe I'm full of shit. And she took a breath, let it out and placed the bowl of fresh cream on the table, so thick the spoon stood up. Next—the sugar bowl. The good, white china—her mother-in-law's—gleamed against the red oilcloth.

She contemplated the scene as a still life painting, as a wild, pure beauty; a warm enticement; a warmer invitation, and lifting a tablespoon from the drawer, Caroline dipped it into the thick cream and then into the sugar. She brought this to her mouth and swallowed, feeling, then tasting, the smooth/gritty sweetness, and she closed her eyes with pleasure.

The oven timer dinged. *And . . . Jake's coming this summer,* it reminded her. Caroline sighed again and laid the spoon in the sink.

God, let him come.

Grabbing two pot holders, she lifted out the casserole and moved the steaming dish to a trivet on the table, placing a serving spoon beside it. She laid a clean tea towel over the dish. It smelled good.

"This is ready, hon," she called to Rufus, just as she heard boots on the porch outside and a light knock. "Come in!" she called.

The three hunters entered the kitchen, greeted her, removed their stocking hats, vests and coats and sat down in their usual places. Gabe followed shortly.

Rufus broke the ice—if not literally, then close to it in the cold silence. "Gabe, you remember these guys?" He did. His antenna had picked up a vibe when he met them last year, a slight twinge from the larger man in the group, but nothing came of it and he was glad. The youngest was in his early twenties, with short blond hair and a two-day scruffy beard. *Kind eyes,* he remembered. The third was scrawny, *but big-hearted,* he recalled.

After hanging up his jacket and hat, Gabe slid the chair from under the wall phone, as his seat was occupied. Before sitting down, he leaned over and shook each man's hand, "Mornin.' Good to see you again." They repeated their names in succession: Gil, Rory and Pat.

"You know where to go by now—is that right?" Rufus asked their spokesman, the large bearded man named Gil, whose hand around his mug dwarfed it like a child's piece of pottery.

"That casserole's gonna be cold if you don't get after it," Caroline announced. They all made sounds of apology and Gabe handed the serving spoon to Gil.

"Help yourself," he told him and they passed the dish around the table.

Casserole devoured, they complimented Caroline and she refilled their coffee mugs.

"Gabe's helping me out this year," Rufus repeated. He'd stated this the night before, when they arrived, but they'd started drinking, so he mentioned it again.

"Yeah . . . good deal. So, how's that going, Rufus?" asked Gil, pointing to the bum hip.

"Well. I mean . . . well, it's *going*," Rufus said. "That's all I can say. But stay clear of that ram. He's a man killer." He spoke in a serious tone, concentrating as he rolled his first cigarette of the day. Flecks of tobacco dropped to the table. He swept these off with the side of his hand. When he looked back up, his audience was gaping at him, except Gabe, who hid a smile behind his prodigious mustache and new beard.

Rufus chortled. "Christ, I'm just kidding. You should see yourselves," he said. "Gabe'll be around if you need any help with anything. Same routine as usual."

One of the two quieter men spoke up. "You have cell service here yet, Rufus?"

"Are you hunting—or gabbing?" he asked, not waiting for a reply. "Hell, I don't know, but Gabe does. Where is it, son?" he asked in Gabe's direction.

Rufus caught the slight cough from Gil at "son," then Gabe said, "I walk down the road a ways, about fifty feet from the car gate. There's clearer range from the tower."

"That's 'cell tower,'—not *Devils* Tower," Rufus added, with an all-knowing wink to the young hunter named Rory. "Why? You expecting a call? They can always leave a message here with Caro."

"I was only wondering," the kid said. He sat back in his chair. The third hunter, named Pat, met his friend's eyes, giving him a sympathetic look.

"Rory has a new baby boy at home," said Pat. "Two weeks old. His wife didn't want him to come this year. We sort of dragged his ass—uh, sorry, ma'am—away . . . but his in-laws are there, so—"

Well, congratulations!" Caroline said. "Your first?"

"Yes, ma'am," said Rory. "I hope I can fill soon and get back. I drove separately." They all lived in Minnesota, a hard, twelve-hour drive.

Gil looked out the window and said, "We'd better get going. Thanks for breakfast, Caroline. And Gabe, if you'd set us up?"

"Sure. But I need to feed first." He looked at Rufus. "And I suppose I need one of those vests . . ." he added.

"Caro'll get you mine, and nah, go on. They'll be all right for a while. If you don't come back before 10:00, the wife and I can manage. I think the old girl remembers how—" and he ducked, waiting for the swipe that never came. She'd left the room.

CHAPTER 13
THE HUNT II

G abe grabbed his jacket and vest, then pulled on his hat. He tipped it to Caroline, who'd just returned to the kitchen. She moved to clear the table.

"Thanks for breakfast, and wish us luck—they'll need it," he said, then winked.

"You'll do, Gabe," she said, turning toward the refrigerator to return the cream.

The hunters had wanted to go to their trailer first, and Gil told him they'd meet him outside. The indigo sky had lightened, but it was yet dark enough to be well-timed, if they managed to get to their hunt areas soon. He knocked lightly on the trailer door.

"Yeah, we're coming," called Pat.

The plan Rufus and Gabe had discussed seemed simple enough: Gil and Pat would park themselves above a known trail. Whoever saw a deer he wanted to take, and said, "Got it," first, would sight in and shoot. *Simple.*

Gabe left them, visible in their hunter orange, sitting beside some cover, then he led Rory farther down a canyon in the opposite direction. Rufus had told Gabe to make sure they were all shooting downhill. Into the hillside, in other words. When they spotted the old stock tank that sat smack in the bottom of a converging three-ridge valley, Gabe whispered to Rory that he often saw deer here in the mornings. They needed to get settled quickly. A thick-trunked ponderosa stood beside them and would do fine.

Too late. *Maybe.*

Gabe moved to touch Rory's arm and quietly pointed with his chin. Through the trees, off the trail, and snapping twigs as he went, a large buck was slowly ambling toward the tank, only forty yards away. A five-by-six, with a drop tine on the left antler. Gabe's senses fired at once in an explosion of adrenaline.

"*Oh, wow,*" whispered Rory. Gabe carefully stepped behind him, out of sight. Rory slowly pulled his rifle around and leaned the barrel against the tree for support. The buck moved broadside to them. *Lucky,* thought Gabe. *God, he's beautiful.*

The gun fired. In the same instant, a shaft of morning sunlight split the air, illuminating the steel sides of the water tank, momentarily blinding him. While the shot's loud report trailed away, he heard Rory exclaim with quiet jubilation, "*Got 'im.*" And he had. The animal lay still beside the tank. No movement. What his boss would call a good shot.

Gabe's sensibilities were undergoing some mighty dissonance, but he took a breath and said, "Let's go see, shall we?"

Rory's aim had been true, behind and below the facing shoulder, into the heart. It was a magnificent animal. Rory's expression conveyed wonder and, to Gabe, an inexpressible quality. He'd have to think about this. Perhaps it was something only a hunter could recognize in another. But some of it was infectious and he felt a growing joy for the boy. *Boy? Hell, he's got a newborn at home.* Gabe snorted, then did what he imagined he was supposed to do in this case. He slapped Rory on the back.

"Good job, kid."

The kid beamed. "I never thought. . . I—I've never gotten such a big one, and a non-typical!" A drop tine was a rare thing. The third tine on the left antler curled down. One could continue to grow toward the buck's mouth, to eventually prevent the ability to eat, leading to starvation.

"Let's, ah, drag him away from the tank to gut him, all right?" said Gabe. "I'll go back for the four-wheeler. . ."

Rory sat back on his heels to examine the deer. Whitetails embodied the noblest characteristics of the deer species, Gabe believed. They were somehow more beautiful in their expression than other deer; even elk. Definitely more so than moose. But then, he'd never been that close to either.

The buck's eyes had glazed over, and his tongue protruded slightly from his mouth. "Thanks," said Rory, as he continued to stare at the buck's head.

"No need—"

"No. I—I'm thanking *him*," he said, still regarding the face. Then, he stood quickly and, moving to the rear hooves, grabbed them and began to drag the beast toward a grassy patch. Gabe stepped in to help. When they were sufficiently removed from the tank area, Rory took out his knife and set to work.

"Uh, I've never done that, so—" Gabe said.

Rory looked up, "Hey, I've got this, and yeah . . . thank you, too. I—"

And here, Gabe stopped him to say he wouldn't be long.

Meeting Pat and Gil on the way, Gabe explained how to reach the tank and turned for the ranch.

"Our turn now?" called Gil. Gabe felt his gorge rise. He ignored the comment as if he hadn't heard.

Rufus met Gabe as he was backing out of the shop on the four-wheeler.

"Heard the shot. How'd you do?" asked Rufus. He held a jar of milk for the barn cats. "I fed . . . but I have trouble with the hay, if you'd do that?" He still required a cane for balance.

"Sure, boss. As soon as we get back. Uh, the kid, Rory . . . got a nice buck. With a drop tine—isn't that what you call it?"

"Oh, yeah? Well, good for him! He really wanted to get on home to that new baby. Nice job, Gabe. Where?"

"That tank at the bottom of the three draws. Not quite sure how it'll be to get down there in this—" The four-wheeler. "He's dressing it now. The others are with him. Do you really think they'll have any luck this morning after that shot? Won't they have scattered—the deer?"

"You'd be surprised. No, not necessarily. But by the time you get it up here and hung, and the kid skins it—he is going to skin it, right? It'd cool out better for the trip home. . . Anyway, it'll be lunchtime, tell 'em. Might be better to wait till late afternoon or evening, so . . ."

"That Gil's antsy. But I'll do whatever you want, boss. Oh, good. . . I see you brought the cats more milk. Greedy little things, aren't they? Well, we'll see you when we see you. Later." And he turned the vehicle toward the track that ran along the far fence.

Beyond the *putt-putt* of the engine, he heard a far-off shot, then another. The day was sunny, but cool. Gabe took a deep breath. It felt good to be out with the wind in his face. He idly wondered if he'd shave off the beard before leaving for Italy. When he reached the place where the trail petered out, he looked ahead then decided to get off and walk a few yards. He didn't want to get into a squeeze. After several of these reconnoiters, he was able to ride unhampered the rest of the distance.

The three hunters were in the midst of taking photos and in good spirits. A good sign, thought Gabe. The deer lay on its side; a thick stick propped the rib cage apart to allow for cooling. A hot tang of blood reached his nostrils, then he spotted the gut pile off to the side. A good, clean job of it, he noticed. . .

Rufus liked to tell a story about two hunters from back east who didn't field dress; who instead hauled the animal back to the ranch to hang and then proceeded to gut it into a trash bucket they'd brought all that way for the purpose.

Pulling up, he turned the four-wheeler around to face the right direction and switched it off. He grinned at the boy.

"Ready?"

"Yep. Oh, first, I want a picture of you and the buck with me. You mind?"

"Nope," Gabe said. "My first guiding experience. Say, email me a copy, will you? My dad would be tickled."

"You betcha," Rory said, handing his cell phone to Pat.

"Say cheese," said Pat as he pressed the button. Then he passed the phone to Rory for approval. "Now that's a good one."

"Take one more, will you? And Gil, come get in this one," Rory said.

"Nah, nah . . ." he said, putting up his hands, palms out. "You want just the two of you in it, but thanks anyway."

Gabe noticed the man's eyes flick in a manner he'd learned to recognize with dismay, then he glanced at Rory, who lowered his eyes.

92

"Well, let's get him loaded on," said Gabe, and Pat, with Rory's help, hoisted the animal onto the rack of the four-wheeler.

"Rory," Gabe called over his shoulder as he started up the hill, deer secured behind him, "drive the truck back, will you? Since I'm hauling your animal?"

They hung the carcass in the yard, under the shade of an old cottonwood, some of whose golden leaves still whispered in the breeze. Rufus had repurposed an old swing set and attached a pulley to ease the chore; the buck was heavy. After ooh's and ah's, directed at the *trophy* animal (Rufus's assessment), and cups of spiked apple cider, Rory asked Rufus if he'd mount the head—if it was him. Caroline arrived with warm cinnamon rolls, telling them to help themselves.

To Rory's question, Rufus asked, "Your wife, Rory; what would she think of a dead animal's face in the house?"

Strange they hadn't had this conversation before, thought Gabe. Stricklands exhibited two mounts in the house. One, a pheasant in flight; and the second, a big mule deer. The pheasant graced the living room, and the muley was downstairs among the other stored antiques and cast-offs. But he *was* on a wall. . .

Gil took a large bite of roll and, still chewing said, "And what's *that* got to do with anything?"

Gabe's head swung around, then back to Rufus quickly, to ward off an ill-considered response. *Figures*, he thought.

"Well now, let me think about that a second," said his boss. "Cause that's all the time it'll take. . ."

Gabe smiled and caught Caroline's eye. She stood by waiting to see if her husband was going to need the cavalry.

"Caro," said Rufus, "answer the man, will you?" and he grinned, took a drink of cider and, after tasting the pastry, his eyes closed with pleasure, or, was it anticipation?

In his mind, Gabe envisioned Caroline winding up her arm like a big-league pitcher. *Oh boy, is she going to let him have it.* He waited. They all waited. Rory paused in his skinning chore, lowering the knife to his side.

"Hunh," she grunted. Then, "I figured you smarter than that, Gil," she said, wearing a wry smile, adding, "You plainly *like* to hunt, don'tcha?"

Gil nodded. Gabe saw him swallow, his large Adam's apple rising and falling through the scruffy neck hair.

"Well, if *I* was your wife, and you came home carrying one of those mounts, then stuck it up on *my* living room wall or wherever, and never asked me about it? Well, I'm afraid I'd feel a tad sore—more than a tad. And, if it was me, and I'm glad it ain't, I'd probably cut you off for oh, say, *twenty years?*" (Nervous laughter from Pat.) Then she glared at Gil, next, Pat and Rory, turned, and made her indignant way back to the house. Where she was busy preparing their lunch.

Gabe knew Caroline was sore just thinking about it. *Now why would anybody want to go and mess with the cook?*—remembering his mother's penchant for threatening sabotage in the kitchen.

He saw Gil crack a wary smile as Rufus leaned over and jabbed the man's shoulder in jest.

"Well, there you go, Gil," said Pat, finishing off his second roll and licking butter frosting from his fingers.

"Rory," said Rufus, still regarding Gil, "you best have a little talk with your sweetheart before doing anything . . . just salt that cape well; I'll get the Borax—and cut it deep for the taxidermist. Besides, her being a new mama, your woman's liable to still be, ah . . ." and he winked at Gil. "Ornery."

Gabe mentally applauded his friend's aplomb.

"Yeah, I get the point," the kid said. He resumed his task. The hide easily pulled away from the carcass. A game sack and the good layer of fat would protect the meat until he could get it home.

That night, as Gabe lay in bed, he reviewed his day. He'd never make a hunter. To his relief, Rufus could resume guiding next year. His boss didn't limp as much, so the hip must be improving.

He reached for the notebook he kept on the small refrigerator-bedside table. Sitting up, he jotted down some thoughts before they swam away, as they would, if he didn't catch them quickly enough. Like the slippery fish they were.

Often, the act of writing down a word or phrase prompted another and he'd wind up with a passage. As now.

The image of the buck—alive—was imprinted on his mind like a thing you cannot un-see. *And why this particular buck?* He'd seen dozens and dozens in the wild. Gabe spent the next forty minutes recording the circumstances: his and Rory's careful way through the woods; scent of decaying leaves; hint of vanilla from the bark of the ponderosa; the happy trickling of water issuing from the tank pipe, which he only now recalled—all juxtaposed against the explosive sound of the shot, so final and incontrovertible an action.

The sighting of the animal, combined with their intent, threw him back millennia, to the origins of humanity and the sheer necessity of the hunt.

When, if ever, had he *consciously* affected a comparable outcome? It wasn't so much the taking of the animal's life—he ate beef with no qualms, and chicken, etc., so what was it? The kid's utter single-mindedness? *That sounds corny*, he thought. He considered Rory's sincerity; his tone, his gratitude to the deer and the respectful manner with which he'd taken *care* of his responsibility.

Ownership. Maybe that's it. The deed was done with a kind of authority. *Not "kind of,"* his inner editor corrected. Gabe missed seeing Rory set the knife point to the animal's sternum and crack open the cavity, but he expected it was duly performed with reverent awe. The necessary violence in life felt both repugnant *and* poignant to him. A paradox.

Contrasting these events with the other hunter's attitude brought distaste, even if only for a moment, and Gabe said aloud, "Nope, not going there." He returned the notebook to its place, set his alarm for four-thirty a.m. and turned off the light.

His thoughts drifted to a mental list of tasks he needed to do soon: get the passport, buy a few pieces of clothing for the trip, look over his finances and review the short story file one last time before sending it. *Oh, and look for an engagement ring. . .* As well, he'd promised Francesca they'd do something on her last night in the Hills. He fervently hoped the other hunters would fill soon. He'd visit with Rufus in the morning. But what he sorely needed was a five-mile run. And soon. Too much clamored for his attention, and he sensed a growing discomfort welling in his person, as if he'd recently eaten a seven-course meal. A bursting surfeit of energy roiled in his cells. *Tomorrow, sometime,* he resolved, and with that Gabe recited his *God blesses* and fell sound asleep, to the loud hum of the bedside refrigerator.

CHAPTER 14
SEBASTIAN'S PLACE

Sebastian Hansen retired from an advertising firm in Copenhagen where he'd worked as principal photographer. His oversized photographs of natural settings and examples of old architecture had since garnered him a certain respect in the European art world. The queen had recently bought one of his large-scale images for Marselisborg Palace—that of an ancient oak tree in winter; stark lines against a white background, conveying strength, stability and survival. Perhaps a cliché in description, he'd lamented, but the image *was* arresting.

His new work qualified as passion, appealing to his sensibilities far more than using his skills to market merchandise. He believed he had justly earned this era of inspiration, and fancies hounded his early morning tasks. He recalled, hazily, something from his childhood—that grace needn't be earned; it was freely bestowed. *But you must allow it—the crux*, he remembered. *And what difference does it make—how Truth is parsed?*

Senga would arrive shortly and show him the improbable arrowhead. The thought was giving him a headache. He had confirmed that the large vertebra he had found in the shale layer above the dry creek bed near her cabin was *Archelon ischyrus*. An extinct sea turtle was a matter he could reconcile; a Horatio, he was not. But part of him felt a slight jab of envy around her discovery—*more* than simple discovery; a vision, evidently. *With evidence.*

No, he argued, *I am not like this; I am not an envious man.* Had he not said this to her? No, again; they were discussing *jealousy*—an altogether different animal. But when one's rival is quantum physics, or seemingly timeless Indians. . .

Sebastian laughed out loud, acknowledging and banishing his foolishness. It was merely what Senga attracted. *So what does that make me?* he wondered, chuckling.

Was she his muse now? Did he stand at the crossroads of yet another expression of his work? And then, he saw it; rather, he saw Senga. Through his view finder. A three-quarter view of her face, in black and white, wearing that sometime inscrutable expression.

"Would she?" he wondered aloud. *A collaboration.* And his heart quickened.

The oven timer dinged, startling him. The artichoke quiche, made with Brie, was baked.

He used oven mitts to remove the dish and set it to cool on the stove. Warm smells of pie crust and heady cheese permeated the air. The table set earlier, there remained only the bedroom to straighten.

The name of his home meant *peace* in Danish. His aunt and uncle's bed in the breezy loft of *Fred* commanded the entire space, due to its size. They had found they slept better on the wider mattress. Sadly, it had been purchased only six months before Uncle died, and Aunt had wished to return to a smaller one, but there was no help for it. One week, she simply began alternating sides, to soak up every advantage, to sense her husband's having slept there, and, to be able to go longer between sheet changes. Sebastian had smiled when Aunt related this solution on his last visit.

He had just plumped a pillow when, below, car wheels crunched the gravel. The loft's windows, facing the front of the house, were open to fresh air. Sebastian quickly glanced into the bathroom to see if anything was amiss and, satisfied, he stepped down the spiral staircase and reached the artful front door, just as he heard the knock.

"What does the mermaid say to the old beached sailor?" he called out.

They had initiated the riddling upon seeing one another after an absence. It was play. After a moment, he heard Senga's reply.

"Ahoy, you crusty old son of a beach!"

He laughed quietly and opened the door to her. She wore the forest green turtleneck sweater he came to associate with her; the usual blue jeans and the old leather jacket. Hair braided as always.

"Come in, come in—let me take that from you." First, he leaned down and kissed her cheeks, then took the bag that held her travel items. In her other arm, she carried a cloth shopping bag. She shook her head when he reached for it.

"Can you take a passport picture of me?" she asked abruptly.

"Yes. . . This is simple, Senga. And where is Gabe making his?" he asked.

"You know, I'm not sure. . . I just got him the application, but I don't think it'll be too hard to find someone to do it, as long as they print it correctly. Who knew it was this complicated?" She sat down at the foyer bench to unlace her boots, while he carried her overnight bag to the loft.

"I remember you haven't traveled very much, Senga," he called down.

"Something smells good, Sebastian, and no, I haven't. From the mountains of western North Carolina to Wyoming's Black Hills— that's me, but I've always wanted to. . ."

"It largely depends on one's temperament," he said, as he descended the staircase. "*How* one responds to a little, and sometimes great, aggravation. *Diabolic* might be the word I would use to describe travel today." He stoked the woodstove and mentally gauged the stack of logs. "Since 9-11, it's become a tiresome business. Or, can be. But forgive me, my dear. . . I do not wish to curse you with unnecessary concerns," he said, when he saw her expression, and he curbed his speech. After a moment—

"We are going to review some, ah, necessary guidelines, while you are here. Would that be helpful? I don't mean to frighten you, my dear . . . so! This evening's activities are set in stone."

Still seated, Senga took a deep breath and reached around to hold his legs, as he stood before her. "As long as we're horizontal for some of it, Sebastian."

"A given."

When she released him, he saw she had found the knitted green slippers. He pulled her up into an embrace and felt all the strain of his own travel preparations fall away. Then, he felt himself harden against her.

"*Hmmm*. . ." she said.

"Ah, we've missed you. . . I dread this separation, Senga," he said, tightening his grip.

99

"It's not so long until Christmas . . . and the absence shall be doubly compensated by joy. Now there's a seriously sappy sentiment. . ."

He laughed quietly and kissed her pout. It was emptiness he made the opposite of joy. Not sadness. But he was philosopher enough to know things evolve. Eventually, even stagnation will move.

"Come. Our quiche is ready."

She followed him into the kitchen and removed several items from the sack: a pint of fresh cream, a coffee cake she'd evidently baked and a variety of apples from the orchard. She crossed to the long farm table, with benches on either side. At one end sat the carved arm chair Sebastian had inherited from his uncle. The privilege to sit in it too. While not quite a throne, it conveyed presence, with its turned oak legs and dark green, velveteen cushioned seat and back. At the far end waited his aunt's chair, of the same vintage as his uncle's, yet created along more graceful lines.

Whenever Sebastian had sat with them, his aunt had taken a seat on the bench, to his uncle's left. It was her *place*, and Sebastian had come to suspect the habit held more significance, if tacitly. But, his aunt did employ the chair at the end of the table—outside of mealtime. There, she paid bills, or knitted, or made lists, or engaged in any number of tasks that required a surface. It served as her *working* chair of sorts, and perhaps spoke to her other roles in their long marriage.

"Sit, sit. I'll bring it," he said.

Senga sat at her new, usual place: on the bench to his left, "So I can see the room and the fire, she had explained.

First, he brought over a chilled bottle of Sauvignon Blanc and filled their glasses. She smiled at his industry. Next, he set the quiche on a trivet and asked her to cut it, which she did. Then, he returned to the refrigerator for a green salad. She asked for a glass of water. Finally, he took his seat.

"Cheers, my dear. I am happy now," he said, meeting her eyes, and he waited for her response before drinking.

"To a bearable absence, Sebastian," and she touched her glass to his, holding his gaze. They drank and set down their wine, and he served her a portion, then himself.

When they had eaten, Sebastian suggested coffee, ". . . to accompany this new dark chocolate I discovered in town—with cherries and chili pepper."

Senga beamed. "I've had that! From Marie's."

"Yes, that's where I found it . . . on the day of your workshop."

"It's great. Spicy. And, thank you for this. . . It was all so good," she said, as she rose from the table and kissed his cheek when he returned for the glasses. "I'll be back in a moment," she said.

He watched her make her way toward the hallway and bathroom, to disappear within, and he occupied himself with the dishes and coffee. When Senga returned, she held a small red pouch and set it on the table.

"Can I help with anything?" she asked.

"No, my dear. It is finished. Is that it?" He nodded to the pouch.

"Yes. I'll get the cream."

Sebastian handed her a porcelain creamer, hand-painted with violets. She filled it from the pint jar, then joined him at the table.

After tasting the coffee and chocolate, and making appropriate sounds, Senga opened the pouch and removed the arrowhead. She set it on the bag—reverently, he thought.

"May I?" he asked, pausing as he reached for it.

"You may," she said, smiling.

He turned the point over several times, examining the shape and workmanship. Of particular interest were two perfectly symmetrical notches where sinew was wound to attach it to the shaft. A beautiful example. His eyes shone and his mouth curved into an involuntary smile. Senga noticed.

"What do you think?"

"I think you have a treasure," he said, setting it back on the pouch. "Now, tell me everything."

She did, during which they drank another cup of coffee and ate four more squares of chocolate.

Evidence of mystery does not diminish the mystery, he thought, as he struggled to resolve the event, or, Senga's interpretation of it. He told her he would have to think about it or, barring that—because of its impossible nature—he would, as well, consider it grace, what the Franciscan had called it. (*At the very least*, Sebastian added silently.)

After, she suggested a walk, as the day called for it. She wanted to further explore the National Forest road beyond his turn-off. New territory. "Moreover," she told him, "I need *grounding*." Recounting the point's discovery, she explained, had left her feeling disconnected from reality—"No," she corrected, ". . . from *matter*. Not reality. . ." His eye twinkled as he suggested another form of exercise, but no; Senga required Earth beneath her feet, and they set off.

Later, they drove into Spearfish to have dinner. By her response, after he told her he had made reservations at a restaurant, he gathered it was an unusual event for Senga.

"*Really?* Now there's a unique idea. But I didn't bring fancy clothes, Sebastian. I, um, don't own any. . . Well, there's a long skirt. But I didn't bring it—"

"*Shhh*," he interrupted and said she was perfectly well-dressed for the place.

Her eccentric sense of novelty was refreshing and he tried to experience the evening through her sensibilities; sitting at a table among others, having someone ask what you would like to drink; to pore over a menu, and then order what pleased you. He considered all with new eyes.

They did not speak, as much as soak in the busy ambience of the restaurant. And, of one another. He had worn his teal blue sweater, the same as when they met in the gallery. Senga reached for his forearms, bared for having pushed up his sleeves.

"I feel such *well-being*, Sebastian. It's a compelling place, isn't it?"

Sebastian cocked his head, but kept his eyes trained on her, then gazing beyond to other diners, he said, "It has a comfortable atmosphere, my dear, and your meal, is it good?"

"Silly bear," she said, recalling a line from *Winnie the Pooh*, ". . . Yes, my halibut is *very* good, but that's not what I meant."

"What then?" he said, as he reached for his glass of Malbec.

"*Well-being.* Do you know this phrase?"

"I do—'to feel content and healthy.' I would feel the same if I did not have to leave on Monday, but—*ahh, I see* . . . *well-being* as a compelling place. . . Yes, my dear . . . or, are you Christopher Robin this evening?" he said, having caught the reference. He smiled down his nose at her as he sipped more wine.

"Let's just say 'Robin.' I like that; I may adopt it," and she returned to her eggplant. After, Sebastian ordered chocolate cheesecake to share, feeding her bites from his fork.

Upon leaving the restaurant, Sebastian suggested an after-dinner cordial. They entered a crowded "hole-in-the-wall" pub. He spotted a just-vacated table and guided Senga to it, ordering *limoncellos* as he passed a waiter.

"I think you will like this drink, my dear. It is considered a digestive in Italy. Usually served after dinner in small, ornate glasses or cups." He had to speak loudly over the din. They settled and Senga grinned.

"I never even knew this place existed, Sebastian. How'd you find it?"

"I explored this part of town last week, and it simply—*appeared*. Quite extraordinary," he teased, immediately regretting the reference. She either missed it, or chose to ignore it. "They have music, and I believe so tonight. Anyone can get up and play, I was told. It is common in Europe. . . *Senga?* What is the matter?"

She sat in near catatonia, blankly starring and immobile. He swiveled in his seat. She was fixated on someone talking with the bartender.

"Sebastian." She spoke his name quietly, eyes still on the man at the bar. She slowly rose from her seat, lifted her jacket from the chair back and headed toward the door, having to once again weave through the milling crowd. Having stood after Senga did, he remained, nonplussed. The waiter arrived with their cordials and, shaking his head, Sebastian laid some bills on the table with, "I am sorry." He glanced once more at the man Senga apparently wanted to avoid, made a quick appraisal, turned and caught up with her.

"Take me home, please—I mean, your home," she said, as she strode briskly to the Volvo.

"Wait, Senga, please. Who was that person?"

She said nothing until they were in the vehicle and driving toward the Forest Service road. A few side-long glances confirmed her turmoil. She kept her face turned to the window.

"Senga . . . please? You are frightening me."

"That—was Rob McGhee, Emily's father." On the last word, she turned her face to his and he saw the tears welling in her eyes.

"I'd forgotten how much she resembled him. That's all, Sebastian. I—I'm sorry I scared you. Please say he didn't see me."

"Ah, no, my dear . . . he seemed engaged with the barkeep. I watched him. Why . . . why do you think he is here, apart from making music? I mean—you have told me he is a musician."

"I don't know, Sebastian. He knows I've probably received that package . . . it was Rob who put all those things in the box for me, do you know? The album, the letters; even one of his CDs."

"Ah, I see." He did not; his mind was a jumble. "Let's go home and find Aunt's bottle of *limoncello*—I'm fairly certain she kept one—and we'll try to. . . No," he demurred then paused. "What would *you* like to do, Senga? Do you want to speak with him? If so, I will turn around. . ."

"No, Sebastian . . . oh, Jesus. . . No; not tonight. I need to sleep on it. . . Do you know what I'd *really* like to do?"

He smiled at her change in countenance and felt relieved. "No, my dear, and what is that?"

"I'd like to have a long soak in that bathtub. With oil and candles and music—that tune you played for me the first time. . . I can't remember the last time I sat in a tub."

"'The Immigration Tunes.' And I'll bring your cordial on a silver tray, if you like. You can pretend you are in a fabulous spa. But tomorrow we begin the travel lessons. Agreed?"

"Agreed. *I love you, Sebastian.*"

Unexpected.

The force of her words and their intent arrived like a soft blow to his chest; her love as wind, his breath remained intact, and not knocked from his body. A second force dueled with simple acceptance of her declaration. He pushed through the opposing pressure and replied in an even tone, "I love *you*, my Senga," and he banished the musician from their evening.

The spacious bathroom glowed with candlelight. She discovered a collection of body oils in a drawer and squealed. He watched her undress, then pour an amount of sandalwood oil into the steaming water as the room bloomed in a cloud of scent. He watched her arrange her hair on top of her head and carefully step into the tub, to lower herself slowly. Sebastian heard a groan as Senga lay back into the deep water, her head propped against the sloping tub. He handed her a rolled-up towel for her neck and she smiled with eyes closed, as he swished the scented hot water over her body.

He perceived the scene as through a lens, each frame a still life.

She reached low and touched herself and he mentally discarded the camera. He watched her undulate in the water like a fish, water sloshing like a wave. She reached behind her for the curling lip of the tub, the dark silky hairs of her armpit, another nest, another secret place, and lifting her pelvis, she spread herself wide and invited him, her eyes now searching his.

Kneeling down, he peeled off his sweater to a t-shirt, leaned over and, plunging his arms into the hot water, he folded them under her to lift her to his mouth, an oyster on a shell, pearl and liqueur both present, and she made the sounds and he raised his head to observe her features—not catatonic—as she gained her joy, and then he watched her return to herself as the water stilled.

"*Mmmm,*" she sighed.

He stood, dried his arms and face, excused himself and went in search of the lemon cordial. He certainly wanted one. In the back of the freezer, he discovered a sufficient amount left in an old bottle and he emptied this into two crystal glasses, placed them on the promised silver tray and, returning to the bathroom, set it beside the bathtub.

A sky light allowed a view of the stars, there being no moon tonight and city lights at a remove. With the strains of Loreena McKennitt's music surreal in the shadows, Sebastian found himself beset with nerves. Unusual for him.

Handing Senga a glass, he considered and said, "To Love."

"To Love," she repeated and took a sip. "Oh! This is *good*," and she took another sip, he his first.

"Yes. But not as luscious as you, my robin," and he leaned over and kissed her forehead.

"Should we try some, you know, *down there?*"

"*Limoncello?* I should think it would burn terribly . . . the alcohol?"

"Mmmm. Still. . ."

"You need no enhancing, my dear." He laughed quietly, then, "May I photograph you, Senga?"

"Here? *Now?*"

"Well, it *is* tempting, but no. I have something else in mind."

And he spent the next fifteen minutes describing his proposal, with Senga's silky answer coinciding with her silky exit from the bath, wrapped once more in Aunt Karen's silky robe, now hers.

CHAPTER 15
CARRYING ON

Senga stirred. It was morning. Had she dreamed it? Had she'd seen him at a bar? Sebastian was there . . . even the hint of Emily, like a softly billowing curtain, sheer. The heavier drape; Rob—her father. . .

The bed was immense. Senga reached for Sebastian, turned toward him and opened her eyes to—no one. She experienced a moment of acute emptiness. He'd lowered the shades, she saw, to prevent bright sunlight from disturbing her.

It wasn't a dream, she recalled, and then she shuddered, pulling the duvet back over her shoulders to retreat once more into oblivion.

A hand on her back and the smell of coffee roused her senses.

"Is that you?" she asked.

"I hope so, my dear. Did you sleep well?"

"I did. But I woke earlier and you were gone. It felt . . . lonesome."

He'd set down the tray and sat beside her in the bed, pushing a strand of hair from her face. "I wanted to make some calls to Denmark, and early morning is a good time."

She pulled him down, to rest his head on her chest. The weight of him keeping her wolves at bay.

After the near-euphoric calming effect of a recent hug, Senga researched their physiological benefit and learned an embrace can release oxytocin in the body. A hormone, it encourages prostaglandins and may, in turn, stimulate uterine contractions. "*Hmmm*," she murmured, now feeling a tug below. *But it must have a corollary in a male,* she reasoned. The possibility dawned. . .

"*Coffee.*" She spoke the word as an edict; Sebastian chuckled and she released him.

He stood and crossed to the shades, raised them and light flooded the loft. Then, he cracked the window open to allow fresh air and returned to the bedside.

"Here you are," he said, as he stirred the cream and sugar. He had brought the French press, creamer and bowl of sugar cubes; a spoon and a napkin too. "But breakfast is served below," he insisted.

"*Bien sûr, mon capitaine,*" she saluted then raised the mug to her lips. "What do you want to do today?"

"Discuss your travel arrangements, as I mentioned last night . . . and . . . have you thought about our seeing, ah, this man last night? You may have forgotten. . ."

"When I first woke, I thought I'd dreamt it. Oh, I don't know, Sebastian. Sleeping on it doesn't seem to have produced a—" She paused, having arrived at a three-way crossroad. *To turn back? Go right? Or, left?* None were possible. Then, a shimmer interrupted the image and she saw another path, barely visible against the dark, contrasting ruts of the other directions. It led forward, beyond left, right or backward, and she groaned. Grannie stood with Emily, beside this new, ethereal way. To their right, the juniper; the very one near her cabin. She felt confounded. "But, it's always been the one at the falls," she spoke aloud.

"What did you say?"

"Oh. Nothing . . ." she said, but glimpsed the hurt pass behind his eyes. She couldn't hurt him. "No, I'm sorry. I'll tell you," and she related the image.

"Do you . . . know what it means, Senga?"

She wouldn't bother him with speculation, so she took his hand, kissed the palm and held it, and then, shaking her head, said, "Just a picture yet. It'll come. I'll let you know, but—I'm ready to get up," and she finished the cup of coffee, thanked him for bringing it and he stood so she could climb out of the vast bed.

They met below after a quarter hour. The telephone rang and Sebastian answered it. He covered the mouthpiece with his hand, told her he'd be a moment and passed into the study. Found below the loft, the room was located beside the small guestroom where Senga had slept the night of their—*what to call it?* she'd wondered. That would come to her, too. It seemed important to name it. *Reunion* sounded absurd, she thought.

A gentle *click* signaled Sebastian's closing the door to the study.

This she noted. So, they both held privacy sacred, and she conceded the fairness of it, the necessity even, releasing the light sting of feeling dismissed. Granting privacy in one quarter permits the space to explore in another. She carried her second cup of coffee to the wall of books behind the sofa and began a perusal. Her hand reached for a thick spine almost immediately. A classic. *The Travels of William Bartram* was an early botanical study of the American Colonies. She moved to the sofa and curled up with her find.

After several moments of trying to concentrate on the text, Senga allowed her thoughts to drift. To the night before.

Would Rob go to Sara's Spring to look for her? And why? Or was he simply touring the area and it was mere coincidence, nothing more, that she happened to see him? But she didn't truck with coincidence, she reminded herself. What was *more* significant was her decision to avoid him altogether. It was this she needed to examine.

She sorted her sentiments. (Such as they were.) She had once asked to be released from his affections. This was how she'd worded the request, not to Rob. To God (or that which she grew up calling "God"). Her intention had been honored. But, some residue obviously remained, if merely seeing him produced such a turn in her.

Unfinished business? Seeds of love are eternal? Nothing's lost; nothing's wasted—as he had suggested?

She would store the questions in an unlocked drawer of her mind and wait.

"What song does the mermaid sing in the morning?" she heard Sebastian ask.

"Hmmm. . ."

"Quick! Else she will disappear under the waves and we shall have no joy—"

"Oh, Sebastian," Senga sighed.

"You are correct, my dear. But . . . with perhaps more enthusiasm," he chided, crossing to her, and, sitting down beside her, he lifted her book to inspect the cover, made a sound and put it down. "Hungry yet? May we have some of your cake? What kind is it?" he asked, beaming.

Senga thought he sounded too cheerful and wondered what the telephone conversation had revealed. She would ask. Privacy be damned.

"It's an apple cake—what else? Who were you talking to?" adding, "O *Sebastian*," in a purring tone.

"Aren't you the coy one . . . but you can do better. I have *heard* you. . ." He paused, looking down his nose at her, in a dare, waiting for a demonstration. Hearing none forthcoming, he smiled and continued, "My son-in-law, Peter. He has just returned from Saint Petersburg—"

"Russia?" she broke in.

"Yes. He has clients there. Actually, to the east of the city. A town called *Naziya*. One of his contacts mentioned travel to the United States, to retrieve his sister. . . She had gone missing for five years after leaving Russia for a proposal of marriage in Idaho—the destination on her flight itinerary. Her family had heard nothing from her and last week they received a telephone call from the sheriff in Sundance—yes! *Wyoming*—" he confirmed to her widening eyes. "The name of the brother is Alexandre Ivanovich; he is called Sasha."

Senga blinked. "Jesus."

"It is most strange, I agree."

"I'm reeling from all these gears turning at the same time, Sebastian. That's what it feels like," said Senga, placing her head in her hands, then rubbing her forehead. Looking up, she said, "You? Any thoughts? Please—I'd like to know. I need some perspective—apart from mine, I guess."

"I want to warm your apple cake first—may I?"

"Of course. Now *you're* stalling."

"Yes. I am. . . To think before speaking is wise, my dear. More coffee?"

"Please. What does your son, um, Peter, *do,* exactly?"

Sebastian said nothing for a moment, then, "He owns a small electronics business, but he also—ah—how to put this. . . He works as an international *copper*, my dear. That's the simplest description. With Interpol. A "business trip" is a euphemism we employ."

"Oh, I see. . ." She didn't. "So, is he searching for these traffickers?"

"I do not concern myself with his affairs. Best for my nerves—and those of my daughter—if we allow Peter to do his work. . . But we support his efforts where we can. I only tell you because it relates to the woman found near that guest ranch, yes?"

"It must. What are the odds?" she added, expecting no answer.

"And something else. Peter also told me the sheriff spoke with this Alexandre this morning—his time—to say the man who had taken his sister—"

"Larissa—"

"Yes . . . well, the man was arrested at their place in the mountains. He was alone. The police surprised him before dawn yesterday. He is in custody, to be questioned. . . Peter sounded very glad of it."

"So the other three are still out there?"

"Ah, only two. . . One of them, an older man, was found dead in a motel room in *Belle Fourche* (he pronounced it with a French accent) yesterday morning as well. Natural causes, they believe."

Senga sat quietly absorbing the information. Sebastian busied himself in the kitchen, setting out plates, forks and butter. The coffee cake, warming in the oven, filled the room with scents of apple, honey and cinnamon, lending a certain symmetry to the morning.

So, Yellowtooth and his brother are still—she forced herself to process the thought, not knowing what to do with it. *At large* and mulled the nonsensical phrase. She hadn't told Sebastian about the incident with the man she'd dubbed Yellowtooth. *A slur for a slur?* He'd called Gabe *nigger* behind his back. In defending her friend's dignity, she'd lost some of her own.

On the surface.

Her actions were predetermined before she pushed the man against the cooler in the store and pulled her digging knife on him after he added yet another insult. "I had no choice," she'd admitted to the town cop. *If you accept modern neuroscience.* And she did. It had to do with conditioning and the subconscious.

Enough! She shook her head from right to left to banish her thoughts.

Sebastian was watching her from the kitchen. He smiled one of his sad endearing smiles. It was the expression she longed to imprint behind her eyelids, to beckon when alone. *You could just take a picture of him,* came the thought. "When you take my passport picture," *and whatever else you have in mind,* she added silently, "let me take one of you, please?" she asked, the non-sequitur clearly registering on his face. But she would forget.

She rose from the sofa, laid the book on the table before her and walked into his outstretched arms. "It will sort itself, Senga. Not to worry." She rooted her nose into the crook of his neck, his weathered skin roughened to a texture, *like resilience,* she thought. She inhaled the woodsy citrus fragrance he wore on occasion, but, far more; this place, *her* place—this particular nook on his body—she equated with safety, with comfort and with being cherished. And they stood fast together, fixed, while their respective chemistries quietly carried on.

CHAPTER 16
AIMING AT STARS

*S*ome think the passage of time is like the flight of an arrow: Time
doesn't flow; it merely is. So why does it exist at all? Past, present
and future are only illusions.

Balancing her journal on her knees, Senga wrote, She then
copied a quote by Octavio Paz from a thin book she'd
discovered on the bedside table in the loft: *"Time is no longer
success and becomes what it originally was and is: the present in which
past and future are reconciled."*

Among physicists, poets and philosophers, there existed a
plethora of theories to chew on. *To reconcile...* Senga corrected,
as she strove to cipher the arrowhead's meaning: *And if something
merely "is," then what's the use in...No. The argument demands to know
whether time is illusory. A* mirage, *as it were. Was the Indian a mirage?
A "time" mirage? An imprint?*

The journal stowed for the time being, Senga reached across
the bed to straighten the duvet. She'd discuss her notes with Joe
in her next letter. *And Sebastian?* While he possessed a capacity
for wonder (of this she was certain), she wondered if he wasn't
mired in four-square reality, the kind that excludes the abstract.

Even his photographs are in black and white! She dismissed the line
of thinking for now.

He had last minute errands to run before leaving for
Denmark tomorrow. She chose to remain home, repeating the
word as she made the bed and put away clothing.

"Home . . . *sweet* home. . ." Tentatively speaking the words,
she realized. *Why?* Wasn't *Starwallow* her home?

Rob's reappearance rattled for attention. But she shook her
head in her way and resumed her task.

At breakfast, Sebastian had reviewed airport information—explaining Customs procedures, and her and Gabe's change of planes at Schiphol Airport in Amsterdam. Francesca would meet them in Florence. Sebastian entreated Senga to pay attention to her Italian friend and ask questions—to not simply "defer" to her expertise and be led. She saw the wisdom in this, to take a certain responsibility.

She'd only recently discovered, however, or *re*discovered, the freeing—if abdicating—principal of deference. How lovely it was to relinquish control! *Life as mere conveyance; nothing to steer. Now there's a thought,* and she swallowed. *It could be a raft, or a horse . . . but not a car . . . and I'm still trapped in linear mode. What if it's more like an exploding star, with pieces bursting in all directions? Hmmm. But the flight of an arrow . . . could be . . . one of those bursting projectiles.*

The phrase about the arrow returned like an earworm tune and she heard it as such, in a way; the shaft's quick whistle through air, creating its own music through time. And she remembered she *had* heard it that evening; her east window had been cracked against sealing-wax fumes. Well, if not music, then at least sound. *The sound of Time.* Like that of a song, a composition, a recitation of a poem. The image of the Indian reappeared in her mind's eye; his tall, burnished beauty, his expression of intent as he drew down on the buck. *Will.* She'd never forget it, and she wondered if this was how God might appear when planting a seed in our mind; *sharing consciousness?*

Recognizing the fanciful, she rolled her eyes at Cupid's bow and his lethal love arrows. . .

Her thoughts turned to Sebastian (naturally), and how his absence might unravel her. This met with the knowledge of Rob's presence. *What presence?* she countered. She'd require presence of mind to weather it all.

Senga inhaled and blew out slowly. Bed-making as meditation. A respite from stimuli.

Chore accomplished, she stepped back to regard her work. The colorful appliquéd quilt, done in red and white hearts with matching shams, and bolsters—in European custom—created a cheerful sight. She spied a wrinkle in the spread and moved to smooth it. The room needed freshening, so she walked to the window and opened it wider.

Her eye fell to the telephone beside the bed.

Call Gabe and ask about the arrest. Did he know? He was guiding for Rufus, so perhaps not. But Stricklands had a scanner, so chances were good. She dialed the number.

"Hey, how are y'all?" she asked Rufus.

"Just fine, Senga. And you?"

"I'm good. In Spearfish with Sebastian—I'll be taking him to the airport on Monday. . . Say, do you know anything about that Berry place guy's arrest?"

"Yeah; so one less thing to screw up my day."

Senga could hear her friend's crooked smile through the phone. "The other two . . . um, they know where they are?"

"Nah. But keep your eyes peeled, girl. Lock up at night."

"I do, Rufus. You know that."

"Yeah, well. . . Gabe's out with the last hunter to fill. The other two got nice bucks. One was a five-by-six drop tine. A nice one—" he added, and she broke in:

"A drop tine on the left antler? A five-by-six?" she repeated.

"That's it. Why? You've seen him?"

"I—I did. A couple weeks ago by the pond." A sense of loss gathered in her gut.

She hadn't disclosed her experience to her neighbors. Not even to Gabe. She was saving the story for the long flight to Europe. As a captive audience, he couldn't dismiss her as easily, she figured. This was tongue-in-cheek. Senga expected Gabe to be intrigued and awed. He allowed for the numinous. He courted it.

"The kid who got 'im has a new baby at home, so he took off," said Rufus.

"How's the hip? Need more of this arnica salve?"

"You know, I could use some. It helps. I have another therapy appointment this week and it always hurts after. . . So, can I ask you a question?"

"What's on your mind, Rufus?"

"Two things, actually: when you want this lamb, and this man you're seeing. I'm just curious—sorry—but Caro says he's good for you. You sure he doesn't have someone back in Sweden, or wherever he's from? You know, like some do nowadays?"

A whole other family, she heard him imply.

"Denmark, Rufus," she corrected.

"What's that?"

"He's Danish, not Swedish and, no, he doesn't have someone else. Don't ask me how I know; I just do. Without getting all mushy, I know him. . ." Here, she paused, ". . . like the back of my hand, Rufus, and I don't want you and Caroline fretting for me, please?"

"Well, if you're sure . . ."

"I am . . . and the lamb—how about Wednesday? If Gabe can help you load it, can you bring it? Or, Gabe can when he returns from Rapid. I'd have rather done it this weekend— waning moon—but it'll have to wait. And, thank you for your concern, Rufus, as always. It means a lot. . . Oh, and please tell Gabe to expedite his application for the passport. Has he gotten the pictures made yet?" she remembered.

"I took one with his cell phone and he's going to print 'em up. Got the application filled out, too, but I'll let him know to— what was that? *Expedite?*"

"Yes . . . and thanks."

"Sure is a lot of comin' and goin' these days. . ." he said. Then, "I gotta go, girl; I hear Caro yelling for something. No rest for us old farts," he laughed, and she said goodbye, then replaced the phone on its cradle.

She descended the spiraling stairs and walked beneath the loft into the kitchen to fill the kettle with water for another cup of coffee. When this was made, she took the cup into the hallway to view the gallery of photographs once more. She wanted to see a photo of Sebastian's daughter, Erika. He'd shown her the small one in his billfold, which included Jytte, his granddaughter, but Senga remembered another photo beside that of Sebastian and Elsa, with the bronze of the *Little Mermaid* in Copenhagen's harbor shining in the background.

"There you are," Senga said when she recognized the girl's face. Taken several years ago, apparently, when Erika was younger, she was her father's daughter in appearance: a pale complexion, light hair (*much like Emily's,* Senga noted), the same dissimilar eyes as her father; his nose, but the mouth resembled her mother's—a bit crooked when she smiled. She wore an endearing gaze for the camera.

If it was her father, who made the photo (which almost certainly would have been the case), the girl's expression confirmed it. Senga peered more closely. Erika was standing in the sunshine and shielding her eyes with upturned palm against the glare, having just twirled (apparently) and seen the photographer. Perhaps he'd called her.

Yes, there it is, and Senga read the clear message in the girl's eyes and felt the chill of feeling outcast, of being interloper, or worse. But surely, by now, having a daughter of her own and a husband, Erika had found fulfillment in motherhood and marriage, and her father might be free to pursue his own . . . *his own what?* and she heard the front door open behind her.

"Where does the mermaid hide her treasure?" he called, not yet having seen Senga.

"Are all your riddles double entendres, Sebastian?" she answered from the hall.

"What kind of answer is this, my dear? But of course they are! If you're *willing*." He chuckled as he set a package on the long farm table, crossed to the kitchen and set another sack on the counter. "So, I repeat, where—"

Not missing a beat, Senga replied, "Where the crusty old sailor hides his."

"*Touché!*" he said, "I used to sail when young . . . so that should be 'young sailor,' if you wish to be accurate."

Senga had come into the kitchen; he saw her eyeing the package on the table. "And who named *you* the crusty, um, *young* sailor?" she asked, grinning and inspecting the package. She lifted it, to gauge its weight.

"I did, my dear . . . *and do not shake that!* You are a child at Yule, you are. But yes, open it. It is for you."

"A present? *Really?* But I don't have one for you, Sebastian, and now you're leaving tomorrow . . . this isn't fair . . . but, thank you."

"Please, just open it."

Senga pulled away the heavy paper to uncover a box with a photo of a smart phone printed on it. She looked at Sebastian. "How useful!" and she beamed at him. He'd stepped near her and, taking the box from her hands, he lifted it above his head.

"My dear. It is only as useful as you choose to make it. I thought long and hard of what to give you before leaving, and knowing you don't have a mobile and are going on this trip . . .

117

I decided it was the wisest thing. It has been set up for use in Europe, as well as here, and the monthly charges will be billed to me. The woman entered my numbers; I hope I'm not presumptuous."

She glared at him.

Ignoring her expression, he continued:

"As well, you may use it to find information—and directions! The Internet, you know? Marvelous invention. Email?"

She was warming to the idea, and reached to grab it from him. "This is just so unexpected, Sebastian. You . . . this is . . . oh my, *thank* you. Let me have it!" she said, reaching for it. He bent down and kissed her, still holding aloft the box.

"Only if you concede the crusty, *hmm, old* sailor is none other than myself."

"Uncle; I concede," she said, stepping up on the table's bench for the box. He lowered it behind his back.

"*Uncle?* That would be incest, my—"

"No, no. . . That's a saying, you know; 'cry uncle,' when you want to give up? I suppose you don't say that in Denmark?"

"Something different, but the same principle. Have you used one of these?"

"Well, not really. . . Joe calls them 'tech meth.' He's sick of seeing people glued to them—worse than cigarettes, he says."

"An apt analogy, that. He is quite the social provocateur, is he not, your Joe?"

"*My* Joe? He isn't *mine*, Sebastian. . . He's the Cheyennes' . . . and Christ's."

Here, Sebastian surrendered the box. They straddled the bench, facing one another, then she removed the phone and glanced up at him. "I don't have a clue about these things. But Gabe uses one, so if I get stuck, he can help me."

"I can show you; it's quite simple. And the camera is a wonderful tool." He looked at her, wondering if he had made a mistake in its purchase. It was not romantic at all, he realized, but he believed Senga not particularly subject to such sentiments. He sat lost in thought, when she reached over and placed her hands on both sides of his face.

"Silly Pooh Bear," she said. "This is the *best* possible gift, and I love you for it. It is perfect. Thank you, Sebastian," and she edged forward, climbed onto his lap, a leg dangling on either side, and he felt his cock respond, and he wanted her now. *Upon this very table—forgive me, Aunt.*

An incongruous personal ritual, perhaps signifying his taking ownership of his aunt and uncle's dwelling. Perhaps not? *Definitely.*

He neatly lifted her off his lap and set her down on the bench before him. "What?" she said. Wordlessly, he replaced the phone in the box and set it aside, on the cushion of his chair to his left. Then, gathering the pair of candlesticks and the table runner, he placed these on the chair as well. He stared at Senga . . . willing her understanding.

She began with the top button of the chambray shirt she wore, slowly, with a sensuality uncommon to his growing years. She leaned over to remove the slippers and socks then stood to unbutton her jeans, while holding his gaze. She unzipped the jeans, ruching them down by degrees and stepped out, to leave them a puddle on the floor.

She enjoys this, he realized, a taunting strip-tease. Her facial expression alone masked such mystery that he envisioned it frozen, framed and behind glass. Her movements were erotic and beyond spectacle: the woman was performing a sexual mystery play designed to beguile, captivate and conquer. As though she were lifting the seven veils of Science Herself (adding the component of a conscious mating ritual), Senga slowly pulled the tank top over her head, revealing the soft, dark underarm hair, and he felt his cock shudder.

An old, old memory awakened in the base of his brain: an ancient image of coupling, triggered by seeing Senga's long braid cover a breast and the dark, silky pelt of her body. Her nipples were hard, beseeching touch, and he reached to brush his thumb across one and the other. She groaned. He cupped a breast and gently kissed it. Reaching for her panties, he slipped these down, smoothly, matching her rhythm, and she lightly lifted first one foot, then the other.

His disrobing proved less deliberate, and they soon stood naked, facing one another, the sunshine streaming onto their bodies. Sebastian smelled her nakedness. Perhaps the warmth of the sun through the windows activated some feral memory about her, he wondered in passing. They simultaneously inhaled and exhaled.

He knelt and pulled her to him, his arms entwining her buttocks and the curve of her back, his face buried near her thatch of dark hair, and he kissed and mouthed her lower belly, behind which lay her womb. She groaned again in supplication.

"You . . . are . . . so *very* lovely, my dear," he said, his voice low, gravelly, and near choking. "*I am filled with you, Senga; you are . . . wine to me and . . . I am drunk with you. . .*"

She sighed and knelt down against him, "May I hear that in Danish, please?" she whispered.

He repeated his declaration in his language and she kissed him thoroughly in reply.

Glancing over her shoulder to the farm table, she moved to recline on its thick polished planks, and Sebastian spread her to his love and hunger and love again and, after her paroxysm and cries, she reached for him, and they lay together a moment, their breaths coming in short bursts.

"I'll do it," she said to him now. "Photograph me however you like, Sebastian; *my* parting gift to you." And she parted her legs once again.

Why the mermaid yearned to be human, he remembered.

He would ponder and question her next comment for several months: "You are now free to pursue your own . . . passions," and he listened as her breathing returned to normal, and then she reached for his cock, sat up and leaned over.

He gasped in helpless surrender and to the utter incredulity of his life.

After several moments, he entered her and his release met with her second, and they rode the hard boards home together. When he heard Senga breathlessly say, "Ahhh, *le petit mort,*" the French reference to sexual release and its aftermath, he could have indeed died and judged his life complete.

"But I am not yet dead, my dear," he said aloud, ". . . and, happily, neither are you."

They passed the remains of the day, and long into the night, in creating and making photographs. Sebastian found in Senga a natural model: utterly unselfconscious, free from constraints and oddly talented with movement and style. The silk robe featured in many of the shots, as did a setting of an old clock on the sideboard, the simple background in the foyer, and the *altar* of the dining table. (His emphasis.) They worked outdoors too, with snow rendering the canvas stark.

She did not care to view the photographs, she said, in order to approve or disapprove. He told her he would create a series and show them to her when he returned in December. She had smiled and said nothing. *Naturally*, he conceded.

CHAPTER 17
JIGGIN'

Rory left after breakfast for home, to his wife and new baby. He planned to drive it in one long leg. Gabe had helped to arrange his gear and deer carcass in the pick-up bed.

He liked Rory. *His heart's in the right place,* he thought, as he waved goodbye and ambled back to the house. Gil and Pat were eager to get going. Gabe had ridden horses who jigged less. He mentally apologized to the horses.

"You ready?" he asked, as he downed a quick cup of coffee, adding a thanks to Caroline.

"Did you tell these boys you're busy Tuesday night and Wednesday, Gabe?" she asked.

"Uh, no, Miss Caroline, not yet, but I guess you just did."

Gil looked at him, then the floor, then up to the ceiling and said, "Well, looks like we'd better take something before then, right?" and he looked at Gabe, who didn't know if he was supposed to answer, so he didn't.

Pat said, "I feel lucky this morning," and with that, they left, Gabe smiling at Caroline as he closed the door behind him. He heard her calling Rufus to come finish the pan of oatmeal and the terse response. He knew his boss didn't much care for hot cereal.

Gabe drove the hunters to an area he and Rufus had discussed the night before. Gil and Pat were familiar with it, making it easier to plan. They drove in silence, to Gabe's relief, and he used the time to mull the news about the arrest at the old Berry place, of the person who was with the kid at the bar and who may have pulled most of the strings.

He wondered if Senga knew. She was in Spearfish with her new "sweetie," as Caroline called Sebastian. Senga had dropped off a passport application for Gabe, but he'd been out guiding. Maybe they'd have some luck today, and Pat had a good feeling. This always, well, *occasionally* helped, he thought.

The graveled road wound through a dark valley that ran east-west, and he could just see the horizon's hint of dawn. He was driving Rufus' extended cab pick-up, and Pat was seated in the back, behind Gil.

"Look at that. We don't see views like that in Minneapolis," Pat broke the spell.

An amber streak divided land and sky.

"We're not going to be in place if we don't get a move on," Gil stated for Gabe's benefit. He ignored it. Gil added, "So . . . you ever find it hard being the only, um, black man in the county, boy?"

Staring ahead, Gabe took a breath, exhaled and said, "Do you know who W. C. Fields was, Gil?"

"Well, yeah . . . hated kids, I guess. Why?"

"Maybe. . . He said something I kinda keep on my short list for certain situations, like now: 'It ain't what they call you; it's what you answer to . . .'" and he nodded in Gil's direction then back to the road. Pat squelched a snort.

"Here's the fork," said Gabe, as he veered onto a track and pulled up at a gate. Pat jumped out to open, then close it, after Gabe drove through. This led into a large pasture, at the end of which Gil would wait near a haystack, while Gabe and Pat hiked up a trail.

Pat's presentiment proved accurate. He'd been lucky. At lunch, Gabe told Rufus and Caroline it'd been a "pretty" shot, while Pat wore a wide grin. Rufus, ever the polite host, asked Pat to tell it, so he did. Gabe noticed that Gil just looked constipated.

"Well, Gabe and I wandered up that trail above the haystack where we left Gil—you know, Gil, it could've just as easily been you getting that shot," he added as an aside to his friend. "Anyway, Gabe and me, we were just hiking up that way when

Gabe put out his arm to stop me, and I almost spoke out loud, but he put his finger to his mouth, then pointed, and I saw it. This four-point was moving through the trees, slowly. You could barely make him out—it was that dusky. He hadn't seen us. So I sat down quick, aimed and fired. I was lucky, like I said. Could've just as easy killed a tree." They laughed.

Caroline passed the bottle of Jim Beam for the requisite celebratory swig. Gabe passed, but he noticed Gil took one. They wouldn't be going back out until three or so, so Gabe let it lie. Rufus looked at him and raised his white beetled brows.

"If y'all don't mind," Gabe stood and said, "I've got a couple things to do before we go back out. Temperature's dropping, so that deer should be all right."

Pat had skinned it earlier. He wanted to do a European mount with the buck's skull, so Caroline had brought him a large canning kettle and a hot plate. An outdoor project, if ever there was one, given the stench. It would take a day to boil the skull, and another to scrape it clean. He would then bleach it.

Pat told them (after their lunch settled) about taxidermists using *dermestid*, or flesh-eating beetles, to clean the skulls; *nature's forensic scientists*. Gabe actually preferred the stark skull and antlers to other mounts. More artful, he thought; *or, are they simply more powerful an image?*

Rufus followed him out to his room in the barn. Gabe had wanted to have a short lie-down. *Maybe later.*

The old rancher's hip was mending, but slowly. The doctor had told him at last week's appointment that it could take longer than first estimated. This depressed him to no end. Gabe noticed his friend's demeanor had suffered since the run-in with the ram.

"Uh, something going on with Gil, son?" Rufus asked.

"Nothing that can't be endured, boss. . . Why?"

"Oh, he just seems, you know—*pissy*. Can't stand pissy people, Gabe. They make me wanna puke. Into their bowl of oatmeal," he added for good measure.

"Aw, he just wants to fill and get on home, I think. For some reason, he's in a toot, or something, and . . ."

"And what? Spit it out, damn it. Can't stand pussy-footin' either."

"Nothing, boss. Nothing at all; at least, that's the weight I put on it, and that's how it is, you hear?"

Rufus heard and understood. They stood regarding each other for a moment, and Gabe crossed to the bathroom in the corner of the room.

"I'm going to fill out this passport application and I need a photo made. Would you mind doing that for me—you can use my cell phone and I can crop and print it. . . I think it'll work."

"Well, sure. I suppose I can do that. I used to take pictures, you know, but nowadays. . ." he said, letting his thought drift off.

When Gabe returned, Rufus was seated at his desk, gazing out the window. "It's nice here, isn't it? I mean for your writing and all. I'm wondering what you're going to do after you and Francesca are married, Gabe. *That* weighs on me. I need you— well, Caroline and me both."

Gabe had to look away. He'd never heard Rufus express a need, much less a sentiment toward him. He grunted.

"That's a ways off, Rufus," he said, "We haven't set a date, or even discussed living arrangements. I'm sorta flying by the seat of my pants these days, if you haven't noticed."

"Yeah, well. . . It goes by fast—I'm here to tell you. Enjoy every moment you can with your sweet Francesca," he said. Then, he stood and gingerly stepped down into the aisle of the barn, his cane used for balance, and Gabe watched him, through the sparkling clean window, head back to the house

PART TWO

CHAPTER 18
LA NONNA

Lucca, Italy, November

Market day in the church *piazza* in Lucca attracted throngs of visitors and housewives. Contrasting smells assaulted the senses, even before one stepped into the large, open space, as stalls of flowers, fruit and aged cheese competed with fresh meat and fish. It was noisy, vibrant and smelly.

Muttering to herself, Maria Teresa Barone negotiated a gawking group of tourists tripping through the square. The trick, the old woman knew, lay in guarding your step on the cobblestones, even as you took in the surroundings. *A bit like a chicken's gait.* She snorted as she watched an impeccably dressed Italian guide holding aloft a fluttering green, red and yellow standard for identification. The woman was gathering her chicks, who had apparently scattered.

Maria Teresa sailed past the chestnut vendor without her usual greeting. She would not buy today and didn't want Gianni to catch her glancing at his tempting sacks of just-roasted nuts, and their luring scent. You were doomed if vendors caught you looking, she knew. And no smiling; rule number two. Tourists smiled too much.

Sailing past is how she once might have avoided the chestnut man, but, "waddling" described it more accurately today. Her knees. The uneven footing. And her tricky balance. The doctor had pleaded with her to wear a hearing aid, but she'd primly declined. She'd moved to more sensible shoes long ago.

It required much to pry her clenched, remaining teeth into a full grin anymore, but one excuse was returning home soon. Francesca Albinoni. Maria Teresa allowed herself a quick beam of delight and continued toward the outdoor market. Setting a trajectory toward the tents (with attention paid to cobblestones), basket firmly balanced on an arm, her little dark-dressed and determined presence parted the throngs, like Moses—the Red Sea.

Travel to Tuscany in summer remained popular, but more and more tourists had discovered this autumn shoulder season for lower air fares, better hotel rooms and, supposedly, fewer tourists. Maria Teresa scoffed at this reasoning, declaring the *pazzo* tourists part of the problem.

Crazy people. . . But winter—he approaches—and life will calm. Maybe. To move to a more natural rhythm. A familiar and more regulated tempo. And, her Francesca was returning. A child of her heart. . .

Maria Teresa Barone had met James Munro during the U. S. Military's "mopping up" in Italy at the end of World War II. Following a hasty wedding in her Tuscan village, they moved to western North Carolina and, there, raised their only son. Andrea—"Andy" to everyone else—met Lucy Cowry in high school. A *strange* girl, Maria Teresa thought; haunted, afraid and prone to moods. *But then, so am I,* she admitted. Lucy and Andrea married and had a daughter, Agnes Maria (who later changed her name to Senga, she learned). Her son served two tours in Viet Nam, getting himself killed on the *very* day the United States began evacuating, April 30, 1975. Her husband died the same year.

Too much.

Returning to Italy was not so much a decision as a compulsion, and here she'd lived all these years. *Thirty-eight years now I am orphan mother and widow . . . but I have Francesca.*

Her granddaughter Agnes—this *Senga*—she no longer knew. They were once close, exchanging letters, even after her move to Wyoming in the American West. *Use olive oil on the body,* she recalled writing in a letter.

And then, the child's child had died.

My great-grand daughter. . . Too much death. Now, what was her name? she asked, not seeking the answer, as much as waiting for it. *Ah, sì... Emily—la dolce bambina.* Maria Teresa often confused Agnes with Emily.

"*La Nonna Maria Teresa?*" she thought she heard, halting in the midst of pre-school children being herded, their teacher flashing a frustrated look. The black and white habit appeared in stark contrast with Maria Teresa's own uniform, the dark silk dress she wore every day.

"*La Bella Signora Barone!*" There it was again. Who was calling her now? And with such cheek! She pursed her lips and twirled around, coming face to face with Francesca's younger brother, Carlo.

"Ah, Carlo, *come sta?* How are you? What do you want?" Maria had learned to be direct, or perhaps always had been. Her abruptness and raised voice were accepted by everyone now. Being ninety-two years old held the advantage.

"I am well, *Nonna, grazie . . .* and you?"

"*Bene, bene, grazie.*" She fixed her gaze on him, waiting.

"Will you come to dinner on Saturday of next week? After Francesca returns? Mama asked me to find you. She says there is to be an announcement. May I tell her you'll come?"

"Of course, Carlo. I'll be there—if I am not dead." And without waiting for a rejoinder, Maria Teresa turned and toddled off.

"*Ciao, Nonna!*" he called after her.

The news distressed rather than delighted. It could mean only one thing; the girl had found love in America. She would leave them. Her steps slowed and she wished to sit down. Luckily, a bench waited a few steps away.

Feeling her age, she lowered herself to the seat, first carefully smoothing her dress beneath her and feeling for splinters. It would not do to snag the silk. Maria Teresa placed the basket on her lap and leaned back. Checking her watch, she calculated she had forty-five minutes left to shop before the market shut down for the day. She had time to sit a few moments.

The *piazza* was bathed in the clear, bright autumn light of morning. Cobalt blue sky hung as backdrop for sweeping flocks of birds. They ranged back and forth between the church heights and the trees across the square. *Pigeons and sparrows,* she noted. *Always the sparrows. They wait near café tables for the dropped morsel. I am the sparrow.*

Then, she admitted that, in Italy at least, the sparrows ate well.

"*Ahhh, sì!*" she said aloud, and a passer-by turned her head in question.

"*Niente, niente . . .*" Nothing, she muttered to the woman, who then stepped up her pace.

The façade of the church rose to her right, an example of Gothic Romanesque architecture, in polychromatic rose and green marble; bright, glorious, uplifting. Italian odes to joy. In this city of one hundred churches, this was her favorite, likely for its proximity. It was *her* church. *L'Annunciazione.* Never mind the neighborhood children whispering *strega* to her back. Witch. She resembled their idea of one now. No matter. Crones in Italy, she knew, easily fit the description; all of them *La Befana;* what of that? But then, she read Tarot. *Yes, well. . . We must have our amusements, mustn't we?* This stated tongue-in-cheek.

Maria Teresa watched as the tall religious paused at the church's massive doors, and nod to each child as they trooped past her. When the last pink-smocked little girl (boys in blue) entered the shadowy space, the teacher turned in Maria Teresa's direction for a moment and stared, finally pulling the tall door behind her and disappearing into the church.

"Old bat," muttered Maria Teresa, tossing it like salt over a left shoulder.

Realizing she hadn't pondered Francesca's announcement, and accepting this as gift, she prepared her knees to bear her weight and pushed off the bench.

"*Maria Teresa!*"

The hand reached under her elbow to assist her rising and, when steady, she turned to thank—

No one. It didn't surprise her.

A swift breeze cooling her face lifted a piece of tissue someone had dropped. She watched it rise and spiral in a whirlwind, then gently alight several yards away near a trash bin.

"Humph." She stepped over to the litter, bent over to pick it up and, thinking better of touching someone's used tissue, she spotted a fallen leaf and used it to pluck the paper, depositing both in the bin.

"That will be me soon enough," she declared, strangely amenable to the prospect, and, turning in the direction of the noisy market across the *piazza*, Maria Teresa looked both ways, her path clear of tourists and children for now.

CHAPTER 19
IN PLAIN SIGHT

Nearing Sara's Spring, Dale instructed his little brother to ask the clerk at the grocery store the whereabouts of, "that root digger, Senga *something*"; where she lived. That he needed to see her about a problem, and to add he'd heard she was *good*.

"Why, Dale?" asked his little brother.

"Just do it, Joey. You ask too many questions," he said, lighting another cigarette. After exhaling, he rubbed a hand over his raspy face, catching a glimpse in the side-view mirror. Sighing, he thought, *I feel old*.

Earlier, in the country store at the base of the Bear Lodge highway, where the road flattened out for several miles before entering another canyon, Joey had told him he'd overheard the owner tell a customer about a man's arrest at the old Berry place. Joey had left without buying anything, for fear of being recognized. They had spent two cold, miserable nights in the truck cab. Joey never complained, but Dale was angry and out of sorts, feeling the rug had been pulled out from under him and Joey. He just wanted to feel warm again.

What the fuck do I do now? The question looped in his brain, over and over.

The image of the crazy woman, who had objected to his language two weeks ago in the store, flashed in response. He took it as a sign and headed toward Sara's Spring, where they avoided the main street and parked in an alley to avoid being seen.

"So what do you want with her, Dale?" Joey asked, as he climbed into the truck with a sack of food and drinks.

"I just need to see her, Joey. Give me that sandwich, will ya?" he demanded.

Dale tore the cellophane from a pre-made ham and cheese and reached for a can of Coke. Joey devoured a granola bar with a pint of milk.

"I need a toilet," the boy announced soon after. "*Now,*" he insisted.

"There's a porta-potty around the corner. Near the park. Hurry up."

The clerk had told Joey where Senga lived, and she'd also told him that, *by golly*, he was, "the second person come looking for her," and she'd tell him what she told the other guy: Senga wasn't home right now; she was away for a couple days and wouldn't be back until tonight. Dale grinned after Joey relayed this.

"Now don't go doing something stupid, Dale," his little brother muttered.

The day before, Rob McGhee had found Senga's cabin easily enough. She still worked at the library in town, after all this time, and her supervisor, who recognized him when prompted, had simply given him directions. He'd told the woman he was Emily's father, and this seemed to allay suspicion. Earlier, the store clerk had told him Senga wasn't home, and wouldn't be until the next day. He hadn't asked where she lived. Their former home stood a block away, in need of painting.

When he arrived at Senga's cabin, he in fact found no one home. *Well, I'll just wait,* he decided, *and sleep in the van if need be.* His next gig wasn't for two weeks; he had some time. He'd explore the environs. Senga lived in the middle of nowhere, he decided. A break in the heavy cloud cover bathed the scene in a surreal glow. Four black crows perched atop a feeder beside the garage, daring him to disturb their snack. The juniper tree caught his eye; rather, flashes glinting off dozens of small mirrors and ornaments did, and he moved forward, entranced. A light breeze caused a faint tinkling, and then he sat back on his heels. Only his Senga could have created such a memorial. For their Emily.

He'd been away more than present during her short life, but he couldn't deny her white-blond hair and those eyes; she was his daughter; their love-child. And the girl had clearly adored him, present or not.

"You are a will-o-the-wisp," Senga had once told him, and she'd explained him to Emily this way, to protect the child from false expectations.

He studied the various trinkets in the tree and his eyes, at last, fell to the small red chair beneath the bottom branch, upon whose top slat was inscribed, *For Emily-Who-Loved.* Beneath the chair, the ground mounded, and Rob wondered if his daughter's ashes lay buried there. Senga had written she'd used a Walker's Shortbread tin to hold them, as these were their daughter's favorite cookie.

He waited a moment longer, in emotional perplexity; then, reaching into his pocket, he drew out a worry stone. A smooth pebble from the Chattahoochee River near his home in Georgia. After kissing it, he placed it on the red chair seat. Rising, he looked about, spotting a red strip of cloth tied to a twig across the ravine. He'd save its exploration for tomorrow, and returned to his van to make a cold supper and to turn in early.

Rob slept late on Monday. He must have needed it, he thought. Musician hours are brutal, if you must wake early. He thought he may as well stretch his legs and, after heating water for instant coffee on a camp stove, he set out in the direction of the red cloth.

The late morning air felt and smelled cold, while the sun played hide and seek.

In *The Wizard of Oz,* Dorothy wakes to Technicolor, while this was simply an enhanced lighting effect, caused by sunshine burning through clouds. Bird call pierced the stillness. He heard a turkey squawk. Cooing doves. *Senga inhabits a magic land of anticipation,* he decided, catching sight of the high, curved rim that rose behind the cabin. *And there's the sleeping giant's brow. . .*

A distant rifle shot startled him, followed by another. He reached the red cloth and pondered its purpose for a moment, then continued to climb.

"She ain't even there, Dale. So what's the point?" said Joey, as they drove toward Senga's cabin. "And somebody else is looking for her . . . which could be trouble, you know?" he added.

"Yeah, somebody probably looking for one of her medicines, you moron; besides, she *could* be there. You didn't think of that?"

"I told you not to call me that."

"Yeah, you did. So, we're just going to check out her place. Besides, I'm curious."

They drove the rest of the way in silence. At the mile marker the clerk had indicated, Joey began to watch for the cabin. The clerk also mentioned a rock outcrop. It loomed to the east and Joey told Dale to watch for the turn-off.

"These are fresh tracks going in," the boy said, when they arrived.

Dale turned off the highway, pulled up and peered past Joey in the cab, to see if he could make out a vehicle through the trees. Yeah; a green van. He decided to drive in, feeling adventurous; or, was it frustrated? He usually just felt confused.

Putting the truck in gear, he rolled forward. Lowering clouds presaged weather, their darkening mass hovering like a puffy, steel gray quilt spread above them. Chilling air, passing through Dale's open window, had a bite to it.

"Smells like snow, Dale," said Joey, to his brother's utter nonchalance.

Parked behind the van, they sat for several moments to see if anyone would appear.

Joey was intrigued by their surroundings, and after several minutes, they both stepped out. *It's like a kid's secret fort, almost,* he thought, *or a trapper's cabin. Homey.* He wanted to find a warm corner, curl up and fall asleep. Instead, he approached the gate to a fenced-in area. Trees and a garden. He stole a glance at Dale, heading toward the cabin. Joey unlatched the gate and stepped through, closing it behind him, having read in hunting magazines to always leave a gate the way you found it.

He was tired. Bone-deep tired. Just seeing the orderly rows of trees and the sleeping garden (how he saw it) engendered a peaceful feeling, and he remembered something from long ago, when he was small. His body begged to rest, *just awhile,* in this place and he slid down against one of the fence posts, his legs splayed out before him. His stomach was making sounds again.

The respite was not to last long.

"Hey, Joey! Get a load of this!"

He hated the loud interruption. The unnecessary shout. Joey turned his head toward his brother's call. The deckled edge of a tree, peeking from behind the south side of the cabin. He waited for his eyes and brain to make sense of what he was seeing. Even Dale was simply staring at it, not touching it, or messing with it. *Yet.*

Why did his brother always mess with things he didn't understand? *Curiosity's one thing, and foolishness another,* he remembered their mother saying, or was it their grandma?

Joey knew Dale wasn't only foolish, he was—

"*HEY!*" he heard from somewhere, followed by another *hey.* Then, "*WHAT ARE YOU DOING?!*"—*doing . . . doing.* The word bounced against the canyon wall behind them, making it difficult to judge direction.

Joey swung around and rose, then let himself out of the enclosure. He thought the voice was directed at his brother, as usual. Beside the tree, Dale stood holding up an ornament in his hand, like a fresh-caught fish. Caught red-handed. He froze.

"*Put it back. Now,*" the voice stated quietly but evenly. Joey heard a Southern accent and an undertone of threat in the demand. His brother slowly raised the bauble to the branch and reattached it.

"*Who are you?*" asked the voice.

"*Where are you?*" Dale spoke to the woods, backing from the tree.

Joey reached the cabin, a painted *Starwallow* above the door, and, with his back against its wall, moved to the north side to see if he could spot anyone. He peered around the corner, into the woods across the ravine. Then, he bent over, arms clutching his mid-section. "*Dale?*" he whispered.

CHAPTER 20
MARIA TERESA KNOWS

Lucca, Italy

She drew the top card from the first stack and laid it face down on the table, followed by a second and a third. Then she sat in silence for several moments. A first-quarter moon, visible from the open, tall window to her right, illuminated her workspace, though she required the light of a candle—in the interest of protection. Her intentions considered the will of God. The beautifully colored Waite Tarot deck simply elucidated that will more clearly to her. Why did everyone not grasp this?

Her great Aunt Serafina had taught her to read the cards. It had grown into a prayerful exercise, but Maria Teresa had scrupled with the old argument—that the cards were evil.

No more.

She would cite Jesus' terse reply to those detractors—that it is not what goes into the mouth that defiles a person, but that which comes out. She insisted the teaching covered her use of the cards as tools. Much as one might employ knowledge of, say, harbingers of spring, such as tongues of jonquil, piercing hard, late winter soil. Or, the coming winter's flocking of wild birds.

But her *last winter?* Of this, she felt certain. She had read it. Moreover, she knew it.

She contemplated Francesca's coming announcement and wanted to appear equal to anything when she heard it on Saturday evening. Maria Teresa had ceased to enjoy surprise many years ago. Not all revelation is welcome, she had learned.

She tried to live her life—and diminishment—with acceptance and dignity, but still needed to prepare for contingencies. So, the cards. About these, she ignored all criticism and condemnation. This eased with ageing.

Old age, even given its mounting difficulties, had proven oddly liberating to Maria Teresa. Her mind was still sharp and she could more easily leave yesterday's vale of tears behind. She lived for and in the present, for the most part, though her anticipation of Francesca's return from America had awakened in her an emotion of longing for the future once more. She had believed she was done with pining.

No help for it but to occupy her mind, which she now proceeded to do.

Then, the cat meowed.

"*Accidente!*" she swore, rising from her arm chair. As she did, a gust of night air blew through the window, extinguishing the candle and strewing cards onto the floor. (Naturally, a portent.) Only two cards remained where she had laid them. *Present and Future.* Maria Teresa studied these, head over her shoulder, as she crossed to the cat. She lifted furry, white *Bianco* to the window sill, then pulled him back to her chest to cleave to a moment. He was growing old himself and welcomed the affection; he tolerated assistance.

The feline's habit entailed tentative steps along the balcony, then beside the windows, hopping to a waiting tree branch and disappearing, to eventually return to this second-floor apartment window. If closed, he would patiently wait for his mistress, mewing if he saw her.

Maria Teresa stood, stroking the white fur, feeling the breeze, and listened to evening sounds of a close neighborhood: a baby crying, occasional laughter, a television broadcast, a radio program, the bark of a dog, an argument. City smells of grease, diesel and sour garbage abated, to be replaced by night-blooming flowers. She smelled sweet jasmine. Moon-lit clouds scudded across the sky, putting all these events, or signs of life, into order and place.

Leaning over, she released the cat. *Bianco* lazily stepped over the sill, his thick white tail flicking like a metronome. He paused, waiting for what, Maria Teresa didn't know.

"Go on then. . . Go," she said in Italian. The cat made a sound, then moved to the ledge, proceeding slowly. She watched the cat reach the linden tree that anchored the corner of the building. Then, closing one side of the window and locking it in place, Maria Teresa left the other open five inches, bracing it with a brick.

The tall, paned casement window was one of three in her home. All faced south. Bright examples of the Italian Renaissance, they married function with beauty. The increased availability of glass met with simultaneous need (or wish) for more natural light indoors—a great boon for painters, among others. France adopted the style after the Great Italian Wars of the early 16th century, when they were renamed "French." *To the victor belong the spoils, tut, tut,* Maria Teresa had once quipped. French *cuisine* owed a debt to Italy too. She kept a list.

Despite their origin, or perhaps because of it, she had formed relationships with each of the three windows (if the word could serve).

Illuminating her kitchen was *Rafael;* Bianco's window was *Gabriele*—and the third, *Ariel.* Two named for archangels and one for a conjured spirit *and* an archangel. Maria Teresa envisioned the tall panes as glorious wings; yes, this was how she saw them. No need to persuade herself. Whenever she closed the great structures at night, she saw enfolded wings, embracing these beings of light, at night—opaque. A long bamboo pole stood in the corner of the room, with which to adjust the sheer, blowsy curtains, or *raiment.* The fabric would invariably catch between sash and jamb. Everyone knew where Maria Teresa lived, by the bight of white peeking out.

Identically constructed, each window rose seven feet in height, five feet in width, in perfectly symmetrical proportions, with small, glass panes seated in leaded mullions. Each side, encased in dark wood, hung on polished hinges. She regularly oiled the mechanism on the egg-shaped brass knobs.

For this reason, Maria Teresa would not be removed to a retirement home. She had duties as caretaker. . .

The windows' main purpose? To *flood* the rooms with as many photons as possible, even into the interior rooms.

Maria Teresa's kitchen was tiny, but well-lit during the day (by *Rafael*).

The larger room featured a small fireplace (no longer of use), with a lovely, carved mantel. Above, tilted at an angle, hung a gilt-framed mirror. This reflected her dining table, four arm chairs, a love-seat, chest, radio, book case and two radiators, both painted bronze. A large bedroom (which had once been two) and a bathroom completed the floor plan. She kept few mementos, and those, she venerated. On the chest stood silver-framed photographs of her husband, her son and one of her granddaughter and great-grand daughter taken together. An old wooden frame held her parents' wedding picture. Beside it, in a Baroque frame, smiled out Francesca Albinoni.

When Maria Teresa moved to these rooms in 1975, she ordered the interior painted a deep rose. The color had faded with the years. . .

The cards called her back to her chair. Seated once again, she relit the candle and turned over the first card, the Six of Pentacles, ignoring the windswept. *Is it time, then, to depend on others?* She looked at the second. The Knight of Cups. It could mean a visit, but it held other possibilities. She gazed at the candle and waited for clarity.

A soft rustle alerted her and she turned. No Bianco at the window. She raised her eyes to *Gabriele.* A breeze knocked the pane against the brick door stop; the rosy-blackened sky waited beyond the glass, above the moon. The soft lights of Lucca prevented most stargazing, but on this night, she was given to spot three, *There, just there*—and she wondered if she'd imagined them. She stepped to the window and, yes, they shone high in the sky.

An impression brushed her cheek and she turned back to the table. Bending to the floor, she collected the fallen cards, arranging them as they had lain, some upside down. Finally, she returned to the deck the two cards from the table. Beside the white candle that burned until bedtime, she stored the box of cards on the mantel, wrapped in a square of white silk,

So, a visit. *And none too soon,* she thought, as she prepared for bed.

CHAPTER 21
UPON MY WEAKNESS

Black Hills, circa 1820

She Who Bathes Her Knees watched her sister as they moved through the forest toward the cliff. The air crackled in the crisp autumn morning and her cheeks tingled. Her sister appeared to be struggling, by the expression on her usually placid face. Lona must have sensed eyes upon her and turned.

"I cannot be with him, you know. It is impossible." Her betrothed in the tribe.

When High Wolf heard this, he looked over his shoulder to his wife, and by silent communication, told her he was moving forward a few paces, to grant them privacy.

Bathes Her Knees nodded to him and her husband advanced in two long strides.

"Lona," said Bathes Her Knees, "you find yourself in a difficult place. This *Little Eagle* man—would *he* wish this pain on you? If he cares for you, as you say, why does he not leave . . . and return east to his people?"

Lona stopped in her tracks, and sank to the ground in one fluid motion. A sound came from her and her sister feared she would set up a wail.

"Please, sister, let us be careful. My husband—" and Bathes Her Knees looked to High Wolf, who slowed his pace. She knew he would give them several moments.

Lona covered her mouth to stifle her cries, and Bathes Her Knees dropped down beside to rock her and croon quiet words; to offer comfort. Presently, Lona took a deep breath, wiped her eyes with the back of her hand and said, "My tears have passed

. . . thank you, sister. Let us not keep High Wolf waiting upon my weakness," and she brought herself to her feet, held out a helping hand and they scurried forward.

High Wolf looked to his wife to gauge her sister's state and, with a curt nod, Bathes Her Knees indicated their hike could resume. She looked to Lona and a chill passed through her. She read an expression of blandness, as if the girl's soul had deserted her.

CHAPTER 22
HERE WERE YOU BORN

The envelope Sebastian had thrust in her hand, after their embrace at the regional airport, lay on the seat beside her; his cursive *Senga*—a siren's song. *What did the sailor say to the mermaid before he sailed away?* The riddle's answer lay inside the robin-egg blue envelope. *Must be his aunt's stationery*, Senga guessed. She'd save its reading for bedtime.

They'd enjoyed two days and nights together. *The concentrated dose*, she considered it; *dosage and frequency*, both, oft-repeated protocol, à propos to several situations. Senga smiled at the memory of Sebastian's enthusiasms. His god-within. Their *collaborations*.

On the heels of this arrived a thought of Rob. She was approaching the Wyoming border, when she wondered if she should turn around and find him.

Was he still performing at the bar?

Did she *want* to see him? Yes and no, she reasoned.

She knew Sebastian harbored reservations about the man; and . . . there was the matter of their relationship now—hers and Sebastian's. She knew the *truth* of it . . . yet something. . . . *It's Emily of course,* and she understood, or at the very least perceived, the tug from the musician.

She noticed cars passing and realized she'd slowed down in her reverie. Increasing her speed to the posted limit, she continued west, soon passing the *Welcome to Wyoming* sign. In a few miles she'd reach the place where she'd given birth to Emily under a moon and starlit night in 1984, on the north side of the borrow ditch.

She was made dimly aware of the roadside cross, where someone had met their death. Strange she'd never considered the obvious: a *birth* marker for her Emily. What was the symbol for it, she wondered, if death was a cross? *A circle?* The birth canal, to a sentient infant, would appear circular, wouldn't it? She'd have this information in one of her books.

Grannie used to watch *Ben Casey* on television, and Senga remembered the opening credits: the older physician (whose disheveled hair resembled Albert Einstein's) drawing glyphs on a chalk board and naming them. Senga recalled *infinity*, the recumbent figure-eight. Time turning in on itself in a continuous looping, like an automaton. *What was Birth? Or . . . was it Life?*

As she approached the site, she slowed. Far on the northern horizon, reddish hills shone. Nearer, tall dry grasses waved lightly under the bright sun. She pulled over, after activating the Honda's blinker. Here was the location she'd acknowledged countless times between home and Spearfish. She squinted—at a recently placed object; else she would've spotted it earlier. Something. Squatting in the grass.

Hunh, she grunted, *like I did,* and she stepped from her car and crossed the dip of land to the spot.

It was subtle. And was meant to be. *To prevent detection,* she reasoned.

A roadside crew might remove it as a danger, but perhaps not. And Senga figured Rob must have placed it there, just in the last few days. *Who else?* The grasses lay flattened where he'd trod. *Had Emily been his only child?*

Senga peered over her shoulder to see if a car approached. One might stop—a common courtesy in the area—but no; she was utterly alone, at least for this stretch of time and highway. Long enough.

She was only aware of it for knowing an exact position.

It was a bowl. Simply a bowl. Of pottery, painted a light sage-green on the outside, with sky-blue interior, and fired to a gloss against the elements. It rested, like a nest on a wooden plinth of sorts, well-seated. Its diameter—ten inches at most. Tall grass partially obscured it, but Senga wondered what might happen in winter, when it'd be exposed.

She approached with reverence and discovered the water-covered letters on the bottom, shimmering in the light; they seemed alive. Painted inside the bowl in gold were the words:

> *Here were you born,*
> *Flaxen-haired Child,*
> *Under the Stars,*
> *But O! In the Wild.*
> *8 October 1984*

Tears sprang to her eyes. She leaned over and touched her fingers to the liquid. *Rain water?* Then touched her lips. *Holy Water. How for granted we take your gift* . . . she heard in the breeze and up from the earth and in the light of the sun's rays. And then she sat down, and then she wept.

After several moments she wiped her eyes, then again touched the water. She rose and bowed deeply to the bowl, and the memory, with love, then turned toward her car. A vehicle sped past. She waited until she saw no other cars or trucks and walked around to the driver's side, climbed in and drove away with trembling heart.

In the rear-view mirror, she sought the shrine. It had vanished into the roadside's landscape, like magic. Perhaps it wasn't there at all. . .

CHAPTER 23
NO HEDGEHOGS HERE

As he wiped his face and neck after his run, Gabe leaned over his table to examine his photograph, the one Rufus took for the passport. It had printed out well. He'd cut two copies to the correct dimensions to submit with the application. Caroline thought the kitchen's white refrigerator would make a good backdrop. *Well,* he thought, *it certainly makes for contrast.* But it would do.

Black as a moonless night, his was one of the darkest-skinned tribes to ever arrive from Africa. *And they do still,* he amended. Both his parents were blue-Blacks, named for their gleaming, near-indigo skin. He hadn't smiled for the photo, having read somewhere it was discouraged; it made some people appear crazy, and that wouldn't do, not anymore, when boarding a plane was such a charged affair. But he'd grown used to seeing himself with hat and scarf and felt a mite naked without them. His hair was cropped short, but he kept the great, as in *wide,* mustache. No beard for the picture.

Peering at the photo now, he recognized himself. Rather, he recognized his mother, and through her himself. He saw her gazing at him whenever he caught himself in a mirror. And here she was again. Behind those heavy-lidded and *snappin'* black eyes. Warm. Merciful. But how she could flash them in anger, and had. The righteous sort.

He'd mail the application today and hope Gil filled his license soon. Rufus told him if the hunter had no luck this evening or in the morning, he'd (Rufus) set him up behind the barn, "on stake-out." But Gabe knew Gil, at least his kind, and he doubted any old deer would do. Gil had already passed on a decent buck, in case a "better" one came along.

It was Monday. He'd give the man his best until tomorrow afternoon, around 4:00 p.m., and then he'd be off, having promised his sweet Francesca dinner at The Cottonwood, where Barry was preparing a special dinner. They would drive on to Rapid City for the night. She'd fly out the next afternoon, to arrive in Lucca by Thursday. Her brother Carlo was meeting her in *Firenze*, she told him. Florence.

Gabe folded the application and placed it in an envelope, along with the extra fee to expedite the process, as per Senga's instructions. He took another quick look at his photo and spotted a glint in his eye, remembering Rufus' "Think of Francesca!" just before he pressed the button. "Ha! The old rascal," Gabe said aloud. He'd printed off two more copies: one for his father and another for Francesca.

While not vain, Gabe always wanted to look, and put forth, his best—the Catholic Sisters' insistence on excellence inculcated by the end of eighth grade. The gulf between pride and humility, when it came to distinction, had confused him when young. *Maybe it's the proverbial razor's edge,* he wondered now.

He grunted, then muttered, "It'll do," slipped the photos inside, the check, and licked the envelope. Caroline had told him she needed to go to town and could drop it by the post office; the rural mail carrier only delivered on Monday, Wednesday and Friday, and had already passed by.

He grabbed his gear after filling the cats' bowl with milk outside his door in the barn aisle, nearly tripping over two of them as they raced for it. "Who's yo daddy?" he called after them, as he pulled aside the barn door to step through. Gil and Pat leaned against the pick-up. Waiting, it appeared. He slid the door closed.

"Be right with y'all," Gabe said as he walked past.

"Oh, no hurry. We can shoot the shit all day, can't we, Pat?" replied Gil.

Gabe looked at Pat, who looked at his feet. He didn't share his friend's sentiments.

"How's the mount coming?" Gabe asked Pat over his shoulder as he continued toward the house. The stink from the simmering wasn't as pronounced, and Gabe wondered if the deed was done. He hoped so.

"Oh, it's getting there. I'm letting it dry before the peroxide . . . and it looks good, Gabe," Pat said with obvious pride. "It's getting ready to snow, so I'm glad it's pretty-much done, anyway," he added.

Gabe told them to go ahead and get in the truck, that he'd be right there. Pat didn't need to accompany them, but wanted to. He couldn't carry his rifle, but, "I've got eyes!" he reminded them.

"Hey, y'all," said Gabe, after Caroline yelled, "Come in, damn it!" when he knocked.

She and Rufus were sitting at the kitchen table, nursing cups of coffee. Caroline had a checkbook out and looked to be paying bills. Rufus shifted his weight on the chair, to find a more comfortable position.

"Now Miss Caroline, you seem in a snit, as my mama used to say," said Gabe.

"Snit, shit," she replied. "I keep telling ya to just come on in, Gabe," she reminded him. Rufus made a sound and took out his cigarette makings.

"Here's that application, and thanks for mailing it for me. I think it's enough postage. What do you think?" Gabe asked.

She lifted it off the table, "Yep, that should do it," she said and set it among her other envelopes. "I 'bout forgot to pay the damn taxes. . . You two'll tell me when I get feeble, won'tcha?" She kept her eyes on her work.

Rufus and Gabe glanced at one another; eyes rounded, each knowing what the other was thinking, "*Like hell. . .*"

"Uh, they're waiting for me in the truck. Wish us luck. Hope he'll settle for something besides *Monarch of the Glen.*"

Rufus raised his brows.

"An old series," Gabe explained, ". . . about a venerable *old* patriarch," and he grinned at Rufus. "A huge stag figures. Naturally."

Rufus snorted, licked his cigarette paper and put the roll-your-own between his lips. He struck a match and lit it, blowing the smoke in Gabe's direction.

"Wait," Caroline said as she stood from the table, not having followed the exchange, apparently. Gabe had braced himself for sarcasm, but none materialized. Instead she said, "I've got a Thermos made up for you."

"Why, that's nice . . . and I needed a pick-me-up. Thank you, Miss Caroline. I'll just grab another cup, in case they want some." He stepped toward the counter, away from the cigarette smoke.

"The *son-of-a-bitch* won't drink from the same *cup?*" Caroline demanded. Gabe noticed she hadn't brushed her hair yet. It stuck out all over, like a hedgehog.

"Oh, now, *that* I don't know . . . maybe it's just my own preference," and he winked at her. Slipping the Thermos bottle under his arm and dangling the extra cup from a finger, he picked three gumballs from the dish, popped one in his mouth and stepped through the door.

CHAPTER 24
AN EARNEST REGARD

At the Blue Wood guest ranch, Francesca helped Carey with lunch dishes, then poured a cup of coffee. She resisted creamer, resuming the Italian custom of none after lunch. Mary sat curled on the sofa before a blazing fire in the hearth. She was idly leafing through a magazine, a cashmere throw draped casually over her legs, and appeared content, thought Francesca. Sun streamed through the large picture windows, accentuating the blue veins in the tongue-and-groove paneling on the far wall. Mary's hair shone like a torch, red as it was.

They had passed the morning reviewing early bookings for the following season: three families from Rome, two couples from Tuscany and ten individuals from Umbria, Sicily and the Venice area, including Vicenza. Clearly, Francesca had been enterprising.

"Can I bring you more coffee, Mary?" she called from the kitchen.

"No, but thank you. I drink too much of it. It's interfering with my sleep. So . . . are you packed and ready to go home?" she said as she studied a page.

"I am packed, *sì*, but I am two minds about leaving. It is, how do you say—"

"Bitter-sweet?" Mary glanced over her reading glasses in her friend's direction.

"Yes, this is true. I want to see my family of course, and now, *Nonna* . . . I wonder how she will accept this news that her granddaughter is coming to see her, after so many years."

"Oh, I expect it will seem like no time has passed at all. Families, you know. We just pick up where we left off, like your

150

knitting after a summer. *Can* you take your needles on the plane? It'd be a shame to lose the opportunity."

"*Hmm*, I don't know, Mary. Something to ask at the airport. . . But after thirty-eight years? This is a long time. How do I tell her, Mary? Will you help me?"

"Well, sure . . ." The picture of comfort set aside her magazine and shifted to face Francesca, who had sat down in one of the club chairs beside the sofa. "She should be sitting down. . . How old is this woman? And you should be alone with her. She may fall to pieces; I know I would."

"*Nonna* is, I think, ninety, ah . . . early nineties. Maybe more. But she still walks everywhere; and upstairs to her apartment, which she takes care of herself. No, that is not correct. A young woman comes once a week to help. I'm glad. Mamma told me *Nonna* will be at dinner on Saturday night when I tell everyone about my, my—"

"Engagement, Francesca. Is Gabe getting you a ring?" she asked as she stared at Francesca's left hand, bare of jewelry. "Would you like to look at my collection and pick one, just to have something to wear until then?"

Francesca looked at her employer as if she were *pazza*. Crazy. "That is—"

"Yes, yes, I know, *ridiculous*, but here's the thing: unless you are wearing a ring, your family won't truly *believe* you are engaged. At least that's the way it is down South. It's a protocol thing; *de rigueur*, as it were." Mary's French accent was Southern.

Francesca's eyes grew wide once more.

Mary continued: "You know—*tradition*. Come on, I'm *serious*! I know it's silly, but it's just the way it is." And she threw off the throw, swung her legs to the floor, and pushed herself up.

"You are kind, Mary, but—no; I could never do this. Perhaps I am . . . *ah, come si dice?*"

Mary sat back down and sighed. "Superstitious. No, I understand. At least assure them you are shopping for one?"

"Yes, Mary. I will say that. It is not so important to me, a ring."

Carey peeked around the corner from the kitchen. "I'm finished, ma'am. I'll be taking off soon. Anything else?"

"No, Carey. And thank you. Those hunters arrive later tonight, but they'll have eaten in town. We'll see you in the morning. Enjoy your evening."

"You, too, ma'am. Bye, Francesca. You don't leave for another day, right? I'll see you tomorrow."

"Yes! *Ciao*, Carey," she said, as she pulled her knitting to her.

Mary sat back as though in trance, her eyes focused on the periwinkle wool yarn. The quick clicks, like crickets, could be heard over intermittent pops in the fireplace. She watched the metal tips dash back and forth through her friend's nimble fingers.

"Mary?"

"Yes?" she replied, only raising her eyes when Francesca's hands paused.

"Are you . . . okay?"

"Oh! I was day dreaming, wasn't I? Yes . . . *right as rain*, as they say." Mary gathered her wits. "It's just warm here in front of the fire, and . . . Oh, Francesca, I will miss our conversations. You've been a friend, do you know? And I'm wondering what will happen when y'all get married. Will you still work for us? I hope so! But where will you live? And I am *so* sorry. I don't mean to go on like—like a silly old woman—"

"Mary, *you* are not old. . . *Nonna,* she is *old*," and here she laughed, to lighten the mood. They both turned as the great, carved door behind them swung open, and in walked Jim and Lee.

"Francesca says I am *not* old, Lee, so *there*," Mary declared. Lee looked at Francesca, then at his wife.

"It's only a state of mind—age," he said, ". . . And no, sweetheart; you are a fountain of youth, and we've come for a drink." He smiled at her, then at Jim, who looked uncomfortable.

Evidence of the recent blizzard still covered the ground, with new snowfall adding another six inches in the high country. The men were dressed in orange hunting vests; Lee wore a near-fluorescent ball cap, the better to be seen. After chucking their overshoes near the door, they crossed to one of the tables.

"Carey and Lupita are gone for the day, so you'll have to fetch your own coffee," said Mary, now hunkered back down into the sofa. Francesca had risen to add another log to the fire.

"Well, you haven't asked about Pete," said Lee.

"What—did he get one?" asked Mary, a hint of disbelief in her voice.

"Oh, he got one, all right," said Jim.

Earlier that morning at the safe house, or "shelter," as it was called, Larissa Ivanovna had trembled with excitement, rising from the chair every few moments to look outdoors. Tanya busied herself on the bed with a doll, jabbering in a half-English, half-Russian conversation.

Larissa's brother Sasha was due to arrive soon. Deputy Carter had offered to meet his plane, on his own time, at the regional airport, and Larissa had been moved by the gesture. She kissed his cheek, shyly, when he told her. The last several days had provoked a whirlwind of activity. She and Tanya were seen again by the nurse practitioner at the clinic, who told them what they already knew, that they were doing much better. Larissa wondered if Americans always stated the obvious.

Their bruises, while less apparent, still ached, but the nurse told Larissa the internal damage would take more time. Physically and psychologically. Larissa understood the honest assessment. The nurse recommended she continue the *sitz* baths, and had her refill a course of antibiotics against possible infection. She also advised physical therapy for the arm once the cast was removed. The multiple breaks would have weakened ligaments, tendons and her muscle tone. Their health in general improved, due to the care they received. Nourishing food, good hygiene, counseling and simple goodness in the persons of their hosts rallied their forces, and Larissa felt once again—*human.*

At last, a car pulled up to the gate. After a moment, this swung open and the vehicle passed through, coming to a stop a few yards away. The retired couple, whose shelter this was, came out of their home to meet Carter and Sasha. Larissa watched them shake hands and she felt a wave of joy wash over her.

"Tanya! Come and see who is here . . . now—up you go!" using one arm to lift the child so she could see her uncle. "That is your Uncle Sasha, my darling. Isn't he *beautiful?*' Larissa took a long moment to fully recognize her brother. How much he had grown, changed and matured! He was not as tall as Carter, but he was stouter, with thick brown hair combed back from his high forehead, and clean-shaven, with the strong bone structure of a Slav. His complexion was ruddy and he was smiling. His eyes as well. Something she had not seen in a very long time.

Tanya stared out the window, wearing a perplexed expression of both wonder and expectancy. Then, with softened eyes that saw only love, the child matter-of-factly said, "*Da*. He is, Mama. Beautiful." Larissa caught the earnest response, spoken with pride and perhaps awe. She reached for the small hand of her daughter, who jumped off the chair and opened their door and they went out.

Jim, the wrangler at the Blue Wood, who'd discovered Larissa and Tanya in a snow bank two weeks ago, hadn't known when Larissa's brother might arrive. She'd asked him if there was room at the guest ranch for Sasha, as she didn't think he could stay with her and Tanya at the shelter. Jim said he'd ask, but he'd put it off. It wasn't like him to procrastinate, and he wasn't sure why he had.

Pete had wanted to hunt this year, which pleased his father, but having never shown an interest in the sport, it was left to Jim to teach him. The guest ranch usually booked at least one novice hunter a year, so this was simply a warm-up for the wrangler-guide. He had set aside an afternoon to go over principles of shooting, which Pete quickly absorbed, even excelled at; then, it was simply a matter of paying attention, to Jim in the field, in this case, the woods, and, well, *paying attention*. He emphasized the point. Pete told him he *got* it, perhaps a bit too testily. The boy was going to carry his father's Winchester .30-06.

Guest hunters were arriving that night, so Jim had wanted Pete to have a chance to hunt without the extra distraction, but they'd gotten a late start. It was cold and they'd bundled up. Jim wanted to hunt the area adjacent to the old Berry place, now that no one was occupying it. It would be a good bet for unsuspecting animals. They would have grown used to less interference.

Now is that right? he heard in his head. *Since when can you read the minds of deer?* He chuckled. His mother used to say he was

154

attractive when he smiled, but he seldom did. Running the guest ranch (despite the owners' welcome participation) largely fell on him.

"What?" asked Pete quietly, as they trudged along the logging road.

"Nothin' . . . do your thoughts sometimes argue with themselves?" he asked the boy.

"Ha. Isn't that the definition of youth?" answered the youth.

"*Shhh*," they heard from Lee, who was bringing up the rear. He added in a whisper, "*Foolishness* is the definition of youth . . . it's when you're *supposed* to get it out of your system."

Jim snorted. He was enjoying this. *Something different, anyway.* He had a connection with the kid, making it more important that Pete be successful. He didn't much care if guest hunters filled or not. Though he worked at it. No, today's hunt included an added ingredient.

They approached the wire fence between the old Berry place and National Forest land. It was electrified, but Jim didn't know if it was still hot.

"Touch it and see," he told Pete.

"*You* touch it," Pete replied, grinning.

"Y'all are being too damn loud," said Lee, reaching out to check the wire. Nothing. "They must've unplugged it."

"You're wearing gloves," said Pete.

"Shouldn't matter," said Jim. But he pulled his off and lightly placed a finger on the wire. "It's off," he said, and they continued up the line. Through the trees, Jim could barely make out the old house and trailer. A preternatural quiet accompanied them. No bird call, no chatter of squirrel; not a sound. Then, as if to protest the vacuum of silence, they heard loud cracking, such that Jim recognized it immediately, and it jolted his heart.

Too loud for mere *deer* antlers and too much force behind the racket, there before them, in a glade seventy-five feet away, two bull elk fought. Antlers knocked and crashed into the other, in a duel between a six-point Royal and a younger four-point, possibly the challenger. Jim raised a gloved hand to stay his party, and they hunkered down quickly. It was elk season, but they carried deer licenses. Jim looked at Pete, whose eyes burned with adrenaline and excitement. Lee's bearded face had broken open in a wide grin, and Jim was happy for the father and son, who were able to share this thing, and would have it to share forever.

Then came the shot.

A loud bellow followed. Spooked, the old bull pivoted and dashed off through the woods, his magnificent rack weaving in and out among close aspens. The four-point dropped, front knees first to the ground, and then over, onto his great side.

"What the *hell?*" Jim muttered, standing up, Pete and Lee rising after him.

From the old Berry place came a shout, and then, a curse from another voice. Jim, Lee, and Pete watched as a man appeared through the trees, brandishing a hand gun, and rushing up behind him was Deputy Carter, who grabbed the weapon to replace it in his holster.

"*What the hell, Carter?!*" exclaimed Jim, more forcefully.

The elk was still alive. The great head and antlers whipped around. Another shot rang.

Jim and Lee turned and looked agape at Pete, whose expression broke their hearts. He still held the rifle to his shoulder, having put down the animal.

CHAPTER 25
THE GUEST HOUSE

Snow was falling as Senga drove into Sara's Spring. She was happy to return before night fall. Dusk would arrive within the hour and no moon tonight, she remembered. Roads would quickly ice and her thoughts flew back to her grandfather, the tall, wiry man everyone called Papa; how one night, he'd quietly walked through the front door on their mountain top home in western North Carolina, to slowly make his way to the coat rack to hang his green felt hat and coat. Without turning, he'd told his wife that their daughter Lucy had just died in an accident, having run off a slick, snow-covered highway on her way home from town.

Senga felt cleaved from her body.

Avoiding his wife's countenance altogether, Papa had merely looked at his granddaughter without speaking. His expression conveyed all. Then, he'd shut himself in his bedroom for the night, seeking no comfort and giving none, leaving wife and orphan to console one another. Eyes stinging with tears, Senga had allowed Grannie to guide her to the old sofa, while she withdrew to the kitchen to brew a calmative for both. *A large pot, it was,* Senga now recalled. The old healer's hand had trembled as it reached above her head for the tied bunch of hanging herb—catnip, with its rose-purple, dried flowers among green leaves and stalks.

Senga didn't want to think on this now, but refrained from dismissing it.

Why had it come unbidden, like an uninvited guest? She recalled a line from a poem by Rumi, *The Guest House*, about welcoming the uninvited; that they all have something important to impart. . . *Be grateful for whoever comes, because each has been sent as a guide from beyond.*

So, what was it?

Senga pulled into the store parking lot. She needed coffee and oatmeal. And eggs.

"Hi, Ellie, how are things?" she asked the clerk.

"Good. Ah, you expecting company, Senga? Two guys asked about you; one yesterday and one today. Today's was looking for the "root digger," and the other asked for you by name. I said you wasn't home and got chewed out for telling the one where you lived. But he said he wanted to see you about your herbs and all. . ."

Senga stared at her. "One of them chewed you out?"

"I'm sorry; no, not *them*. The boss. I know I shouldn't have."

"No, it's all right, Ellie . . . I just can't think who—" And then she did. She remembered Ellie calling her a *root digger* to Yellowtooth, the man who'd made the remark about Gabe that day in the store. And the other could only be Rob.

"*That* guy? The one I, uh—"

"Nope. I woulda known him. This one was younger . . . maybe sixteen. Bad gums, I remember. I kinda felt sorry for the kid, actually. Not sure why."

"Damn," Senga said under her breath. "Sorry, Ellie. I've gotta go. Put this stuff on my account, will you?"

"Okay. Senga, do I need to call Charlie? Is it bad?"

"I don't know. Yes, would you—no, wait—when, today?"

"About two hours ago, more or less. You think they're still up to your place? Why don't you ask Gabe to go by?"

"No. Look, it'll be okay. Actually, I have a new cell phone. What's Charlie's number? Oh, never mind. I'll just go see him. Thanks, Ellie, and don't worry."

Declining a plastic bag, Senga gathered up her few items and walked out to her car, where she deposited them. Then she crossed the road to the small police station—snowflakes swirling around her. The Cottonwood Café and its bar were doing good business. *More vehicles than usual,* she noticed and remembered it was hunting season.

Charlie's police SUV was parked in front. She knocked on the door unnecessarily, turned the knob and stepped in.

"Well, what's happened now?" Charlie asked from behind a messy desk.

"How do you find anything?" she asked, looking down at the stacks and disorder.

"I have a system," he answered, "What is it? You've got a look brewing," the large man said. The Chief had dropped a few pounds in the last three weeks, but he needed to lose several dozen more.

"Hey, Charlie. Um, I think someone from the Berry place has gone up to my cabin, and Emily's father went up yesterday, too. I'm concerned, is all. Ellie at the store just told me. I heard one of them was arrested at their house?"

"Yeah. He's being questioned now. By the DHS— Department of Homeland Security to you," he added. Charlie made a gesture toward gathering a stack of papers, for form's sake. "Glad they've got it, personally. That whole crew gave us the willies . . . you know one of them was found dead in a Belle Fourche motel?"

Senga eyed a chair and sat down. "Don't mind if I do," she said absently, ". . . And yes, Rufus told me."

"You want me to drive up with you?"

"I don't know, Charlie. I guess I'm concerned for Rob. He's liable to do something stupid if provoked."

At this Charlie put a little finger in his ear to scratch an itch, and then squinted in her direction, "Ah . . . kinda like *you?*"

She glared at him from under her brows. "Yes."

"You think they might get into it?"

He meant a disagreement; not the cabin, she deduced. "Hell, Charlie—I haven't seen Rob in twenty years . . . well, not true, I saw him just Saturday night in a bar in Spearfish."

At this, Charlie's eyes sprang open. "*What?*"

Senga and bars had not always sounded oxymoronic and she lightly blushed. "I was there with a friend, when, uh, I saw him. He was going to perform. I think."

"You have a *friend*, Senga? Well, good! Male or female?"

He was enjoying this far too much. "Now you're just pissing me off, Charlie, though I'm beginning to understand why some women give up on men. War comes to mind. . . Anyway, Rob didn't see me, and I left—*we* left."

"Your friend and you."

"My friend and me."

"Okay. Here, call your number and see if anyone picks up." Charlie turned the phone around to her.

"I left the cabin locked, Charlie."

"Yeah, and I suppose you hang the key on a nail across from the door on a post."

She made a face at him. "And you're too fuckin' smug. . ."

He snickered and she dialed her number.

After the second ring, it was picked up. Silence greeted her. Senga said nothing, and she held out the receiver so Charlie could listen. After a moment, a tentative "Hello?" was heard.

She was about to speak when Charlie quickly put his hand over the end of the receiver and shook his head. He lifted it to his face and said, "Howdy. I'm looking for Senga Munro. Can I speak to her?"

"Uh, well, she ain't here. Can I, uh, can I take a message?" said the voice.

Charlie's eyes opened wider to Senga, as if to ask, *Do you recognize it?*

Scrunching up her mouth, she shook her head and Charlie spoke into the mouthpiece, "No. No need. I'll call back," and he hung up.

"Well, somebody's in your cabin. Let's go." He stood, plucked his hat off the nearby stand, pulled on his jacket and made sure he had all the trappings of his trade by patting his pockets. He looked once more at his desk, with a baffled expression, thought Senga.

"But . . . you don't have jurisdiction, do you, Charlie? And I just thought of something else . . . I've got caller I.D. on my phone."

He smirked, "Going as a friend," ". . . and don't worry; I hit the private number feature before letting you punch in yours," he said, tapping his temple with a forefinger.

Charlie followed Senga out of town through heavier snow fall, and they turned onto the highway which led to her home. He'd called his off-duty officer to come in, and filled him in.

Charlie's thoughts swirled like the snowflakes. *The hunters will be happy,* he reflected. *Not if it keeps up . . . the deer will lie low for the duration,* came the argument.

If this was a breaking and entering, which it sounded like, what the hell was he going to do? And her old boyfriend? What was that about? Charlie took a deep breath, exhaled and called the sheriff.

Senga's Honda slowed in front of him. Within eight miles, they were in the middle of a white-out and he barely made out the delineator poles on the side of the highway. Her brake lights flashed intermittently as she slowed then continued. He gave her more road and, at last, he spotted her mail box ahead.

She pulled over and left the car to retrieve a bag of mail from the box. *Only a woman would think to do that in this weather and with these circumstances,* he thought. She waved and climbed back into her car, to drive the quarter mile to the cabin. As he proceeded, he noticed recent tire tracks in the snow, rapidly filling in, either coming from or turning north, toward Montana.

A van was parked near the garage. No sign of the dually pick-up from the old Berry place. If these people were in her cabin, would they have seen them drive up? *Yeah, by the headlights,* he answered himself, adding, *Idiot.* He'd never been to Senga's, and didn't know how the cabin stood in relation to the drive. *So, just maybe . . . but improbable.*

She'd stepped from her car and was heading toward the garage, when Charlie hustled out of his, making a nondescript noise. She turned and nodded. Stepping up beside her, he unsnapped his holster strap and motioned for her to return to her car. This she did, if stubbornly, he thought. He quietly pulled open one of the garage doors, gasped and jerked backward.

He drew his SIG Sauer and trained it on someone in the back of the garage. Dim, gray light from a small, adjacent window fell on a featureless figure, its head-scarf askew, its arms raised. In supplication? Was it holding a bundle of twigs in bony hands? Charlie finally identified the scarecrow—its purpose fulfilled. He shuddered, and then, he swore. The place smelled of apples, he thought, and—pot; its musty-pungent smell strangely married to that of the fruit.

He whipped around to a sound of amusement.

"Gotcha there, didn't she?"

The chief didn't recognize the voice, but the face rang a distant bell. About twenty years ago, when Charlie was a state trooper, he'd helped deliver a baby on the side of the road in the middle of the night. Senga's and this man's.

He swore again and holstered the gun.

CHAPTER 26
MEMENTO D'AMORE

*D*earest Senga,

The sea turtle vertebra is Archelon ischyros, from the Cretaceous—145.5 to 65.5 millions of years ago— a late period of the Mesozoic Era. It is indeed petrified, which you knew. I wanted to write these figures and names down for you before I leave. It is the middle of the night as I sit here at the table. A candle burns. The woodstove offers heat by its red coals, but I am warmed by our love making and I may never be cold again. This from a man who returns to the frozen north of Europe in a few hours.

I watched you sleep before rising to write these thoughts. Do you know that you snuffle? Yes! But quietly. Like a cat, purring.

I would say so many things to you, but they all seem paltry and unnecessary and bland, compared to how I feel.

I love you, Senga. Is it enough?

You said tonight is the new moon. A time for beginnings. I stepped outdoors for a few moments just now. How bright the stars are! In my country, I would have to travel far for such a view. Or be on the cold sea. When I am in Copenhagen and think of you, it will be with this sparkling crown above you. Senga's stars.

Forgive my effusive sentiments, my dear. It must disturb the pragmatist in you.

*Now I will tell you some things I want you to know,
but about which I have difficulty speaking.*

Senga shifted positions, to gird herself. She read on:

*In the intervening years, between our first meeting
and a fortnight ago, when we met again, this man you
call Sebastian was different than he is today. After Elsa
died, I was dead to the world and merely put in my time
at the agency, making photos for advertisements. I can
tell you this because you have walked the same valley.
My ennui was beyond words. I was not present for my
daughter, but she somehow understood and took refuge
with an aunt, her mother's sister. She lived away from
me for several years, only returning when she entered
university.*

*My Elsa died from a cancer. Uterine—a
particularly painful sort. Even the morphine did not give
her relief in the end. It was a mercy when she finally
died. The suffering of a loved one affects us
psychologically as much as their physical pain, I believe.
I may be wrong. I never wanted to repeat the experience,
this I know. But this is life, and I would rather be alive
and feel, than be dead and numb.*

*After your Emily died and I held her, I demanded
from God, Why? Not, why did this beautiful young girl
have to die? But, Why did I have to undergo another
trial in feeling someone's pain? And I felt yours, Senga.
Perhaps this was my penance for asking such a selfish
question. I may have felt it even more acutely than after
my Elsa's death, because Emily's was so immediate and
your grief so complete.*

*So, I beg your forgiveness for this shameful
admission. If it is any consolation, the image of us there,
beside the falls with your Emily, has accompanied me
all these years. And it has only abated—yes, I use this
word—upon your discovery in the gallery. The image by
the falls, formerly a memento mori of sorts, has come to
underscore Life, instead of death. Do you understand,
my dear? You quite literally saved my life. As in, "laid*

it aside," to be picked up and examined and deemed useful, even loved.

After my father and I returned to Denmark, my photos (for the agency) became more "edgy," as is popularly said. More immediate, my employer suggested. As though I had been given to glimpse the fragility and absolute phenomenon of living. I say this only now, much after the fact. I did not notice it at the time—exactly. I heard comments about my work, yes, but they flowed over me as so much flattery—or nonsense.

I continued in this vein, working long hours, ignoring most interpersonal relationships, save those with my Aunt Karen and Uncle Harold, through letters, and, with my Erika. But my daughter did not want to be further hurt by the negligence I had visited upon her while Elsa was sick—and afterward—so she held me at arm's length. Still loving, but cautious. A pitiful combination.

Since her marriage to Peter, and with Jytte's arrival, Erika is much happier, and has managed to embrace my presence again, for which I am grateful. I expect she has difficulty forgiving me for depriving her of a father, when she'd lost her mother so irrevocably. And I will not pretty it up for you; I am not at all certain how she will accept you, Senga. But know that it does not matter.

I can hear you now. Of course it does! With eyes flashing.

I mean to say, that however my daughter receives you, it could never make a difference in how I feel about you. You are now my life. My muse. My Senga.

A muse is an artist's god, Senga. Or goddess, in your case. There is God, and then there are the gods. I suppose they could be called any number of things: angels, divine inspiration, fancy, electricity, and wonderment—even mystery. I do not mean to reduce you to mere function; you are so much more. . .

Your comment, that I am now free to pursue my own passions. . . But I pursue you, Senga. Only you. In all your guises. I wish to uncover (if this is the appropriate word) inklings of your essence. No one has a right to the thing itself, save one's soul, yet we follow bread crumbs—to borrow from a fairy tale—leading to one another's suchness, and this is what I wish to explore. For the rest of our lives. I did not understand your statement about passion when you made it, but this is my response.

So I thank you for last night, and all the days and nights which preceded it. I will think on you, and this remarkable gift that has been given me.

Please use the mobile to reach me anytime, day or night. Copenhagen is eight hours ahead in time, but I'll answer anytime. If I can. If not, I will return your call.

May you be safe on your travels, and may you have a marvelous reunion with your grandmother. Kiss her on the cheek for me, please, and tell her that I love you.

Now I am weary. But I am able to blow out this candle and return to our bed for the rest of this sweet night.

May God—and all the gods—bless you, Senga, and keep you, and may you know how very much you are loved.

I already miss you,
Sebastian

P.S. The arrowhead is a brilliant reminder of your exquisite nature, my dear, my nature mystic.

Senga carefully folded the letter along the exact creases Sebastian had made, replaced it in the blue-lined envelope and held it to her heart. She leaned against the headboard, wrapped in a blanket against the chill, and turned her gaze to the stalwart candle flame keeping darkness at bay. It wavered against the occasional gust pushing against the less-than-airtight window.

Sebastian would be somewhere over the North Atlantic by now, she thought. *Safe journey, love,* she prayed into the light.

Having read the letter for the third time, she felt the words shift previous information aside, request—not demand—room, to finally settle into her cells; these were gracious words. Enriching and nourishing words. She remained still as death, not wishing to disturb the spell he'd cast. An antidote to earlier events.

Abracadabra, she mused.

So, she was a muse. She, who had heretofore embraced *All Else* as muse; *what goes 'round comes 'round*, she quipped and shook her head. *Not the time for being glib*, she chided; and tranquil, unmoving, she rested.

Rob McGhee occupied the other room, keeping the woodstove fed during the storm, which wasn't expected to let up until after midnight. She'd invited him to stay, rather than send him out into the weather. He'd accepted. They'd arranged a pallet and his sleeping bag on the floor.

Their reunion had been awkward, and Senga wondered if she'd regressed to a former incarnation, wherein she was even *more* socially inept. She'd spoken to him simply, wanted to be kind, though she would have preferred to have been alone this night. (Alone with the absence of Sebastian.) But *here* was the guest, and she would practice hospitality. *After all, we had a child together.* This served to rally her will.

For reasons unknown, she said nothing about the roadside shrine, holding it sacred. The speaking of it might cause it to disappear or, as with efforts to recall dreams, to retreat beneath consciousness and reality.

Mulling all by candlelight in her bedroom sanctum, she allowed her mind to drift.

Rob hadn't changed much; he'd filled out and wore his white hair shorter. In fact, it was nearly shaved off and his hairline had receded. He was still attractive, and she was acutely aware of him. By cat-like aquamarine eyes (whereas Sebastian's were sapphires). She idly wondered if Rob McGhee could see in the dark. Emily's eyes had been identical and therein lay the rub, as they say. Senga saw her in Rob. It proved disconcerting, and she'd finally excused herself to retreat to her bed, where cool sheets smelled of lovemaking and Sebastian. After a moment, she turned to the afternoon's events.

Rob reintroduced himself to Charlie in the garage and suggested they go to the cabin, where it was warmer. He told the policeman two guys showed up while he was taking a hike—that they'd let themselves into the cabin. Apparently, one of them, "needed to use the facilities," (how Rob phrased it), "And by the odor," he'd added, "it must have been dire."

She'd snorted, and set about applying much cleanser to the toilet, followed by vinegar.

Charlie asked what his business there was, and what he was doing in Senga's garage. Rob had merely glared at the former trooper and refrained from answering.

"He was smoking pot, Senga." Charlie turned to her, "Unless you've taken up vices?"

"Circumstantial, Charlie," she said. "Could have been the other guys. . ."

"Hell, I know when someone's been smoking. Anyway, let it go for now; what happened?"

Rob related what he knew; that he'd been exploring above the cabin, when he heard someone drive up. Thinking it was Senga, he'd turned back.

"I saw one of them messing with Emily's tree and yelled at him. They got spooked, it looked like. The younger kid was peeking from the side of the cabin—trying to spot me, I guess. I was just there—" He pointed east, high on the slope, above the red scrap hanging from the ponderosa twig.

Senga sighed. "How'd they wind up inside, Rob?"

"Just what I was gonna ask," said Charlie.

"I *told* you; the kid said he needed to use the bathroom and, from where I was, he looked desperate. I said the cabin was locked and to go in the woods. Then the other guy told the kid he'd found the key. . ."

Hanging on a post opposite the door. Senga squirmed.

". . . And they wouldn't be long. So, I let it go."

"When was this, exactly?" Charlie looked more than a little disgusted.

"I heard the phone ring. One of them answered; it sounded muffled through the walls. That was about an hour ago. Maybe more. They were gone before I made it back. I thought they were friends of yours, Senga. Sorry."

"Um, *no*, Rob," she said, and inspected her surroundings for possible theft. When finished, she drew a deep breath, made silent thanks and told Charlie it looked all right. Frankly, she was surprised but relieved. The bathroom was the only casualty. It could have been worse. She resolved to find a different hiding place for her cabin key.

Charlie used her phone to call the sheriff, to apprise him of the situation, and to say that the two men from the Berry place were probably somewhere between Broadus, Montana and Belle Fourche, South Dakota for the night, adding he wouldn't have wanted to be driving after dark in this storm.

After Charlie left, she made supper, which amounted to egg noodles, butter and parmesan cheese—her quick and easy meal. They spoke little, but she noticed Rob stealing glances at her. She wondered if he could smell Sebastian, evidence of primal, territorial marking. After reading Sebastian's letter and doing her nightly recollection of Emily, she fell asleep with Charlie and the scare crow on her mind. He'd excoriated her for displaying such a thing, obviously embarrassed by his reaction. She'd explained how Hermione had been her and Emily's doll to dress up over the years. The encounter led to a dream. . . .

"Get a blanket, Senga!"

She rolls down her car window and hears Charlie calling. He looks as he did nineteen years ago. Slim. Wearing his state trooper hat. She rolls the window up, opens the door and steps into deep snow.

"The sun shines low behind the snow, an alpenglow," she rhymes to herself. Before reaching the open doorway to the garage, she senses someone on the path, watching her. Turning, she peers through dense flakes to make out the person of Rob McGhee, also appearing as he did nineteen years before—his white-blond hair, long.

"Hello," she says.

"Hello, Senga." Quietly.

He must be cold, she thinks in passing; he's not wearing a hat or coat.

"Go on back inside. You'll catch something."

"No, I'm all right. I see you have a cop with you. Good. That guy's nuts."

"If it's Yellowtooth, then, yes, I know that, but what am I going to find when I walk in there, Rob?"

He looks away, with clouded expression. "His little brother's in the cabin. A good kid, I think. Wants out of this—whatever they're into. It's a long story, Senga. The cop needs to hear it." He makes to return to the cabin.

Charlie appears. *"What do I need to hear?"* He narrows his eyes at the man. *"Who are you?"* he calls, *". . . and what are you doing in Senga's cabin?"*

"Charlie, this is Rob McGhee. Remember? Rob—Chief Charlie Mays, of the Sara's Spring Police Department. Don't y'all remember?"

But they don't—as though Emily was never born, now that she was gone, and Senga struggles with the lie. Like a torch, she holds Emily ablaze in her mind.

"What's going on here," Charlie asks Rob, with a chin nod to the garage.

"I had to do something," Rob faces Charlie. *"The guy was getting ready to cut down Em—uh, Senga's tree—"*

"What?!" she cries and bolts toward the juniper. Rob calls after her.

"It's all right, Senga! I caught him in time."

The words mix with swirling snowflakes, creating a maelstrom of dark energy, as the sun drops below the ridgeline. She needs light. Rushing to the electric cord on the porch, she plugs it in, as the glow lights the gathering flakes. She bends to see under a swag, sucking her breath at the wound where a saw's jagged teeth began their work. The bow saw lies abandoned beside the trunk. She lifts and casts it away where it disappears into the snow.

Her healer's mind quickly makes an assessment: *I can mend you with bee's wax,* she tells the tree. And then, she roars. Emily's red chair has been pitched aside, but the spot remains untouched where her ashes rest. Rob is at her side in an instant. He gathers her in his arms. *"It's all right, Senga. The tree's all right."*

He has not grasped the gravity; rather, he cannot. Gravity eludes him, she reflects. He is one who floats endlessly through life. . .

She permits the embrace for only a moment and pulls away; then, leaning over, she picks up the small red chair to replace it where the Walker's Shortbread tin lies buried. A stone, visible near the chair, emits a strange, blue pulsing glow. She stoops to pick it up and settles it on the chair, where it returns to mere stone. Standing, she rearranges her face into something resembling her feelings and trudges back to the garage, where Charlie stands just inside the open door.

"You okay?"

"No. I'm not; where is he?" she demands, and Charlie steps aside to reveal a sight.

"He needs a blanket, Senga . . . ain't fittin'," she thinks she hears him add, under his breath and she frowns.

Yellowtooth is tied up. He is naked. His tattoos take on a gruesome air and begin to writhe, pulsing from his neck and down his torso. His penis lies flaccid against his groin, then suddenly springs, hard now, toward her, in accusation, in defense, in anger, or so she thinks. It is tattooed as well, with black, zigzag designs. It proceeds to spew a mess of ejaculate.

Senga groaned in her sleep and turned over.

"Come on! Untie me!" the man cries. "Where's that fuckin' witch? T-tell her to t-take it back, all of it!" And Senga hears his teeth chatter. His skin in the low light appears milky and mottled where it isn't covered in ink. He shivers violently, and squeezing his thighs together, he turns away from her. "She told me to do it; it was her fault. She cursed me . . . it's all her fault," he sobs.

She is conflicted; she had wanted to hurt this tattooed man, but he is clearly deranged. She grabs one of the quilts that covers a pallet of apples and passes it to Charlie. She looks away. When the crying ceases, she regards Yellowtooth again. His eyes are fastened on the scare crow and wild with fear.

Did Rob do this? she wonders, even as she realizes he did. Gravity hounded him and ran him down at last.

"Where are his clothes?" Younger Charlie asks Younger Rob, who appears in the doorway.

Senga watches him step to a pile of clothing and hand it to Charlie. "I—I couldn't let him—I . . ."

"Shut up!" cries Charlie, who's just about had enough.

"He needs to be warmed up, Charlie . . . we should all go inside," she says.

"No, Senga. Listen; go turn up the heat in my outfit. I'm taking him in. He'll get warm on the way. Now I've got to make a call and you have shitty cell service out here, so I'll be using your phone; is that all right?"

"Yes, of course."

"Let's get him dressed," Charlie snaps his holster strap down, in case the man has any ideas, and he squats to untie him. The knots are difficult. Rob has secured his hands behind his back, with the bight of the rope on a hook on the wall. His feet are tied together and the rope hangs from a steel table leg, making it all but impossible to move. He is sitting on bare cement. In a wet spot, she notices. He's pissed himself.

Senga shuddered and moaned again, trying to cry out in her sleep. She was caught in a night terror, as tightly bound as

Yellowtooth, the nightmare sitting squarely on her chest like a succubus. *Gravity,* indeed.

"*Damn it, you think you could've made them any tighter?*" *Charlie asks Rob.*

"*Just cut the damn rope.*" *Senga says.* "*I'll make him something hot to drink.*"

She awoke. Thirsty and cold and needing to use the bathroom.

CHAPTER 27
FLARE-UPS

Caroline and Rufus had left for his physical therapy appointment, leaving Gabe to feed Gil and Pat the noon meal and see them off. Caroline had prepared a pot of venison spaghetti the night before—with chops, courtesy of Pat. It warmed now on the back burner. Gabe stepped to the refrigerator for the butter, salad and assorted dressings. Two loaves of homemade bread lay on the counter.

"White or wheat?" he asked the men.

"Oh, white, I suppose," said Gil; with a smirk, Gabe noticed.

"I'll have wheat," said Pat, not missing a beat.

Gabe placed both loaves on a cutting board, along with the knife. "Help yourselves."

They ate in silence. The snow had ceased during the night and the sky shone blue through the windows. Before leaving, Caroline had driven the truck out to the mailbox, returned and deemed the road passable. The plows would have cleared the highway.

"Rufus asked me to remind you about the landowner tags," Gabe said as he placed the pot on a folded towel on the table. The subsidy, provided by the Game and Fish Department for deer taken on private property, went straight to Caroline. Her "mad" money, she called it.

"Yeah, we know," said Gil, who reached into his front pocket to extract the form. Pat did the same. "You have a pen?"

Gabe plucked one from his shirt pocket and handed it to him.

As a first-time guide, he was glad this hunt was over. Gil had wound up with a two point, only because he'd missed the four-by-four he wanted, shooting instead the young buck standing directly behind. A gut shot. Not good. The hunter suggested they "just leave it." When Gabe mentioned this to Rufus, his boss only said, "Well, that rips it."

The phone rang, pulling him back. Gabe stood and crossed the kitchen to answer it.

"Hey. . . . Yes, I'll be leaving here about 3:00 . . . have a few things to do first. Okay . . . see you later, *chère*," and he nearly bit his tongue. *Damn.*

"*Chère?*" spoke up Gil. "You have a *sweetheart?*"

"Not that it's any of your business," Gabe said with a wide smile, to deflect possible escalation. He wanted no discussion, so he employed one of Senga's tricks. Misdirection. Or changing the subject, as it was politely called:

"Uh, Pat, that skull needs to be rinsed off—or do you want to leave the paste on 'til you get home?" Gabe ignored Gil, who, he could tell, was mulling the phone call.

"He'll leave it on, won't you, Pat?" the big man spoke for his friend. "So where does she live, this girlfriend?" he pressed.

Gabe looked at him now. A long, level gaze. Then he smiled, without humor. Pat placed his hand on Gil's forearm.

"I'm ready to get going, Gil," he said, and started to rise. Gil reached around and pulled the man back down.

"Sit. I'm not ready to leave, Pat. So, black man, where does she live? *Africa?*"

Gabe hadn't thought this through. He'd hoped he could complete the hunt without incident, for the Strickland's sake, but they weren't here. So he prayed. To Gabriel, his saint. *I need help.*

Gabriel heard him.

Pat rose from his chair, all one-hundred-and-thirty pounds. His face took on an expression Gabe had seldom seen on anyone, let alone a timid man. Pat leaned over and spoke into Gil's face from four inches away, "I'm heading out. You can quit being a jack-ass and join me or find another way home!" and he turned toward the door, hands in pockets. Apparently it was his ride to command. Then he stopped to face Gabe.

"Tell Caroline and Rufus I had a great time . . . and, I hope to see them next year. You too, if you're around. And thanks for the help." This last sentiment was spoken to Gabe, but directed at Gil, as a lesson. Pat then strode over to Gabe and held out his hand. Gabe stood and shook it, and the man turned and left. Pat had slipped something into his palm. It went into his pocket.

He glanced at Gil, then away. The man's eyes had appeared to glaze over. *Was this a first?* Gabe wondered, as he moved the pot of spaghetti back to the stove to cool. Supper tonight for Caroline and Rufus, he figured. When he turned back, Gil was rising from the table and Gabe studied him covertly—his attitude and expression, knowing he'd have to get it on paper soon, before the scene evaporated. Big men seemed to deflate more spectacularly than slighter ones, but how the slender form of Pat had filled with nerve! Yep, he needed to write it down. . .

Thanks, Gabe spoke to the unseen as Gil opened the door and stepped through, not turning back for a fare-thee-well. Gabe expected none. "Goodbye, Gil."

He reached into his pocket and pulled out the folded bill.

"Well, ain't that nice," he said, returning the tip to his pocket. "Francesca—dinner's on Pat tonight!"

Senga woke to unfamiliar noises. Then she recalled the nightmare and rubbed her hands over her face to dispel it. But no, the image of Yellowtooth in her garage was firmly embedded. She moved her head to the left not once, but twice, in an effort to dislodge it, then swung her legs out of bed and quickly stood. Dizzy, she sank again to the mattress, waited a moment and bent over her knees to perform her stretches.

Out her east window, a patch of blue peeked through the trees and rearranged her thoughts. *The snow's quit; good.* Wearing her tattered blue robe, she crossed to the bathroom, greeting Rob as she closed the door. "Mornin'."

He replied the same.

Another unfamiliar sound jangled from the sitting room. "I can get that, if you want," said Rob, and before she could respond, he'd picked up her new cell phone and said hello.

Senga slipped back into her robe and rushed out the door, "Give me that!" she demanded. "*Hello?*"

It was Sebastian. *Naturally. Who else has my number?*

"Senga?"

"Hey! You're going in and out, Sebastian," she said, moving to the window.

Renée Carrier

"Who answered the phone?" Sebastian asked first, then, "Do you work today? It is Tuesday."

"Yes, I'm leaving soon. Um," pause, "that was Rob. He came by yesterday and there was a snowstorm, so I asked him to stay until the roads cleared."

Silence.

"Sebastian?"

More silence.

"Are you there?" She glanced over to see Rob studying her. She frowned and stepped into her bedroom where there was more static, so she returned to the main room, opened the door and stepped onto the porch, finding the south side clearer.

"Sebastian? Please . . . don't do this."

"I am not doing anything, my dear; you are," he said, in a tone she found chilling. It didn't sound like him, she thought, but then she hadn't considered consequences, from his point of view.

"Well, I'm not going to argue, or, defend it, so we'll have to talk another time. I hope your trip went well and I'll talk with you later, I hope." She hadn't learned the buttons yet and held the phone away to see which one ended the call. She heard "*Senga—*" just as she found the button, pressed it and the phone shut down. Then, she felt foolish.

From the porch, she noticed the path was once again covered in snow, and drifting in front of the garage. She must shovel it. With a sigh, she entered the cabin and ignored Rob, who looked uncomfortable. He bent to roll up the sleeping bag.

Senga reached for the blanket pallet, then stood, at a loss. Breathing audibly, she moved to her wing chair and there deposited the blanket, then walked to the sink to fill the kettle. At last, she returned to the bathroom.

"I'm sorry!" she heard Rob call.

She growled.

After making her toilette, she slipped into her bedroom and drew on her usual jeans, sweater and thick socks, then sat on the bed to lace her boots. The kettle whistled.

"Do you want me to get that?"

"You've done enough gettin'; I'm coming."

They drank their coffee in silence. She glanced at his face from time to time. Compelled to do so. *How like Emily . . . no;*

how like her father was Emily, and she sighed. Rising, she asked Rob if he'd like toast with jam. He did, so she prepared four slices for the toaster and set them on the table with butter and chokecherry jam.

"What are your plans?" she asked. ". . . I have to go in by eight-thirty—but I have some wash to put in first."

"Wash? Um, could you throw in a few things for me?"

She cocked an eyebrow then regretted the reaction, even if silent. But she was *sore.* Mostly at herself. "It won't be done 'til after lunch—when I put it in the drier. At the Laundromat?"

"Oh!" he said, after it dawned on him she lacked the washing machine.

Rob's expression moved her to pity as he gazed out the window for a long moment. He'd be in his mid-fifties now and he looked tired. *So damn tired.*

"Can we talk, Senga? Nothing earth-shattering. Just, well . . . you know we never really did after Emily died." He continued to stare through the window.

Senga didn't want to be having this conversation. *She* had spoken with someone—Joe Rafaela up on the Cheyenne reservation. And he had helped her.

(The horses pulled again, bits in their teeth; one headed one direction, and the other—)

"I am with someone, Rob," she blurted.

He turned and considered her.

"That was him on the phone, and . . . it's . . . it's like a *young* thing, you know? Tender? *Fragile?* I'm sure you can understand that. Now I'm going to have to explain what you're doing here. . ." She finished her coffee and stood. "Okay. I'm going into town; give me what needs to be washed. . . Stay tonight and we'll, ah, talk." *Though it'll be you doing most of it,* she assured herself.

After removing the small plates and her mug to the sink, she rinsed them off and set them to dry in the rack. "There's more coffee. You want it?"

He nodded absently, resuming his wool-gathering. "What's the red cloth up there?" he asked.

"Nothing," she muttered under her breath. Immediately sensing a sting from somewhere, she amended her reply, "I hung it to measure something I saw."

"Hunh," he said. Nothing more. Then, he rose and told her he'd get the bag of clothes, "There's not too much, and thank you," he added, "for everything."

The image of the roadside shrine bloomed in her mind, but she couldn't mention it yet. No, not yet. *However* . . .

"Rob," she began, "I owe you an apology, and thanks. . . What you did, putting those things in the box with Colin—"

He sharply turned his head toward her and hope, like a butterfly's shadow, crossed his face, she noticed and continued—

"Well, we'll talk this evening. I get home about 5:45. Help yourself to whatever food you can find, and a shower. I'll see you later."

She paused to study him a long moment, then surprised herself by walking up and embracing him, not out of pity, she hoped, but for their shared history and tragedy, and for gathering the mementos.

Rob clung to her, then they stepped apart simultaneously. He held her eyes but said nothing. His were moist, she saw. Then he turned to the door, opened it and, spotting the snow shovel, began to clear the path to the garage.

"You need your coat," she said, leaning out the door.

He shook his head, bending to the chore.

Indoors, Senga grabbed her sack of wash, checked her jacket for her wallet, wrapped the lavender cashmere scarf around her neck (a gift from Francesca) and stepped out the door. She turned and peered back inside, as her wont, to make a quick appraisal. . .

Something had disturbed the fabric of the room's atmosphere; this she knew in an instant.

She spotted her new cell phone on the table and reached for it. Spying its instruction booklet, she tucked this in her pocket as well.

Rob shoveled the area in front of the garage and pulled opened its wide doors. She backed her car out and thanked him as he opened the passenger door to set his bag of laundry on the floorboard. "Thanks again," he said, flashing the brilliant smile that had once lit her heart like a flare.

CHAPTER 28
TORTS AND TORTES

F rancesca took her time with the ritual: first, she attended to her skincare, then carefully applied her make-up and, last, dried her hair. Her mother had taught her only daughter three principles: the old Latin exhortation, *Carpe diem*—to seize the day, to be bold; and, finally, to take pains. Tonight would be the last she and Gabe enjoyed together for several weeks. The distance looming between them added another concern, and she assured her own sensibilities that this was indeed a *singular* evening.

Having earlier prepared her travel bags, she waited in the commons with only the warm, blazing fire for company. Everyone was busy elsewhere. The first time she left them, bidding Goodbyes, Jim had stopped her: "Nah. . . We say *so long* in the West, Francesca. You'll be back."

She was sitting transfixed by the flames, when she heard the great door open and felt a draft of cold air. Turning, she saw Gabe close the door behind him. A wave of mixed emotions followed. She noticed the dark purple silk square she'd given him, tied stock-fashion at his neck.

"*Gebb*," she said, her accent not allowing the long "a" of English. She rose and walked around the sofa into his arms.

"Sweet Francesca," he said, then kissed her, his hat brim interfering. "You look beautiful," he added, holding her by the shoulders and looking her up and down, pausing for a long moment at her décolletage. She wore dressy jeans, high boots, requisite scarf—or "neckwear," as it was now called—left untied, and her buttery-soft Italian leather jacket.

"I am ready," she said, ". . . and thank you." She wore a favorite blouse, one that accented her breasts, "Like baby watermelons," Gabe once told her and, the most recent analogy, each gloriously reminiscent (he had teased) of the dome of the cathedral in Florence. His comparison had come in response to her calling his cock a Chinese cuisine spring roll, or *teed beet*, as she pronounced it.

"Is this it?" he asked, looking at the baggage neatly parked near the door: one large suitcase, a smaller one and another large bag that carried her "necessaries,"—items she wouldn't chance to checking.

"*Sì, cara mio*, this is all. But they will be heavier when I leave tomorrow. I want to look for gifts for my family when we are in Rapid City. *Okay?*"

"Okay," he said, and they rolled the bags out the door and into the bright sunshine to his waiting pick-up. Jim had plowed the road and parking area. They had a room in Rapid City for the night, but first they would have dinner in Sara's Spring, where they had met sixteen months ago.

The Cottonwood was crowded and Gabe was glad he'd made a reservation. Their table stood by the window, so they could gaze out, even if only onto Sara's Spring's main street, lined this evening with pick-ups and trailers. He'd relaxed his rule of choosing a place in the back of the room. This was clearly the best table. After Annie brought the wine and antipasti, Francesca mentioned Pete's hunting story. He'd been permitted to keep the elk, but the deputy was dreading the consequences of allowing someone to snatch his gun.

"I expect so," agreed Gabe. "So tell me what happened."

"It is a long story, but *okay*—" Francesca pronounced the word with no diphthong, making it sound entirely foreign.

"Mary and I were sitting in the commons, when Lee and Jim returned from hunting," she began. . .

"Where is Pete?" his mother had asked Jim, as Francesca stowed her knitting materials. She stood and held out a hand for Mary, who was trying to rise from the sofa's deep cushions.

"He's coming," said Lee, whose expression seemed peculiar to Francesca. *Something has happened.*

"Looks like we're going to be eating well this winter," said Jim.

"Oh, he *did* get a deer!" crooned Mary, her smile vanishing when Lee's eyes dropped to his footwear.

"The warden's coming, Mary. Let's have fresh coffee ready when he gets here."

"What?" She frowned and looked from Lee to Jim and back to Lee. "What on earth?" And they told her, after removing their jackets and hats. Francesca brought them a carafe of coffee when it was ready. They sat at one of the long tables.

Lee explained that Deputy Carter had taken the Russian woman's brother to the old Berry place, to show him where his sister had been held. Apparently, the man had demanded to go, after seeing her at the shelter. As they trudged through the snow from the house toward the trailer, Sasha heard, then glimpsed the pair of bull elk through the trees— ". . . And this is where the story gets weird," Lee told them.

"Carter said something about it being elk season. Says to the Russian, 'Will you look at that?' and the guy calmly walks over to him, unsnaps Carter's holster—just like that," Lee snapped his fingers, "and grabs the gun before Carter knows what's happened—then he sprints toward the elk, kneels in the snow and pops one off—"

Here Francesca made a sound of dismay.

"He'd only wounded the bull and Pete, well, he did the right thing, putting him down, but there'll be hell to pay, I expect. Maybe not. We'll see. . . The kid isn't exactly celebrating, Mary, so, well . . . you know. . ."

"All right. I won't go on about it, but where *is* he?"

"On his way over. Carter's the one who's going to be chewed out. Maybe worse. Not sure what happens to the Russian. Boy, I tell you what—like that Caroline Strickland said the other night, *'When it rains'. . .*" No one completed the saying. They exchanged glances, not knowing what to say.

"When's the warden coming?"

"As soon as he can get up here," said Jim. "Look, I'm going to find Pete . . . he's still pretty shook up."

"Thanks—yeah, would you?" said Lee. "And the elk's in the pick-up outside, if y'all care to see it," he told his wife and Francesca, "But the warden takes the antlers—needs to, he told Carter—anyway, the one that got away was the biggest animal I've ever seen—outside of the ocean," he added, with a wistful look on his face. . .

"And this—this elk was *so* large, *Gebh*. I have seen these animals when we trail-ride sometimes—but never this close, and to think, the other was larger!"

"Hunh. Poor Carter," said Gabe. "That's not good. You're taught never to let someone take your gun. At least that's what a cop once told me. Where's the Russian now?"

Francesca wiped her mouth daintily at the corners with her napkin, then lifted her wine glass by the stem to her lips. He spied her bosom heave as she took a breath. It was the *prettiest* thing, he thought.

"This is a good chianti," and she smiled, setting it down, watching him watch her, eyes communicating all, and he answered with his own suggestive gaze, leaning back in his chair.

"I asked Barry for the best he stocks when I made the reservation."

"*Mmmm*. . . Sasha—that's his name, the brother of Larissa— he is staying at the Blue Wood—*sì!*" to Gabe's surprised expression. "He told Carter he was *so angry* when he saw where they made her live that he was crazy when he took the gun. He was very sorry, and he would make, ah, res-ti—"

"Restitution. . . For shooting the animal or grabbing the gun?"

"*Sì*, this is the word. The sheriff spoke with this, ah, *game warden?*"

"Game warden."

"And they agree the circumstances were, *bah, come si dice?*"

"No, I get it, Francesca . . . so he's at the ranch?"

"Until Larissa knows what she will do. It is difficult to explain the law in English, *cuore mio*."

"You speak better English than some I've met. . . So what's he like?"

"Oh, you know; Russian," and she reached for the bread sticks.

"No, Sweet Francesca, I *don't* know, and shame on you," he said, but with a smile.

"Oh, you are right, *Gebh*; but I have met several, and those I have met were very similar—well, except the one, *mmmm*. . . He was a poet. Do you know the words, 'he sings' in Russian is close to *po-et?*' Here she paused and gazed out the window for a long moment.

Gabe was glad he'd insisted on the window seat. For this very reason. Reflection requires space *through which* to reflect and process. Windows in classrooms, for example. *And in a barn's tack room doubling as a bunk house and study,* came the second thought, and he continued to study his lover's face in three-quarter profile.

He fell in love again.

The warm lighting from the ceiling heightened her complexion. She was a strong woman in size and carried her weight well. "*Forte!*" she'd once joked, holding out her arms to show her biceps. She reminded him of the frescos of women painted on the walls of Pompeii. But there was something regal about his Francesca. Oh, yes; her dignity. Now *he* was doing it . . . making generalizations. *Is it merely human?*

She was remembering someone, he sensed. "*Hmmm*, I smell a story in there. . ."

Turning back to him, she grinned and lifted her glass. He raised his and they lightly clinked. "To *amore, il mio amore.*"

Their dinner was presented with a flourish and Barry visited their table. Gabe had given the man license to prepare what he wished—within certain parameters; they couldn't take leftovers, as they weren't going home this night. But Gabe knew his girlfriend—*fiancée now*—had *buon appetito*, so he wasn't too concerned.

Barry waited for their reaction and wasn't disappointed. The lovers *oooh*'ed.

Annie had placed the tureen of Tuscan *Ribollita* soup between them, so they could return to it, if desired. An au gratin side dish and a salad would follow. For desert Gabe requested

Barry's dark chocolate torte, with vanilla ice cream. *One for each.* Francesca loathed sharing her desserts; he loved that about her. He knew he'd feel uncomfortably full for the drive to Rapid City, but they could sleep in. Caroline had told him not to worry; she could easily feed in the morning and when he was away in Italy next month. So that was settled.

They tucked into their meal, but saved the desserts. No one interrupted them, for which Gabe was exceedingly grateful.

The old hotel boasted a history and a ghost, informed the brochure on the bedside table. Francesca liked the room immediately. It felt European in its décor and ambience. They were on the ninth floor and enjoyed a view of the town. It was full-on dark now. Fallen snow lent the lighted streets mystery, but also a warm feeling, when viewed through a window.

She hugged herself, took a deep breath and twirled around. Gabe was arranging his Dopp kit in the small bathroom. She was disappointed there was no bathtub, but not overly so. Yes, this would do.

From her suitcase, she lifted out a nightgown in a delicate shade, of a fabric reminiscent of a wedding night. They had not set a date, and would not, until they had made other decisions and learned what her parents might expect. As sole daughter, Francesca's mother would likely prefer a grand affair. *Wait and see,* she told herself. She hinted to Gabe she would need the bathroom for a few minutes. It was a strong hint.

He backed out and she closed the door.

After thirty minutes, she emerged, wearing a stretch lace gown. A single lamp shone across the room. The windows reflected street light from below, washing the room in a pearly glow. Gabe was sitting up, nude, against the upholstered headboard of the queen-size bed. His skin gleamed against the off-white (grayish now in low light) walls, curtains, comforter and turned-down sheets. Her eyes met his and she noted his astonishment, or was it wonder? she wondered.

"*Gehb,* you look . . . so—*funny!* Or, do I?" she asked, frowning and looking down at her attire. She raised her head.

Holding her gaze, he swung his feet to the floor, rose and walked around the bed to her; leaning over, he lifted her off her feet into his arms. "Funny? *You?* Never, but I . . . *oooh,* you smell *good!* And *I* have me a princess, *whoo-ee!* Always wanted one of those." And he pivoted to the bed, where she waited to be laid down gently.

He paused; she looked at him expectantly, doe-eyed.

"Nah," he said, watching her face, and he dropped her onto the waiting mattress. She bounced once then settled, giggling, and she held out her arms, into which he fell.

As she'd heard Jim once mutter to Pete, "it was all over but the shouting." After, they ate their chocolate torte, soaked in the long-melted coffee ice cream, and then they fell asleep, with Francesca extolling the exquisite pairing of chocolate and coffee.

CHAPTER 29
BEGIN THE BEGUINE

Lucca, Italy

Maria Teresa had slept poorly for a week. Even her nightly passion flower tisane did little to calm racing thoughts, her mind a carousel, spinning round and round. Why, she heard strains of music in the background—the hurdy-gurdy kind. *What is this?* she demanded.

The clock beside her bed read 3:55 in the morning. *May as well get up,* she thought as she threw off the light blanket; then, turning to her side, she swung her legs off the bed, pushed herself up with her arms to a sitting position and remained so for several moments to gain her wits. Her habit was to fix her eyes on the window she called Ariel, the one visible from her bedroom. The one that watched over her as she slept.

Its panes, or *wings,* stood open, to allow a breeze. Soon it would be necessary to shut it at night against the chill—her old bones susceptible.

To Ariel, as intercessor, she prayed; one whose face regarded both mankind and God at once. *And woman,* she reminded them. Them. All *thems* of the world who thought they knew everything. *Ha!* The older she grew, the less she knew and, yet, she knew some things. . .

The important *things* included her cat's upcoming check-up this Friday. She would have to coax him into the small crate. No small feat. And before, her housekeeper's appointment to come on Thursday, so the apartment might be tidy and clean for the most important thing: Francesca's return from America. Maria

Teresa hoped, no—*expected*—to see her prior to dinner on Saturday evening.

Her prayers recited, she hobbled to the small bathroom to splash water on her face and smooth her short, white hair with a brush. Her arm had just lifted to her crown when a stabbing pain in her jaw, radiating from her sternum, forced her to lower her arm, and she backed up to the side of the tub to sit. She recognized the angina. Her old friend hadn't made an appearance in years. Why now, of all times? Her habits were consistent. She had not changed her diet, or neglected her daily walk. *But you are ninety-two years old*, she heard whispered in her ear.

With difficulty, Maria Teresa rose and reached into the medicine cabinet for the small bottle of nitroglycerin her doctor had prescribed years ago. She knew it should have been refilled, but *willed* it to quell the pain as she placed a tablet under her tongue and waited. Then, she reached for the small bottle of aspirin, drew one out and slowly chewed it. Leaning over the sink and turning on the tap, she then slurped a handful of water into her mouth and sat back down again.

The pain subsided. "*Accidente.*" She muttered the oath against the bad timing. Then, remembering herself; "*Grazie*" to her helpmate, looking on from the next room. Ariel sent a fresh breeze in response.

Well, she would simply have to pace herself, and this she could do, she resolved. Isn't this how she lived anyway? She recognized what was named "stress" nowadays was the culprit. Maria Teresa had often questioned past judgment of this seeming, present epidemic. Stress had always existed of course, but humanity granted it mostly lip service today and not true respect.

Ahhh, sì; it is a demon . . . she wryly concluded. Moreover, she would not permit it to defeat her old age. Not now. Not while she was trying to wring every last drop of living from her dishrag called Life. She would defy it!

Maria Teresa set about mounting an offense. A scheme—to overthrow this unwelcome entity. A *spell*, for want of another name. She would enlist her sisters—the other old *befanas*—and perhaps an angel or two.

CHAPTER 30
COUNTING FOR SOMETHING

Becuse last night's supper had been meager, Senga decided to prepare a more substantial meal and stopped at the grocery store before returning home. So, Rob was staying another night. *On a pallet! In the other room!* she clarified, in case Sebastian heard her thoughts from afar.

At the library, she'd received a text message from him; an apology for the disagreement. *And that's how these things work,* she thought dryly, then wondered whether to respond. Muriel had noticed her consternation and asked if everything was all right.

"No. But I'm ever hopeful," she quipped, as she stared at the phone. She'd returned the cart-full of library books to their shelves, had chosen a theme for the Thanksgiving display and was taking her mid-morning coffee break.

"Do you turn off your phone when you're working, Muriel?"

"Oh, sometimes. But most of the time, I just set it to vibrate, so it doesn't disturb anyone. I see you have one. I am amazed."

It was a gift, so don't be getting all righteous on me." She half-smiled. "I'm just learning it. What a thing!" she added.

"Yeah. They're pretty handy. You'll soon never be without it . . . like the rest of us sheep, *bahhh*." A patron approached the counter and Muriel swiveled round to assist her.

Senga had emailed Sebastian to say Rob was staying tonight and leaving in the morning. She'd left it there, but signed off, "All my love, your mermaid." She hoped to allay misapprehension. At lunch time, she put the wash in the machine and cursed when she realized she'd forgotten two pairs of jeans hanging behind the bathroom door. She ate her sandwich as she waited. After transferring the wet clothing to the drier, she returned to the library, where she delighted in

188

cutting stencils and pilgrim hats from colored construction paper.

After work—laundry dry, sorted and folded—she walked to the grocery store.

At the counter, Senga knew that Ellie wondered if she'd encountered the two men who'd asked about her, the woman's facial expression obvious. But Senga said nothing, paid for the items, placed them into her canvas bag, smiled coyly and turned to leave. It was a matter of deliberate action. She'd read her Thoreau.

Darkness fell earlier and earlier, as the calendar inched toward winter solstice. At 5:15 it was past the magic hour, where deer stood camouflaged on the side of the road. During hunting season, they acted skittishly and behaved as one might expect. Crazy. Then she remembered that Rufus, or Gabe, was bringing the lamb tomorrow. It would be a long day and she could use some help, wondering if Rob would stay long enough. She didn't know where he was heading; she didn't know when Gabe would be back from Rapid City.

Reaching her mailbox, she turned and followed the snow-covered, two-track road onto her property. The temperature had remained in the high twenties, perfect for her chore in the morning. A steady light burned in the kitchen window (an unusual sight), and the glow from the juniper tree's lights welcomed her. *He must've plugged it in—I can't believe I forgot this morning,* and she frowned. Through the years, she'd unfailingly determined to have the fairy lights burning whenever she returned home after dark. *My candle in the window,* she called it.

Her Cherokee great-great grandmother was named Tall Juniper, Grannie had once told her, ". . . And now you'll remember her each time you see one," she'd added. "That's how they live forever in our hearts."

Senga sent love to her grandmothers, Papa and to her mother as she approached the garage. As though waiting with outstretched arms, the doors stood wide open. She noticed Rob off to the side, wearing a grin and dressed for a blizzard. "Must've seen the car lights," she muttered under her breath, and her thoughts flashed to last night's dream. She moved her head to the left, adding "*Begone!*" With particularly irksome thoughts, she'd learned the fierce word was helpful, sometimes garnering strange looks from passers-by. Even Sweet Jesus employed the tack, she reasoned.

Canvas tote in hand, she stepped from the car after pulling into the garage and shutting off the engine. Shining in the headlights stood Hermione, arms ever-raised in greeting. The scarecrow never failed to elicit a smile from Senga, and the dream reinforced her decision to leave the figure in the far corner. Senga leaned into the car to turn off the lights. Rob removed the bags of laundry.

"Hey," she greeted him, as she pushed the wide doors closed and replaced the bar. He was dressed in a heavy parka and wool stocking hat, his cheeks ruddy from the cold. Perhaps he'd been outdoors a while.

"How was work, dear?" he asked. An old joke.

"Fine. What did you do all day? Write a Grammy winner?"

"I detect sarcasm. By the way, have you listened to my CD?"

"Uh, no. Not yet. I only just got it, you know. But I will." She avoided his eyes and possible disappointment.

They entered the cabin where she thanked him for plugging in the lights. After putting away her laundry, she began dinner: chicken—baked with potatoes and carrots; a salad and her bread. She had even bought a pint of the gelato Francesca had discovered in the store just two weeks ago. It wasn't inexpensive, but this was a thank-you dinner, after all.

Noting the half-bottle of wine on the counter, she looked at Rob and, lifting it, raised her eyebrows to him in question.

"No, not for me. I gave that up. . ."

"But not the pot," she added, acerbically.

"Nope. I like my weed," he said and turned to the sack of laundry. "Wow, you even folded it!"

"You high now?" she asked. "Oh, never mind; of course you are. . . And yes, I folded it."

She poured herself a glass of Pinot Noir, acutely aware it was her favored means of inebriation (if not quite a euphoric), and she needn't judge Rob for his preference. But *dosage and frequency* were bywords she suspected he (still) disrespected, adhering rather to *pro re nata*—"as needed." She would know soon enough, if his behavior and speech became erratic and, well, cloying.

"Cheers," she said, taking a sip, then turning to her task.

After a few moments, he took out his guitar and began to play. She paused to listen, a sad smile turning up the corners of her mouth. What she'd once called him, and he'd learned the song.

"The minstrel boy to the war is gone. . ."

Later in bed, Senga performed her nightly recollection of Emily. She imagined her daughter's face as she stood beside the juniper tree, above the falls, in the sacred moments before she fell to her death. The sequence: first, conjure the image and search the girl's face until the smile came, then tell her how much she loved being her mother. Emily would always grin, and patiently wait to be dismissed into the wherever-land she inhabited. Senga usually fell asleep during this time.

But not tonight. . .

She wanted to review the evening, then she could seek her daughter.

Dinner had been good and they'd conversed amiably about Rob's intervening years—mostly. She'd honored her resolve to let him do the talking. He volunteered that he'd been involved with his booking agent, Sherry, for several years, after Senga had asked him to let her be. It was Sherry who'd carried him through the news of his daughter's death and its aftermath. She'd cancelled his gigs and taken care of him until he returned to the road.

"So what happened?" Senga asked. "You said you were with her several years. Past tense."

"Oh," he said, "It's hard to be a traveling musician and keep fires burning at home, as you well know." He looked to her for some understanding.

"Ah."

"I've had a little success with the music, Senga. Enough to survive on anyway . . . but I'm tired of the traveling. This is my last tour."

"Do you . . . have a home anywhere?"

"Well, that's the thing. I keep a studio apartment in Asheville—how I wound up at your grandparents' place and ran into your cousin. I was out for a drive in the mountains. But I'd like to find something, well, like this—" and he waved his hand at the room. "There're some folklore schools over there where I could teach; I've already been asked. *Seems* like the next thing to do, doesn't it?"

"Yes, Rob, it does." She sensed a quiet desperation in his voice and it wrung her heart. "I think you'd be a wonderful teacher of mountain music. We need you—I mean—the mountain folk need you," she amended, forgetting she no longer lived on the top of a mountain in North Carolina. *But how swiftly our hearts and minds can return.*

They relaxed before the bright window of the woodstove, alternately feeding it split pine and bur oak logs, and refilling their mugs of tea. Senga felt Rob needed more from her but, outside the prompts and short responses, she had nothing to lend, save basic human kindness.

He stood to step outdoors to smoke; "Helps me sleep," he suggested, and she wanly smiled and let it go. As she'd once let him go.

Rising from her wing chair, she walked to the shelf to his CD, then reached into her pocket for her knife, to slip the blade across the shrink wrap and pry open the case. She set aside the liner notes to read later, stooped to the radio/CD player on the bottom shelf and inserted the disc—uncertain as to whether this was the *good* time to listen. His song, "Nothing Lost, Nothing Wasted," was last. She cued it to play first.

In the intro, she recognized his finger-picking style and the sweet sound of his guitar, a 1955 Martin dreadnaught, made for gut strings, but strung with nylon nowadays. It leaned now in the corner behind her, out of the cold. As much an appendage as his right arm, she paired Rob with the instrument, ever since the night she first heard him perform in Blowing Rock, North Carolina when she was fifteen. The silky, mellow tone reached deep inside as she leaned back in her wing chair, the too-facile comparison not lost on her, that her own heart strings were poised to be plucked.

Rob opened the door and made to speak, but she raised a palm and shook her head. He moved toward the bathroom and closed the door, leaving her alone.

'The minstrel boy,' she called him,
When they met in late December,

His songs a-playing on her heart.
But travel is the minstrel's curse,
And the calling road kept them apart.

She waited on a mountain top,
Where thunder rumbled close above,
One night to plant a winter seed.
'Livin' is the wait for love,'
The child was born beneath the moon.

Nothing lost, nothing wasted,
It will count for something later,
All the love, it just turns over,
Like autumn leaves in October.

'Will-o'-the-wisp,' now she called him,
He couldn't stay; the child was left,
But it was she, who could not wait,
And leaving them both sore bereft;
The wind, it bore their child away.

He begged the sky, beseeched the Earth,
Why? Oh, Why? Whatever for?
We sally forth on chosen trails,
Never knowing in our core,
If we'll reach a promised place.

Nothing's lost, nothing's wasted,
It will count for something later,
All the love, it just turns over,
Like autumn leaves in October.

Senga felt the familiar shiver scale her backbone, to end at the nape of her neck. Her body trembled violently and she pulled her shawl from the back of the chair to her shoulders. When she glanced up, Rob stood a few feet away.

"It says . . . it all, doesn't it?" she said. "And in so few words . . . our entire lives. How do you *do* that?"

"Thanks for listening to it, Senga. It means a lot. But no; I expect there's too much there to distill." He sat down beside her on one of the ladder-back chairs. She smelled him, how she remembered it; then, the lingering, acrid scent of cannabis reached her and she rose.

I'll listen again. It's an autumn song, Rob. I look forward to the rest of the album. What were you going to say? Before you went to the bathroom?"

"Oh . . . just to take it at face-value, the song."

"Why would you say that?"

"It's just a tune, Senga. Not some eternal declaration of—"

"Stop—please. You have no right to manipulate my response to a song! You are unbelievable, do you know that?" And she went to switch off the player, crossed to her collection of tinctures, chose one and placed several drops into a glass. Motherwort. *Leonurus cardiaca*. Against anxiety, and for the heart. She added water from the tap.

"Still doing the herbs, I see . . . like me."

She rounded on him in irritation, but took a deep breath to calm herself.

"I'll be back in a moment, then I'm going to bed, Rob," she said and stepped outdoors to unplug the tree and search the sky for peace.

It arrived in the form of a shooting star. *Comet dust*, she corrected. *Still . . . Star bright?* she pleaded and made a wish; two actually: one for Rob's own peace, and one for Sebastian, that he needn't fret while they were apart. Wishes and prayers were comparable in her philosophy.

Indoors again, she banked the woodstove for the evening and bade Rob goodnight. She made her nightly toilette, searched her face for tell-tale signs of stress, resolved to begin an adaptogen in the morning. In bed, the song lyrics reverberated in three-quarter time, to waltz her away. *Nothing's lost; nothing's wasted.* A natural bridge to her nightly ritual. And then, she could sleep.

CHAPTER 31
THE ABYSS

Senga awoke in a mental fog. She threw off the covers, turned from the wall to face her dimly-lit bedroom, clutching Sebastian's pillow to her chest. She inhaled deeply. *There.* She caught his scent and groaned, feeling his absence acutely. This, paired with having neglected her body's other needs, only stressed the psychological benefits of exercise. She passed a long moment simply breathing.

After breakfast, she sharpened a knife on a whetstone, slowly, methodically, meditatively and, testing it on a sheet of paper, declared it would "do," and then, she proposed a hike to Rob, who was polishing his guitar with her lemon oil. The room smelled of citrus and she felt another pang for Sebastian. She would call him, but only after the present guest left. Rob had offered to help with the lamb and then be on his way.

He was amenable to a walk and they shrugged on jackets, hats and gloves and pulled on their boots. Senga remembered her Japanese digging knife, the Hori Hori, and grabbed the diamond willow walking stick from the corner of the room. Rufus had called earlier to tell her he could deliver the lamb on the way to his physical therapy appointment, since they'd be out anyway, he'd added. Her home was *way* out of the way, she protested, and she thanked him and sent her regards to Caroline. She gauged the sky for weather and, deeming it fine, she nodded to Rob in the direction of a lesser-used trail to the top of the ridge. Snow still lay in draws and on north slopes. She reminded him to watch his footing.

"You know this country pretty well, then?" he asked.

"Well enough to find my way back home in the dark."

"Are you out after dark often?"

"No. But sometimes I get sidetracked by foraging—mushrooms, usually. I always carry a bag in case," and she reached into her pocket for the folded cotton sack to show him and replaced it.

"Aren't you afraid of poisonous *shrooms?*" pronouncing it in counter-cultural fashion. The properties of the psilocybin species included euphoria and often hallucinations or *visions*, when ingested toward that purpose. However, white-spotted, red-topped Fly Agarics were deadly poisonous, causing mere hallucinations if the dose was small enough. What was small enough? She had occasionally stumbled on bright collections of them, whose tops had been nibbled, and wondered how the animal fared. *Did they use it medicinally, as dogs eat grass in the spring to purge a winter's digestion?*

"Well, I stick to only a few well-identified varieties; meadows, shaggy manes, oysters, boletus and *morels*—those when I'm lucky. I do recognize the bad ones, Rob. But no, I've never identified magic mushrooms around here. Sorry," and she looked over her shoulder to him, smiled and proceeded across the small field that led to the trees.

The air stung her cheeks, but the sun shone down now, onto her piece of the planet, and sparkled off patches of crusty snow. Living in the valley precluded all-day sunshine, as the two ridges running north and south made for later sunrises and earlier sunsets for her, but she counted it as so much topography to be accepted for the privilege of place.

They hiked quietly. She heard his breathing behind her, not labored, but not *easy* either. "You okay?"

"Yeah. A little . . . out of shape . . . I suppose."

"We'll take it easy. The elevation might be higher than you're used to . . . but thanks for coming. You'll love the view from up there." A distant gunshot reverberated through the air. "We should be wearing orange—I keep forgetting deer season," she said absently.

"The other day . . . I only made it . . . about halfway up this ridge . . . before I heard those jokers . . . at your cabin," said Rob between breaths.

Senga didn't respond, but planted her stick and pressed off a rock, onto a higher shelf. She spotted the deer trail and made her way toward it.

Lona and the Little Eagle man traveled through the darkness. She had left the tipi after her mother and adopted sister had lain down. If the old woman awoke to find Lona gone, she might attribute her daughter's absence to nature's call. The hope.

When Lona did not return after several minutes, the sleepless woman rose and gasped to discover her daughter's *possibles* bag missing from its usual place. She knew it contained the girl's treasures, including her newly-beaded wedding moccasins, a thumb-size ball made of silver her father had given her (a trade item) and dried meat and berries. In its place, she found her daughter's rope of protection, rolled up neatly in a mullein leaf. The man's very right to live in question as a result.

So, Lona had lain with him, her mother guessed, and she wrapped her buffalo robe about her thin, sagging shoulders and crossed the short distance to the tipi of her daughter, She Who Bathes Her Knees, and her husband, High Wolf.

"*Daughter,*" she whispered.

The shapes beneath the shaggy cover shifted and a face appeared.

"Yes, Mother?"

"Your sister is gone. Not too long now. Will you bring her back?"

High Wolf turned toward the moonlit entrance, silhouetting his mother-in-law against the night. "I'll go, Mother," and he waited until the woman backed away and dropped the flaps before he emerged naked from the bedding.

"I am going with you," said his wife, and he knew it was useless to argue.

Dale Scobey left his little brother Joey in a truck stop bathroom, in Alzada, Montana. In short, he was sick. He was puking and had diarrhea, and his face looked pasty. Dale spread the kid's coat on the surprisingly clean floor and handed him a ginger ale—what he remembered helped when you were sick. He bundled the boy in the two sweaters he'd packed and shoved the smaller duffel bag under his head. And there lay Joey, moaning.

The stench in the bathroom was horrendous but, so far, no one had wanted to use it. When he passed the preoccupied clerk at the counter, he told him he was going for help and he'd be right back, knowing it would take more time than he'd led the man to believe.

The root digger, he thought, so he dropped down into Wyoming and made his way back to the woman's strange, echo-haunted valley.

"Yeah, she'll know what to do," he muttered. *But would she do it?*

Rob was breathing harder now, Senga noticed, so she slowed her pace, stopped and turned to him. He lagged behind several feet.

"Let's take a break," she said. She rarely stopped when hiking, choosing to wait until her destination, unless something claimed her attention. She studied the ground and crossed to a pine-needle-covered bowl, beside a south-facing patch of Oregon grape plants, their berries ripened to a dark purple. The holly-shaped leaves blanketed the slope.

Senga harvested their roots for their immune system-stimulating effects. Reaching for the Hori Hori at her side, she knelt and closed her eyes a moment, nodded, then plunged the knife into the ground, twisted it and, with her other hand, pulled away the plant, roots intact. She dug two more and placed them in her carry bag. The berries made good syrup, but today she'd settle for the roots. *Thank you,* she sent the herbs, after wiping her digging knife across grasses and replacing it in the scabbard.

Rob caught up and lowered himself to the ground, letting out a long breath. "Whew!"

She reached for his wrist and he pulled away.

"Your pulse," she said and he was still. It thrummed.

"You're working pretty hard. Let's go more slowly. . . There's a lower trail that ascends at a less steep angle, okay? Or do you want to go back?"

"No, Senga, I don't. You'll think I'm a wuss," he said, glancing away.

She rolled her eyes. "Who gives a shit what I think, Rob? You have heart issues?" she asked him now.

"Not that I know of," he said, starting to rise, but she pulled him back.

"Not yet," she said. "Let's just sit." They did. She listened to his breath, and only when it sounded normal did she rise and hold out her hand for him.

That morning, she'd taken a dose of Siberian ginseng tincture, an herbal adaptogen against stress. She'd send a bottle with Rob when he left, with instructions for its use. She wondered how much he smoked. Could his lungs and arteries be damaged? Or, did he have a family background of heart disease?

"Do you have family history of heart problems?"

He took a breath and let it out audibly. "My dad died of a heart attack, Senga, the year after Emily died. Thought you knew."

She turned to him. "No, Rob, I didn't. . . I'm so sorry."

"Long time ago, anyway. Let's just be quiet—you mind?"

"Um, no, Rob. I don't mind."

She suddenly felt exhausted and wished to curl up in a soft deer bed and sleep for days, remembering herbs do their good slowly.

Bathes Her Knees hoped they could find her sister and return to bed shortly. It was not to be. Tracking by moonlight was difficult, even under a full moon, and tonight's needed another seven days, at least, to reach the bright circle. She bent low in an effort to recognize her sister's footprints. High Wolf groaned in frustration.

"Has she never mentioned a particular place to you, dear one?"

"No. Could they be returning to his people? To the east?"

"Possibly. Let us continue in that direction and, if we see nothing, we will turn back and follow another trail. The one we returned on last month."

She felt a quiver in her gut, remembering . . .

Last month, after reaching the ridge where he had shot an arrow and missed his quarry—a large, drop tine buck—they had searched for the fletched shaft, but their efforts were interrupted by a bear, who had laid claim to a patch of nearby, low-growing purple berries. The grizzly rose on hind legs, lifted his head and nose to the air and sniffed. It might have been comical had they not recently witnessed the horrific outcome of a bear attack—a child left to bleed to death after his arm was torn from its socket. The child's father had discovered him before the beast returned for the rest of its quarry.

With the gruesome image in mind, High Wolf had slowly motioned for his wife and her sister to back away, and the bear dropped down to resume his task, preferring the sweet fruit to them, evidently. The arrow was summarily forgotten in their retreat.

"Do you remember how Lona gazed at the cliff that day, husband?"

"What are you saying?"

"Only that she seemed attracted to the place."

"I believe you are right. I remember . . . yes, we'll turn back. I want to gather warmer clothing as well."

They were soon on their way back to the promontory, accompanied by night noises, the stars and a quarter-moon. And, their fears.

Her walking stick was a great aid in climbing; a friend once called its ball top a "head-knocker," though it didn't resemble the traditional Indian war club at all—an oval stone worked to points on both ends and fastened to a baton. Senga offered it to Rob but he declined, preferring *noble-minded chivalry*.

Their view expanded through the trees, to the south and west, at least 300 feet above the creek bed that meandered in the distance. A glittering pond stared far below, like a great limpid eye, surrounded by pale grasses and intermittent splashes of snow. The top of the old-growth Grannie Tree peeked above a sea of dark green, with separate stands of ponderosa crowning tops of hillocks; great, wide swathes, park-like, rolled away to end at fence lines, these placed perpendicular to one another, like so many interlacing silver threads on a patchwork quilt.

She never tired of the lay of the land from this vantage, resolving to climb the height more often. She was glad she'd persevered this day. What was named *Lovers Leap* on the county map commanded the area. Her imagination conjured the image of an ancient fortress; its southwestern face—the buttress—a sheer drop, until a rock-strewn land—not quite a talus slope—fanned away at forty-five-degrees, due to erosion. If it *had* been a stronghold, its backside was vulnerable, and this was her tack today.

They were nearing a point where it was necessary to clamber straight up a narrow flue of stone, and slabs jutted out to create convenient steps; but both hands were required, so she pitched her stick up and over the ledge and climbed. After retrieving it, she waited.

It was an unavoidable leg, she explained to Rob; otherwise, they would have to hike the distance around the underbelly of the rim and climb the north end. He managed and they paused for a few moments, then, tacking back and forth, they continued toward the summit. The air felt fresh and unusually still. *Preternaturally so,* Senga noted as she moved toward the sedimentary beds of limestone and shale at the top.

She was pointing out a far peak when she noticed Rob, several yards behind her, staring back over his shoulder.

High Wolf pushed them harder through the night, while fear pulled him forward. His wife read his intent and stepped up her pace. They were grateful for the milder weather, as both knew it could change within hours this time of year. *The Moon When the Nose of the Buffalo Calf Turns Brown* brought the cold. The tall warrior hoped they had caught up with Lona and her lover. *What was the man's name?* He searched his memory but could not recall having learned it. He would henceforth think of him as Little Eagle, but a red-tailed hawk came to mind.

If Lona and the man learned they were being followed, would they hide themselves? And *why* were they bent on causing such distress for everyone? Then, High Wolf pictured the other man Lona was betrothed to, and he sighed. Fear and loathing make one do strange things; he could forgive his wife's sister, enough to continue searching for her, and then what? He wondered, turned to his wife to gauge her attitude and, finding her determined as ever, strode on in silence, making prayers to the Creator for guidance and protection from bears. They saw no sign of the couple, but at last approached the place.

Moonlight shone from behind scudding, pale clouds, to reveal the cliff, whose face seemed lit from within, being made of whitish stone.

"Husband, I hear my sister. *Listen!*"

High Wolf cupped his right ear to better hear the keening high above them, like wind through a thin reed.

"How do you know it is Lona?" he asked. "It sounds like a night bird."

"This is Lona's mourning song; she sang it when Father died. We must reach them." She quickened her steps to a trot through the brush and pines, once tripping over timber. After helping her up, High Wolf knew his wife could not sustain the pace to the height, but he allowed her to proceed before him. They did not stop again to listen for the eerie sound, choosing instead to make their way up the ridge, trotting back and forth, to mitigate the danger of falling. They came to a rock chimney of sorts and this they had to scale, the notes of the tuneless wail coming from only a few paces away.

"What is it?" Senga asked Rob.

"*Shhh,*" he whispered. "I thought I heard a motor earlier, then it stopped, and just now I heard something. . . You expecting someone?"

"Rufus . . . later on. Suppose he could be early." She listened for the bleating of a lamb. Nothing. *He'd just tie it up and leave,* she thought, *but we'd hear it.* She turned to continue, summit fever overtaking her. The screech of a hawk split the air, startling both climbers.

"Jesus!" Rob sputtered.

"We're encroaching on their territory," she said with a light chuckle. "A pair of Bald eagles spends the winter over there," and she pointed toward the area. "They return year after year— or their offspring do, I should say; might see them too."

Senga slowly approached the rocky edge, their objective. A breeze wafted from below and she remembered sandhill cranes rising in their *widening gyres,* having caught a warming thermal off the cliff. While she didn't suffer from vertigo when peering down from a great height, her mind always leapt to her daughter's fall, tempering the experience.

Rob stepped nearer the edge, twenty-feet or so away from her, and turning again to stare toward the trees below them, he whispered, "*Someone* is *coming*," and called out, "Hello?"

High Wolf helped Bathes Her Knees up through the chimney rock by standing behind her as she negotiated the climb, only once having to give her a push in order to reach a stone foothold. The keening sounded louder, once they were both above the rocky layer. They looked at one another and moved forward. High Wolf gazed over the moonlit country below and felt a fist clench his heart. He was afraid this night, of what was to transpire in the very near future, and he extended his hand for his wife, to help her ascend the remaining way.

When they reached the cliff, they paused a moment to comprehend the image.

Lona and Little Eagle were locked in an embrace on the lip of the rim, in moonlight one moment, moonshadow the next. The lovers did not know they were observed. Bathes Her Knees gasped and High Wolf pulled her closer to him, shushing her, for fear of startling her sister. Then, he bounded from his wife, hoping against hope to reach the pair in time to pull them back.

Little Eagle saw him first, made a sound and, after thrusting Lona away from him, fell backward into the night. Lona glanced from High Wolf to her sister, and after uttering the phrase *Néstaévahósevóomatse*—I will see you again—she backed to the edge and simply let go of what in time would be named gravity.

Her sister screamed.

Hearing a cry, Senga chanced to see the hawk swoop below the lip of the cliff. Then, she again heard her own scream echoing at Emily's fall; an internal and eternal scream of all who witness a tragedy; who feel their guts turn to soup; who will never be the same. And once again she found herself prone and crawling on an edge of the earth.

Below, as though viewed through a sheen of smoky water, lay two figures; one, a woman—judging by her pale doeskin dress—who appeared to be dragging herself toward the other, a man, dressed in leggings and fringed shirt (not the hunter she'd seen from her cabin window, she was oddly relieved to note). When the woman reached him, she laid her head on his chest and was still. The air rippled like a heat wave in summer, not unlike a mirage, and after, the molecules flattened out to merely a slope and its sage, stones and grasses.

Senga marked the spot as the vision faded, then exhaled, her cheek resting on the ground, facing Rob, who regarded her strangely.

She heard a twig snap, then a curse. Rob gestured to her, finger to lips, motioning with his hand to stay low.

Yellowtooth's head bobbed up, next his torso and legs, as he mounted the path toward them. His expression, grim. His appearance, dissipated. He didn't see her; his eyes were fastened on Rob. *Too close to the rim,* she noted with fear.

"Is . . . that root digger . . . with you, man?" He gasped for air. "My little brother's sicker . . . than a dog at the Alzada truck stop. He needs . . . some help."

"What's the matter with him?" asked Rob.

"He's puking and got diarrhea, and he just don't look too good. Will she come?"

Senga made herself small as she listened. Yellowtooth hadn't spotted her and, studying him, she watched with growing fascination as the man's visage changed. His eyes took on a hopeless look, and his mouth twisted into what Senga would describe later as a scowl when questioned, but even this was too mild a word. It was past description at this point, as the man raised his voice in a desperate plea and lunged at Rob, yelling, "*You gotta help him!*"

She didn't think; she acted. In an instant she was up, her walking stick raised at the man. Swinging the ball end in his direction like a bat, she struck him hard on the shoulder, but not before Rob `had been shoved off-balance, tumbling head-over-heels, not over the edge, but down the north-facing slope they'd just ascended. Senga ran over and sighed in relief as he came to a sudden stop against a grouping of low-growing juniper bushes.

She turned to Yellowtooth, who sat stunned; his expression muted to one of surprise and confusion, pain and then—*Is this remorse?* Senga had never seen a man's features vary so, in a minute space of twenty seconds.

"You stay *right there* for now," she demanded, pointing a finger at him. "We'll go get your brother. . ." she added in a softer tone, and she eased down the hill to where Rob was extricating himself from the shrubs.

"Aren't you glad you dropped by?" She smiled wryly, then examined him for blood or breaks or both. "I expect you'll feel stiffer than snot in the morning, but other than that, I think you're okay," she said, then returned for her walking stick, and regarded—

"What's your name, anyway?" she asked her erstwhile adversary, who was trying to stand, though a little crookedly, on account of the shoulder pain.

"Dale."

"Well, that's a start. . . Mine's Senga. You know I have to call the cop, don't you?"

"Can't we keep my little brother out of it? *Please?* He can't go to jail. . . He just *can't*," and the pitiful face broke into tears.

She remembered her dream, wherein Rob said of the brother, *"He wants out of this . . . he's a good kid."* Squinting at Dale, she considered for a moment. "Hunh," and she held out a hand to his uninjured arm. *"Git* on up."

Her mountain accent had returned with Rob's reappearance.

When High Wolf drew his weeping wife away from the cliff, he sensed further evil. A low growl arose from behind, and when he turned to its source—for it sounded more human than animal—the silhouette of a tribesman approached. Bathes Her Knees whispered, "Lona's betrothed, Yellow Bird."

The man's face was smeared with charred wood, or so it appeared. Better to avoid detection, High Wolf noted. Had he followed them from camp? The blackened visage was fearsome, and in his right hand he wielded a war club, having prepared to do harm this night.

"She is gone. Both are. See for yourself," High Wolf said to the man as he gestured toward the abyss, its edge marked by moonshine on white stone. Inky darkness met their eyes below. The lovers could not be seen. Bathes Her Knees, still weeping, tore from the grasp of her husband and pounded the chest of the challenger with her fists, sobbing that her sister was dead because of him and had he been a man and let her go—

High Wolf gripped her arm to pull her back.

"Cease, woman." Then, he addressed Yellow Bird. "There is at least one bear in this place. I do not wish to leave our sister and her man to it . . . so soon. Will you help me build a scaffold?"

The man's eyes turned to slits, and his mouth opened to bare his teeth, betraying his initial thought, but the eyes softened and he replied, "Yes. I would not wish that upon anyone. Especially her; besides, I must see them. . ." The squint returned, ". . . to be certain you are not lying and they are, in truth, long gone from this place."

High Wolf said nothing in reply.

Slowly, they picked their way down the height, aware, and Bathes Her Knees stifled her cries for all their sakes. The trilled call of a raccoon accompanied their descent; a great horned owl called in the distance.

After discovering the bodies, indeed *gone* from them, they worked through the night, uninterrupted (thank the Creator), dragging fallen timber to a suitable pair of trees, and High Wolf was satisfied he had done what he could for his wife's sister and her lover.

This place will be forever haunted by their spirits, he lamented. It must surely remain a most solitary place, left to the bears, raccoons and owls, and he felt a deep sadness for his wife, as she would recognize this as well. *But,* he reasoned, *they are forever alone together,* and this imparted a kind of consolation. He would remind his wife. When it was time.

CHAPTER 32
ACROSS THE POND

Sebastian could not eat. His stomach. *Or was it his heart?* Whichever, the area throbbed as though he had been "drawn and quartered," he grumbled to Erika, who told him he couldn't *possibly* make that analogy and to stop the drama, that it was tedious. He had come to enjoy a late breakfast with his daughter after his granddaughter, Jytte, had left for school. Glancing at Erika, he thought she must have sensed his utter desolation, for she hurried over and collapsed beside him on her sofa, put her arm around his chest, and laid her head on his shoulder.

"Poor Papa. Love is a terrible thing sometimes, no?"

"No, Erika, it is *everything*, but sometimes it makes you wish you were dead."

He had not heard from his Senga in two days and she must have simply turned off the phone he'd given her. *Why?* Had she returned to this fellow, the father of her child? It was conceivable. *They made a child together, after all.*

"Papa . . . from what you have told me about her, I am certain she has a good reason, and it has only been two days. She has a job, you said, and, well, you know what they say: *out of sight, out of mind*," she teased, pushing her pale hair behind her ears, a constant habit.

"You aren't helping, *min kære*. Oh, I'll be fine . . . I need to return to work—train my mind on something else. I have enough to do, God knows, before we return, in what? *Six weeks?* Oh, Erika . . . I cannot bear it. . ." He turned his face away, then, she reached for his unshaven chin to return his gaze to her.

Erika looked on him with concern. He recalled how frightened she had been by his behavior after her mother died—

207

why she had left to live with her aunt. He suspected she was regarding him with like mind and he needed to alter his sensibilities soon; *now,* in fact. He closed his eyes and breathed deeply, imagining Senga's face before him in one of their closer moments, and he felt his pulse slow. He opened his eyes. Erika still observed him, her expression unchanged.

He tried a smile. His usual—tinged with sadness. "I am all right. Truly. Just a bit nervous is all . . . and that opening reception at the gallery is coming up, so!—" he clapped his hands together, "What time is Jytte home from whatever practice she has this afternoon?" He could always read his daughter and knew she recognized this as so much bravado, but it was better than the alternative.

He had *ardently* wished for Erika's impression of Senga to be positive, and it would be his fault if she felt otherwise at this point. He would simply have to have faith in his nature mystic. *Yes.* Wasn't this precisely what he loved about her? An infernal capacity for surprise? For keeping him off-balance? He smiled again and noticed his daughter's mien relax. She stepped to the calendar on the kitchen wall.

"I pick her up at 6:00 today. Want to come along? It will be a surprise!"

Whenever even insignificant synchronicities happened, Sebastian knew he dwelt in a good place: the *flow*—an English expression he'd adopted, coined by Hungarian psychologist Csikszentmihalyi. He rose from the sofa and raised his arms for his daughter. She crossed the space to him in an instant, enveloping herself in his embrace. "I'm glad you're home, Papa. I've missed you."

Francesca Albinoni gathered her bags from the carousel at the Florence airport and, with some difficulty, negotiated the passage to where her brother Carlo would, with luck, be waiting for her. She had passed through Customs in Amsterdam with little trouble, only having to declare the small gifts she and Gabe had purchased yesterday morning in Rapid City. It seemed long ago. *How distance stretches time as well,* she mused, then remembered a conversation with Senga and Gabe about this when they horse-camped in the peaks. *Yes. A lifetime away.*

"Francesca!"

It was Carlo. Her lovely brother Carlo. They resembled one another, but while his physique demanded restraint and discipline, she could have modeled as one of Italian Renaissance artist, Artemisia Gentileschi's heroic women. Francesca's favorite painter of the period taught her to embrace her own somewhat weighty dimensions, as these might prove vital for some future deed, whereas a lighter frame would be ineffectual.

Carlo was dressed impeccably but casually, in gray slacks, a grey polo sweater and a light jacket. His near jet-black hair was cut shorter. A new style.

"Carlo! *Come sta?*" she cried. It was good to be speaking Italian again. Like coasting a bike downhill. Moreover, it was heaven to hear it.

He briskly walked to her and kissed her on each cheek, and once more just because. Then he stepped back to inspect her, a grin from ear to ear. He twirled his finger and she obeyed, turning around, then laughed.

"You are beautiful, sister, and I have a surprise in the car for you. You will never guess who wanted to come with me to collect you. . . Guess!"

"I cannot, Carlo. The mind is asleep, and this body hopes to catch up soon. It has been a long trip." Having flown all night, she arrived in Amsterdam at 6:00 a.m., and there endured a four-hour layover before boarding the regional jet to *Firenze*. She hadn't yet slept, she explained, a yawn escaping her mouth.

"Then I will tell you. La Nonna Maria Teresa—*Sì!*" he confirmed, after seeing her eyes round and her jaw drop. It could be a tiresome car ride for *Nonna* from Lucca to Firenze. But perhaps the traffic hadn't been too heavy, she hoped.

"She is waiting in the car, Carlo? Oh, how could you? Come—let us go," and she grasped the handle to one of the bags, while her brother took the other, and they moved quickly to the doors.

The streets were wet with freezing rain, and Sebastian caught a whiff of diesel. He stood below Erika's apartment, ready to walk back to his in Vesterbro, a restored neighborhood in Copenhagen. He placed the forest green wool cap on his head, lifted the collar on his pea coat and adjusted his neck scarf against the chill. It felt colder than had the blizzard in the Black Hills, he reflected. *Wet cold.* He'd forgotten. *But you live in the North Sea, young son* . . . His father's oft-repeated message.

The lively city noises (alike everywhere), the peculiar odor of salt and sea, sometimes overriding the petrol, sometimes not, and the familiar, cheerful buildings between his and his daughter's homes, both on *Sønder* Boulevard (if at opposite ends), welcomed him like old friends and his disposition improved with each step.

Erika would pick him up at 5:30 to fetch Jytte. He had the afternoon to work on Senga's photographs (the prospect comforted him now more than he'd anticipated), but only after some business relating to his aunt's estate.

Around the next corner stood a respectable café, *The Four in Hand.* He'd stop in for a cocoa and, what else? That which in America was called a Danish, ironically introduced by Viennese bakers in 1840. Sebastian smiled at the strange habit in the States of reducing everything to origins. *A nation of immigrants, notwithstanding.* Perhaps a simpler method of classification; but how lacking in follow-through! He chided himself. Theirs were the engineers responsible for a moon-landing, after all. *Now, there's follow-through. . .*

The café bustled with neighborhood employees on their mandatory coffee break.

Its exterior resembled an old English pub; a green-and-white-striped awning shaded a mullioned window to the left of the green door. Indoors, he noted neat racks of firewood stacked beneath tall bistro tables; walls painted in a warm palette; and the wait-staff smartly dressed and groomed. Despite an overcast sky, light flooded through high, second story windows. *The room's ceiling must have been removed sometime,* he silently remarked. Gazing upward, he delighted in a curving, narrow balcony that ranged above, providing access to row upon row of books. *Brilliant!*

He'd arrived, thankfully, near the end of a break shift and spied a free table near a window. The server took his order quickly and returned with it as efficiently. The hot cocoa steamed and he poured a stream of cream into it, remembering Senga's—*well, Julia the Cow's,* he corrected. He could tarry at this table all day if he wished, but he mainly wanted to reestablish a connection to the city and his country. The coffeehouse presented the means; *then* he could move on to his projects for the week.

The cocoa tasted like childhood, rich and bittersweet, and the flaky pastry evoked his grandmother. She always provided delicacies when he and his brother visited. It tasted like love—the almond-cream center—but he couldn't make a habit of indulging himself, else he'd be unrecognizable when Senga again saw him.

Sitting here and listening to his fellow Danes chatter on was enjoyable, and the occasional treat could be off-set by the long walk to and from his apartment. They also provided Wifi, so he could write to Senga, or anyone else, from this genial venue.

He laid a plan—*Yes. A good plan.* Something to write Senga about in his first email.

He would show trust. . . No mention of her guest. And so this he did and clicked *Send.*

She had told him she preferred *real* letters, "But," he'd countered, "they take so *long* from Denmark and this is instantaneous!" In the end, he promised he would write her a *proper* missive, if she promised to do the same. "Of course," she'd responded. He resolved to bring his writing materials to this café and begin a letter there, and return to it every couple of days, then mail it, say, in a week. As it was, he had little to say but words of love and longing. *Which might suffice,* he hoped.

Then, he remembered the photographs.

He could describe what he was doing with them. Taken on a digital camera, the old work of developing negatives and prints was over, but between shutter click and print, there still remained a process of artistic development—countless decisions regarding a multitude of effects.

Feeling much improved by his earlier talk with Erika, the cocoa and *Danish*, and, by having arrived at a plan—knowing such are susceptible to circumstance—he finished his hot drink, pressed the white cloth napkin to his lips and the server miraculously swept by to set the check on the table. Sebastian groped in his pocket for some *kroner*, added a small tip (as service was included) and rose to leave with contentment on his face—despite the exorbitant cost.

A handsome elderly woman seated near the door smiled up at him and said, "Come back to see us, Mr. Hansen," at which he was flummoxed, but tipped his hat to her.

Maria Teresa sat quietly in the front seat of Carlo's Renault Clio and stared straight ahead. He had said if someone asked that the car be moved, she was to remain mute, as though she couldn't hear them. She wondered if she had reminded the girl to clean the windows today.

Someone tapped on her window. Maria Teresa raised her chin and turned her head in the opposite direction.

"*Nonna!*" came a frustrated call and this person tried to open her door, but she had locked them all. Someone walked to the front of the red car and waved.

Maria Teresa's mouth opened in surprise and then she grinned.

"*My little Francesca!*" she cried, having called her young neighbor this since childhood.

After Carlo used his key to unlock the doors, the younger woman leaned into the car and gave Maria Teresa quick pecks on both cheeks. Taking Francesca's hands in hers, she kissed the knuckles over and over, her eyes brimming with tears. She fished a lacy handkerchief from her bosom and dabbed her eyes, then returned it.

"*Buongiorno, Nonna,*" greeted Francesca, "I am so happy you came! I see the Clio is still running," she then said to her brother after she was settled, her luggage stacked beside her. The car was an older model, but he maintained it well.

"I hope you don't mind sitting in the back, sister."

"Of course not," she said, as Carlo moved the gear shift into drive, and they pulled away.

"Unfortunately, there will be even more traffic this time of day," said Carlo.

Maria Teresa craned her neck to steal a glance at Francesca. "I have nowhere to go but heaven; how about you, Francesca?"

"*Nonna,* what is this talk?" asked Carlo.

"Only the truth. Now, what is this surprise you are going to tell us on Saturday?" she asked, her left eye fixed on the young woman.

"I love you, *Nonna,* but I will not tell you until then," and she smiled sweetly.

To soften the blow, thought Maria Teresa and she accepted this, after murmuring a series of sounds unintelligible even to her. These locutions were becoming more frequent and seemed to originate from elsewhere. She'd asked one evening, as she recited her prayers, and was given to recall a short passage, citing *groanings from the spirit*: that sometimes, Holy Spirit prays in us; so she attributed the murmurs to this and dismissed it.

The car rolled evenly through the rush-hour traffic and Maria Teresa listened quietly to brother and sister, as Carlo related the family's last eight months.

CHAPTER 33
TEA AND SYMPATHY

E arl had just filled his pick-up with gas at the Alzada truck stop, and what served as a convenience store, in his small community just inside the Montana border. He rapped on the restroom door a third time. It had been locked for a while. *Hell, might as well go back home,* he thought.

"Hey! Everything all right in there?" he called through the door, then rubbed his face. Why, he'd forgotten to shave this morning. *Oh well, Mae likes the rough look,* he figured.

No response from the toilet.

He hitched back to the counter. "Did you lock the crapper?" he asked the part-timer, who needed a shower. *Rough* didn't begin to describe him. *He looks older than me,* Earl decided.

"Uh, no, Earl. . . Why?"

"Well, I've been waiting is all—might as well go use mine," and he turned to go.

"Two fellas were in here earlier . . . come to think—I saw only one of 'em leave."

"What the hell, Ray? You have a key?"

"Yeah . . . here," and the grizzled clerk handed it to Earl, who nearly ripped it out of his hand in disgust. When he leaned over, he could smell the rot-gut whiskey rolling off the guy. Earl recognized liver disease, but not from having bartended these many years. It had killed his old man, a Viet Nam vet. Ray's complexion showed the same jaundiced cast, and the whites of his eyes weren't; spider veins criss-crossed his cheeks and the back of his hands like crazy roadmaps. His abdomen was swollen.

Earl made his slow way to the back of the store.

He and Mae, *mostly* retired bikers—mainly due to an accident that claimed Earl's left leg years ago—owned and ran a bar and diner on the opposite end of town. They'd stopped serving Ray last year when he became more than surly one night. Earl just hoped someone else was doing his buying so he'd stay off the highway.

At the toilet door, Earl knocked again, waited, then put the key in the lock.

"*Damn it!*" he said as he backed out. "Ray, you're gonna need a mop and disinfectant."

"*Aw!* And the girl just cleaned it yesterday! What *for?*" he yelled from the counter.

"There's a kid in here—looks like he's shit himself. . . It's bad. Look, you'll need some towels and hot water," he said as he leaned to better see.

The stench was unbearable. Ray walked over, stuck his head in and out and gasped for fresh air. "Oh criminy! I'll get some." He stepped up his pace. "You think it's catchin'?" he called over his shoulder.

"Hell, I don't know, Ray—at least he's moaning and not dead. That would make for a bad day. Go on! Get those towels now, will ya?"

"Uh, I got somebody at a pump; it'll be a minute."

"Where are they, the towels? I'll get 'em. Chrissake, Ray," and he leaned over the kid's face and lifted an eye lid. The pupils contracted readily to the light. *Good,* he thought.

An hour later, the patient was lying on the bed in Earl and Mae's spare room. He'd been given a shower and Imodium, and was slowly sipping a sports drink, one that replaced electrolytes. Mae reminded him that dehydration is the main thing to worry about. He ate a quarter-bowl of chicken soup under Earl's watchful eye, and promptly threw up, but managed to hit the trashcan Mae had judiciously placed beside the bed.

The kid murmured thanks for their help and told them his name in halting speech; that he and his brother had been camping for a few days when he came down with this, whatever it was, and that he felt horrible. Mae asked him what they were doing camping in November anyway, then gave him two aspirins. He closed his eyes.

"I think it's the flu, kid; at least I *hope* that's all it is," she said, exchanging a glance with Earl. "So where is this brother? He coming to get you?"

"Dale . . . was going for help, he told me. That . . . was . . . *hours* ago," he groaned and turned his head to the wall, then blurted, "*Aw shit!*" and made for the bathroom.

Mae had given Joey one of Earl's t-shirts and a pair of his underwear. She rounded up a couple more pairs, then crossed to the window and opened it. Cold, fresh air blew in.

Earl retreated to the kitchen and poured a cup of coffee, where it occurred to him: *Dale.* That was the name of the crazy-ass who'd shown up at their place two weeks ago and got chewed out by Gabe's girlfriend. The guy with him was older. Gabe called a cop after the two left and Earl had later heard from another customer that four men, one a juvenile, were being sought by the authorities. They'd arrested one up in the Bear Lodge, and another was found dead in a Rapid City motel room. "Of natural causes."

He set the mug of black coffee back down after a too-hot sip. Earl had a feeling.

Senga called Charlie Mays at the Sara's Spring Police Department to explain the circumstances, omitting mention of the absent younger brother. The lawman made the drive to her place in record time, she thought. When questioned about his brother's whereabouts, Dale dissembled, saying he'd left him in Montana somewhere on his own.

"What happened to your arm?" asked Charlie, as he cuffed and turned him toward the waiting SUV.

"I sort of whacked him, Charlie," Senga volunteered.

Charlie swung his head to her, eyes wide. Then, he looked at Rob, who was standing off to the side.

"She was, ah, *defending* me, Officer," Rob offered, then glanced at Dale, now hunched over in the back seat of the SUV, elbows on knees, eyes to the floor. Charlie closed the door and pivoted.

"It's *Chief*," he corrected, sounding more annoyed than offended. He removed his hat, smoothed back his salt and pepper hair with his right hand. *To buy time,* Senga figured. She saw Rob cut his eyes toward the orchard fence and step toward it; Charlie followed.

Senga heard them converse, but couldn't make it out. She walked back to the cabin to gather her possibles bag of remedies and first aid supplies, going over in her mind what the sick boy in Montana might need: tincture of Sweet Annie against diarrhea; Osha for the respiratory system; St. John's Wort (an antiviral and anodyne);and *Echinacea*—against infection. She'd take a small jar of elderberry syrup as well. That's as far as she'd gotten with a plan.

Earlier in the cabin, before Charlie arrived, Senga had examined Dale's shoulder, where a goose egg swelled. He'd stripped down to his tank top. She decided she must have hit the top of his humerus squarely—*If you can hit a round thing squarely*, she wondered. A red welt shone through a tattoo. "*That* is disgusting," she'd told the man she still thought of as Yellowtooth.

Through the left eye socket of a black skull, a penis-like snake emerged.

The macabre images from her nightmare proved all too fresh and a chill passed through her. She jerked her head to the left, warding off the memory. The slight man looked at her and grinned, his mouth a veritable ashtray in sight and smell. He ran his tongue over his front teeth then flicked it out at her, waggling it back and forth.

"*Knock it off, you—!*" Rob raised his voice, but let the pejorative die. Senga shook her head as she stepped to her freezer for the ever-present bag of peas.

"Hold this on it, *Dale*." She pronounced his name with some effort; it sounded alien. "As soon as you and Charlie leave, we'll go see about your brother . . . Joey, right? That's the deal."

A slow but decisive nod. And *there*—she saw it. In his eyes: his all-too-fragile, and perhaps shy, ghost of humanity. It pleaded with her. And Senga apprehended, instantly, that the man was not his tattoos, nor his galling behavior. Moral turpitude aside, she exchanged something with him in that moment. An understanding of loss. At least its possibility.

"And . . . if he's as sick as you say he is we'll figure something out. I don't know what's in your future, but maybe we can do something about his . . . and you've *got* to quit behaving like such a—" She spotted the tattoo of the pissed-off woodpecker, ". . . *dick*," pronouncing the epithet as a matter of fact. She gave him a look, one cultivated since childhood to ward off the occasional inappropriate or unwanted attention. It succeeded when misdirection failed.

He got it and looked away. She caught the corners of his mouth bending in a quick, softened smile, then he took a deep breath and exhaled. "I could use a smoke."

"In a minute, outdoors. . . Well, it isn't broken, but could be cracked," she'd told him as she rubbed arnica oil onto the site, feeling along the length of the bone, and then she gave him a loading dose of St. John's Wort in some water, against the pain. The hematoma protruded through the skull's right eye socket, the other being occupied.

"I—I don't know what got into me, to rush you like that," Dale had said to Rob.

"No worries, man. Could've been worse. A lot worse, ha," and he'd glanced at Senga, whose curiosity was piqued.

"Did y'all hear that scream? Not the hawk; before."

"You heard it?" Dale asked. "Yeah. But I hear shit all the time. No shit—you heard it too?"

"Rob?"

"No. Guess I was too busy wondering what was going to happen after Goober here showed up."

"Hey now . . . I had to find the root-digger—I mean uh, you, ma'am." Dale glanced at Senga then back to Rob, ". . . and then I heard that scream, and I was scared for Joey *and* pissed off, and I thought you were gonna give me shit, so figured I'd better give you some first."

"Oh for fuck's sake. . ." Senga addressed the ceiling. "You're citing me the worst rationale for war: 'Let's do it to them before they do it to us'. . . Dale," she modulated her tone, "what did this scream sound like?"

"Like every one I ever heard. They all sound the same to me. Horrible."

Later, it occurred to Senga that, to Dale, all fearful emotions, including misunderstanding and disappointment, registered as one fearsome entity. A singular *horrible* to be overcome.

Gabe Belizaire chose to return to the ranch from the airport via Belle. He'd stop in Alzada for lunch. Maybe a beer. He needed some *tea and sympathy,* as he called it. Saying goodbye to Francesca had proven more difficult than he'd imagined. Truth was, he hadn't had time to prepare, having been occupied with hunters in the days before her departure.

*But last night was—*He searched for a word, sighing at the memory.

In Alzada, he pulled into the large parking lot hoping Mae would still serve him lunch. It was nearly 3:00 p.m. A green van was parked beside another pick-up; the van's plates read *North Carolina,* while the pick-up's showed Montana's titular mountains.

"Hunh," he grunted, not sure why, and strode to the door.

This was a favorite watering hole for him and Rufus when, and if, they had business in Belle Fourche, home of the nearest sale barn and other ranch-related businesses. Gabe and Earl had become friends, while Mae treated him like a little brother. He counted himself lucky to have Stricklands, Earl and Mae, Senga and Francesca in his corner, in this corner of a largely Caucasian state. *Don't forget the Indians!* his inner editor protested. "Nah. I don't," he muttered to himself, as he pushed open the door and stepped into the large room.

"Well, looky who's needing a shoulder. . . How're you doing, buddy?" Earl called as Gabe crossed to the long vintage bar. Two men sat at the end, their backs to him, watching through the long, low mirror running the length of the bar's back wall. Gabe could see them as well. It appeared they were having a late lunch, too.

"Hey. Yeah, well. . . I'm doing all right, considering. How're y'all?"

"When it rains, they say. . . That friend of yours," he spoke quietly, "Senga? She's in the back with Mae," Earl stepped closer to him, as Gabe eased down on a stool away from the other diners.

He saw Earl cut his eyes to the others, then raise his eyebrows. Meaning, *let's keep this on the down-low.*

"Oh, yeah? Still serving lunch? I could surely use a patty-melt and a Stella, please."

"Oh, I suppose we are . . . can't be too picky about hours, can we?" and he smiled. I'll go tell Mae," but first, he stepped to the cooler and pulled out a bottle of beer, then made his way back to Gabe, handing it to him. "Suck on that for a minute, you *po' chile,*" he said with a snort as he pulled off the cap with an opener, then he stumped through the swinging door into the kitchen. Gabe grinned, grunted and put the bottle to his lips.

He'd about finished it when he glanced up to see Mae's face framed in the door's small window. She was beckoning him. Wondering what this was all about, he set the bottle down, stepped off the stool, walked around the counter and pushed the door open, careful not to inadvertently glance at the men at the end of the bar.

"What's up?" he asked her.

"Earl, go on back out there," she told her partner. "Come on, you," and she gestured to Gabe with a crooked finger. Both Earl and Mae continued to wear biker gear. Mae's graying hair was tucked under a purple bandana, a concession to the food police who would have her wear a *shower cap* (she insisted) when preparing meals.

"Okay. Is—is Senga all right?" he asked.

"Oh, yeah, but there's this kid. . ."

He followed Mae down a narrow hall behind the kitchen. Gabe had never been invited back; the bar and diner served as their living and dining room, he'd surmised long ago. He'd seen the kitchen, having been shown the new, state-of-the-art grill they'd installed last year.

Another man stood in the hall, near the doorway of a second room. Gabe felt a slight pull in his gut. The man looked somehow familiar. Then, he heard Senga's voice.

"Mae? That you? You have a turkey baster?"

"Gabe's here. Just dropped in. What do you need a baster for?"

"Gabe. *Here?*"

The stranger backed against the wall. Gabe eyed him closely, and it came to him. He was Emily's father. One couldn't mistake the blue cat eyes. He'd seen Emily's photograph often enough to mark the resemblance. He nodded; the man nodded back.

Senga was on one knee at a bedside. Someone shivered beneath a blanket, by the looks of it. A waste basket was beside her, and she was trying to persuade the person—*a kid?*—to take some liquid. He was jerking his face away from her in revulsion.

"Joey, if you *don't* drink this, I'm going to have to give it to you the *other* way. Do you understand?"

Gabe didn't think the kid was conscious enough to understand what she was saying.

"How long's he been like that?"

She turned at the question. "Hey, you. Just in the last thirty minutes or so, Mae said. We just got here ourselves. He's dehydrated," and she lifted the cup to the boy's lips again. He again turned away.

"He's been throwing up everything and has the runs—bad," Senga said.

"And you want to, ahh, use a turkey baster to get some liquid into him—" said Gabe, eyes round, to confirm.

"Well, yes. But I'm afraid it's the me doing it that's got him mortified. . . Though I don't think he's in his right mind. He's not doing well, Gabe."

"Why don't you just call an ambulance? He ought to be on an I.V."

"Well, that's the thing . . . and it's a long story. I'll tell you later, but will you help me with this now?" She began working to turn the boy over. He didn't protest.

"You're serious?" said Gabe, eyes still wide. Mae came up behind and handed him a turkey baster, filled with water.

"Hold it up so the water don't leak out, Doc." She winced. "I'll go start your patty-melt," and turned back toward the kitchen.

"Uh, never mind, Mae," he called after her then glanced at the stranger near the door. "Who's your friend, Senga?"

"Oh, sorry; Gabe—Rob McGhee; Rob, Gabe Belizaire."

He switched the turkey baster to his left hand and they shook hands.

"Hello," said Rob McGhee.

Gabe's mind roiled with questions, but he settled into Senga's instructions, which had Rob seeking more towels and steaming hot water—what he hadn't had to produce at their daughter's birth on the side of the interstate nearly twenty years before, Gabe assumed in a strange analogy. But this was a *decidedly* messier business. . .

With Rob's help, they were able to administer two "doses" of water; Mae's anti-diarrhea medication had begun to work, and the kid had lain quietly for almost twenty minutes without a mishap. They each took their time washing up, and *Echinacea* was administered to everyone as a preventative. Senga asked Mae for some clear broth, which Joey sipped quietly, if half-consciously.

"Here's some Sweet Annie, Mae. It's less constipating than what you gave him, though that certainly won't hurt. If he has another bout, give him about five drops in water, then another five if he loses it again; but use your judgment—if the herb isn't effective, use the drug." She placed the small dropper bottle beside the bed.

Senga explained the circumstances to Gabe, and he listened with all pitches of warning bells sounding in his head, not the least of which stood beside him, in the person of Rob McGhee, never mind the fugitive they were aiding. His last long look in her direction clearly asked, *"What. The. Fuck.,"* before she returned her attention to an outlaw kid named Joey.

Earl and Mae offered to keep the boy at their place, at least until something else could be arranged. If the law showed up, they could always just say the kid was near death, which might have been true. Senga remained in the room with Joey, where she told him about his brother's arrest and what he'd wanted: for them to go help his little brother and, to somehow keep said brother out of jail—that none of it was his fault or doing.

Joey had turned his head to the wall at this.

"These are good people, Joey. Let them care for you," she told him. "I'll keep in touch and we'll figure something out, you hear?"

She heard her Grannie, in the hours after her mother had died in the rollover. *You hear?* resounded in her ears; an echo from the past.

Joey took a deep breath. "Thanks for your help, but I gotta be with my brother. We don't have anybody else but us," he said and began to sob.

"Now that's not true," she said soothingly. "We ain't chopped liver, any of us," and she rubbed his thin shoulder. "Look, I've got to get back home, but Mae's going to take care of you. I'll give her a call tonight to see how it's going. You just need to rest and drink some liquids. Just a little at a time. And don't worry about stuff, Joey. I'll let Dale know you're all right. He did a good thing—for a pain-in-the-ass brother," and she heard the boy snort.

"I'm going now. You warm enough?"

"I'm warm," he said, and he gazed at her for a long moment. She thought her heart would break as she left the room.

Gabe's appetite hadn't returned, but he drank another beer and bought one for Rob. The place was empty of customers and quiet, not unusual for a late Wednesday afternoon. Even the twenty-four-hour news channel was turned off.

Senga accepted a ride home with Gabe and she promised him and Rob soup when they arrived, her usual supper. Tonight's was split pea with bacon. Rob followed in the van.

While watching the last two miles pass, she'd hoped Rufus had tied the lamb well, and evidently he had, for there it stood, its horizontal pupils shining in the headlights as they drove in. She remarked his spotted face, unusual in the breed. *A throwback?*

Darkness and cold equal a strange sum this night, she thought as she climbed out of the pick-up and walked over to the bleating animal. *Probably thirsty,* she determined, and brought over a pan of water. The lamb greedily lapped up the liquid. Rufus had left a small flake of hay, she suspected, "to give it something to do," until she returned. She would call him as well.

As they'd driven through darkening miles, Senga had described Rob's appearance in Spearfish to Gabe, his turning up at her cabin and the rest of it (including Sebastian's misgivings). Gabe was a good listener, but she could tell he was perplexed. His slow-to-come advice was, "Call your man tonight, woman, even if you have to get up in the middle of it to do it."

She would. *And Woman? He used to say 'girl. . .' Must be a badge of some kind . . .*

When they finished the impromptu meal, rounded out with bread and cheese, she asked if they were up for slaughtering a lamb tomorrow, "Now that we've saved one, something's gotta be sacrificed." She proclaimed this tongue-in-cheek, but they didn't catch the nuance, and Rob and Gabe glanced at one another and then at their hostess.

Gabe slowly stood, his eyes all the while on her, and he flung down his napkin at his place, turned to his hat and jacket, put them on and, without a word, opened the door and walked out.

"Back in a minute," she said to Rob, whose mouth was still open.

"Oh, shut your mouth," she said, as she shut the door behind her.

Gabe had reached his pick-up and was climbing in. "Gabe!" she called. The lamb bleated. "Oh shit," she muttered, "I've done it again, haven't I?" and she raised her eyes to heaven.

"Gabe!"

He watched her step around the front of his truck. He rolled down the window. "What?"

"I'm sorry. It was a stupid thing to say. Really, I'm an idiot."

"You're not an idiot, Senga . . . just a bit—twisted sometimes. *Sacrifice?*" The lamb bleated again as if it grasped the situation. *Shit*, she thought. *It probably can.*

"You don't have to help. I'm just wrung out from the day. It was . . . an *evil* day, Gabe," and she pronounced this in all earnestness, willing him to understand her intent, her meaning. Enough had transpired to deem it such. But she hadn't related the tragic scene over the edge of the Leap; it was not *The Time* to tell it.

He put his truck in gear and made to back up. "If you get in a bind, give me a call. I don't know why you insist on doing this yourself, but I raised that sheep . . . I'd just soon not be involved with its killing," he said. "Call me soft." And she was left staring after him. She shivered.

"Well . . . we can't hope to be always understood," she spoke to the lamb—a wether—as she passed him. "*Mehhh,*" he replied, dropping down on front knees, then his hindquarters lowered to the ground, and, then, he was quiet.

Starwallow

CHAPTER 34
INDIFFERENCE OF
WILDERNESS

I'm going to see if I can switch tomorrow for Friday at
work," Senga spoke absently as she put away dinner dishes.
"Thanks for staying another night to help me in the
morning, Rob. You still game?"

"I don't know what I'm letting myself in for, Senga. What'll
I need to do?"

"Oh, you can go off somewhere while I—um . . . or, stay
here in the cabin if you like. I'll let you know when I need you.
The hoisting is easier with two people."

Senga gauged his response. Maybe it was too much to ask.
This was her responsibility, after all, one she charged herself
with—*lo, these many years*. He was occupied with building up the
fire.

"Mind if I take a shower?" he asked. "I feel *germ-y*."

"I'm right after you," and she smiled in his direction. "Go
ahead. I think everything you need is there. I've got some phone
calls to make. And Rob, thanks for your help with the boy. We'll
take more *Echinacea* before bedtime; St. John's Wort, too. I'll
send some of each with you, if you'd like."

"Yeah. Good idea. I do need to get going. Have a gig on
Friday night."

Senga studied him as he went about his task. She gave the
appearance of tidying the kitchen area, but took him in, in order
to somehow rearrange her former opinion. She wanted to, at
least. True, she'd released him from her affections, but the lyrics
to his song prompted her to revisit their relationship. He was
older. Rob would be . . . fifty-five? The same age as Sebastian?

That can't be, she mused. But it was so. No, she wouldn't compare them. *Comparisons are odious,* she recalled.

A fire now blazed behind the woodstove's glass door. She drew the drapes at the east window and decided she inhabited a one-person cabin, after all. Though with Sebastian, it never felt this close or tight. *Hmmm.* She counted it as sign.

While Rob showered, Senga made her calls. Muriel agreed on Friday instead of tomorrow. Mae reported their patient felt better, but weak. Joey had drunk a cup of chicken broth, some ginger ale and had eaten a frozen Popsicle. "So far, so good," she'd said, adding the boy needed to stay in bed for a couple more days, at least, and was welcome until something else could be arranged.

Senga had an idea.

She called Caroline with the story, banking on her friend's affinity for strays. Rufus was none too pleased. He took the phone from his wife after overhearing the discussion.

"Senga? Where have you been? Your car was in the garage when I dropped off the lamb, and there were tracks heading north. I wish you'd—Oh, hell, never mind," he relented.

So, she told him, in words similar to those she had spoken to Caroline. When he caught Rob's name, he interrupted.

"Rob? Who's Rob? And where is Sebastian? Girl, what are you playing at?"

"Rufus, quit. Rob's my daughter's father. He's between gigs and, well, I really don't want to discuss this right now. I'm getting ready to call Sebastian, if that makes you feel better, and *why* is my love life, all of a sudden, so damned important to everybody?" She had a feeling Gabe might have said something. Her feeling was accurate.

"Yeah, well . . . Gabe was concerned, is all. All right, bring the kid here. Are you absolutely sure about this?"

"No, actually, I'm not, but I told his brother I'd try to help out. At least there's one less of them wreaking havoc." Her memory flashed on a childhood journal entry, wherein she wrote that havoc was a favorite word. *Wreaking havoc,* the phrase, tickled her fancy. She chuckled.

"What now?"

"Oh, Rufus. It's going to be all right. . ." *I hope,* she added silently. "I'm less quick to say it anymore, but. . . Okay! I'll visit later with Caroline about what the kid'll need, maybe pick up some clothing for him somewhere . . . and, well, something else I thought of—he could help out when Gabe's away. What do you think?"

"We'll see, Senga; I'll talk with Gabe," and did she need to speak with Caroline again? She didn't, so they hung up. What would Charlie say? she wondered. *And is the kid considered a fugitive? Wasn't he as much a prisoner as Larissa, having no means to leave the mountain?*

Senga wanted to use the cell phone, but now it showed "No Service." She'd have to drive up the road, where the range was unobstructed, but it was only 4:00 a.m. in Denmark. She'd write in her journal. The practice helped her sort through events, emotions, philosophies and relationships; the usual flotsam and jetsam of life.

Rob emerged from the bathroom holding the ends of a towel around his lower half. She recognized his body. It felt *queer* (in the Shakespearean sense of the word, she noted) and a muscle memory jerked in response. *Yes,* she remembered this body. *I also returned that body to him,* she reminded herself.

She watched him cross to his duffle, bend to extract a few items, one-handed, turn to her and stop. "You know, when that black guy showed up, I wondered if he was your boyfriend."

She waited, not wishing to interrupt, to see if he was going anywhere with this.

"He seems like a good dude."

She held her tongue.

"Well . . . is he?"

"A good *dude?* You're out West, Rob. That's . . . not how I'd describe him. But he's a good *friend.* The best," and she replaced the land-line phone on its cradle to charge, then stood from her wing chair, conscious of having articulated a hitherto, seldom-considered fact.

"My, um, *boyfriend,* as you call him, is in Denmark. He's a Dane. He—"

She hesitated.

Did she wish Rob to know that Sebastian had been the one to lift his child from the rocks onto which she'd fallen, and then cradle her precious body in death? No. She held this sacred. She would not say it.

"How'd you meet?"

Of course he'd ask. She'd supply the second meeting. "At a gallery in Spearfish. He's a photographer."

"Ah. Well. I wish you well, Senga, you know that. And—"

He didn't finish, but simply regarded her for a moment, dropped his gaze and returned to the bathroom with his clothing. Senga watched him go, taking the measure of his long back and well-formed calves, conjuring an idea of wilderness: a landscape of hidden mysteries and peace, culminating in the complete, clinical indifference to that which observed it. She laid this notion beside that of an oasis, not in contrast to wilderness, but as *nourishment*, in an obvious sense. *Sebastian.*

Her attention was drawn to the south window. The glow from the fairy lights illuminated her reflection back to her. This woman sorely missed someone, but she also saw one who very much needed to come to grips with what she was.

"And what *is* that?"

She opened the door and took in great gulps of cold autumn air. *Is the answer on the air?* She descended the porch steps and walked to the lamb that stood as she approached. *Mehhh,* it bleated and butted her gently with a black nose. She scratched the hard place between his eyes. "Hey you," she said, making sure the lead wasn't too tight, and that he had water.

"Goodnight, lamb," she muttered and turned back to the cabin, taking in another deep breath, to inhale a possibility, if any were forthcoming. Yes, she'd write for an hour or two (notes and a letter), then quietly leave the cabin, go to her car and drive until her phone magically connected her with her lover.

Hoo-hoo! Hoo! said the owl.

Renée Carrier

CHAPTER 35
LIGHT AND BLOOD

Journal

This evening I upset Gabe. Seems a pattern lately, with everyone. Grannie would ask, What's gotten into you, child? Usually she called me dearie, *unless she was serious, or scolding; then it was* child. *The more clinical title.*

So. Gabe. He has a problem with my personally giving death to a sheep he raised. I don't feel obligated to justify this to him, but I must remind myself, just to turn a light on it. It's been a while since I reviewed my rationale, such as it is. . .

I eat meat. It nourishes me. An animal must die in order to feed me. Papa taught me this, which is why we hunted rather than raised a cow to butcher. We did butcher chickens, every fall. Not my favorite thing. It took a week—and a month after that—to rid the stink of wet feathers from my nostrils.

Papa showed me how to eviscerate a deer and, when I took my first one, he stood over me, keeping his hands clean, while I bloodied mine. He always spoke respectfully around a just-killed deer. No joshin', as he called it.

We give birth; we give death, he'd say.

It's a holy responsibility, and not one I'm wholly comfortable explaining to someone. That would demean it somehow, I figure. If Gabe persists in judging me in this, I may say something, but only if he brings it up. I know he doesn't have the stomach for it, especially hunting. And that's fine. Chacun à son goût, *as Madame taught in French class. . . To each his own.*

When I moved to this cabin and decided to buy a yearly lamb from Rufus, instead of hunting, I discovered a humane way to do this thing, if that's the word. (Probably not, given our species' propensity for inhumanity. But, there it is, and it'll do for now.)

We examine the blade (before sharpening) for nicks, as these can cause pain. We use a long-bladed, just-sharpened knife. We pull the sheep to us and lean it backward against us, straddling it as when shearing, or, we can sit against a tree; then, with the swiftest motion—no hesitation—we lay the blade against the throat and cut across the carotid arteries—the jugular and the trachea—all at once. (Sheep and goat carotids are both located in the front of their throat, rather than on each side.)

Its head will naturally drop, so we lift it during the cut and hold open the wound to allow the sheep to bleed out, as this in turn mitigates pain. We are mindful never to carelessly prick with the point of the knife.

We observe the sheep's pupils and, when they are completely dilated, we know the animal is insensible, usually after about 15 seconds, give or take.

We give birth; we give death.

This is the kosher technique, practiced for thousands of years. I wish I'd learned it before I encountered the trampled antelope on that cattle drive in '95. . . To be cont'd. . .

CHAPTER 36
BISCOTTI AND SECRETS

Lucca, Italy

They called themselves, in jest (though not strictly so), *Le Befane*, plural, in honor of the legendary crone who declined to accompany the Three Wise Men to the Holy Child. *La Befana*, as she came to be affectionately known, her name borrowed from *Epiphany*, was adopted, if tacitly, into Italian popular culture.

On the feast, the crone brings presents to children—to this day—as she resumes her quest to find the Christ Child, having realized her blunder in not going when called. Her image was originally less fearsome than that of a Halloween witch, but the devil of advertising took advantage of marketing prospects. She retains, however, mystery and its inherent appeal. Usually depicted in a shawl and wielding her twig broom, she is associated with either The *Constant* Housewife, or, The Witch.

Maria Teresa flitted about her home like a butterfly, from one bloom to another. Her friends, Sofia and Nadia, were expected soon for a coffee and chat, to discuss their strategy to reduce this *demone* named "stress," in their lives, especially in *her* life, as she was the only one to suffer from a heart ailment. Maria Teresa needed their assistance to work this intent. She had invited Francesca, but the girl had other obligations, having only returned home yesterday.

"*Buongiorno, Gabriele,*" Maria Teresa muttered to the great window, as she pulled open its tall panes to the air. A fresh gust greeted her, followed by the distinct aroma of roasted chestnuts. The vendor must be nearby, she decided. It was Friday, market day in the piazza.

The window named *Gabriele* framed an animated painting: puffy white clouds scudding across a cerulean blue sky; two large flocks of pigeons winging over housetops; Lucca's medieval towers, including the iconic, tree-topped *Torre Guinigi*, all shimmering in the distance. On the breeze, a disembodied voice practiced a libretto, in descant with a crying child and scolding mother from another apartment.

Maria Teresa gave the tableau a half-smile and returned to her purpose—the table setting. She waddled to her tiny kitchen to place demitasses, miniature spoons and small square napkins on a hand-painted Florentine tray. She had bought the biscotti when out on her early, daily bakery errand. The veterinarian had permitted her to bring Bianco early for his yearly exam and leave him to retrieve later.

Creamer and tiny sugar bowl in place, she was ready. She carried the tray to the table as a light knock announced her friends.

"Come in, come in!" Maria Teresa said in Italian. Sofia called out that the door was locked. "*Ah, sì, sì,*" Maria Teresa called back, having forgotten, and crossed to the door.

The two, only slightly younger women entered the foyer, and both in turn gave Maria Teresa kisses on each cheek. They untied their colorful, silk head scarves and slipped them into their coat pockets, then removed their wool coats; Nadia's, a dark charcoal color, and Sofia's, a lighter gray. The women wore similar silk dresses, cut nearly identically to Maria Teresa's; Sofia's was steel gray, Nadia's indigo and, Maria Teresa's—a deep purple. Their only concession to variety was their footwear, determined by common sense, if no longer fashionable.

When seated, the women sipped from dainty cups of espresso and dunked their almond wafers while listening respectfully to Maria Teresa's account of fetching Francesca from the airport near *Firenze*. None spoke after, having apprehended Maria Teresa's qualms regarding the girl's pending announcement. Sofia and Nadia reached across the table and laid gnarled, silky hands on the forearms of their friend.

Then, they settled down to the business at hand: banishing a demon.

Francesca and Carlo sat behind the two-story villa on the *terrazzo;* a quiet area, bordered on three sides by a tall, vine-covered, rose-colored wall. They had brought their coffee to the wrought-iron table. Her eyes sought and found the wooden door at the very back of the yard, reestablishing her connection. Partially hidden by swags of green, it invited means of escape, and had served on many occasions by the adventurous Albinoni children.

The sun shone into one south-facing corner of the yard much of the day, where her father cultivated his garden. Her mother grew herbs and flowers wherever she found available soil. A venerable plane tree shaded the sitting area, its old roots cracking the travertines laid around its trunk and surrounding area. Someone had recently repainted the chairs a glossy, forest green, Francesca noticed.

She had reverted to her Tuscan wardrobe, having laundered the contents of her suitcase and stored the Wyoming clothing for the interim, save her best jeans, the tall boots, her favorite blouse and her leather jacket. She needed, on occasion, to see herself as Gabe saw her. Today she wore her brown woolen slacks and a beige V-neck sweater against the slight chill. An off-white scarf coiled around her neck and shoulders. She felt recovered from the long trip.

It was Friday morning. Her mother had left early to run errands—mainly to shop for Saturday night's dinner. She might be away for hours. Carlo was a computer technician and his day did not begin until 10:00. It was he who helped Francesca arrange tourist trips to the Blue Wood Guest Ranch in Wyoming.

Her father taught sciences at the upper secondary school, while her grandfather spent most of his days sitting, either on the terrace, or beside the front door, to better participate in the street activity. If too fresh outdoors, he could be found inside, reading or watching television. Her *nonno* lived between misery and a guttering hope. Francesca was aware the old widower carried a torch for their neighbor, Maria Teresa Barone. Everyone else knew as well—save the old woman, it seemed.

Older brother Marco lived in Pisa, a short distance away. Gianni, the youngest, lived in the country and worked for a vintner.

Theirs were a lively mix of temperaments and dispositions, and Francesca wondered how Gabe might be received, after all.

Bursting with her news, she dreaded the grilling that would follow her announcement. She decided to tell her brother Carlo, who still lived at home, but knowing Marco and Gianni would feel excluded if they found out, she made Carlo promise discretion.

"Carlo, I *must* tell you, but you cannot say a word to Mamma or Papà, or *anyone*—at least not yet, *capisce?*"

He nodded solemnly, not incongruently with his choice of clothing, she noticed. Carlo preferred to wear gray, accented by the color purple. Today, his shirt.

"*Bene,*" she said. Good. "I am engaged to be married, and his name is *Gabriele*. He likes to be called *Gehb*." She searched the widening eyes of her brother, saw humor grow in degrees and his lips curl up. She added, "He is . . . ah . . . a *wonderful* man. . . Look—I have a picture," and she rooted in her pocket for the extra passport photo. His eyebrows shot up, then he puckered his lips and whistled as he reached for the photo.

"*Beautiful!* Big sister's won the lottery!" and he leaned to kiss her cheek.

Carlo, in both senses of the word, was gay, but he could play the somber card when appropriate.

Francesca passed the next forty-five minutes recounting her and Gabe's meeting in Sara's Spring and his background. Carlo commented on the shine in her eyes as she spoke.

"And he rides the bulls, you say?"

Francesca nodded. She knew this impressed him more than Gabe's MFA from a well-known university, though Carlo admitted he loved that the man was a writer. At an early age, her introverted brother had found solace in the worlds of literature.

"Has he talked about *Mithras?*"

Francesca detected a hint of veil clouding Carlo's eyes, as if she were viewing them through gauzy film. "No . . . never—*wait!* Yes, I have. *Mmm*. After we watched *Gehb* ride last June—and he won the prize, little brother—" she added proudly, ". . . Senga—remember I've spoken of her?—she asked him if he had heard of Mithras. My *Gehb*, he looked at Rufus, his *capo,* do you know? in that way that says they share something? and my lover answered Senga in a tone, as though the question was insulting. Senga—she said nothing and left shortly after."

Carlo reminded his sister that mythology and religion had always intrigued him, and, that Mithras, in particular, fascinated him, even now. She listened, with a growing sense of confirmation, now more than inkling, that Gabe embodied a certain spirit; of what—she did not know.

Carlo alluded to several practices by devotees of Mithraism; undergoing a false death, for one. The religion spread from Persia to Rome in ancient times, its tenets popular with soldier-legionnaires. By the fourth century, it was largely replaced by Christianity and virtually suppressed. Believers lingered; "As with all paths," her brother added, cryptically.

When he completed his short lecture, she took a deep breath and exhaled loudly.

Carlo said quietly, "I would not question him about this, if I were you. It may be he holds it private; it *was* a mystery religion, after all. *Secrets,* do you know?"

"Well, I do not need to know anyway," she dissembled, making a moue with her mouth and reaching for the coffee she had allowed to cool.

CHAPTER 37
BIOLOGICAL IMPERATIVES

Late afternoon the following day, Senga stepped back to witness the peaceful waning of light, the shadow behind Emily's juniper tree lengthening by degrees. From a branch, like a medieval queen's graceful sleeve, a unique item dangled close to the trunk, unique among those suggesting whimsy and child-like joy. This object signified mystery.

The image of the Leap's lovers, prostrate on the sloping base of the cliff, returned for a moment, then faded. She linked the events: the "impossible" arrowhead and the hapless souls. She'd slipped the point into a small muslin pouch once used to brew tea—that it might serve as a prayer bundle for them. But why was *she* privy to the knowledge of their fate? She needed to write to Joe. The Franciscan could usually dig his way through her conundrums. *Like a holy badger,* she added, as she stepped back inside the cabin.

Senga looked about in consternation. The dropping temperature insisted she throw on a wrap or jacket, if only to walk the short way to the garage. She pulled on an ecru hand-spun hat; her Grannie's oft-repeated warning resounding in her head, "If you frown or squint like that for too long, it'll stick, dearie." She pressed a finger to the place between her eyes and rubbed it. The malaise passed.

The mid-autumn sun dipped below the western horizon behind the ridge, and her environs now lay blue in shadow. She halted before the batten board shed, swung open the wide left door and inhaled, transported to her grandparents' small garage on the mountaintop in North Carolina. A sense-memory. Now the sweet fragrance of apples hung in the air, like a high note piped above a drone—the usual, musty old smells.

She greeted Hermione, who remained mute.

Senga needed to be about her herbs, her refuge. She sought to perform one herbal task a day; *the bare minimum,* she called it. It returned her to her center, where the doing was its own reward.

Strung across a clothes-line, each bundle in their own brown paper sack against the cold, she tested one, listening for the crisp note of readiness. *Snap!* went the stem, indicating it sufficiently dry. She laid the plants on a large tray, each turned the same direction, as Grannie had shown her. Tension eased from her neck and shoulders, and her breathing slowed.

Each sense came to bear as she inspected with her eyes, heard the familiar pop, and inhaled the aromatic, spicy scent on her fingers and in the air, merging with that of the apples nearby. There was taste, as she laid the crispy leaf on her tongue and bit into it. An odd, *old* flavor and smell arose, those senses being married. *As one might expect from a just-opened mummy's tomb.* Unfortunately, cold had nipped some leaves, leaving black spots on several. *Harvest earlier,* she resolved.

Senga could do this blind-folded. But, if she had to explain it to someone, it would take some effort, as when called upon to teach. Akin to teaching one's native language, how to impart something ingrained and part of one's being?

She carried the wooden tray into the cabin, where she'd cleared the table.

Thus, began the work of *garbling,* a word she'd thought funny when Grannie said it; sounding too much like *gargling,* Senga had giggled.

She was five years old.

The old woman had looked askance at her, as if the child were *tetched.* There had to be a good reason to laugh in the Hills, else you were thought deranged. A smile was one thing, but a baring-your-teeth grin was suspect. Senga smiled at the memory and continued her work. She reached for a large bowl and placed it on the table. Then, she began to carefully remove the short string ties from each plant in succession, setting them neatly aside to reuse.

She lifted a stem, its olive-green leaves and purplish flowers well-dried, and stripped it, the work prickly, but strangely comforting. A meditation on the art of patience. No need to hurry. No sound but rhythmic small *pops!* as each leaf came away. She included some flower tops, not all.

The scent of *Ocimum basilicum,* or Holy Basil (sometimes called St. Joseph's Wort), could not be mistaken. Some likened it to cloves. Cultivated for 5,000 years, it originated in India, *possibly,* she'd read. Its uses were myriad, even against boredom and insanity. She'd snorted at this. Called "the king of herbs" in several countries, every summer she looked forward to making pesto and freezing it in ice trays, then bagging it to use all winter as a breath of sunshine. Dried herb waited until fall, until now. When finished, she plunged her hands into the bowl and crushed the brittle *materia medica,* rubbing her hands together, until the action produced a heap of dark green. She sat back and waited.

For the serenity.

For the sense of connection.

For the singular shiver and glimmer of joy. It may have resided in the fragrance (*Boredom, begone!*); or, in the color (*Viriditas!*); or by virtue of simple touch, wherein the basil's molecules exchanged with her skin cells. In any case, working with the herb brought pleasure and peace of mind to her regained solitude.

She placed the garbled herb into paper bags, labeled them with name and date, and set them on a shelf.

Journal Entry, cont'd. November 7 (I am combining last night's and tonight's entries. They are related—)

Once again, I am alone in my cabin. Rob left after lunch for Billings. We have forged a prevailing peace between us. I am glad. I mouthed Thank you *to him (for Emily's roadside shrine) as he drove away; I wanted to acknowledge his thoughtfulness, but he may not have read me; he merely smiled. Oddly, we never did speak of it.*

I was able to reach Sebastian on the cell phone last night. He answered in an unfamiliar tone. It spoke fear, and when he asked if Rob had left, and I said no, he was silent. I became testy. "How dare you question my behavior—" He said nothing. I heard him take a deep breath, then he simply said, "Senga."

I fell apart; I actually sobbed into the phone, remembering his body on mine, his hands, his beautiful, strong hands on me, and I saw his eyes boring into mine, and . . . I fell apart.

It didn't ease his level of concern.

He may have wondered if I were crying tears of guilt, or remorse. He repeated my name two more times, his voice warm as—well, a hot-water bottle, and I calmed down. "What is the matter, my dear?" he asked, and I couldn't say. I didn't know. I only knew—I only know—that I feel somehow split asunder by this distance. Not a feminist view, but there it is.

I told him I loved him. I told him I was waiting for the passport, and hope the documents come in time. I told him I look forward to the trip, but, more, to being with him again in December. In other words, I abandoned any and all sense of autonomy I may have earned in the last, oh, twenty years—since I moved to this cabin.

The hour was early in Copenhagen, or Vesterbro—his neighborhood (as he corrected me). Awake for only a short while, he was making a cup of coffee. He's been steadily working on the photographs, and is pleased. "Pleased." The way he says this word imbues the meaning with so much more than I've ever associated it with—until now. I could hear his pleasure in it. He didn't want to say more about the photos. Naturally, I am curious.

His routine: he's discovered a café a "good walk" from his apartment: "Better to earn the pastry before I arrive!" And there he writes, or works, on the computer; or, he reads. It's his social outlet, I gather. His daughter and granddaughter sound most involved with his life. I wonder how it will be when we finally meet. . . But I don't mention this to Sebastian. We hung up after I told him I'd write a letter, an explicit *letter from the mermaid, and he laughed.*

Senga set down her pen and rose to tend the fire. She put water on to boil, then stepped outside to light the tree. After a moment of contemplation, she refreshed her cup of tea and returned to her task.

I am stalling. . .

So, this morning Rob and I ate breakfast—the usual oatmeal, made like Papa's. After washing up, I inspected my Kosher knife again, and slipped it in the scabbard I usually reserve for my Hori Hori. I donned an old shirt and work apron while Rob set about gathering his gear. He seemed distracted.

I walked to the garage for the hoist and carcass hanger. These I hung from the cross-bar beside the garage. The lamb stood by, quiet, occasionally bleating. All that remained of the flake of hay Rufus had brought were a few stalks of sage-green. Sheep pellets lay sprinkled on the ground. Like shit Raisonettes.

The air was crisp, the sky blue, with little or no wind. The leaves on the ash trees had fallen; I hadn't noticed when. Strange. I've been inwardly self-conscious lately; not outwardly so. It's exhausting. . .

The cottonwoods along the creek stand nearly naked, their blizzard-ravaged limbs more pronounced. Oaks grip their foliage the longest.

Rob was busily arranging his gear in the van. I furtively watched as he worked. I'd thought to mention his substance use (as it's called), and why it had finally decided my change of mind—and heart. His desire to be stoned interfered with our relationship—not from his point of view, but from mine: he'd preferred an altered state of consciousness to grim (?) reality. Emily and I were that reality, at least in part. He would have insisted it "enhanced" that reality.

For my part, I didn't much like him when he was stoned. Simple as that. And it finally eroded the love (or what passed for love at that tender age). So, I'd prayed to be able to let him go, and he went back on the road—for good.

I wondered if the cost of my answered prayer was Emily's death, but I've long since dismissed this notion as stupid and wrong-headed.

I agree with Rob's song title, that nothing's lost, nothing's wasted. And today, if it isn't exactly a spark, there's warmth between us, and that's better than coldness, or a wilderness of indifference. I ignored the topic of his self-medicating. He's not mine to take to task.

Rob caught me watching him and smiled that smile. He asked me if I'd been able to reach "what's-his-name" in Denmark. I felt ornery enough to withhold a name. I'm a jealous lover and only answered, Yes. He didn't press for more.

"Well, I'm ready to do this, if you want to step away, or go inside," I told him. His eyes grew wide.

He looked at the lamb, contemplating us with a blank expression, and regarded me again, frowned and simply said, "Fuck, Senga," and slowly made for the cabin. I heard him step onto the porch, but he didn't go in. He must have settled on the south side, near the juniper tree, I thought, for I heard the tinkling of one of the wind chimes.

I let out a breath, stepped to the lamb, untied the lead from the tree trunk, and, grabbing his neck wool in one hand, and back wool with the other, I guided him toward the ponderosa next to the garage. I made my peace with the animal: soothing words of gratitude and comfort. (I'd done this a dozen times.) My mind went both quiet and hyper-focused at once.

Best to be deliberate.

I quickly leaned against the trunk, inhaled and, intoning a prayer for help, I took hold of the lamb's head at the jaw and drew the long knife from the scabbard. The lamb rested against me in trust. In absolute acceptance of his fate. I saw his pupils clearly from the angle by which I held his head. The lozenge-shaped light within burned.

And then, I fell to pieces. For the second time in as many days.

Rob was there within seconds. "I . . . can't . . . do it!" I cried. "What's happening to me?!" But I knew. Even as I crumbled to the pine needles, having tossed the knife away, I knew: the sound of the gear's deep "clunk" resonated. I had experienced it when I first found myself with Sebastian, after the incident in the gallery.

I am no longer who I was. Who, or what I am now calls.

I heard Caroline's voice (not Grannie's). The recent conversation with my old neighbor about "the change," or, menopause, fell into place (like gears), similar to the phenomenon of finding oneself suddenly fluent in a new language after long study. (I wouldn't know—but for the language of herbs.) I am 47 years old, and it's simply (merely?) time to perceive things in a different light, as they say.

Ah, the ever-mysterious "they." I wonder if I'll ever make aftr atheir acquaintance. . .

Senga pushed away from the table, stood and stretched. She picked an apple from the bowl beside the sink and bit into it. The crisp, sweet taste of fall. She resumed her ruminations, apart from the apple.

Another topic for Joe; our evolution—the biological invitation to a new perspective. I suspect he'd claim it's simply a human imperative, in order to grow, mature and ripen into wisdom. I recognize it's hard-won—this so-called understanding. It wouldn't be called wisdom if it weren't.

No, it wouldn't.

So. After I allowed Rob to tend to my wracked sensibilities (or insensibilities), and catch the wand243touff lamb (none the wiser to his reprieve), I asked my erstwhile lover if I could have a few minutes alone in the cabin. I called Stricklands and asked if Gabe would come for the lamb, then I picked pine needles and bark out of my hair and rinsed my face. In the mirror, I saw swollen and tear-filled eyes. For someone who hasn't been able to cry for so long, I've made up for lost time these past few weeks. My reflection, haggard and seemingly struck by some unseen force, watched a long moment, considering me; last night's question to the stars in answer.

I am meant to be stronger now, *I heard in my mind—twice. In an altogether odd voice, foreign to my ears, as if someone else uttered it. Not Caroline. Not Grannie. And there it was: someone* else *had, and she lived within me. I understood differently upon second hearing, the "I" accented.*

I am meant to be stronger now. . .

CHAPTER 38
AY-TOO-FAY AND GINGER ALE

Wanna come to supper this evening?" Caroline waited for Senga's response. It was taking some time, she thought. "You there?" she spoke into the telephone.
"Yes, I'm here." Another pause.
"Don't worry about it, hon—but I wish you would; Gabe's gone and made a shitload of something and I need eaters."
Senga laughed. "*Mmmm,* sounds so enticing, Caroline . . . what is it? What he made, I mean,"
"Something that sounds French. You'll love it. See you around 6:00." She hung up in her usual abrupt manner.
"So, she coming?" asked Rufus. Caroline shrugged her shoulders. Her husband was on his third cup of coffee. The kitchen once again smelled of onions, garlic, tomatoes, herbs and—the sea. It lent the room a Cajun feel, at least how Caroline imagined it. A lot of the color red was involved, starting with McIlhenny's Tabasco sauce. *Okay, orange-red,* she self-corrected. The walls bounced in their brightly flowered pattern, and the countertops and tablecloth were red. *Music's missin',* she lamented.
"This kid . . . you putting him downstairs?" Rufus asked, interrupting her reverie.
"Huh? Oh, I suppose. I'll clear away some of that stuff . . . been meaning to for a while, anyhow. And we'll be needing the room for Jake anyhow, so. . ."
"That's true. Need some help?"
At the stove, she pulled the lid from the gallon pot and stuck her nose over the simmering contents; then, she picked up a long wooden spoon and stirred the—"What'd he call this? And no, I'm good, hon."

"Shrimp *ay-too-fay*," he exaggerated. "Come on, you've had it before. Remember that auction in town for the little girl with heart problems? Somebody cooked up a pot of it. You *liked* it, as I recall." He looked up at her, then back down to his cigarette paper as he finished rolling it, swiping his tongue along the edge to glue it and put it to his lips.

"Oh yeah, I did. Well, good. Something to look forward to . . . *unless there's sex in the near future,*" she muttered under her breath. In the next beat, "How's Sadie doing?" Her horse had suffered a near catastrophe recently and was stalled for the time being. Only Gabe's levelheadedness—and the mare's trusting nature—had prevented the worst. She'd stepped into one of the ranch's car gates after the first blizzard.

"She's fine. Could be put out anytime, I expect . . . just a slight limp. Maybe Senga'd want to take her out sometime . . . see how she goes."

"You think Jake rides?"

"Now that I don't know. Ask his mother." Rufus had a hard time saying their daughter's name. That Leigh hadn't fought more for their involvement in their grandson's life remained a sore point.

"Well, at least he's coming," said Caroline—the resignation sprinkled with optimism. "Okay, I'll work on that room today . . . and hon, you leave Senga alone about that fella who was here; it's none of our business," she said in a slightly imperious tone, even as she heard Rufus nearly spurt out his coffee. He wiped his mouth on his sleeve.

"As if you're going to ignore it. *Christ,* Caro." He twisted in his seat, lifted his cane from the chair back and steadied himself to rise. "So . . . what time is 'near future'?'" he asked the ceiling, rhetorically. Caroline snorted and he shuffled toward the hallway. She watched him (his back turned to her) stop once to raise his cane and jab it playfully at the air three times before continuing down the hall.

Francesca filled Gabe's head like a fever. He felt homesick for her, a condition he'd never anticipated, and he'd had to rally his will to get on with his responsibilities. Only three and a half weeks until Italy. He needed to shake off the lethargy and be about his work, for both the Stricklands and his editor. While not *formally* a balance to strike, he weighed each purpose carefully, as far as accountability.

He'd completed his chores. They'd slowed, now that some of the sheep had been sold, but his boss kept a running list of repairs and such, and Gabe endeavored to keep up, depending on the weather, the season and further vicissitudes of life. There would forever and always be something to do on a ranch; *even if it was nothing,* he added with a sigh. As hired man, he usually enjoyed the rhythm of ranch work; the job description meshed well with his writing. At first, he'd dreaded middle-of-the-night lambing in February, but discovered he didn't mind it so much, once he was awake. Freezing night air stimulated his senses. He counted it *holy*—being present with the ewes and new-born lambs, as they lay ensconced in their personal enclosures, or, *jugs.* At the very least, it felt primordial.

He'd overslept only the one time. A gruff bark roused him. Gus, the Great Pyrenees, had fetched him to the lambing shed, a short distance away. The enormous white dog had never enjoyed a second chance to upbraid the human, and Rufus never let Gabe forget the incident. Hence, exchanged looks between Gabe and the dog had since taken on a curious air, as though each were sizing up the other's intentions. Gus clearly regarded the sheep as *his* and this human was, well, the hired help.

Gabe had time to do two things this afternoon. First—go for a run down the road and back, which would serve two purposes: help shake off his ennui and allow him to check his cell phone for an email from Francesca. Second—look over the last two stories, before emailing the complete file to his editor. He changed into sweats and running shoes, pulled on a stocking hat and grabbed the phone off his desk, along with the plastic bag that held his small notebook and pencil. These he stuffed into his heavy sweatshirt's pouch pocket.

The air smelled fresh and cold and he predicted snow. He was glad he'd left off shaving again, after making the passport photo. Ahead, the graveled road unrolled like a ribbon, broken by intermittent patches of snow. Clusters of mustard and brown leaves lay matted in the ruts. *The land's quenched,* he thought. *And saturated.*

He waved at Caroline, who'd stepped outside with something destined for the freezer. She waved back dismissively, shaking her head. He laughed.

After the first one hundred yards, Gabe found his stride. His motivation lay in reaching his turn-round point, where he'd connect with his sweet Francesca.

From the dresser's bottom drawer, Senga pulled her long skirt, as her only three pairs of jeans were now in need of washing. The skirt was old, one she'd worn as a high school senior in North Carolina and the same she was wearing when Emily was born, hiked up over her swollen abdomen. It had survived the years, as she rarely found occasion to wear it. Made of heavy, olive-colored knit, it draped well, but she felt nearly naked without the familiar jeans, so she pulled on long johns for added warmth.

Her lace-up walking boots felt good and sturdy. Into a skirt pocket, she slipped her pocketknife.

With few clothes, as it was, Senga thought she'd better reinstate her workday routine of patronizing the town laundromat before heading for the library, and the ever-burdened cart of returned books. After packing her usual peanut butter-and-honey sandwich and an apple, she remembered the two bottles of tincture and salve for Muriel.

The drive into Sara's Spring whipped by and the washing task, as well. After placing the wash into the drier, she walked to the library.

"Well, look who decided to dress like a girl today!" the quiet, deep voice called.

Senga wasn't prepared for the ribbing. Her supervisor wasn't alone. Chief of Police and Muriel's boyfriend (well advanced of *boy*), Charlie Mays, was bent over the counter toward the librarian, as much as he *could* lean, given his girth, which had decreased, Senga noticed.

He cut his eyes to Muriel, who frowned at him. He ignored her, adding, "You clean up *good*, Senga," and he gave her a once-over.

"*Charlie!*" Muriel scolded in a loud whisper.

"Well, look at her. Doesn't she?"

"Hey, Muriel. Charlie," Senga said, lifting her hand to make a rude gesture, but thinking better of it, she lowered it discreetly and continued across the room to her desk. She removed her scarf and jacket to reveal a peasant blouse—a vintage style she'd also excavated from the bottom of the drawer.

In short, Senga looked . . . feminine—how she'd viewed herself after arranging her appearance for the day. It had felt unsettling, but at the same time, not undesirable.

"Thanks for letting me come in today instead, Muriel," she said, as she took her lunch bag to the refrigerator.

"Just means your pile got bigger," said Muriel. "You have that *Echinacea* for me?"

"Yes. Here you go." She pulled two amber bottles from her pocket and placed them on the counter. "And here's the salve." She half-smiled at Charlie, handing him the jar, then she turned back to her desk

"Thanks. I like this stuff," he said. "Uh, what do I owe you?"

"Muriel's taking care of it," Senga said, glancing at her supervisor.

The librarian nodded and opened the bottle of tincture to put a dropper of the liquid under her tongue.

"You should have water with that, you know," Senga said.

"I know. Just wanted to try it. You know, you can tell its strength right away; and Jeri had the flu, so. . ." Her sometime housekeeper.

"I need to use the computer before I start." Senga stepped around Charlie and settled into a chair before a terminal. She turned on the computer and logged onto her email account. The name **Sebastian Hansen** appeared in her inbox and a thrum vibrated her thoracic cavity. She sensed Charlie coming up behind her. Reaching over, she switched off the monitor, turned in the chair and asked, "What's on your mind, Charlie?"

"Well, I guess I'm wondering where that kid's brother might be, Senga. Dale's? He says he left him in Montana."

"And you think *I* know?" She turned back to the screen. "Excuse me, Charlie; I need to take care of something here," waiting until she heard Charlie step away before switching the monitor back on.

"See you later, Muriel. You, too, Senga," Charlie called as he headed for the door.

249

Joey lay in bed feeling drowsy and, for all the world, like a seven-year-old; a memory surfaced of being sick in bed and she was there. His mother. And then, she wasn't. He wallowed in the unlikely emotion of feeling treasured, of being cared for, of having his needs met by simple human kindness. The rest mattered little—the soup, the iced ginger ale, the toast and soft-boiled eggs; *heck, not even the clean sheets,* he mused. But the gentle way Mae treated him. . .

He felt guilty for being unable to endow his mother with the same quality of mercy, but it was easy to attach excuses or explanations: his mother was just so overwhelmed by everything.

Yeah, that's it, she was . . . is . . . He sighed and let it go, turned over and fell back to sleep.

When he woke two hours later, a fresh glass of ginger ale sat on the bedside table within reach. Someone had also provided several Saltines on a plate. *Earl,* Joey thought. The man had visited him several times when Joey was awake. *Why am I sleeping so much?* He wondered. He hadn't realized he was so darn tired.

Just then, the old biker stuck his head around the door, left ajar in case Joey needed help. "How's it going?" asked Earl.

"I feel like I've been asleep for days. Doing better. Haven't, uh, had an accident in a while. . . Look, I hate being such a pain," and Joey turned his head away.

"Folks get sick, kid, and you must've needed the sleep. Glad you're feeling better. Mae thinks you might want to sit up—or you'll stop sleeping at night. What do you think?"

"Yeah. I could do that."

"I'll move that chair over." Earl entered the room and crossed to an old arm chair beside the window. He scooted it to the bedside. "Here you go . . . need some help?"

"Nah." Joey managed to swing his legs over the side of the bed and sit up, but feeling wobbly, he collapsed.

"Dizzy?" asked Earl.

"Some. I'll just sit on the side of the bed a minute," he said, as he pushed up with his arms. His equilibrium felt completely upset, as though he was on a small boat in rough seas. Not that he'd ever been.

"You hear from my brother Dale?"

"Uh, nope, but that Senga called to see how're you're doing, and . . . to say a cop's asking about you. She doesn't think he's going to drive up here, but with you being a juvenile, well, there is some concern, Joey. . . Her neighbors are offering you a room for the time being—until you feel better."

"I feel all right, not great, but—"

Earl interrupted him. "You'd better stay here another couple nights, then we'll see. Gabe'll probably come get you. Remember the black guy who helped out the other day?"

Joey's eyes rounded. "What about him?" He remembered the turkey basting.

"*Ha!* Yeah, well," Earl chuckled, ". . . he works for those people I mentioned. He's *good* people, kid. . . Okay, gotta get back. You wanna sit up a while like that? Or try the chair?"

Joey looked at him and forced back tears. Darned if he was going to cry in front of the man who'd earlier shown him his prosthetic leg; Joey had asked why he limped.

"I'll just stay here for now," he said, ". . . and, thanks." He picked up the glass and drank deep.

"Now you'll have to go piss in a few. . . All right then; see ya later."

The man smiled and Joey felt a warm presence hovering somewhere over the man's head, with fiery tendrils curling down and around his puny-feeling self and embracing him.

CHAPTER 39
THE BISON
IN THE REAR-VIEW MIRROR
IS CLOSER THAN IT APPEARS

Jim and Pete hauled the elk to the county seat's meat locker to be processed. The Blue Wood Guest Ranch was expecting a group of hunters, so they skipped lunch at Higbee's, munching instead on Lupita's hearty sandwiches. She'd packed the meal with care and attention, Jim noticed. He knew she was sweet on Pete and figured the sentiment was returned, but he stayed out of it.

"So—that cop in trouble?" asked Pete.

"I don't expect. The sheriff probably just glared at him, and that would've been enough."

"He staying—the Russian—until his sister testifies?"

"Can't say."

"But that could be months away, couldn't it?"

"Yep."

"I can't quite figure him, you know?"

"Who's that?"

"The Russian, Jim—the guy we're talking about. *Geez.*"

"Winston Churchill thought the same thing."

"How's that?"

"Well, he called the Russians—oh I'll probably get this wrong—something about an enigma, wrapped in a riddle, inside a mystery . . . something like that."

"He's defensive as hell."

"Might have a right to be. I'd be mad as hell if my sister went to Russia and wound up as a sex slave forced to work in a meth lab, then almost dies with her little girl in a blizzard while trying to escape. Wouldn't you?" Jim took a breath and looked at Pete for a long moment as they waited for a truck to exit the gravel pit. He hadn't strung so many words together at one time in— well, he'd done more jawing than usual lately.

"Yeah . . . absolutely," Pete replied. "Mom told me he's leaving this afternoon before the hunters arrive. . . Going to stay at that shelter with his sister."

"That's what Lee said. He's driving him in now. I offered, but your dad wanted to come down, I think."

They ate their sandwiches quietly. Jim wadded his wrapper and stuffed it into the truck's litter bag, then took a swig from his coffee mug and said, "Sasha's an interesting guy. Damn good with a pistol." He gave the boy (how he considered Pete) a side-long glance. "That was a *long* shot. You know—and this is just for future reference—sometimes after you fire, if you just sit back and wait, the animal goes on down, Pete. But I get it, what you did. No harm, no foul."

"Oh. Okay. And I wondered about that—I mean his being so good. Are they allowed guns over there?"

"Don't know. Seems unlikely. Why, you think he's a spy or something?" Jim grinned.

Nothing surprises me anymore, Jim. I'm what you'd call *jaded,* at eighteen years of age. Pathetic."

"Hey, save some room for surprise, kid. That elk, for instance. *Huge* surprise."

"Yeah. That was something, wasn't it?"

"You did good. And the Game and Fish are being fairly decent about it, so, another surprise there. Kid, you abound in luck!"

After driving through the late fall landscape—gullies bright with scarlet and burgundy from hawthorn, burning bush and chokecherry—the sleeping bison silhouette of Sundance Mountain retreated behind them, and they turned onto the county road leading to the guest ranch.

He hadn't realized it until this moment, when the image of the mountain in the side mirror tripped a connection and he felt a *ping!* Of nostalgia, uncovering a yen to see Larissa and her little girl, Tanya.

What the hell? He thought.

253

Larissa sat in an armchair in the shelter's living room. She gazed out the picture window, watching dark clouds gather over the town. The temperature had dropped several degrees since she and Tanya had strolled around the yard. The child had run and jumped into their host's efforts at corralling the fallen leaves, her high giggle piercing the thin air.

The Jamison's dog had kept his distance and a watchful eye on them. Larissa wished the dog were friendlier, for Tanya's sake. The child had only ever known George's two hounds and they were devils. *Like their owner,* she'd decided. He'd trained the dogs to patrol the area near their trailer and house in the woods, preventing any hope of escape, until that day before the blizzard. When told the man had died, Larissa had said nothing, her face impassive. The man deserved nothing—her intent.

Tanya chattered in Russian and broken English to her doll, a gift from Carter. He'd brought it yesterday. He'd also told Larissa what happened at the old Berry place after he showed her brother where she had lived. Larissa asked if Sasha was in trouble. Carter didn't think so, given the circumstances, but he didn't know for sure.

She was worried. Sick. Her intestines roiled.

Sasha was coming to stay with her and Tanya. This she'd learned from her benefactor at the shelter. The former nurse had readied a room for him, available for only a short while, as they were expecting another resident soon. Larissa expressed her gratitude by reaching for the woman's hand with both of hers and kissing the knuckles several times, the way her grandmother had when overwhelmed at some kindness.

Her broken arm and insides healed slowly. "Normal," the nurse at the clinic had reminded her. If she survived the ordeal with only the damaged arm and privates, Larissa might consider herself fortunate, but in her heart, she feared the evil remained unseen and she would simply have to shut it away, or banish it somehow from her life. She thanked God for her daughter and recognized the girl would save her in the end. She was mulling all this when there came a knock on the door.

CHAPTER 40
EATS SHOOTS AND LEAVES

The light over the kitchen table cast a mellow glow on the friends. Gabe's shrimp *étouffée* was declared a success and each enjoyed seconds, Rufus, thirds, and Senga begged the leftovers to take home.

"You seem a tad *giddy*, Gabe," she observed, never mind the bottles of beer.

"Well, now . . . I suppose I am," he told everyone. "I finished my edits . . . heard from Francesca, *and,* I got in a run!" He took a deep breath for emphasis.

Caroline was clearing the table and Rufus had just rolled a cigarette and put it to his mouth, when a deep, loud bark startled them.

"Now what does he want?" asked Rufus.

Caroline stepped to the door and opened it. The large white dog sat back on his haunches and barked a second time.

"Is Timmy in the well?" Senga quipped, then spied concern on Caroline's face and held her tongue.

"Guess you better go see, Gabe. Gus doesn't generally bullshit," Rufus said, after blowing out a plume of smoke.

"Want to come?" Gabe asked Senga.

"Sure," and they both stood, screeching chair legs on the flooring. Caroline set down a small container of the shrimp dish at Senga's place.

"Better take the rifle, Gabe, and a flashlight," said Rufus, but when Caroline crossed from the sink to the .30-30 Winchester propped in the corner beside the door, she handed it to Senga.

"In case it's a lion. Or the boogey man," she said and grinned. "It's loaded—and half-cocked. Be careful. Lions attack from behind."

They pulled on their jackets and hats and headed out. "Since you're carrying the rifle, I'll walk behind," Gabe proposed, as they crossed the yard to the paddock, where the sheep were penned.

"Deal," she said then inhaled deeply, to see if she could detect the cat. "Smell anything?" she asked.

"Rufus' tobacco is all."

"That'll do it. Ruins taste buds, too." They advanced toward the sheep and saw Gus raising his snout in the air to sniff.

"Have you ever seen him do that?" she asked. The dog then growled low.

"Nope. But he's on to something. . . You stay here and I'll check the sheep. Uh, and don't shoot me."

She chortled and slowly turned, barrel pointed up, and then she caught it—a slight whiff of beast. The sheep began to bleat; one, two, all and a fiercer growl set up from Gus' throat. It was full-on dark now, and whatever phase the moon was in, it mattered little, as thick cloud cover hid any star or moonlight. A yard light cast long shadows and Senga was glad of it.

"We could use a little more light," she spoke quietly to Gabe, whose form bobbed between the milling sheep, most of which had stood from their repose and were now agitated. He switched on the flashlight.

"Damn," she heard him mutter.

"What is it?"

"One of the lambs. Gus must have interrupted the cat, or whatever it is . . . it's—"

Out of the corner of her eye to her left, Senga caught a quick flick of a long tail and it was gone, back into the night. She lifted the rifle to her shoulder, but it was too late; the cat was out of sight.

"It's a cat. I just saw the tail. I'll help you put them up if you want."

"Yeah, guess we'd better. . ."

"Hey, you okay?"

"I will be. *Damn.* We could use Caroline—you want to go get her?"

"Why don't you, since I'm holding the gun?" she countered.

"All right . . . yeah . . . guess you're right. What a waste," he said, then tossed the light at her feet, the bright beam illuminating sheep hooves. She picked it up and wondered how she'd manage with the rifle. *Drop the light if necessary,* she heard.

When Gabe turned toward the house, Senga walked around to the back side of the paddock where he'd been. She kept the rifle at the ready in case, and muttered continuously, a form of whistling in the dark, in hopes of discouraging the lion from returning.

The sheep lay on its side, unmoving. Dark blood soaked the neck wool, the gash horrendous. And with a sickening jolt, she recognized the animal, for its sweet, spotted face.

"Son-of-a-bitch," she mumbled into the darkness. "*Son-of-a-bitch!*" she repeated, louder this time.

Another snarl emanated from Gus, who stood by the sheep inside the pen, the thick hair on his back raised in warning. The musky smell returned, mingled now with the hot blood, and she heard a throaty, strangled sound just out of the light's halo. The cat plainly wanted its kill. She dropped the light into her pocket and raised the rifle.

A cacophony of banging clatter caused her to pivot toward the house and she saw Caroline and Gabe crossing the yard with all manner of noise makers; *the entire kitchen battery?* Senga wondered, lowering the barrel. No; just two pots, their lids and their respective bangers.

The sheep weren't comforted by this manifestation and raised frightened voices in further protest. Then, Senga heard a loud whinny from inside the barn and for a moment she froze, wondering if the big cat could have found a way inside, where Sadie was stalled. Horses fear few predators, and one stalked nearby.

She raised the rifle to her shoulder again and sighted through the scope along the edge of darkness. Nothing. *Which means nothing,* she thought. Noise from Caroline and Gabe persisted, along with *mehs* and *bahs.* Another neigh from the barn, and Senga decided a door had indeed been left open. The air now smelled of coming snow; cold burned her nostrils.

She hurried around and pointed to the barn when Gabe and Caroline saw her. The great sliding door was open, if only enough to permit entrance. The mare's screams more insistent now, Senga quickened her pace.

Gun barrel leading, she slipped between the sliding door and jamb and crouched down on a knee, the long skirt a nuisance. Thanks to the dim lighting, she spotted the lion immediately and pulled back the hammer, aimed and shot and, after jacking the lever, aimed and fired a second time. The cat lay still, outside the mare's stall. Sadie screamed again.

"Hey now, it's all right, girl. . . You're okay," she assured the horse. Senga rose to her feet, just as the wide door slid to the left, to reveal Gabe and Caroline.

"*Damn*," cursed Gabe, for the third time in an evening.

He admitted sheepishly he'd left the barn door open—"For the cats," he said with a straight face. Senga watched Gabe nearly break up when he saw his boss's expression.

"Don't *do* that again," said Rufus, eyes boring into his hired man's.

Senga dropped her gaze to the aisle's dirt floor. "You want the shell casings, Rufus?"

"Nah. I don't reload anymore. Well, I suppose we need to do something with this old *señor*. Ever seen one, Gabe?" his boss asked.

The beast *was* impressive, if dead. Senga sighed, then squatted to examine it, noticing how compact the head appeared in proportion to the body. Her mind leaned way back to the mountaintop in North Carolina, to the "cat" biscuits Grannie had her form with left-over dough; then, forward several years, to Emily's presenting her with one; "*Wook!*" the child had exclaimed. Some called them "cat-head biscuits."

Senga sighed once more and returned to the present conversation.

Gabe was saying, "No. Well, actually—yes. Just the once . . . in east Texas. A buddy and I were headed to Port Arthur to a rodeo, and we looked over in time to see one crouched near a creek bed. We pulled over to get a better look, and that cat proceeded to leap to the other side of the draw. Must've been close to twenty feet, we figured."

"Yep, they can go twenty, maybe more. Wouldn't want to test it," said Rufus. "And thanks, Senga. Nice shooting . . . for a *girl.*" He winked at her with his good eye; the other couldn't manage it. "I expect you'd rather not have done this, so, I appreciate it even more for that." He reached for her with the arm that didn't end with a cane, and pulled her to his side.

Caroline beamed at her, at a loss for words, for once.

Gabe dragged the animal outdoors and Sadie ceased to circle her stall.

"What do we do with that lamb?" Gabe asked Caroline when he returned.

"Haul it off with the cat, Gabe . . . and what are *you* starin' at, hon?" she addressed Senga. "We can't *eat* it—at least *I* won't. Damned parasites, or god-knows what. You still want it?"

"Um, no, Caroline. It . . . it just seems like such a waste."

"If it hadn't been your lamb, it would've been another."

She made no response.

"Come on, girl," Caroline gestured, "You need a shot."

"I'll be there in a sec, Caroline. I want to check Sadie. Mind if I take her out of the stall?"

"She'll still be spooked, Senga," said Rufus. "I wouldn't quite yet, and we need to clean this up—Gabe, get the four-wheeler, will you? Then we'll put down some of those wood shavings. . . Oh! And do we have any cat litter? To soak up some of this blood, Caro?"

"There's a bag in my room," said Gabe, and he turned for it.

After accepting Caroline's offer of a drink and tossing the jigger back in one swallow, Senga, in Strickland's truck, followed Gabe. Large wet flakes danced in the headlights and shovels clattered in the back. When Gabe rounded a curve, she could just make out the sheep secured to the front of the four-wheeler. The cat lay fastened to the grill with bungee cords, overhanging it. The predator had measured longer than Gabe's reach. Snow fall played hide-and-seek with them.

She wondered why Rufus had insisted they take the animals away on the four-wheeler, instead of simply in the truck. But both she and Gabe had learned not to ask too many questions of the man. *Shoot, shovel and shut up,* advised an old Territory mantra.

The chore took almost an hour.

"In the barn, you looked like Karen Blixen in Africa, or *Out of Africa*," Gabe later told her. Both were sweating from having dug a pit in hard ground, and counted their luck it hadn't yet frozen. When they returned wet and cold to the house, Caroline handed each a hot toddy and they thawed before the fireplace to warm feet and fingers, and, to dry their clothing. Senga left for home soon after.

No further mention was made of the incident. The subject lay buried, like the spent autumn landscape, under snow.

CHAPTER 41
SOME WONDROUS THING

At home, Senga shivered as she built her evening fire. She felt chilled and chided herself for accepting the toddy, though it felt restorative going down, never mind further lowering her body temperature. After the log ignited and a good blaze followed, she closed the woodstove door and straightaway dosed with an *Echinacea* tincture, including a half-dropper of St. John's Wort, against a cold, or whatever Joey was fighting. She recognized when her immunity stores were depleted.

Wearing a shower cap, she allowed her plumbing's hot water to soothe her rankled spirit. Killing the lion had upset her, but there was nothing for it now but acceptance. She would not so much dismiss it, as count it necessary, and stow it among other difficult *necessaries*. The "memory palace" model intrigued her, though she hadn't adopted it. However, in this instance, a nook under imaginary stairs might serve.

At last warm and feeling calmer, Senga threw on her shawl over her robe, then pulled on her stocking hat. She'd wear it to bed, borrowing a friend's old-time protective against sickness. The latch on her door was sticking and, after a third try, she succeeded in lifting it. She'd soap it tomorrow.

The fairy lights twinkled through the flurries, casting an otherworldly glow near the cabin to further warm her—despite the temperature. She reached for the broom to sweep the porch and steps and was interrupted by a piercing cry. How she'd once heard it described—as a child's wail—proved true to her startled ear. Sound carried poorly in these conditions and this seemed distant, but she guessed its source could just as easily be found in the adjacent canyon. She lifted the wool from her ear and cupped a hand behind to better hear.

Silence.

The lion's mate? she wondered and sent *Forgive me* into the thickening air, resolved to further practice care when outdoors.

After unplugging the tree lights, she stepped off the porch and raised her face to the flakes. She imagined Sebastian, not so much as conjured him, his presence, in whatever form this might take. Inhabiting snowflakes as plausible as any. His letter—*email*—she corrected—waited on her bedside table and her heart lifted. Then, she blessed the evening, every facet, and returned indoors.

> My dear Senga,
>
> I wish you were here. There, that is out of the way. I want to show you my country someday. You would love it. I know it.
>
> I am sitting in what you would call, "a quaint coffee house." It exudes *hygge* (I'll explain when I see you) and geniality—along with its fragrant confections and coffee. I am attaching a photograph of the view before me, via the mobile phone. Have you learned to use yours yet? It would seem not, since I hear so seldom, my dear. Yes, I am complaining. Yes, I am lonely and lost without you. Yes, I want you.
>
> A certain elderly woman frequents this place (be forewarned!), who knows who I am. She has me at a disadvantage, as I do not recognize her at all, and will probably be mortified to learn she was my professor or, god forbid, a nanny, at some juncture in my life. No, I haven't had the courage to simply ask. I'm letting the mystery lie for now. She merely may be familiar with my work. Speaking of which, I am happy with the collection so far. I work daily and have such a subject! It requires more time than you might think to achieve my purpose and what I hope may be a fascinating work. At the *very least*, "important," as they say now. The critics.

My intent, if you wonder, is to depict the
(a?) truth and mystery of beauty. In so many
words. None actually. Which poses the
challenge. You see, I worked in advertising for
so long, where the newest, shiny example of the
next thing is often disguised as *the truth*. Perhaps
I am simply making amends.

I am attaching one of the finished
photographs to show you an example. After
studying over two-hundred photographs from
that day and evening, I have chosen thirty to
further develop—not in the old sense of the
word; I use enhancing software, although no
overt disguises; they are all you, my dear.

Save it to the photo file on your mobile,
then you may open it whether you have service
or not. I call them *Intuitive Portraits* for now.

Senga set down Sebastian's email and stepped from her bed
to add a pitchy log to the fire. After taking another half-dropper
of the herbs, she retrieved the phone from her jacket pocket and
slid back into the warm bed. She pressed the correct button,
waited and considered the collection of icons. She tapped *Photos*
and three thumbprint pictures miraculously appeared.

She tapped one. Using her thumb and forefinger as Sebastian
had shown her, she enlarged one he must have made for her
before leaving; she sucked in her breath, as if beholding some
wondrous thing.

Magic, she declared. She couldn't tell if he'd taken the
photograph of himself, or if someone else had. Maybe the clerk
at the store; *yes*—as it lacked a quality of self-consciousness. The
photo pictured him from the waist up. *There's the counter line,* she
noticed; hands stuffed in his pockets, she guessed, by how his
shoulders hunched. He was wearing the teal sweater he'd worn
that day in the gallery, nineteen years after their initial,
heartrending meeting. His eyes—whose pupils were a shade
lighter than the pullover—sparkled like blue ice; stars in a cold,
moonless sky.

In the picture he looked . . . *happy,* she thought. *No; content,
and* . . . (she couldn't help herself) *beautiful. . . Yes, Marie; you're*

right, she sent the health food store owner. But he looked weary. Deep furrows creased each cheek, beside commas at his mouth. Senga had seldom witnessed such an animated face conserve its movements so well. He smiled more than laughed.

She groaned as she touched her finger to the image, wondering if he'd been thinking of her when the picture was taken. *There must be a name for such a thing. A recorded thought bridge?*

A second image portrayed the interior of the coffee shop; its white marble counter and a gallery of books high above, behind a brass balcony railing. She tapped the third and, recognizing it immediately, drew a quick breath.

A profile. Of her, seated—nearly reclining—in one of the low-backed arm-chairs in the loft bedroom of his Black Hills home. An austere background, his canvas; devoid of *noise,* as he called it, or, *distracting influences.* In black-and-white, he'd frozen her just as she'd leaned back to face the ceiling with eyes closed. White shoulders at rest, her tanned forearms lay on the hard armrests, her left hand evoking a languid gesture.

Owing to the position of the photographer—in line with the arm of the seat—the visible, delicate, rounding curve of one bare breast peeked out, the dark areola and nipple punctuating the light-and-dark play. The second breast remained only a suggestion. Her expression, even in profile, radiated contentment by the slight upturn of her mouth. Her long braid, mussed, added texture and streamed behind the chair back like a rope—*No, falling water,* she decided, with a turn.

Senga studied the photo for a long moment, and again, as with Sebastian's laser-like eyes; one, to see if she could, and two, to determine if her response might elicit a desirable intent. She could and it did. The image was decidedly erotic. If this was his intention, he'd succeeded. But Senga didn't believe this his sole aim. *Too easy; too banal,* and she considered it again with a wider audience or purpose in mind.

"What else does this say?" she asked aloud.

She wished the image were larger, but she wouldn't ask Muriel to print it at the library. *Gabe has a printer,* she recalled. He wouldn't have to see it. *Would I mind?* She nearly choked in response.

How much does Sebastian mean to enlarge them? she wondered. In strictly artistic terms, the photo depicted a nude, seated in a chair, with light and dark vying for prevalence. *Or relevance; which is it?* That was the short version, abridged. *Art-lite.* Her lover would have been disappointed by her lazy analysis. *Dig deeper,* he'd say. *What else is there?* It was a visual medium, after all. *No,* she corrected herself, putting words in his mouth: *What do you feel, Senga?* It was, foremost, an emotional medium.

She felt it down to her womb, at the erotic, yes, but more; at the simple, yet elegant, proof of *life.*

It was a human sensation; *a conscious, living one,* and she smiled at his genius. Setting the phone on her bedside table with her right hand, she reached for the print-out of his email with her left, and continued.

> . . . I imagine you examining the photograph and wonder how you receive it. I sent this particular one because I love it so; I absolutely do. Please call soon to put my mind and heart at ease, Senga.
>
> Now I find myself daydreaming of mermaids and composing silly riddles during opportune moments. (There is a fair amount of waiting when one lives in a city.) I think of you each time I pass *Den Lille Havfrue,* what we Danes call the mermaid in the harbor. In fact, I have instituted a daily *devotional* walk (except on Sunday, ironically, when I spend the day with Erika and her family). I am devoted to you, but will send you a photo of her, our *havfrue.* We photographers are terrible at snapshots, so I will endeavor to simply take, not "make" a picture. *Perhaps not.* I see your smiling eyes and I want to drown in them. Love me, Senga. *Keep me in you.*
>
> What did the mermaid say to the passing lovesick sailor as she sunbathed on the rock? Waiting for your reply,
> Sebastian

She leaned against the pillows for several moments and listened, then played a childhood game. Sense detection. The refrigerator clicked on, a hum she'd grown accustomed to; a white candle sputtered as it burned on the dresser across from her, throwing light onto the Waterman print of a mermaid, a favorite image. The sharp, sweet smell of Aunt Karen's lavender soap rose from her skin, a gift from Sebastian, whose aunt had collected scented bath notions. Finally, Senga tasted the nutmeg she'd sprinkled into her hot milk, the spice warming and soporific.

All these sensations conspired to ease her spirit. She folded the paper, placed it in the drawer of the small bedside table with his first letter, then rose to snuff the candle flame. As she'd already made her toilette, she walked to the cabin door to check it, then returned to her bedroom, where she would first bring Emily to mind, to say goodnight, and then fall asleep, listening for the siren's comment to the passing lovesick sailor.

At 4:00 in the afternoon (Denmark time) on the following day, Sebastian studied the photograph he had just printed, its dimensions the great size he preferred. It was fastened to foam board, and propped on an easel. His apartment's living room doubled as his studio (having acquired it for the purpose, on account of the room's tall windows). He tore away his gaze to mind the kettle.

He poured hot water into a waiting mug and returned to the black-and-white. Senga again, now seated on sheepskin, posed accidentally like the harbor mermaid. It was uncanny. He'd wanted sky as backdrop, so they had risked the outdoors, never mind the chill. He had arranged the rug and her placement to include an expanse of blue—rendered light gray now. The effect could have been duplicated indoors, using an ironed sheet, but this demanded a truthful background.

Sebastian looked on his lover's image, willing a response in his core. He inhaled, exhaled and waited.

Legs folded beneath her, she represented a perfect three-point triangle: head to right arm and hand braced on the rug, to a third point of her calves and feet stretched out to her left. The other arm rested in her lap. A tumble of loosed hair, the white streak in contrast to mid tones, fell over the left shoulder and covered a breast—in marked departure from the famous bronze sculpture. The second breast seemed to ask a question and answer with an, *Oh?*

The image evoked the simple, spiraling statement of a mountain and . . . something else: her stare, directly into the lens, betrayed no opinion (not even love, he noted) except that which the entire body made; Senga's portrait stated, *I am.*

His mobile beeped. He distractedly pulled it from his pocket and raised it to view, eyes still fastened on the photograph. "Oh!" He gasped as he pressed the button. "*Hej?* Senga? Is that *you?*" he asked, backing to a chair and lowering into its hard contours.

"It is I—it's *so* good to hear your sing-song-y voice, Sebastian! But first, the riddle. We must respect our, ah, tradition."

He grinned.

She continued, "To the lovesick sailor . . . the mermaid said nothing . . . however, she cupped a bountiful breast in each hand and raised them to him in greeting."

"*Oh ho!* Brava, my dear! Brilliant! Do you know, that is one pose we did not manage to shoot?" he said, then "How are you, Senga? It is just a little after 8:00 a.m. there, yes?"

"Yes. And, I am well, so far. I may be catching something—a cold, or some virus. *Bah!* So, I am wearing my knitted hat all day. . . And thank you for the email. I finally printed it and brought it home last night."

"I sent it days ago, Senga."

"I know, and I'm sorry for my slow response. It's been, well, hectic."

She relayed the incident on the cliff, including the mystery of the two people lying below—which she had yet to contemplate, she added. He did not comment. Then, Dale's injury at her hands and his brother's predicament and temporary shelter in Montana; her failure to kill the lamb, followed by the encounter with the mountain lion, at which he cried out, "No, you couldn't have!"

"But I did, Sebastian. It was threatening Sadie and the Strickland's sheep. . . Had *already* killed one. Please, no more talk of it. To change the subject—the photographs are wonderful—especially the one of you. Thank you for that. And what a coffee house! Nothing like that hereabouts."

"But what do you think of the photograph of *you,* my dear? Oh, it's so *very* good to hear you, Senga. I'm truly lovesick. My daughter feels sorry for me. . ."

"I want to meet her. Does she know you're taking nudes of me, Sebastian?"

"This is Scandinavia, my dear. Where the body is exalted. I love a quote by your playwright, Tony Kushner: *The body is the garden of the soul,* yes? Do you know this? We are perhaps, ah, healthier than you Americans in this respect. But no, Erika has not seen my work lately."

"Ah, well. And, no, I don't know that quote. I like it—*and* my photo. It is quite, um, *sexual,* Sebastian. Was this your intention?"

"But that is simply *you,* my dear. I wanted to . . . to . . . *ach!* I cannot find the English word; oh, marry? Yes, marry the soft lines of your body to the hard, straight lines of the chair and, with that, the light and dark contrasts. The sensual nature is simply the overall impression. You are a natural muse, my dear, and I am most fortunate."

"Aw shucks and you're looking for 'juxtapose,' I think."

"What is that? I do not know this expression."

"Which?"

"*Shux.*"

She laughed at his pronunciation. "It's just a response to being overly praised, Sebastian. Humble, I guess. But back to the photograph—what are you planning to do with them?"

"Why—exhibit them, of course! This is what I do, after all—and hope people might like them well enough to pay us for them. . . I am sorry—you did not know this? I won't show them if you would rather I didn't—but they *are* extraordinary. . ."

"Hmmm," she said, going silent for a moment. Sebastian wondered if he had been mistaken in his zeal.

"Well," she began, ". . . it's not as if I have relatives who will be mortified by the notion, and I suppose they wouldn't be shown—oh, wait, are you thinking of the local gallery? Relatives or not, I'm not sure our area is ready for this much, ah, exposure to the body, garden or no."

"You may be correct, Senga. Perhaps it is time?" He heard her snort on the other end. "I am joking," he said. "No; but I am considering Denver, Los Angeles, Minneapolis, Chicago . . . ah, New York, of course, and possibly Atlanta. Naturally, Copenhagen and Paris. We see how the collection is received at the first two exhibitions." He paused. "Senga? Are you there?"

"Phenomenal," she spoke quietly into the phone. "Never thought of myself as an exhibitionist . . . and all those fancy places my picture gets to see. Makes me wonder if tribal taboos against having one's photo made has some merit—as in, will I astral-travel to these places?"

He chuckled. "This is all, ah . . . what is the word? . . . *hypothetical* yet; but if they are well-received, you could accompany me to opening receptions."

"Oh, let's not get ahead of ourselves. There is too much on my saucer right now as it is."

"I thought the word was 'plate,' and what are you doing today?"

"A plate is too large, Sebastian. Couldn't handle that. I'm a *simpler,* remember? It's a play on the word."

"Yes, I understood." A pause. "I miss you so, Senga . . . Tell me the dates you will be in Italy, once more. I will update the contract on your mobile so you may use it in Europe. It will be helpful. Does Gabe have one?"

"Yes, but he hasn't mentioned getting service there. I'll ask. I'm sure Francesca will insist, to stay in touch—and . . . I miss you, too, Sebastian. I'm, uh, not very good with sweet talk, but a *real* letter is coming, I promise."

"I will look for it." Pause. "So! What are you doing today? You never said."

"First, we are leaving on December 3, to arrive on the fourth in Florence. Our return flight is scheduled for December 18. Then, you will be here with your family on the twentieth? Or the twenty-first?"

"The twentieth. It will be marvelous! Erika is excited; Jytte as well. Peter, well, he does not wish to be away for so long and will return home earlier. His work, you see. By the way, I almost forgot—he asked about the Russian woman and whether her brother arrived."

"Long story made short: Sasha, the brother, shot an elk with the deputy's gun, and he's waiting to see if he'll be charged." She heard Sebastian groan. "Larissa and the girl, Tanya, are still at the shelter. Dale, as I said, was arrested. The boy, Joey, well . . . less said the better," she finished.

"The Wild West," said Sebastian. "Peter is acquainted with this Sasha. Could he somehow offer a good word?"

"I don't know, Sebastian. Want me to ask?"

"Yes, do. And tell me what you're—"

"Okay; I'm going to make an herbal infusion—oat straw this time—then I may write to Joe, remember him? The Franciscan?" she teased him. "And I have to soap my door latch—it's sticking; and then I'll make my weekly soup—"

"What kind," he interrupted.

"Winter squash, with apple and carrot. I sprinkle blue cheese and walnuts on top. Come by for a bowl. You'll love it."

"If only I could; it sounds divine. You must make it for us during the holidays—would you?"

"I would," she said, then paused. "So, what did the brilliant artist shout to the libidinous mermaid as she floated on her back beyond the surf, catching raindrops in her open mouth?"

"Oh, my dear, you grow more clever and bold at our game. I'll have to note this—wait; I need a pen." Another pause. "This demands thought. I will think about it, yes?"

They said goodbye and Senga hung up first. Sebastian stood for a moment studying the words of the riddle on the paper. He sighed, then smiled, jotted something down and returned to his work, surrounded by images of a would-be mermaid. For a brief moment, it led him to consider past lives.

CHAPTER 42
THE WHISPERERS

Lucca, Italy

*L*e *Befane* sat around Maria Teresa's table. On the mantle, a white taper burned beside the Tarot deck's draping, white silk cloth. As they were three, a fourth chair was moved aside. The great windows shut against city sounds and chill, she rose once to open *Gabriele* to Bianco, after he appeared at the pane and loudly meowed.

"We may begin," said Maria Teresa, after situating herself.

They held hands as each breathed deeply to calm their minds, their eyes riveted on the steady flame of the taper. Maria Teresa spoke the invocation, being the eldest:

"Madonna, gracious Mother of us all, who grew old as we grow old, we seek your assistance. Listen to our plight; we beseech you—who crushes the serpent with your heel. Come to our aid."

"Come to our aid," repeated Sofia and Nadia together.

Maria Teresa continued: "This *demone* named stress, it assaults us at every opportunity, and we struggle to defend ourselves against it. We await your sweet voice and counsel."

The cat meowed.

"We await your sweet voice and counsel," repeated Sofia and Nadia, together. All three watched the flame for several moments.

Maria Teresa's eyes watered and she wanted to wipe them, but dared not break the circle. Finally, she raised an arm and rubbed one eye with her right forearm and the other with her left, not breaking the circle, then she sighed. Sofia and Nadia maintained their concentration. Maria Teresa resumed her gazing. The flame flickered, once, twice, three times—the sign they had been heard. Releasing their hands, they relaxed in their chairs. The cat meowed once more.

"I will put him in the bedroom."

Upon her return, several books and a notebook lay open before Nadia. "This is what I found, Maria Teresa," she said, "and Sofia brought several other remedies. . . La Madonna desires we address this thing, as it is an epidemic, apparently, and greatly interferes with the lives of the aged. It is largely responsible for heart disease, as well. You know this?" Nadia waited for her friend's nod and resumed.

"So! What we have learned from these books, Sofia and I, is that stress differs from *distress,* what the *white coats* name the real demon, but *I* believe we must learn to recognize when ordinary stress progresses . . . or, just before. There must be a subtle sign of sorts. I believe this is what we must uncover here today."

When she concluded her statement, Nadia sat up straight and her mien took on a satisfied air. She pursed her lips, but smiled with her eyes. Her expressive eyebrows, jet black and strong, remained the single most defining characteristic of her face.

"*Grazie,* Nadia; I agree," said Maria Teresa. "And what is it you have there, Sofia?"

The woman tried to appear serious, but possessed of a naturally cheerful disposition, she blurted, like so much custard between layers of puff pastry. Giggling, "Oh, just some samples of teas," she said. "For one thing, we drink too much coffee. I know we all love it, but we *could* limit our cups. Herbal teas are the answer, whatever the question!" She grinned—her long front teeth lending her a rabbit-like appearance.

"This," she proposed, "is a very common calmative; lemon balm. And catnip grows everywhere. Remember we used to give both to our *bambinos* to help them sleep? If we would simply do this one thing, replace some coffee with a calming tea, *il demone* would flee. Of this I am certain!" She laughed. "And—*laugh* more, my sisters! Look at you; so *glum! Laugh* at the old devil! We surely did when we were younger; it was not merely childish foolishness. Ah, but we were bolder then!"

Maria Teresa and Nadia turned simultaneously in their chairs toward the angled mirror on the mantle behind them. It was true. The dour expressions on their faces attested to Sofia's claim. They considered one another and both broke into wide grins, if not full-throated mirth.

"And I have another suggestion," added Sofia. "We *must* walk outdoors more. Even if slowly," she addressed Nadia, whose arthritic knees ached. "Perhaps meet somewhere for *tea,* or lunch at a *trattoria* requiring at least fifteen minutes of walking. Enjoying one another's company is also a remedy, my point," she emphasized and sat back, closing her lips over her toothy bite, to indicate her conclusion.

"I like all these ideas; thank you for them," Maria Teresa said, "and I *do* walk, yet my heart complains. Well, I could drink less coffee, it is true—" and they all sighed as one. "It *is* beneficial though, you know . . . against the dementia, I read."

"There must be a middle ground," said Sofia. ". . . somewhere between crazy and anxious," and they sighed again.

Then, Maria Teresa wondered if not being able to laugh at oneself was the subtle sign Nadia wished to uncover. She offered this.

Sofia raised a crooked finger and her friends grew quiet. "*Il riso e la migliore medicina!*" They all nodded, chuckling.

Laughter is the best medicine, indeed, Maria Teresa agreed.

"*Nonno,* how are you?" Francesca asked her grandfather. He was sitting outdoors, his high-backed chair perched precariously against the rose-colored stucco of the house, beside the front entrance. Startled, he jumped, bringing the chair's front feet back down to the pavers.

"Francesca! You could have warned me you were there!".

"I am here. How are you?" she asked again.

"Not bad, not good, and you?"

"I am very well, thank you. Are you ready for the dinner tonight?"

"What's to get ready for? We eat, we shit, we sleep and we do it all over again the next day."

She frowned. *This is not good.* She squatted to look at him. "*Nonno . . .*" He turned away. A wild, white beard, begging to be groomed, dominated his face. He wore an ancient fedora whose rakish brim was pulled low against the sun.

"Oh, look, Francesca, here come those two old hags, Nadia and Sofia. Don't look at them or you will turn to stone," and he dropped his gaze to the ground.

"*Nonno,* you are so—*Buongiorno, signore!* How are you?" she asked the pair as they halted before them. Her grandfather did not lift his head.

"We are well, Francesca, thank you. Maria Teresa is so pleased you have returned to us." *Nonno* lifted his face at the older woman's name, but just as quickly lowered it. Francesca noticed his eyes darting this way and that, as though examining his limbs for any sudden change.

"Yes, she is coming to dinner tonight. I look forward to seeing her," said Francesca, and the two women nodded and smiled. Sofia squinted at *Nonno* and reached out her hand to his shoulder, but, thinking better of it, discreetly returned it to her side. Francesca caught her eye and each made a conciliatory expression.

Nadia spoke. "Well, Sofia, let us continue. The stationer closes soon. *Ciao,* friends. Enjoy your evening."

"And you," Francesca replied, and they watched the pair amble off, arm in arm. Slowly. She stood, turned to look at her grandfather and spoke in a lighthearted tone, "You know, I *could* trim your exquisite *Babbo Natale* beard for you, *Nonno.* If you wish. Mamma doesn't need me yet."

He twisted in his chair and shot her a look. "And why would I do that?" he asked, his liquid brown eyes saucers, and then they softened. "How does Father Christmas stand it," he muttered, as he sought his cane; then, standing stiffly, he said, "Good. I will let you. It itches."

"Mamma, Maria Teresa is nearly here!" Francesca shouted as she climbed the stairs, pausing at the narrow window that gave onto the street. The old woman could be spied walking carefully, negotiating the uneven stones, her gaze ever directed to her steps. Francesca resumed her objective; she needed something from her room.

She had dressed carefully in a brown silk tunic and a long, navy blue skirt. A blue shawl rested over her left shoulder, as she had seen Mary Rogers do. Her brothers were all present, with

Gianni bringing his girlfriend, Paola—a timid young woman originally from Vicenza. They worked at the same vineyard.

Francesca rejoined her family after setting an item on the foyer table.

Nonno's newly-trimmed beard and mustache (and shaved neck) gave him an entirely different appearance. "Socrates?" his daughter-in-law addressed him, when he stepped onto the *terrazzo,* where they gathered.

"Well, you finally recognize my *sagesse,*" he said, using the French and smiling. Then, he shuffled to his chair and sat, expectant as a sphinx, cane propped between his legs, hands folded over its handle; his back, ramrod straight.

"Everyone, Maria Teresa has arrived," Francesca's mother announced. The elderly woman appeared in the wide doorway to the terrace. *Like a painting,* thought Francesca. Having left her coat in the foyer, the woman was dressed in her dark purple silk, dark hose and shoes; her short white hair styled neatly away from her face—which showed remarkably few lines (due to olive oil). The only makeup she ever used was a rose lip balm, once telling Francesca the color cheered her. She groomed her eyebrows regularly, and this was the extent of glamour.

Francesca watched as Maria Teresa perused their faces, her expression solemn. She found *Nonno's* face and paused. Her grandfather, Francesca noticed, magically lost twenty years. *Maybe thirty,* she decided. The man pressed on his cane and rose to his feet, glanced at his grandsons and they popped up, having forgotten their manners. Francesca heard *Nonno* grunt, then he reached to doff his hat, which he wore to protect his bald spot from Tuscan sun, even if beneath shade. "Welcome to our home, Maria Teresa. You honor us. Please sit, anywhere . . . but it is most pleasant here under the tree."

Beside me, Francesca added to herself. *He actually has a twinkle in his eye,* she noticed. *Nonno* replaced his hat. Remembering her mother needed her in the kitchen, she started toward the house, but this transformation in her grandfather transfixed her and she paused by the door.

Carlo addressed Maria Teresa.

"Thank you for coming, *Nonna,* and helping us celebrate our sister's happiness," he said to her and everyone; then, he crossed to the table, where his grandfather sat, and pulled out a chair for the woman, who spoke for the first time, "And what is this happiness?" she asked. Rhetorically. For now.

"*Ah, sì, la bella signorina!*" her grandfather exclaimed, meaning Francesca, yet he gazed at Maria Teresa. Gianni and Marco tittered, and she saw Carlo shoot them a look.

This might be an evening of looks, Francesca decided.

She helped her mother serve aperitifs and *anti-pasti*, with Carlo helping where needed. Her father finally arrived, apologizing for his tardiness; the traffic, he explained, and they sat down at the long table, *al fresco*. Above them, strings of lights swayed gently in the soft, night air, er father and mother at one end of the table, her grandfather and Maria Teresa at the other; everyone else, in-between. A shawl magically appeared on Maria Teresa's shoulders. *Carlo,* thought Francesca.

The hall clock chimed nine times through the open doorway as they finished the first course of roasted tomato soup. She had grown used to eating dinner at an earlier hour on the ranch. It would take weeks to train her appetite to wait.

Francesca sat across from whom she now knew to be Senga's grandmother, and a tingle ran down her back. She furtively sought a resemblance. *Yes,* she decided. *Oh, my. They share mannerisms, and . . . facial expressions!* She grinned and noticed Carlo watching her. He raised an eyebrow and lifted his glass to her.

Francesca believed daughters took after their fathers, who took after their mothers, and so on. . . . *When will I speak with her?* she wondered. *Perhaps after.* Her mother had asked her to pair her engagement announcement with the limoncello and fruit tarts, and then she could walk *la nonna* home and tell her about Senga in the comfort and privacy of her own surroundings.

At her mother's signal, an imperceptible nod, Francesca watched Carlo raise his knife to the glass and ping it, quieting the chatter. "Our sister has something to say. *Papà,*" he asked, turning to his father, "shall I bring up the prosecco? Or pour more limoncello? Anyone?" as he raised the decanter of liqueur. Gianni and Paola presented their small glasses, followed by Marco, and then *Nonno,* who smiled questioningly at Maria Teresa. She shook her head.

"I am . . . engaged to be married," Francesca said simply, then sat back and smiled.

The table was silent for a moment, then erupted with cheers. She sought Maria Teresa, whose countenance seemingly struggled with her emotions. *I want you to be happy for me,* she sent the old woman, who had become grandmother in the absence of her own. She hoped the news of Senga might lessen the woman's seeming distress.

"Tell us about this man, Francesca," her father spoke up.

She noted that no one stole a glance to her hand—and absent ring. *You see, Mary?*

When she finished describing Gabe, or, *Gehb,* concentrating on his background, educational and otherwise, and, his work, including bull riding, ranching and the writing, she produced the photograph from the foyer table to pass among them.

The table fell silent once more, except for Carlo, who nearly purred.

Nonno snatched the photo from him and held it out, in order to better see it. Still inspecting it, he lowered it to his lap and began tentatively, almost in a whisper.

"On December 26, 1944 . . . not so long ago now, it seems . . . our family was trapped in our home during a bombardment. I had returned from the fighting to pass Christmas with them. But it was hellish . . . no joy. On this night, we had no warning and had just finished supper—all of us together around the table, like *this*." He stared at the tabletop and then returned his gaze to his lap, where he beheld the photograph.

"We were crouched beneath the table, huddled together, as the mortars continued . . . the walls and ceiling crumbling around us . . . the dust made it difficult to breathe." He raised his eyes to them, "I lay on top of little Pio." Her great uncle.

Francesca glanced at Maria Teresa, who sat rapt, her eyes moist.

"Somehow that oak table held. I do not know how. The noise was so very loud, but above it, I heard someone yelling and wanted to run out and see, but my father held me back. I suppose he thought we were safer together than apart.

"I heard the shout once more. As if someone were looking for someone. And there, peeking around the corner of the house's front door frame—the wall destroyed beside it—stood a soldier. American. And very much like this man." He brought the photo and his arms to the table's surface, tapping his finger on Gabe's image.

"He was wearing his helmet, but it had been struck by something, I remember thinking—I saw a deep dent. Well, my father gestured wildly for him to come—there was room; I . . . I can still see him motioning for the man to join us, where he might survive this . . . this *evil*. And just as he started across the room—well, he didn't make it. . . I will say no more, but I have never forgotten him . . . and the other *neros* like him who risked, and gave, their lives for us."

He raised his eyes to Maria Teresa, "That was near Sommocolonia where I was brought up," then he lowered them to continue. "The battle was one of the Nazis' and Mussolini's last victories. The American soldiers were called *Buffalo Soldiers,* a regiment of Black men. I remember the patch on this man's shoulder. A bison. Many of them are buried in the American cemetery," he spoke to Francesca, ". . . about 400 of them, among the others."

Her eyes blurred with tears. She knew this.

She recalled her personal and national history and felt a strong fist clench her heart. Her *Nonno* had fought as a *Partisan*— a guerilla fighter—against the Germans, and, against his own countrymen. How she and others had allowed the great sacrifices to molder away. Well. She would show Gabe and Senga the cemetery when they came.

"Little Francesca," her grandfather turned to her, "I bless your choice. If you chose him, then he is certainly worthy." There followed a male chorus of *Sì, sì!* And *Bravas.*

Settled again in her own home, Maria Teresa permitted Francesca to brew a late pot of tea. "The chamomile, please," her old friend called out. They had not spoken on the short way back, as both concentrated on their footing or thoughts. While true the street was well lit, the task of walking required attention. Carlo offered to return for her in thirty minutes. He was an attentive brother.

"*Gehb?* This is his name, Francesca?" Maria Teresa asked.

"A nickname. It is Gabriele, *Nonna,* you know, like the angel?"

Maria Teresa then peered at her and, backing to her arm chair, slowly lowered herself into its contours. Her eyes never left the girl. "*Gabriele?*" She repeated the name. To be certain.

"*Sì, Nonna.*"

"When . . . when the photo was passed to me at table I felt confused for a moment, as if I were somewhere else, do you know?"

Francesca did not, but nodded from the kitchen, where she was arranging the tea pot and cups, with saucers, on a tray. She opened a drawer and withdrew two small spoons. The water kettle whistled and she whisked it off the burner, then filled the pot.

"But I felt the *lightest* hand on my shoulder and heard a whisper in my ear."

Francesca stopped and gave the woman her full attention.

"I heard, 'It shall be *fine*, Grandmother; all shall be well.' I thought it was you, but when I looked up, you were across the table . . . and your grandfather was drilling a hole into me with his eyes, so I knew it wasn't him. He looked concerned. Do I look *pazza* to you?" she asked Francesca.

"*Nonna* . . . No, you are not crazy," she said as she lifted the tray, crossed the room and placed it on the table. "How long for the tea?"

"Seven minutes. So he is the one, eh, *bambina?*"

Francesca nodded once again, with a smile, remembering childhood tea parties in this room, and happy chatter among her dolls. . .

"Then I am happy. Ah, happiness. . . Even when you return to America. But you *will* visit." This said imperiously. "I do not think your family would survive without little Francesca in their lives." Little Francesca. What she had called her since she was born. Hearing the irony; she was no longer little. *But I am strong.*

"Ah, *Nonna*, I have something else to tell you," and immediately sensed her friend's alarm by her sharp intake of breath. "*No-no!* No *bambino* on the way, yet, so no worries," she said and laughed. "May I open the window first? Just a little?"

"*Sì, sì,* that one." Maria Teresa pointed to *Gabriele.* Her Francesca had apparently forgotten the windows' true identities, or merely counted it as a childhood game. Some things were better (*or, was the word, "stronger?"*) if left alone.

She watched the girl (in her mind Francesca would always be a girl) cross the room to the window, and there stood Bianco on the sill as if summoned, his white tail gesturing. The child of her heart turned the brass knob, pulled open the sash; the cat sat down, looked up at her and waited.

"What does he want?" she asked.

"For you to pick him up and put him down on the floor! You keep me in suspense, *cara mia.* And the tea is brewed. Hurry up!"

Nonna heard the voice whisper, *No need of hurry, Grandmother; she has all the time there is. Calm yourself.*

She closed her eyes a moment.

Francesca propped the window open, after taking a deep breath of night air. "It is so soft, the air here, and so many different smells!" She returned to her chair and tea. "So, do you want to hear the long version or short?"

"*Accidente,* girl!" *Calm yourself.* . . She rolled her tongue in her mouth three times and her wits grew less rankled. "Then, *please* . . . just get *on* with it," she directed, quietly.

"As you wish," Francesca said, then sipped from her cup, set it on its saucer and both to the table. "I recently learned that I am friends with your granddaughter, Senga, in Wyoming, and she is coming here—with Gabe—in three weeks, to see you."

The girl smiled coyly and reached again for her cup and saucer, obviously enjoying the absolute stupefaction on the still-smooth face of Maria Teresa Barone.

CHAPTER 43
LEGEND, MYTH AND
FAIRYTALE

The oat straw infusion, a nervine, steeped in its mason jar on the counter, to be strained this evening before supper. After bidding Sebastian so long and pressing "off," Senga checked in with her body and decided a walk wouldn't do any harm. On the contrary, it might dispel the congestion and perhaps some loneliness. Before Sebastian, she'd embraced the emotion. Nourished it. *Or, more likely, it embraced me.* Now, she felt his absence acutely; it was like waking in a frigid cabin.

Yes, a hike would help. But first, the door. The soup and letter to Joe could wait.

She rubbed the end of the door latch with a bar of soap, tested it and applied more where the tongue met the guards. The apparatus worked better. She grinned—delighted to have solved a mechanical problem.

Just as she reached for the handle of the door to leave, the phone rang. *Naturally,* she thought.

"Is this Senga Munro?"

"Yes."

"Marie at the health food store in town recommended you. Can I make an appointment?"

"Ah, well, what's the problem, if I may ask?" Senga said, sitting down at the table and pulling a notebook and pen from the drawer.

"I have several . . . do you have an office or something?"

"No, but depending on what you need, I can meet you in Sara's Spring at the café, or you may come to my home, if it's more complicated."

"It's complicated. Where do you live?"

Senga recorded the woman's information and they decided on next Wednesday. She might call Marie and ask about the referral. An ingredient in the woman's voice felt off, like the taste of old lettuce.

Finally outdoors, she admired the cerulean sky, now devoid of clouds, then startled at a loud *caw!* followed by another. Swiveling, she spotted the black birds in a tree, beside the orchard gate. "I see you! I suppose you're hungry. Okay, okay; y'all are spoiled, you know," and she crossed to the garage, where a small metal can held a bag of sunflower seeds.

In lieu of a dog, Senga relied on guardian crows. *Sometimes the magic works, sometimes it doesn't,* came the refrain, one she'd heard Joe use, quoting Old Lodge Skins, from the film *Little Big Man.* The crows left the odd bauble now and then on the platform feeder, but only when she faithfully provided treats. They could be louder than a pack of coyotes.

Birds fed, she resumed her objective and turned south in the general direction of Strickland's ranch, pushing off with her walking stick through an accumulation of five or six inches of snow. The air opened her lungs and her cheeks stung in the biting cold. It felt good. She was soon striding below the cliff, and then halted. Where it felt as though something stopped her.

Turning toward the base, she peered through scattered pines, oaks and ash. The white flag of a doe's tail flashed, then another. Reminded of hunting season, she cursed at forgetting, *yet again,* a bright piece of clothing. But it was the time of day when most hunters gave up until late afternoon. Papa had taught her that deer lie down at midday. *Unless surprised,* she reasoned.

She sank into a snowy draw and climbed the other side, her goal a large copse of oaks. The tang of autumn from wet and decomposing leaves, to the faint scent of rutting deer, drew her nearer the sloping base of the cliff, trying to determine where the two persons had lain, from her earlier vantage above. *It may have all looked differently, then,* adding, *probably . . . definitely; these trees wouldn't have been here, for instance.* Joe had wondered, by the younger appearance of the man resembling Catlin's 1832 painting of High Wolf, if she may have *seen,* or experienced, something from an earlier decade. "Or not," he'd added with a grin.

A screech broke the quiet, and she searched the high blue gaps among the tree tops. Possibly the same bird she'd seen on the cliff, she thought, but no; this was an eagle, a young one, and black, save the white band on the tail. Swooping toward her, he tucked wings and rolled in flight like an airplane, to continue past. She stood, locked in amazement, watching him rise. He made another call, then flew to the top of an old, topped-out ponderosa. The branch gently swayed with the weight, and a dusting of snow sparkled in the cold blue air.

Where you stand is sacred ground.

She heard this inwardly and, noting the conviction, she raised her hand to her forehead in soft salute, turned and retreated to her oft-used trail.

"Rest ye well," she muttered to the spirits.

Sasha was made to feel welcome at the shelter, but Sue Jamison, Larissa's host, reminded them that she needed the room on Tuesday. Someone had sent a character reference to Sheriff Miller on her brother's behalf. The charge of poaching was dismissed and he was free to return to Russia.

Larissa had again asked the sheriff about her responsibilities and learned that in the United States, a defendant is entitled to face his accuser and be cross-examined. "I don't know how it works in Russia," the lawman told her, ". . . but would you mind staying on through the trial?"

She had agreed, and later asked Carter to explain it all a third time, which he had: After the initial hearing, it was decided Jacob Brady would be tried in federal court, charged with kidnapping, unlawful imprisonment and drug charges. The state had dropped domestic abuse and rape, as leverage, with the understanding the U. S. Attorney intended to charge the subjects federally. Homeland Security Investigations (HSI) would investigate the allegations, and look for evidence of human trafficking—the upshot that Jacob had indeed "bought" her, but had not *sold* her. She had been forced to work, however, and this could meet an element of the crime.

The second defendant, Dale Scobey, was in custody and would likely face charges of conspiracy. Both were remanded to the U. S. Marshalls.

Larissa understood most of Carter's explanation, but it was much to contemplate, so she did not. She needed something useful to occupy her time, mainly for distraction and, it came to her one afternoon, as she mindlessly watched television. Their English could be improved, she'd decided, even if she returned to Russia, and she set about developing a curriculum of sorts, recalling her earlier classes in school. By the end of the first day, her head ached with the effort, but she'd made progress; Tanya, more quickly. Larissa asked Sue if the child could somehow meet other children, and the retired nurse, now advocate, arranged it with the local day care. "Children are often the best recourse," Sue told her, and chose another word at Larissa's frown. "Remedy?" Larissa nodded and smiled.

Sasha made preparations to leave without her and his niece.

"Mama will be heartbroken that you aren't with me. She looked forward to meeting her granddaughter, and seeing you, of course."

After struggling with the English, it felt good to speak her own language.

"I don't like it either, Sasha, but I must see this through. It was five years of my life. And now it will be more, but you do understand, don't you?" She looked at him with her heart exposed. They had employed this telepathy since childhood, and he returned her gaze with love.

"Yes. I do. But it is still difficult. Please come home when this is over, Lara," her brother said, with feeling. He sat across the table and reached for her hands, which he opened, to kiss each palm.

"Who contacted the sheriff about you?" she asked, after rubbing her hands together, then blowing the kiss back to him. An old game.

He sighed and ran his hand through his hair, then leaned back in the chair.

"Want some tea?" she asked him, granting pause. She had learned patience in captivity.

"Yes, please. Do you have any jam?"

"I do. I get funny looks when I stir a teaspoon into my cup." She stood to go brew a pot.

"His name is Peter Jensen. A Dane. We do business sometimes. He owns an electronics company in Denmark.

Seems his word was enough for the judge—or sheriff. What a country! I have emailed him—Peter—to thank him. Just two weeks ago I told him I was coming for you, and about, ah, *the situation.*"

Larissa shook her head, his two-word description mournfully inadequate. He began to apologize.

"*Niet,* Sasha. Please, go on," she said.

"Well. . . But this is fascinating, Lara: Peter then told his father-in-law about it. Seems the man is involved with a woman who lives in this area . . . small world and all that; but isn't it *strange?*"

"Yes. It is. . ." *More strange that we survived at all.*

The water boiled and she counted to fifty, then added it to the pot, checking the time. She placed the jar of raspberry jam on the table with a saucer and two spoons.

"Tanya? Do you want a cookie?" Larissa called in English to her daughter in the bedroom, where she feared the child played a tragic and twisted version of house, with the doll Carter had given her. Her entire life, up until a fortnight ago, had been one of unspeakable cruelty, outside Larissa's nurturing.

"Yes, please," the child responded. "*Vasilisa* wants a cookie too," she added, running into the room, her bright red curls bouncing.

Larissa smiled at her and then the brother who'd once recounted the fairy tale so often that she could tell it to Tanya, omitting the darker scenes, some of which were upsetting even to her, given their ordeal. *Vasilisa the Beautiful* was the Russian heroine whose doll, a gift from her mother, saves her life. Tanya was Larissa's very own doll.

"Of course she does . . . and you?" she asked Sasha.

"*Da,*" he said. "Two."

Her neighbor was toting her sun-dried laundry to the front door when Senga gingerly stepped across the car gate into Strickland's yard. She'd decided a longer hike might lend perspective after such a week, so she'd continued through the snowy landscape, hoping she hadn't made a stupid mistake with her health. She was perspiring.

"What the *hell* are you doing?" Caroline called to her friend.

"Trying to catch pneumonia, I suppose. . ."

"Well, get on in here," the older woman said, as she tried to negotiate the doorknob, a full basket, and Gus's large body sprawled against the door. She nudged him with the toe of her overshoe. "Move it, ya big lug," and the massive white animal raised up slowly, stretched, moved a foot away and collapsed, head resting on front paws, eyes rolled up to his mistress.

"How come he isn't with the sheep?" asked Senga. "I heard another cat last night—snow made it hard to tell how close."

"You're kiddin?" Caroline raised her eyebrows. "Nah, Rufus and Gabe have 'em in the shed for now. Well, shit. I suppose it's the mate; but lions usually hang alone after breeding. You could've called to tell us, instead of hiking over, hon. Really. Come on in," she said as she entered the house.

Laundry basket deposited on the couch, its contents to be folded later, Caroline shrugged out of her coat, hung it up, stepped out of the overshoes and pulled off a wool hat. Senga did the same, then leaned over her laces. "Leave 'em on, leave 'em on," said her neighbor.

"They're wet, Caroline," she explained and continued. "I've got a question," she said as she pulled off the second boot, her socks next.

"What's that?"

"Know anything about *Lovers Leap?* I mean the reason it's called that?"

"Doesn't take a whole lot of imagination, Senga; there's one in nearly every state of the union."

"Yes, well, I mean this one. Do you remember hearing anything about it when you were young, for instance? Think. It's important."

"Hunh, is it?" She made a sound like *mmph*. Caroline crossed to the refrigerator, opened the door and stared into it. "I'll have to think about it. Rufus and Gabe'll be coming in soon and there's plenty here, so stay, will ya? Looks like we're all running late for dinner today."

"Thanks. I may ask Gabe for a ride home. Think he'll mind?"

"After last night? Uh, no," she said, with a look expressing disbelief at the question.

Senga asked if she could help with anything. Caroline had her set the table, while she removed a pan of biscuits from the oven, the warm, buttery smell filling the kitchen.

"Syrup?" asked Senga.

"In the cupboard," said Caroline, pointing beside the stove.

"Oh, yum." Senga set the Log Cabin on the table. Most of Grannie's meals had included biscuits and syrup. Sorghum most of the time; molasses, sometimes. Log Cabin would have to do.

After several tell-tale stomps, the kitchen door opened to Rufus, followed by Gabe. "Well, howdy, girl! How's our Annie Oakley today?" the old rancher asked.

She smiled, then sneezed.

"Close the damn door. Hurry up!" Caroline demanded. "Senga, there's a pair of slippers there beside the door. Put 'em on, hon." Both men hustled in and began removing their gear.

"Hey, Senga; back in a minute. My wash." Gabe greeted her, then disappeared downstairs. She reached for the terry scuffs.

"Rufus, what do you know about *Lovers Leap*—why it's called that?" Caroline asked her husband. "Ain't it something about a couple of Indians? A Cheyenne and a . . . *oh, hell,* I can't remember. Different tribe though."

He drew his brows together, as well as he could and, peering at Senga, his face turned to present the unscarred side, he said, "Why do you want to know?"

CHAPTER 44
BROODY AND SNEEZY

Gabe gave his passenger a side-long glance as they rounded a gravely curve. They were approaching the highway. Senga stared out the window.

"A nickel for your thoughts, adjusted for inflation," he quipped.

She turned her head and smiled. "Cute."

"Not enough?"

"Hardly. This is the twenty-first century, buddy . . . and what do kids get from the tooth fairy these days, I wonder?"

"You know, I don't know. I guess I need me some kids in my life."

"You and Francesca planning a herd soon?"

"Cute," he parried and swerved to miss a dead raccoon in the road. "Well, shoot, that's a shame."

"The coon?" she asked, twisting to look behind them.

"Yes, the coon. We all *coon-asses* gotta stick together, you know."

She made a sound. "They steal my apples. . . I thought coon-ass was naughty for *Cajun*, but I've heard Blacks called coons too. Which is it?"

"*We'z* coons, *they'z* coon-asses," he said in his best Louisiana drawl. Then he laughed.

"Cute," she repeated.

"You going to tell me about the Leap, and why you've got a burr under your saddle about it?"

"How about I save it for plane conversation?" she said. "It'll pass the time."

"Okay . . . but to answer *your* question—I suppose we'll wait a while before kids. You know, we haven't really talked about

288

uh, *bambinos*. Truth is, we haven't really talked about living arrangements either. Rufus just asked me. Hopes I'll stay on, but not sure how we'd do that. The tack room isn't exactly honeymoon-grade, now, is it?"

Senga snorted. "Just needs a wider bed. Speaking of which, how are you going to manage that—a honeymoon?"

"My agent wants to meet, and his office is in New York, so I'm thinking that could be a possibility."

"Hunh. Yes, I could see that. I've always wanted to see the angel statue in Central Park, myself. It's haunting. Or haunted. You know the one I mean?"

"Yeah, I do! In the fountain."

"That's it. But, what about Yellowstone or, the Tetons? Or both? Camp, or stay at Old Faithful Inn. I've always wanted to do that, too, but enough about me; what do you think Francesca would like? And how's she doing, anyway? You haven't said."

"Oh, she's fine. . . All right, I'll tell you," he said, then sucked his cheeks, a habit when sorting his thoughts. "She's told her family about us, and your grandmother about knowing you. And—our coming."

"Ah." Senga turned to the passenger window and said nothing for several moments. "And?"

"Well, I guess it's all good, Senga. They were happy for her— she said. Her grandfather set the tone, I gather. But she waited until she was alone with your grandmother for your news." He stole a glance in Senga's direction. Still gazing out the window. He continued.

"She told me the woman sat there for a moment, like a statue—like you right now—then stood up and walked across to one of the windows in her place; let's see . . . she opened one wide, both panes, and this is interesting—Francesca said she— your grandma—"

"*Nonna,*" Senga interrupted.

"What's that?"

Gabe didn't mean, *what's a nonna?* The phrase meant "excuse me?" He hadn't heard her.

"Grandma in Italian; *nonna* . . . what she wanted to be called."

"Oh yeah, you mentioned it the other night; sorry, *chère* . . . Well, as I was saying, *Nonna* spread her arms wide to the night sky—it was dark—and she . . . well, she said, '*Gabriele!*' Like that;

uh huh—my name in Italian. Strange, I know," to Senga's expression. "I asked Francesca about it, and she told me she'd forgotten the woman has a thing for the angel Gabriel, and to your granny—news of you must have come like the Annunciation or something; you know what an annunciation is?"

"I was raised Catholic, Gabe, so, ah—yes, I do. You mean, as in something's coming! Yes, don't you see? Very cool. But we're hardly the second coming." She chortled.

"Francesca said your, ah, *nonna* just stood there for a while, then turned and, still holding out her arms, grinned, and Francesca went to hug her. She also told me your grandma sees the actual windows *as* angels, and I don't know what to do with that. You think she's, um—"

"Absolutely not! On the contrary. Well, good. And she knows we'll be there on the fourth?"

"Yep. Oh, and Francesca's finding us rooms. Hope those passports get here."

"They will. Have some faith. So, did Francesca tell you this today? And you've waited till now?"

He threw her an exasperated look. "Just before we came in; we'd driven out to the road to get yesterday's mail, and Rufus suggested I call her. I think he's sweet on her," he flashed his wide Buddha smile in Senga's direction. She sniffled, rolled down her window, spat, rolled up the window and rubbed her nose on her sleeve, lacking a tissue.

"You know it's eight hours later there." Gabe checked his watch. "Let's see, right now it's 3:10 so, 11:10 p.m. there. Anyway. . ." He leaned to adjust the heat in the cab.

"How about we go get Joey and take him to Stricklands," asked Gabe. "What do you think? You have time? And don't be getting sick on me, girl."

"I'll be all right. Ah, we ought to call Caroline . . . see if she's ready. Let's do that first."

They did and she was. So, they passed Senga's turn-off and drove through Little Missouri River country, dotted with juniper, sagebrush, antelope and not much else. Senga would disabuse him of this notion, for the myriad herbs growing tenaciously low to the ground on the wind-swept plain.

They reached the Montana border town to find the boy feeling better, if weak. "To be expected," said Mae, who'd taken a liking to the kid, she told Gabe, and that she wasn't sure she wanted him swooped away quite yet.

Earl shot Gabe a look that told him it was time. "She's l' *broody*," he whispered out of earshot.

Gabe grinned. "All right, man, you got it," he told his friend.

"Have time for a beer?" asked Earl.

Gabe surveyed the empty roadhouse and said, "Sure, why not? Senga can get his gear—whatever he's got. Oh, that's right! We needed to pick up some more stuff for him, didn't we? Shoot."

"Taken care of. Mae went to town yesterday morning and got him a few things. He'll do for a while, I expect. Nice kid, though. Bring him up sometime, will you? I mean, if he's going to be staying with you for a while."

"Will do. I need to show him a few things before I leave for Italy. And we've got hunters coming at the end of next week. Hope it works out . . . wish us luck. What do you suppose he had? The flu?"

"Mae thinks it was some virus. So, vitamin C. Lots of it. She swears by it. Gets it by the pound. Ascorbic acid."

"You sound like Senga and her potions."

They drank in amiable silence for several moments, until the door to the kitchen swung open and Mae entered the room, carrying a trash bag.

Gabe hopped off his stool, "Where do you want it?" he asked, reaching out.

"It's the kid's shit—I mean *gear*, Gabe. And I've put a small jar of ascorbic acid in there."

"I told him about it," said Earl.

Senga appeared with Joey in tow. The boy looked wan and tired, but better than the last time Gabe laid eyes on him. *Funny haircut though.* At least he looked clean, he thought. Caroline would appreciate that. She had no patience for willful filth, she'd once told him. He'd wondered if she equated filth with *trash,* the derogatory kind.

He set the bag down and drank up the rest of his Stella Artois, then reached for his wallet.

"Your money's no good today, Gabe. Put it away," Earl said, then to the boy, "You come back and see us. Deal?"

Joey half-smiled and said, "I will and thanks a lot. Um . . . I owe you."

Mae added, "Just stay the *fuck* out of trouble while you're with Gabe's friends, or we'll come find you and, well . . . sorry; can't help the language." Then, she scrunched up her face, as if considering something difficult, and wrapped her arms tightly around the boy. "Be good," she said, "and take it easy for a few more days. You don't want that *sh*—uh, crap, to come back." She walked to the cooler.

Gabe wanted to pull out his notebook to record an impression, but decided against it. It would keep.

"No, I sure don't, ma'am, and thanks," Joey answered as Mae handed him a cold can of ginger ale for the drive.

"Open wide," Senga told him, then squirted a dropperful of *Echinacea* under his tongue. He made a face. Mae listed what the boy had been able to eat, and Gabe thought Caroline had such on hand. They waved goodbyes and Senga stifled a sneeze as she climbed back into the pick-up. She said, "Wait," and told them she was going to beg a dose of vitamin C.

"Make it a double," Gabe called after her, "and bring me one!"

Caroline held open the front door as Joey passed through. Gabe followed. Rufus muted the volume on the television, then looked over his shoulder from his recliner.

"Well, here's the young man himself," he said. "I'd get up, but I'm settled. Bum hip. Come here," he gestured, then addressed Gabe, "Senga with you?"

He shook his head. "Dropped her off."

Joey set down his sack and crossed to Rufus, who held out his hand. The boy looked at Gabe.

"He's wondering if he ought to, boss . . . getting over some virus and all," Gabe explained.

"Caroline can douse me with Clorox after. . . Gotta shake, don't we? I mean, I hear you're going to be living in my damn house for a while." He continued to hold out his hand and the boy took it. Caroline noted the firm shake and exhaled. Rufus abhorred limp grips.

"Good to meet you, sir."

Had Gabe coached him? Wondered Caroline. "That's nice and all, son, but just call him Rufus, please. We ain't fancy people, are we, Gabe?" She winked. "And, I'm Caroline," she said, walking over to inspect her new boarder more closely. "Well, Joey, you still look puny. What'd you eat today?"

"Um, some chicken soup, crackers, ginger ale; but I'm feeling a lot better, ma'am—sorry; Caroline. Just tired is all."

"Gabe, take him on down to his room and get him squared away, will ya? We'll uncover that well window tomorrow . . . won't seem like such a cave. There's beef vegetable soup for supper. Think you can manage that? We eat around here after evening chores are done, and they ain't been, so . . ." She quirked an eyebrow in Gabe's direction.

"Gotcha," he said. "Come on, Joey. First, I'll show you your digs."

Gabe couldn't believe the transformation. Caroline (by herself, he supposed) had cleared out her junk room, the warren-like space where she kept an old sitting chair for solitude. *Where'll she go now?* In its place, a twin bed had been set up with a low chest beside it. The second Tiffany-style lamp glowed warmly from it. The battered copy of *The Solace of Open Spaces,* by Gretel Ehrlich, lay beside it. A quilt done in blues and green covered the bed, and a crisp, white pillow case waited for the boy's head. She'd placed a second pillow at the foot beside another blanket, two towels and two washcloths. Her chair sat in the opposite corner.

Gone were the boxes of knick-knacks, culled books, memorabilia, four broken ladder-back chairs that Rufus hadn't repaired and two foot-lockers of archives. Gabe wondered where she'd stowed it all. When he showed Joey the bathroom, it occurred to him to check the unfinished cellar room, and there it was, in a heap. He didn't know how she'd done it alone and felt badly for not having been around to help.

He'd figure out how to make it up to her.

"Joey," he began, as the boy moved about the room, looking at this and that. "These are my friends. I don't just work for them. I want you to understand that from the get-go. You treat them nice, they'll treat you the same. You disrespect them . . . well . . . you'll have me to deal with. Got that? Just so we're clear."

He had similarly indoctrinated his first-year English students back at McNeese. Or, yearling colts. You set parameters early on. You show safe boundaries and point out pitfalls and consequences. And he watched, gratified, as the boy's expression grew soft; as though he'd been awaiting such direction all his life and could finally be at ease.

"Yes sir, I got it. . ." he said, looking Gabe in the eye; then, Joey moved his gaze to a framed print on the wall, of a sunset scene with horse and rider. "So, when you told me Rufus got burned, I guess I didn't . . . I didn't think it would be so—bad," Joey turned back to Gabe. "Which eye do you look at?"

"Oh, I guess I don't worry about that anymore. I don't even think about it—you'll see." Gabe tried to appreciate the kid's position, vis-à-vis his circumstances. While it wasn't exactly a "predicament," as Joey *was* safe and warm and among decent people, he felt a twinge of sympathy for the kid. Gabe smiled and stretched out his hand to lightly squeeze the boy's shoulder. "It'll be all right, kid. Relax."

He was banking mightily on hope.

Joey sank down on the bed and slowly moved his hand over the smooth fabric, looked around again, and up toward the darkened window, and then, he sighed.

Gabe heard all he needed to hear in it.

CHAPTER 45
SOUP TO NETS

After Gabe dropped her at her cabin, Senga plugged in the tree lights. "May it go well for Joey," adding, with a breath of uncertainty, "May this be a good thing to do." She spoke into the glowing green fragrance of the leaves.

Lifting the door latch, she noted the ease with which it worked and congratulated herself. She would make the soup, having postponed it for the walk, which had turned into a day-long excursion. But the boy was on his way to Strickland's and they'd do right by him, she knew. *He'd better do right by them,* she amended.

Gathering all ingredients on the counter and table, a habit she found useful to the ease of cooking, Senga settled into the familiar activity and allowed concerns to fall away. The dark green peelings of squash left her knife and dropped into the sink. Next, carrots; though these she merely scrubbed, then sliced. She added the cut-up vegetables to the pot of boiling broth, waited for a second boil and turned it down to simmer. Grated, unpeeled apple and a small handful of herbs lent color and taste.

When cooked, she'd mash the winter squash and carrots, then sauté chopped walnuts in butter, to add as garnish with the blue cheese. *Yes,* she'd make this for Sebastian and his family.

As the soup simmered, Senga moved to her wing chair and reached to open the thin drawer in her father's table, stopping in mid gesture. She recalled Gabe's words. *Your grandma.* It was *Nonna* who'd arranged to have this very table and captain's chair delivered to her in Sara's Spring, after learning of Emily's birth. They corresponded regularly in those days, she and Nonna; it was only after Emily's death the letters ceased.

In her numb state, she'd never wondered why. A wave of regret washed over her, and she recognized its cousin, *grief.* She held her head in her hands for a long moment.

The furniture must have been in storage in North Carolina. Senga realized she'd never questioned their provenance. "How odd. . ." she muttered, as she laid her hand on the table, then ran her fingers over the familiar grain of the walnut wood, smooth as glass. She opened the drawer fully and lifted out a sheet of paper, an envelope and a pen. The ritual warranted a cup of tea at hand and, given the weather, a warming fire beside her. She followed the same protocol when writing to Joe on the reservation, but this evening she recognized a distinction: *intellectual stimulation and love are different animals. . . It isn't so much intellectual, as* spiritual, *with Joe, but Love is spiritual, too. So what is the difference?*

Biology, she heard, whistling like a fireworks display before the *boom!* and she chuckled.

After a moment's silence, her mind settled and she acknowledged the message with a knowing calm that reached deep inside. She rose to heat water and built up the fire. As clocks had returned to Mountain Standard Time, it grew dark earlier and fairy lights shone through the south window. She wondered what time darkness fell where Sebastian lived. Something to ask him. . . "Dear Sebastian, have you ever taken these kinds of photos? Idle curiosity on my part."

The hissing of the pitchy log spoke beyond the periphery of her senses. It beckoned her, and she entered the writing, as one enters a landscape, a territory, a frontier; and there she traveled feverishly through the landscape of her longing. The cup of tea sat ignored. She felt, rather than thought; she saw Sebastian's face and hands, rather than imagined them; she tasted his mouth and smelled the clean linen scent of him; she touched him and he touched her. . .

At letter's end, she drank the cooled tea, then finished making the soup and enjoyed a bowl, its creamy texture a comfort. After a long, hot shower, she towel-dried her hair as well as possible, braided, then twisted it into her woolen hat, pulling it low over her brow. She followed this by drinking another cup of honey-sage tea, to which she added *Echinacea* and St. John's Wort tinctures. Sitting in her wing chair, she waited for a thick log to catch for the night, then she closed the woodstove door and fell into bed, where she said goodnight to Emily and slept the sleep of the cherished.

> *. . . and I fasten my hands on both sides of your face, to see you for you to see me and we are tossed together into the drink but the net is still attached to the wench above and we are saved.*
>
> *What time does darkness fall in Copenhagen now?*
>
> *My love,*
> *Your Senga*

PART THREE

CHAPTER 46
ANNUNCIATION

From her warm bed, Maria Teresa listened as early Sunday
morning church bells pealed over Lucca, in a riot of tones
and vibration, calling the faithful to Mass. *And am I not
faithful?* she asked silently, as she had every Sunday morning
since her return in 1975. Maria Teresa did not attend Mass,
preferring other devotionals: one, to enter the cool interior of
her neighborhood church and step intently to the candles. There
she would light five, for her sacred quintet: husband, son, her
namesake Agnes Maria (who went by *Senga*, last she'd heard),
granddaughter Emily and, finally, Francesca. She would then
bend slowly to the kneeler and make fervent prayers for each,
offering her suffering knees as penance.

In recent years, the age-old tradition of lighting waxen
candles had been replaced with an electronic alternative. The
larger churches—those mainly frequented by the tourists—
provided these, "in the interest of safety," explained the priests
and maintenance personnel. Maria Teresa was glad this was not
the case in her church, named for the *Annunciation*, "Where God
still speaks through burning bushes, and flames still dance above
heads at Pentecost," she once confided to Sofia and Nadia, who
did attend every Sunday.

She lay still. Her windows were closed against the cooler
mornings, but the peals crossed the glass membranes like light.
"*Bene, bene,* I rise," she said, taking a deep breath, then
remembered what Francesca had told her last night. Senga was
coming, and this fiancé named *Gabriele*.

Maria Teresa lay back down and pulled the cover to her chin.
With eyes to the ceiling (to blurry evidence of peeling paint), she
muttered to herself, in gibberish designed to provide her

company more than anything else. She allowed Francesca's information time to steep and, when she felt settled, pushed the covers off and turned to her side to rise at last.

The angina prevented her.

Pain in her jaw gripped like a vice, and she reached to the bedside table, where she kept a small glass of water, a bottle of aspirin and a pill box containing her tablets. She put one of the latter under her tongue and lay back on her pillow to wait. When the clenching continued, she chewed an aspirin, coughing from its dryness. She reached for the glass, coughed again and spilled water down the front of her nightdress.

A mewling sound escaped her lips and she looked about in confusion. "A little . . . more time, please. Just a . . . little," she mumbled, then pushed from the bed and padded to the bathroom. She cupped a hand under the faucet for a drink, then, feeling better—the jaw pain having subsided—she gazed long in the mirror, *"Grazie, Madonna,"* she whimpered and removed the wet gown.

Senga glanced at her bedside clock. It read 1:12 in the morning. She'd been awakened by a nudge from her old squeeze, *angina* in the Latin. She sat up, took a sip of the water she kept by her bed and the sensation relaxed.

"Hunh," she said aloud. Awake now, she stepped into her slippers and old blue robe and shuffled into the sitting room. The coals burned orange-red, and she opened the door to add another log, then blew to ignite it. She left the door open a crack, to allow air, until the pine caught.

From a shelf, she pulled down the bottle of brandy, poured a capful into a cup, and heated water. When the kettle whistled, she added it to the cup, with lemon juice and honey, and took a warming sip. *"Ahhh,* just what the witch-doctor ordered," and found herself perusing her shelves, where she kept her medicinals, books and other keepsakes. The cedar box holding the letters summoned her.

She set the mug on the table, then lifted the box from the shelf. Crossing to her wing chair, she sat down, clutching the old, miniature Lane chest close to her own chest. Then, reaching across, she set it down beside her toddy.

She took another sip. The smooth, fiery heat soothed her throat and quieted her senses. Grannie's letter lay on top of the packet, waiting for her. *And who else?* she responded to its silent allure. But she froze, lifting no hand to the note, and an image came. Of a doe, standing in a field like a statue, its head raised and trained on her. The buff shades of surrounding grasses, and the like-colored coat of the deer blended so perfectly, that spotting the animal came as surprise. This happened on her hike yesterday, yet only now had she remembered it. *Why?*

Misdirection, her strategy of choice, whenever she needed such help, had been used against her. The swooping eagle had prompted her to abandon her—*mission?* Yes, to leave the base of the cliff.

What was she supposed to examine, but was pulled away? *And now?*

The doe signifies the obvious in the hidden. She turned her head to the fire, blazing through the woodstove's window, and let impressions arrive unfiltered. Wishing to be nearer to the source of heat and light, she sank to the floor, sinking cross-legged, her back against the side of the chair. A draft chilled her ankles, and she reached for her shawl to cover them.

Senga waited, eyes penetrating the flames, and there it was, more correctly, there *she* was, at eight-years-old, leaning similarly against a cement-block wall. She heard Grannie's voice, droning, from inside the small house where Senga and her mother had lived, during her father's last deployment to a far-away country called Viet Nam. His funeral had been on this day.

Yes.

She'd crept to an open window, to better hear her grandmother describe what had happened to her mother after the burial, while Senga and her grandparents visited the post stables. The softly-spoken, dark words spilled over her, like the black paint her mother had evidently splashed everywhere in their house and had wiped on herself, her hair, her face.

She went crazy, she heard her eight-year-old self from the past tell her.

Yes.

And you hid it; you hid knowin' it, like that deer in the field.

Yes.

Everything around you's the same color.

301

Yes.

Except this man . . . What's his name?

Sebastian?

He's blue.

Well, he likes that color.

No, I mean, he is blue.

What do you mean?

In her mind, Senga experienced, more than merely *saw*, the early evening sky, its calm indigo rising, humming like a single bee, but instead she heard:

Like the sea.

But the sea can be green.

Maybe . . . but he's blue.

I still don't get what you mean.

True Blue. True Blue. True Blue . . .

Ah. Now you're playing with me.

Just trying to get your attention.

Well, you've got it.

Good. Now, you let go once.

Excuse me?

You let go, 'member? "Once and for all." Once you've let go, you can't do it again—let go, I mean. Don't you see?

No, I don't.

Kinda dumb for a grown-up, aren't you?

No. I am not. But you're kinda sassy for an eight-year-old.

It got you out of some messes, didn't it?

I suppose. What do you mean, I can't let go again?

Look, one time you grabbed holt of a rope, dangling from a hot air balloon, and you held on for dear life, 'member?

Yes.

Then, just a few days ago, you let go of that rope. I was there. And if I 'member right, you kind of fell down, down, down.

Yes, I did.

Well, did you land?

Yes.

Where?

CHAPTER 47
THE PURPOSE OF PURPOSE

Caroline stood at the bedroom window, meditatively sipping a second cup of coffee. Snow lay *soft*, like the white-down comforter on their bed, blue in shadowed creases. A blade of early morning light highlighted a missed rumple on the spread, she noticed . . . *and the land,* she added, glancing up, to the west beyond the car gate, in time to see Gabe jog by.

It never failed to amuse her, his horseless trotting.

In her day, spending ten hours in a saddle counted as exercise, and it wasn't even called that. It was just work. Work counted for most everything. They didn't ride as much as before, she lamented, what with the four-wheeler.

When had they last ridden? She couldn't remember. A damn shame, it was. "The horses need purpose!" she remembered her father-in-law preaching, often. *Hoped we'd get the hint,* she thought, then grunted. *And not just for the sake of the herd.*

"Hello?" came a voice from the stairs. Joey.

She swung around. "Good morning! You're up. How's it going?" she asked, moving into the hall.

"I'm better. Took a shower. That felt good," he said, as he appeared in the kitchen doorway.

His short sandy hair, still wet, looked as if a two-year-old had cut it. He wore the new jeans, hitched with a belt from his having lost weight, Caroline figured. *That plaid flannel shirt looks cozy.* He still appeared pale, but a hint of blush in his cheeks was proof *some* blood circulated.

"Who mangled your hair?" she asked. Bluntly.

He automatically raised a hand to his head and rubbed it. "Oh, my brother. He uses an electric razor. But it's grown out some. George told me to shave it all off, 'cause of nits—" He caught the possible misunderstanding and added, "No! I don't mean I *have* 'em, 'cause I don't."

Caroline was staring at his head, eyes wide. "Can I look, uh, just in case?" she asked.

"No, *really,* I don't, but you can check."

She gestured for him to take a seat and stood over him, inspecting the shorn head closely. "He sorta got carried away with that thing. You *wanna* look like one of those skin heads?" Then she remembered herself and swallowed hard. "You ain't one of those now, are you?"

She waited as Joey seemed to be asking himself.

After a long moment he said, "I . . . I thought I was, once. But I'm not. At least, I hope I'm not. I'm not even sure my brother is, and he's got all them tattoos."

She finished her inspection just as Rufus limped in. "What's this?"

"Joey needs his, um, *hairs* trimmed," she said, winking in his direction. "Grab me them scissors, will ya, hon?"

He opened a drawer, picked up the pair, and handed them to her, adding, "Mornin'" to Joey.

"Mornin'—um, what do you want me to call you again?"

"Rufus will do," he said, as he hung the cane on the chair back and settled slowly into the seat, with a wince.

"We have that appointment this afternoon, hon, remember?" said Caroline.

"Yeah, Caro, I know." He reached into his shirt pocket for his smoke fixings. "They beat me up, Joey. Those people are vicious—in the name of physical therapy. I come back hurtin' worse than when I left. Some doctorin'!"

"He complains about it," she told Joey, "but he's allowed one thing to bitch about, and that's it," she said, glowering at her husband as she tucked a tea towel around Joey's collar. Rufus glared down his nose at her and returned to his hand-rolled cigarette. Caroline made a sound, then proceeded to study their boarder's sorry excuse of a haircut.

Gabe leaned over to brush snow from his calves and shoes. He'd run to the mailbox and back, a new routine. Lifting his knuckles to knock at Strickland's kitchen door, he caught himself. *All right . . . if I'm to just let myself in . . .* But he stomped his feet to alert them, and turned the knob.

"Hey, y'all," he said, as he placed the mail bag on the table.

"*Gub,*" said Rufus, his lips rounded in an O, his eyes trained on a perfectly executed smoke ring.

Impressing the kid, thought Gabe.

"What do you think?" Caroline asked, as she nodded toward Joey, who was cutting a slice of toast in half.

"What—? Oh! You fixed his hair!"

She had. Joey raised his face to Gabe and smiled, then clamped his lips together.

Now something needs to be done about his teeth, Gabe noted. *He's self-conscious.* He mentally made a note to schedule a dental appointment.

"Didn't take much . . . just a snip here and one there, but boy howdy, I've seen worse-looking kids."

"He'll do," said Rufus, taking up his mug of coffee. "Any sign of lion, Gabe? Senga heard one the other night near her place, you know. They roam. You got Gus in with the flock?"

"Yep, I do. I was going to see if Joey feels like going over some things; you up for it?" he turned to address the boy, whose eyes had bugged at "lion."

"Yeah, I'm okay. I slept really good last night. Thanks," he addressed Caroline, "for everything."

Gabe thought she blushed; something in her eyes gave him the notion, and he turned away to prevent embarrassment. She'd just cut the boy's hair, an intimacy in some cultures. They might have bonded, he thought. "I need some coffee," he announced, and stepped to the thermos on the counter.

"Hey, Gabe, here's something for you," said Caroline, holding out a piece of mail.

He took it, examined the return address—from his publisher—and slipped it into his vest inside pocket.

"From sweet Francesca?" Rufus asked.

"Uh, no, boss, it's only been a week."

Gabe didn't know how much Dale had told Joey about their encounter at the Alzada bar. He wanted to avoid the subject, so he gulped down his coffee and told Caroline, Rufus and Joey he'd see them later, at noon. After, he'd show Joey the routine.

"Wait. Here's something else—" called Caroline. He'd just shut the door behind him, but turned, opened it again and reached for the letter.

"Thanks."

Glancing at the letter on his way to his room in the barn, he half-smiled. A letter from his father in Louisiana was always a welcome sight, but with it arrived melancholy for the elderly man. He wasn't prepared; no, not this day.

CHAPTER 48
PREVENTIVE MEDICINE

I *feel light, as air breathing light. Undulating waters swell and withdraw around my floating form and I extend my arms for balance. I seem to have landed from a waking dream, like a feather.*

The surrounding sea smells of oily fish and I taste salty brine on my upper lip. With one ear cocked beneath me, I hear deep calls of a whale, sounding for all the world like an elk I once heard. From the sky, I hear the far-off screech of a gull; no, no gull—an owl—a great, white snowy owl. He's come a long way, *I think to myself.*

Out of literal blue, two bald eagles swoop toward the water, and the approaching owl banks left to soar away. Both eagles' great wings foil, slowing their descent, in a perfect ballet of grace in motion. I recognize them; rather, I recognize their soul as one—the lovers of the Leap.

A makeshift litter, constructed of hastily lashed-together ponderosa saplings, floats into view on the moving waters, and the eagles alight on this; first one, then the other. They bob with the movement of the waves, cocking their magnificent heads this way and that; their forms, imperious, like colossal sculpture out of Egypt.

I am acknowledged silently, by a look, as I peacefully drift. The smaller bird lowers its head, opens its bright yellow beak and an object drops onto the litter-raft. I hear it roll between two poles and drop somewhere, out of view. The second raptor makes a single, high-pitched cry, and with the next swell, both unfurl their mighty wings and lift away. I follow their flight until they grow small in the sky. Reaching over, while treading with my right arm, I blindly run my hand along the rough length of the litter, discover the object and pluck it away.

A deluge from nowhere breaks the sky.

Thirsty, I open my mouth to ropes of rain, which obscure a descending outline of the returning owl. It becomes a man. He hovers over me, pink-

skinned, naked, arms outstretched like wings. His form, as cover, prevents the pelting drops, which pour off his suspended silhouette. The keening of the whale rises in volume, as I sense its ascending presence and, with no fear, I wait, wait, wait—and cry out. Then, a tremendous whoosh! *and sucking sound, and I lie pinned on the quivering back of the humpback whale, the man resting upon me now, his weight strangely absent.*

Desire calls to desire.

His eyes, as blue and shrewd as were his erstwhile owl's seek mine, and he fastens his mouth on mine and I wake.

I'd slept well and was reviewing reverberations of the *particular* dream (those that treat me sensually), when the phone rang. I answered it cheerfully.

"Hello?" I didn't recognize the name on the caller I.D.

"Uh, hi . . . is this Senga Munro?" said the woman who'd made an appointment to see me later in the morning.

"Yes; is this Cathy?"

"Yeah. Just checking directions again before I set out."

I described the route and, when I hung up, my earlier mood had evaporated. Heaviness now gathered about me.

"What the *fuck?*" I muttered aloud, then moved my head to the left, as was my wont, to dispel disturbing thoughts.

The woman had admitted to "many problems." So, I'll earn my consult fee on this one, I thought glibly, and shook my head again, regretting my unkindness.

No sense borrowing trouble, Grannie would have counseled. But I didn't hear the platitude in her voice . . . I heard it in my own. *Hunh?*

I banked the fire, ate my oatmeal and drank my coffee, brushed and braided my hair, smoothed olive oil onto my face, neck and arms and cleaned my teeth. After putting things to rights, I pulled on my hat, scarf and coat; grabbing my walking stick, I took my pesky apprehensions on a hike, whereby they'd usually abandon me for some other shiny object. . .

A mile up the road, I pulled the cell phone from my pocket and called Sebastian, my own shiny object. Voice mail answered—charmingly, in Danish—and I left a message:

"Hi. It's your land-locked mermaid. I have a new client coming this morning—send luck, as she seems scattered. That's code for possibly nuts.

*Tough ones to crack. Sorry—I'm speaking in idioms again. Anyway . . .
I'll try again later. Oh! Met you in my dream last night. Mmmm. Why I
was calling. . . I miss you, Sebastian. I love you. Bye."*

I hadn't meant to disclose the client information, so it must
have weighed on me, and I quickened my pace to ditch the
qualms. My health having returned, I decided I hadn't caught the
same malady as Joey. Normally, I don't catch viruses. Recent
human interaction, the culprit? *Yes, ma'am,* I heard. (Again, in my
voice.)

Grannie?!

The cell phone chimed in my jacket pocket, startling me. I
answered, "*Mmmm.* Hello, you." Sebastian.

"*Mmmm* indeed? So! In answer to your latest riddle—where
is it . . . Ah! Yes. *What did the brilliant artist shout to the libidinous
mermaid, as she floated on her back beyond the surf, catching raindrops in
her open mouth?*" He paused for effect. "I will meet you in our
dreams, and paint you as a raindrop on my tongue, and then, I
will swallow you, and you shall be reborn in our own shared, salty
waters."

"Well, now I'm wet, Sebastian . . ." I wasn't sure he caught
my meaning. "Did you just make that up after you heard my
message?"

"What message? Did you leave one? I only called hoping to
reach you."

I wondered if he was pulling my leg, and decided to allow for
magic instead. My footing felt oddly disjointed, as if I weren't
used to legs. . .

He spoke of Jytte's piano recital the night before, and I told
him about the boy, Joey, being taken in by the Stricklands. We
said goodbyes and I felt equilibrium return and, dynamic
disequilibrium or no, I welcomed it.

My client arrived fifteen minutes late, but I dismissed it as
miscalculation of distance. I watched the woman park and
stepped from the porch to meet her. Of medium height, she was
enclosed in an army-surplus overcoat, too large for her—and *she*
was large. I took a deep breath, smiled and held out a hand in
greeting. She reminded me of someone, but whom?

"Hi, Cathy. Senga Munro. Did you have any trouble finding me?"

"No. I know I'm late. Sorry."

"Come in. Would you like coffee? Or tea?"

"Coffee, please. Thanks." Distracted, her eyes flashed from this to that. "Quite a homey little place you got here," said the woman, "Kinda *weird,* too."

I said nothing to this and sought to remain equal to the prospect of an interview. I cranked my head to the left and back.

"Got a crick in your neck, or what?"

"A little."

I took the woman's heavy coat and hung it up, then indicated a chair, which she ignored. "*Rough,*" I judged her appearance, and sadly lacking in self-love. She proved more interested in her surroundings and snooped about. In general, I don't mind if someone shows a measure of interest, *polite* interest, but this bordered on nosiness.

"Let's get started, shall we?" and the woman moved to the captain's chair; I handed her the cup of coffee, then sat in my wing chair. "Tell me the problem," I said, open notebook and pencil in hand.

"First, can I ask you some questions? I mean your—ah, qualifications and all?"

I was mildly taken aback. In all my years of practice, so few had asked.

"Well, Cathy, herbal medicine isn't regulated like the medical profession. It's largely an educational model . . . at least those of us who practice hope people learn what we're, um, teaching."

"Where'd *you* learn it?"

She didn't appear to be actively confronting me; she seemed merely nervous, and curious. Better that than combative. Though I hadn't heard what her "problem" was as yet.

"From my grandmother." I answered. "She was a healer and herbalist. You got my name from Marie, at the health food store, right?"

"Yeah. You're right. She referred you. Sorry; I'm *pissy,* I guess. Part of the reason I'm here. Go on—what do you need to know? Oh, first, what kind of money are we talking for this?"

"I work from a sliding scale, Cathy, based on your income."

The woman's lips pinched together and then she nodded.

I changed my tack and asked her to first fill out my standard questionnaire, detailing prior and present medical issues, medications, supplements, diet, exercise and personal/social habits, and, by visual assessment, I determined the woman indeed needed some *shoring up,* as I think of it. But I needed to touch her, to ground our purpose, so I reached for her wrist, for a pulse reading. "May I?" It was fast. The hand was icy; the cuticles, jagged and torn. I squeezed her fingers and smiled. *Calmatives for nerves,* I listed on my pad. *Rapid pulse,* as well.

"What's the trouble, dear?" I asked the woman, who'd reverted to staring at the ceiling, then down to the floor, then out the window. She was avoiding me.

Denial appears in many guises, so, a different approach:

"*Where* does it hurt? Can you say?" This elicited a response, and she turned to me, her expression one of deep sadness. *At last,* I thought.

"My life sucks," she said, "I got me two kids at home with no pa to speak of—he's gone a lot, and another kid ran off with his older, dumb-fuck half-brother, who got mixed up with some *real* trouble this time . . . got hisself arrested again, and I don't know where the younger one is—could be dead on the side of the road or something. . ." Her eyes clouded up.

Oh shit, I thought. *Okay, treat the client, not the problem,* I reminded myself. My usual consultation technique might not work this time—to help clients see how they were already intact and whole. But, viewing oneself as victim was (inconveniently) the most common self-assessment. The art lay in guiding them to reconsider their perceived predicament as a place of power, opportunity and, in time, *beauty.*

"Um, do you live in the area, Cathy?"

"No. Idaho. My sister's taking care of my kids. I got a message from Dale—that's the son that's been in jail, and who was just arrested again . . . said he'd left Joey, the younger one, up in Montana, but he thought he'd be okay on his own . . . better than with him, anyway."

Shit shit shit. I inhaled slowly to three counts and exhaled.

"May I ask how you happened to wind up at Marie's? Were you seeking a remedy for something?"

"Yeah, I was. I *am.* My nerves are shot, lady," and from her ample lap, she raised a hand. It quaked like a cottonwood leaf.

She placed the other over it and lowered them. I studied her face for tell-tale signs. *Visible capillary veins, bad complexion, rheumy, yellowish eyes. . .*

"And may I also ask. . ." I looked at the form, under *Use of Alcohol,* noting the ten drinks per week . . . *well, maybe. . .* "When do you normally drink?"

"What do you mean?"

"Do you drink in the morning, for instance?"

"Yeah, sometimes."

"Okay. Cathy, I suggest several things. Herb-wise, milk thistle and dandelion can help your liver, though the best thing is to stop drinking. But I expect you know that." I felt for her.

The woman stared at me, took a breath and reached for the mug of coffee, to which she'd added four heaping spoons of sugar.

I continued: "But the important thing is, to identify *why* you want to drink—the soul of the matter—then, we help you see the reason differently. . ." On one level the woman desperately *wanted*, and perhaps needed, to escape reality, but healthier alternatives abounded. Reading came to mind. Or daily walks. I jotted down *St. John's Wort* on my pad, against low-grade depression.

"I got me these kids and I'm falling apart. What's to see? I don't know what'll happen to 'em if I—And my sister's got her own problems."

If she what? "Why did you come all this way?"

"To find my kid! What else?"

"Why now, Cathy? Why didn't you look for him sooner?" I was treading water here, but felt the question important.

"What do you mean, *sooner?*" Her head jerked up. "I just found out he was over here! Fucking George Canton and that lot."

"Who is George Canton?" I asked, knowing I ought to excuse myself and go call Charlie, but I couldn't, so I prayed for help and hoped it would come.

"The fucker's dead . . . Dale told me that. But he's the one—him and Jacob Brady—got Dale interested in all that *white pride* horseshit. Piece of shit—Jacob."

Cathy was getting worked up and I wanted to calm her, so I stood up, reached for her coffee, walked to the sink and poured it out.

"What the hell! What are you doing?"

An unintended consequence—she grew more upset. So, caffeine dependent, too.

"You need something less stimulating, and this isn't it. I'm fixing you something else. You here for some help or not?" I asked, minding my tone, as I reached for the chamomile.

"Yeah, but . . . okay, yeah." She wrung her hands again in her lap. I'd only seen one other woman do this, back in North Carolina, when I'd delivered her monthly sack of yellow dock, or *yellow root,* as it was called.

Yes . . .

Grannie had shown the woman how to bruise the cooked root and apply a soaked cloth as a poultice, against her eczema. I recalled the plant was also helpful as a blood purifier and detoxifier, specific to the liver. I stood and crossed to a large jar on an upper shelf. I brought it to the table, unscrewed the lid and lifted out two roots.

"What are those?"

"Yellow dock. I'm going to show you how to make a tea with it, to which you'll add milk thistle tincture and drink it four times a day, if you want, that is. . . Yellow dock's also good against constipation and you haven't said, but I'm guessing your digestion's slow?"

"Yeah. How'd you know that?"

"A lucky guess," I said over my shoulder, as I returned the jar to the shelf. Grannie would have described the woman as "bilious" and treated her with barley water, judging by her appearance and ornery disposition.

"I quit smoking a couple months ago—haven't been regular since."

"Good for you, and yes, it happens. Now, *watch.*"

She did. With interest, I was gratified to see. I saw the woman's features soften, and there they were—both Joey and Dale. "Hunh," I grunted.

"What?"

"Oh, nothing. Just thought of something." I brought out my pruners and cut several thin slices of the root. "These you'll put

313

in the pint jar, pour boiling water over them, screw on a lid and let it steep for thirty minutes. *Thirty minutes,* that's important. Strain it, add a dropper of the milk thistle, heat it again if you want and drink it. *All* of it."

I stooped to a cabinet next to the sink and pulled out an empty pint jar. After placing the roots therein, I stepped to the shelves and reached for a small, labeled amber bottle. Milk thistle put up in glycerin, not alcohol. I tucked it in the jar and found a lid. Handing it to the woman I said, "Here you go, and be careful cutting the root with a knife—you have pruners?"

The woman looked at me as if I were insane.

"Well, a serrated knife works . . . and Cathy, ah, try not to worry so much. . . I know it's hard, but it just wears you down, the worrying." And here I did something I rarely, if ever, practice with clients. A form of misdirection, intended to turn a person's consciousness toward a more hopeful end. I employed Joe's image of the balloon, calling it *hope* in this instance, with its long rope, dangling over an edge of the basket. Why hope instead of faith, I don't know. It's what came to me, recalling my Franciscan's use of the phrase. I sent Joe a smile and thanks, and resolved to write him soon.

"Thank you," said Cathy, after the visual exercise, "Wow, that was . . . *weird*—how I could see that rope and everything." Then, the woman turned to her sack on the floor, lifted it to her lap and asked, "What do I owe you?"

Traiteurs, the traditional healers in Louisiana, accept no money for their remedies, else they won't work, Gabe once informed me; but in this case the converse might be true. Now and then, a client *needs* to pay, as an exchange of energy, with respect to their dignity, though they might not consider it such.

"What do you make an hour?"

"$8.79."

The questionnaire asked about employment. Cathy worked in a child care center.

"Then that's what I'll charge. And three bucks for the herbs and jar. That all right?"

"Well yeah. I, um, I appreciate it."

She rose, after handing me a ten, and two ones. "Keep the change." She reached for her coat, with which I helped her.

"You know, Cathy, we only addressed a couple of issues. Everything works together . . . health is a combination of factors, I've learned. It might be helpful to find someone to work with where you live. Or, go to the county health clinic, to see if they offer counseling. From what I've picked up, you have a lot on your plate," and I made a point to meet the woman's eyes and hold them, to send my intent and good will, until those eyes turned away.

She buttoned up and I handed her the jar and sack she'd set on the table. I opened the door. A bracing gust rushed in, sweeping away earlier energy I'd felt around my visitor. I ushered her onto the porch and quickly shut the door behind us.

"Definitely weird," muttered the woman as she passed the orchard gate. Two crows lifted off the raised platform opposite the orchard.

What's weird? I wondered, in defense of my environs.

When her car reached the highway, I watched it head north, then I turned to the feeder, to check its peanut stash. As the high platform was mounted on a post, I had to step onto a nearby stump. *Definitely weird* echoed in my mind. Encircled by three peanuts (*to brace it?*) was a half-inch diameter ball, deeply tarnished. I picked it up; it had heft. I slipped it into my pocket, stepped down and went to the garage for more peanuts to replenish the feeder. My heart thrummed, as though I'd just drunk three cups of strong coffee, but I wasn't wired, just awake, and my dream slammed back into my consciousness, like breakers on a sea wall. . .

I returned to the cabin, dug out a piece of steel wool and began cleaning the marble *steely*—what I thought this must have been. But it wasn't corroded, only tarnished. After applying a rarely-used silver paste, allowing it time and then polishing the ball to a mercury brilliance, I decided it was a piece of solid silver. I added it to my growing collection of crow treasure. Then, I called the Stricklands.

"Hey, it's me, Caroline. Uh, is Joey around?" I asked.

"Nope. He's with Gabe. What's wrong?"

"Oh, nothing, but . . . well, his mother was just here."

"*What?*"

"Yes. So this is what I think: she doesn't know where he is, and I didn't want to say. After speaking with her, I think the kid's best off for now with y'all. So, I've got her phone number. Would you tell him to call her and to use that unknown caller feature, where you dial *67 before the number? It'll set her mind at ease . . . and, just to say he's all right and that he'll stay in touch. Should be enough, don't you think?"

"How did you—oh, never mind. Yeah, I'll tell him. Hell, if it gets any deeper around here, we'll need a goddamn boat, Senga. What's the number, hon?"

CHAPTER 49
A GIFT FOR
UNDERSTATEMENT

*H*ave you ever taken these kinds of photos, Sebastian?" he read in Senga's letter, which arrived in the morning post. She and Gabe would arrive in Florence in four days. The letter had been written three weeks ago. *Stubborn woman,* he thought; *she could have simply asked me on the mobile. Why this damned insistence on traditional mail? So much can be misconstrued, or lost, in the time it takes to arrive. As in context,* he added. But he was prepared for the question, as he anticipated her curiosity, theirs being similar. And, it was natural, after all.

Her pointed phrase, *these kinds of photos,* stung, but he understood. The images were meant to be provocative, in the interest of Truth and Beauty, twin goddesses at whose feet he worshipped, if metaphorically. *If sentimentally.* Senga was another matter altogether.

He would reply as well as he could, by email, and consider carefully his response. Yes, he would tell her about a woman he had once photographed, who had modeled at the university for twenty-five years, her absolute composure and professional integrity intact. It was as though she had answered a sacred calling to the work, to assist and *insist* in the honest rendering of the female form.

Then, there was Danica . . .

After a particularly soulless advertising campaign in February of 2004, Sebastian made the acquaintance of a young barista of indeterminate age. He had been studying several photos at his coffee house table, the subject of which he could not now remember, when the barista interrupted him and bluntly asked, "Do you need a model?"

317

He startled and turned to look up at her. She was, in a word, lovely: a pouty red mouth and bold cheekbones, framed by long hair, twisted high off her elegant neck and secured in a chopstick; a firm, willowy body, well suited to any athletic endeavor and shown to advantage by the crisp, neat uniform. He smiled in reply, then asked, "And how long have you been modeling?"

"I've posed twice. You must be in advertising—judging by those pictures. How tedious for you!" she said. "Guess you need to make a living too, eh?"

"And so do you, judging by your uniform. I'd like a café crème, please, and, ah, no, I do not need a model. How old are you, dare I ask?"

"Old enough, mister," she said over her shoulder as she turned to fetch his order.

When he returned the following week, she waited on him again. He noticed she looked tired, and asked if she had worked late the night before.

"I did a shoot for someone, and yes, it was late. Café crème, right?" she remembered.

He nodded, then, "Do you attend university?"

"In fits and starts; I mean, I have, but not at present. My life is complicated. But the offer to model still stands," she said and left for his order.

When she returned with it, he gave her a slip of paper with his name and address. "Can you come on Friday morning?"

She beamed. "Yes!"

When she arrived, he showed her where she could disrobe and slip on a kimono—this to ensure she would not simply bolt after learning his intent. As it was winter, and his apartment's living room wall mostly glass, chill was a constant guest, so he built up the fire. She appeared and tension squeezed the back of his neck, as though a great hand directed him. He sensed unease creep up his backbone.

"I can't use you."

"What? What's wrong?"

"Something is not *right*," he demurred as he stood by, trying to sort out his explanation.

"But it's *nothing* to me," said the girl, "Except a few *kroner*, I suppose," she added.

"You have been mistreated—by a man, or men. Am I wrong?" he asked, in the gentlest way, but not at all comfortable with the frank assessment. The pressure at the back of his neck increased, while the girl's demeanor flashed, first angrily, only to deflate before his eyes. She turned in search of a chair and, seeing one, dropped into its cushioned frame, revealing the top of her naked thigh. She shook her head slowly. "And so?"

"How old are you?"

"Twenty-one, just last month . . . but how did you *know?*" she asked, staring into her lap, then drawing the folds of the kimono tightly around her.

"I *don't* know. It was just a guess." He crossed to another chair, picked it up and set it before her. He straddled it backward, effectively creating a barrier between them, and crossed his forearms on the squared back.

He began, not at all sure of his direction, "You are a beautiful *young* woman, Danica; much too young to be modeling. You do not possess . . . how to say this without offending?" He wished she would look him in the eye, but she avoided his gaze. "Would you look at me? Please?" She would not. He continued.

"You haven't the proper—or *necessary*—sense of yourself for this work. Your youth was my initial concern, but your admission—well . . ."

She glanced at him and he made a face in frustration. "Want some coffee? I do," he said, then pushed off the chair and turned toward the kitchen area.

"Then why did you ask me here?"

"That was a ruse. I wanted to speak with you in private and believed you'd come only if I pretended. I am sorry; please forgive me." He'd turned to her, French coffee press in hand. "Listen, I think you need to visit a counselor to talk through the mistreatment. Have you told your parents?"

"Of course not! They already believe I am lost—and responsible for the attention I attract."

Tricky ground. *God help me.* He looked at her and, slowly shaking his head, he hoped to disabuse a mistaken notion by her parents. Returning to his task, he presently brought their cups into the room on a tray. "Cream? Sugar?"

"Both. . ."

Danica Olsen. He remembered her full name now. Following the coffee, she had dressed (he had turned his back to her brazen disrobing), to leave shortly after he showed her his favorite photographs, two of which depicted the mature female model. Danica's eyes widened as she studied the woman's attitude and bearing.

"She resembles a wild thing," she had whispered.

"It is because she knows *who* she is, Danica. Now, please go home; sit down with your parents and tell them what happened to you. Everything. Ask for help. They will find it for you. I believe this," he said to her, reaching for her chin to gain her attention. "And return to school. There is nothing like academia to sweep away old cobwebs and, for such a lovely young woman, you have too many cobwebs."

He smiled at her when she turned once to look at him.

Sebastian paused from his contemplation. He wondered about the girl, and then wished her well.

Dropping his eyes to Senga's folded letter in his lap, her practiced handwriting, a magical cipher, he wondered if she harbored secrets. Would she tell him, and, did they matter? Of course they did, he chided himself; *we are the sum total of all our secrets—among other mysteries.*

> *Dearest Sebastian,*
>
> *Have you ever taken these kinds of photos? Idle curiosity on my part. You have a gift for isolating the obvious, if this makes sense. I try to view the photos dispassionately—hard to do when I'm the subject— but, even I can recognize understatement. At my age, it's gift to be able to view one's physicality with some surprise, even love. Yes, especially that. And I don't know if it's your love or mine for mine own self, or ours combined. For this, I thank you.*
>
> *I've let several moments pass. The fire warms my left side as I sit near it. It's turned cold again. We've had a snowfall. I'm just now making the soup I described earlier. A long hike, first, to the place where I believe I saw those persons lying. I was given to wish*

320

them well and move on, after a cheeky eagle swooped by
in a roll, then flew to a tree top. He was giving me 'what
for,' as we say here. I had trespassed, apparently. So, I
trudged on to Stricklands, where I ate lunch. I also
asked them about the Leap and if they knew the
history.

Seems a Cheyenne woman and her lover gave away
their lives. (I don't like to say "committed suicide." It
sounds clinical, don't you think?) The man was from
another tribe, says Rufus, ". . . and why do you want
to know?" he demanded. So, I told them I'd seen the
couple. It's the kind of thing they expect from me
anymore and, with Gabe out of the room, I didn't have
to give details. He would have pressed.

Gabe was taking me home, when we decided to fetch
the kid from Earl and Mae's in Alzada. He's feeling
better, but I've come down with the virus. We have a
saying: no good deed goes unpunished. It may be related
to paying the piper. I'm taking my herbs.

Enough of the mundane.

I miss you.

When I saw the photo of you on the cell phone, I
realized I'd dismissed your presence as though I'd merely
(!) turned off a light, and then, there you were, turning
me on. HeHe. That's a joke, son (as we also say. . .).
Seriously, could I fold myself into the cranny between
your jaw and clavicle? Just live there? I won't bother
you, I promise. I have lived missing my Emily. This is
who I am, a woman with a large hole in her heart; but
missing you is different: I know you live. And I know
you love me in this time-and-space-dimension-thingy.
Excuse my lazy description.

My Pooh. I want to lie entangled with your body,
like fishing net; there am I caught, all squirm and
movement, drawn from the depths, gently; wet, cold and
wild; then, lowered onto your body, I tear away your
clothing so we are skin to skin; I cover you with kisses,
my scales slippery smooth against your nakedness. To
feel your cock against me, until you discover the bottom
of my cavern and you touch me there and I holler and

you holler and we pull the net around us and roll over and now from above me you take my breast in your mouth and I feel electric to the end of my tail fin and I buck you into the air but the net holds tight, then I feel you inside all fire and ice and my hair snarls beneath you and you draw it away and then I feel the Thing coming and cannot ignore it and I am pulled and I fasten my hands to both sides of your face to see you for you to see me and we are tossed together into the drink but the net is still attached to the wench above and we are saved.

My Pooh. What time does darkness fall in Copenhagen now?

Love,
Your Senga

CHAPTER 50
HEART-WISE

Francesca tittered. She never tittered and grew impatient with herself. Gabe and Senga would arrive tomorrow, mid-afternoon, in Florence where she would meet the plane and return with them to Lucca. Two rooms waited in a nearby inn, one her mother had insisted upon, as it belonged to a friend. The Italian economy depended upon such loyalties. Francesca knew the woman and expected the accommodations to be pleasant, but asked to take a look, just in case, under the pretext of seeing what else she could provide for her friends' comfort, "above the beautiful and most adequate amenities."

Little might have improved the warm Tuscan ambience of the place, and Francesca was pleased, giving her surprised mother a hug in gratitude.

Francesca had suggested they wait until the following evening to host a dinner, as Gabe and Senga would feel jet-lagged and might require some time to catch up to themselves. Her mother had agreed and asked her to remind Maria Teresa of the time and day.

In the days since her disclosure to Maria Teresa about Senga's visit, Francesca had occupied herself in several capacities, foremost as her mother's daughter. If there was to be a wedding then myriad details loomed, she had warned Francesca. *Sì, Mamma, sì,* she had repeated. The detail which hung in the air like a bad smell to her mother (guessed Francesca) was the absence of a date. How could one plan anything with no date! the woman had complained. But Francesca had other obligations, and it was all simply a matter of logistics—something she happened to be very good with, or so she reminded her mother.

Nonno continued to support his granddaughter with winks, furtive grins and eye-rolling when his daughter-in-law threatened to undermine Francesca's joy. And, she noted, he and Maria Teresa colluded on her behalf as well. Last week she caught them discussing possible gifts. The once-rare visits of the purple-clad *strega*, or witch, as Carlo affectionately (sometimes) called the old woman, grew more frequent, as it appeared she'd altered her route to the twice-weekly market.

Beside the front door, *Nonno* had placed a cushioned chair beside his, and begged Maria Teresa to sit *uno momento* with him. This she now did. It pleased Francesca to see them together, perched like (*Scusi, per favore,* she begged) two old owls surveying their domain.

Nonno had permitted Francesca to trim his beard weekly and she had conferred with the barber who usually cut his hair, that when she was away, he was to inform *il Signore Albinoni* that she had charged him (the barber) with trimming it along with his hair. Her father teased *Nonno* about Maria Teresa, but the banter rolled off the backs of everyone, in deference to the old man. It was expected, the teasing, and, the acceptance of said teasing.

In Denmark Sebastian had lain awake for hours. Knowing Senga was flying over the great water—somewhat in his direction—utterly interfered with his rest. He could not settle. So he rose in the darkened apartment, stoked the fire then stood at the windows for several moments before remembering he was nude. Feeling chilled, he moved toward the woodstove in time to watch the new log alight. Flame shadows flickered on walls, into the large mirror, over the furniture and, finally, onto the near life-size photograph perched on the easel. Of his Senga. The last in the series of thirty.

He had finished.

At the stove he paused to warm his groin, then backside, and then stepped aside to watch the light-play again. The black and white image animated in a *chiaroscuro* dance, and not solely on account of the light—though by definition, photography and light were considered one and the same or, at the very least, "drawing with light," whence came the word from the Greek: *photography*. He had named this image *The Question*.

Senga, awash in ambient light, in a white silk robe, whose colorful pattern of oversized, blowsy peonies seem to pulse in the firelight; her hair, free and wavy, cascades down her back; the flowing fabric loosely cinched around her waist, draping open above, reveals a partial view of a breast. Beside her, the twisting spiral staircase—its own elegant, helix movement, rises up and away, like leftover notes of a song.

In the photo, Senga stands poised to step onto the first rung, pale right hand raised to dark steel banister, her expression one of blithe satisfaction *and* question as she looks over her left shoulder, as if someone has just spoken her name.

As he had. Their session had ended (or, so she'd thought) and her response proved beautifully natural. She had laughed afterwards, ascending to the loft to wait for him.

Her capacity for response was astounding. She was the most receptive woman he had ever known. "You, my dear, are the embodiment of the soft conquering the hard," he addressed the photograph, paraphrasing Lao Tsu. *That the soft conquers the hard, the yielding the resistant, is a fact known by all, yet utilized by none.*

He became hard.

The heat from the fire, in concert with the image, multiplied his depth of feeling; all three conspiring, and he permitted this break with protocol and fetched the tea towel. Then he leaned back in one of his chairs and willed Senga alive in fire light, imagining her face slowly turning toward his, her left hand reaching for him. He closed his eyes and she was there.

When his need was met, he missed her all the more so. Yet the expression on her face reflected the constancy he most desperately needed to see.

Seven days before, as he rose to leave his favorite table at *The Four in Hand,* he heard a woman's voice say, "Mr. Hansen. Would you remember my daughter Danica?" He swung around to the voice and looked down, for its source was the tiny bird of a woman who had greeted him near the door the first time he visited the café. He had not encountered her again, in order to review their acquaintance. And now, he knew.

Danica Olsen stood beside her. Grown now, stunning and clearly still interested. She wore the sentiment like her expensive *parfum,* he remembered thinking. Had she ever spoken with her parents, as he had entreated?

"Danica. Please, sit down," and he held a chair, first, for the older woman, and reached for another for the younger. He resumed his earlier seating.

"To answer your question, ma'am—yes, I remember your daughter."

"Call me Birgitte, please." She was carefully dressed, as particular women of a certain age might when meeting friends for lunch. Her makeup was minimal, mainly because she did not require it. She had taken care of herself.

"Birgitte then." He smiled, then turned to Danica who exuded a lusty and life-affirming presence. "It has been a long time. How are you?" he asked her.

"I am well, Sebastian, thank you, and you?"

"The same. What are you doing these days?" he asked. Pointedly. Searching her eyes. A server appeared, to ask if anyone wished to order. Danica and her mother asked for lattes and he declined. Behind the bar, a loud crash of shattering glass drew the customers' attention, to be dismissed after the hapless server apologized.

"Danica is practicing in Paris, Mr. Hansen. She is a psychiatrist . . . a doctor! Evidently, having you to thank," she added, smiling coyly.

His eyes shifted to Danica, who sat quietly self-possessed, gloved hands resting in her lap. Demure. She smiled and lowered her head. He studied her appearance. She wore an off-white coat, fitted, with a thick brown scarf wrapped around her neck and shoulders. Her hair was smartly styled, now short. Gone was the brash makeup; he recalled the pouty red lips. Nine years had passed. She would be thirty now, he calculated. *She could be my daughter.*

"I . . . I am confident Danica might have only herself to thank, and her parents—Mrs. Olsen, is it?" He looked back to her and she nodded.

"Birgitte, please. Danica returned to her studies and chose psychology after your, ah, intervention, Mr. Hansen—"

"Sebastian."

"Ah, Sebastian then. . . . She told us what transpired at your home; also, what, ah, had previously happened to her. We are deeply grateful for your kindness—and your courage; not many people would have cared."

The coffees arrived, giving the older woman time to compose herself, as she seemed overcome, he thought. He stole a glance at Danica, who was helping her mother unbutton her heavy coat. (The room, he had noticed, was warmer than necessary.) *Why, Danica, you have grown yourself up.* It intrigued him, her transformation. She appeared to be whole, *healed,* and he caught Birgitte's eyes on him as he assessed her daughter. In embarrassment he coughed and asked to be excused for a moment.

When he returned Danica sat alone. "Where is your mother?" he asked, glancing around the room.

"She needed to go, Sebastian. Said we might catch up better on our own."

"Ah. Pity. I enjoyed her, and I didn't say goodbye, Danica. I wish she had waited." He noticed Birgitte's coffee cup sat near full at her place. *Why then did she order it, and at these prices?*

The server approached to remove the mug and Sebastian caught the side-long glance delivered in Danica's direction. It was not an admiring one. *What is this?*

"Do you still live on *Sønder?*" Danica asked before taking a sip of latte.

"I do. But I spend some time in the United States now. My aunt left me a home there."

"Ahh! How exciting for you! Where? New York, I hope?"

He shook his head and the game of chess came to mind. "Are you familiar with a region called the Black Hills? In the middle of the country. Rather rural, but most pleasant. Little traffic."

"No, can't say I know it. . . And do you *like* the Americans?"

"For a psychiatrist, Danica, you should recognize an unfair question." He smiled, and watched her squint for a moment, as if she were taking his measure—*utilizing her hard-won degree,* he surmised, and a yellow flag of caution waved. "I have met more than several Americans whom I like, and have grown to love one in particular." He caught the slightest suggestion of judgment cross her vision. She moved a still-gloved hand from the mug to rest it on his forearm.

"An American woman? Sebastian, how adventurous of you! A fling then, surely."

Caution merged with discomfort and he wished to leave, but she interrupted his malaise.

"I am sorry, Sebastian, how rude of me . . . please forgive me," and she squeezed his arm, then raised her hand to her hair, to smooth an invisible errant lock.

Sebastian recognized flirting when he saw it and now felt annoyed. And, disappointed. For Birgitte—in the main. But this may have been misplaced as well. Perhaps they were similarly scarred—mother and daughter. He resolved to take his leave as soon as gentlemanly possible, and was relieved for having read the situation so quickly, so as not to have disclosed too much of his personal life.

Danica was observing his thinking and it unnerved him; her eyes were eerily vacant.

"How long have you been practicing and living in Paris?" he asked, determined to end this soon.

"I secured my license just out of university and moved three weeks later. So, five years now. I live in the Marais. My office is actually in the apartment as well, so most convenient . . . a beautiful old apartment near *La Place des Vosges*. The building has one of those tiny elevators that were installed later, and for which my clients are exceedingly grateful. I live on the fourth floor, you see."

"Ah. Wonderful district, the Marais. The antique stores, I remember. . . I'm curious—do many French speak Danish?"

"I offer sessions in English, Sebastian. It suits. And I have several French clients who find the language practice helpful—even insightful."

"Yes—linguistics is an art whose secrets are ever shrinking. Are you with someone, Danica?" He immediately regretted the question.

"No. Why do you ask? Interested?"

Queen to Knight—Check.

He said nothing; then, wishing to be understood, he simply and quietly said, "I am in a relationship, Danica," and with his eyes, he sent her an unwavering confirmation of this, then turned to their server who was leaning against the bar, probably within ear-shot. Sebastian made the universal gesture for check and retrieved his wallet from his inside pocket. "Please tell your mother I wish her well. She seems to have found some peace for you, Danica, in her mind. I wish you well, also . . . and—I wish you love. It is the great healer."

Not convinced of his method, or choice of words, he set down the necessary *kroners,* added a tip and replaced his cap on his head. Then, he picked up his satchel, which held his laptop, and stood. He had been writing to Senga.

Danica watched him silently, with only the slightest frown, he noticed. Sighing, she brought her purse to her lap, opened it, drew out a silver card case and extracted one. Handing it to him, she said, "Here is my information, Sebastian, if you should ever wish to reach me. I am available for video calls as well." She smiled, tight-lipped, shut the bag (from *Hermès,* he noticed) with a loud *snap!* and stood.

He offered his hand to her, but she moved into an embrace, from which he managed to extricate himself without seeming churlish. He saw the server in the background shake her head and look away.

"So what do you do with the rest of your day, Sebastian?" Danica asked when they were outside. The steel-gray sky oppressed him. At one time, he had simply grown used to it, but having lived where clear, blue skies were the norm, he found the difference hard to bear. Glancing in the direction of his daughter's home, he quickly adjusted his features and told Danica his granddaughter waited for him. That he was late.

Checkmate.

She had no response to this, saying only, "Then we'll say goodbye, Sebastian. It was good to see you," and she turned in the opposite direction to be soon lost among scurrying pedestrians. . .

What just happened? he wondered, as he made his way up the street. He turned onto *Sonder* Boulevard, happy to see the lovely, familiar, pastel-colored homes, painted thus to cheer and distract the recently discomfited and lonely.

His fire (metaphorical and literal) had burned to low coals and the room grown chilly when Sebastian roused himself from the comfort of the lounge chair. He was stiff with cold and had managed to cancel the euphoria of Senga's nocturnal visit by ruminating on that strange day in the café. He swore and stooped, near shivering, to add another log, his cock in absolutely no danger of being accidentally knocked, having retreated to safer ground. "Castle your King," he muttered, then swore again, against the chill and rose to fetch his robe and slippers. *How does she do it—wake to cold every morning?*

Thinking of Senga, a plan hatched, full-blown or, grown, like Athena from the head of Zeus. "I make no comparisons," he again muttered.

After building up the fire, he checked the time. It was 3:35 in the morning. He made coffee, then settled before the computer to check train and flight schedules to Florence.

"Damned if she sees Tuscany without me," he declared and took a deep breath as a website appeared on the screen. The familiar image of cypress trees and vineyards, their colors lit by early or late afternoon sun, warmed him, and he began to anticipate the travel. He had much to do in the next twenty-four hours, but his heart beat in time to his joy. He calculated he could arrive mid-morning of the sixth. A feast day, he recalled. Old Saint Nicolas.

Indeed. . .

CHAPTER 51
THE FACE OF GOD

I told Gabe about the Indian and the buck. After switching on my overhead light, I drew a quick sketch of the hunter on a page of his small notebook, to show him. I described the non-typical antler and he admitted it could have been the same deer taken on the ranch.

His eyes widened as I described the arrowhead's discovery, and wider still at the news of Rob's and my encounter with Dale on the Leap. At mention of seeing the apparition below, he inhaled deeply, but his expression betrayed nothing in the dim light. I told him about Rob's visit and a little about the song he'd composed for Emily and me. Finally, I described what happened with the lamb. Or, more correctly, what didn't happen. He sat for several moments with eyes closed, then rubbed his face all over with a hand.

"Does this sort of thing happen often?" he finally asked, quietly, so as not to disturb the passengers, ". . . these, ah, *sightings?*"

"No, no, it doesn't, Gabe. Not the seeing part, anyway. I get hunches, like everybody else, I suppose. Don't you?"

"Yep. Okay, well, for the moment all I can say is—well, hell, Senga, I don't know *what* to say. . . Told Sebastian?"

"He was as receptive as you—maybe less—"

"Now I'm not dismissing it, girl . . . I expect *being* there and *hearing* about it pale in comparison, don't you think?"

He searched my eyes for understanding and found it. "Joe's researching some things for me at Dull Knife College. I expect it's a bit hard to swallow. Just wanted to *share,* as they say. I don't like the use of the word. . . Let me rephrase that: *Fuck,* I just

331

wanted to *tell* you," I whispered, "There. So I have. . . I'm going to try to get some rest now." I reached up and snapped off my light.

"Oh, thanks a bunch. As if my blown mind will turn off now, *chère*."

I half-smiled. The auxiliary cabin lights dimmed and the drone of jet engines lulled us to find whatever rest we could before landing in Amsterdam. I arranged the thin airline blanket, sighed, closed my eyes and leaned back. Not comfortable, but fatigued enough to allow thoughts to drift, I settled into a kind of fugue state, the various sounds on board providing strange, shifting backgrounds of white noise. The last two lines from Magee's sonnet drifted up—or perhaps they inhabited this rarefied air, like resident sylphs:

> *And, while with silent, lifting wind I've trod*
> *The high untrespassed sanctity of space,*
> *Put out my hand, and touched the face of God.*

Mmmm. Then came a curious thought; that I was aboard a flying city, racing with the very air to stay afloat. The aircraft seated more passengers than the entire population of Sara's Spring. *Extraordinary.* I pondered travel—the literal, as now, and the figurative, as *memories* and these visions of seeming past events that collide with present experience. Travel, or striking camp, must be in our genes, I decided.

A tone to fasten one's seat belt chimed and I shifted in my seat. The scent of someone's perfume, lightly enough to welcome, wafted by. My mind turned to the previous evening.

I was making a last-minute inspection of the place before leaving. The arresting image of setting sunlight on the Leap— whenever I was in position to view it—had always moved me to stop and gaze, to acknowledge this marriage of stone and light. But last evening's spectacle demanded my soul's attention. Magnified by the spectacular effect of underlit clouds, the rock transfigured to rosy-golden luminescence, and the broad face of the Leap blazed (*like a face of God*). Bright crowns of pines shone, tipped in veritable gold leaf, and I remembered Papa's glowing tobacco barn at sunrise, and his worshipful demeanor.

I only observed the ritual with him the few times, but now I understood why it had so moved him. Here and now, in this peaceful interlude betwixt Earth and stars, he met me halfway. *Thank you, Papa, for everything. Thank you, Grannie, Mama and Emily. I love you.*

Last night, without having read Grannie and Mama's letters, I gathered them together, lovingly retied the pink ribbon, opened the woodstove door and placed them on a burning log. Feeling my own heart catch, the packet burst into flames and the words turned to white ashes that rose up the pipe, into the cold night air.

I no longer need to know, and now I may simply live. *And love.*

The week before he died, when Papa and I stalked deer in the forest, he taught me I needn't know everything, or needn't want to.

He was right. *No; he was wise. . .*

In that moment, and the next and the next, I was Astronaut, traveler to the stars, if only a few miles closer, yet subject to the thinning atmosphere of Earth. With peace and gratitude of my loved ones—my stars of infinite magnitude—I sensed their love winking and reaching out to palm my cheek, *Yes,* and I dozed.

Gabe sipped water as he peered out the window. They were seated in the rear of the plane, far enough that nothing interfered with the view below. A pale sliver of moonlight reflected off the massive wing. He glanced at Senga, whose open mouth suggested she slept. *Good.* He wished he could. It would be a long day. Maybe he could catch a nap in Amsterdam. *Damn,* he needed to use the john but wouldn't wake his seat mate. *Should've gone earlier.*

Her story disturbed him. But not because he couldn't believe it. On the contrary. Her "sightings" weren't anything he couldn't reconcile broadly with science, or even theology; either discipline was prepared to make the case for blips in time. *Well, quantum physics, I suppose, and what's Time to God?* But he didn't possess enough knowledge in either subject to examine her claim(s). He didn't know what he didn't know.

*Claims, hunh? Sounds like I'm the one questioning her stability. . .
And perception is a purely personal process, to do with meaning . . .
Significance is for Senga to parse in the end.* His writer sat mulling the
stranger-than-fiction account.

But if what she told me . . .

He grunted and refocused his gaze. Far below he caught sight
of a smaller aircraft moving in the same direction as they, the
same silvery moonlight glinting off silver wings, their beacon
lights blinking. He imagined near-incandescent, shimmering
ocean waves rolling on forever, when a feeling of incipient doom
bloomed in his chest, a time-lapse of a poisonous flower.

What? He lowered the shade, hoping the void's absence
might help. Acquainted with slow, deep breathing to allay pain,
he inhaled and exhaled from his mouth.

"What's wrong?" Senga asked blearily. The tired concern on
her features, even in the low light, gave him some comfort. Had
she heard his altered breathing?

"Ah . . . *anxiety*," he whispered, continuing.

"Claustrophobia?" She reached to unfasten her seatbelt.

"I *could* use the john," he said, still breathing slowly.

"Wait. Here, try this," and from her liquids baggy she pulled
a tincture bottle.

"What is it?" he asked, not feeling particularly patient with
her potion pushing right then.

"Valerian. Lift your tongue." He did and she squeezed out
several drops.

"That's *horrible*, girl!" His face scrunched in distaste.

"Shhhh now . . . relax, Gabe. I know—it tastes like dirty
socks smell. Come on, relax."

He huffed, then sat back and waited, struggling to slow his
breaths. "I'm better. Thanks. Um, I really do need to piss." He
waited as she screwed the dropper back on the bottle, slipped it
in her pocket and stood for him to pass.

In the tiny lavatory he closed his eyes as he relieved himself
and, after rinsing his hands, he studied his face in the mirror.
The existential fear had passed—*on its own? Or by use of the herb?*
That was the trouble—he never knew. But, he hadn't
experienced a panic attack in, oh, twenty years? Then, it dawned:
the last time he'd flown. *Damn.* It hadn't occurred to him. But it

wasn't claustrophobia. *Nope.* He'd been flying over the Gulf of Mexico, from Houston to Miami. *Water?*

Feels like somebody put a gris-gris *on me, yep.*

So, water. *Deep* water.

A low shudder startled him and he eased down to the seat lid. The unfamiliar sound repeated, seeming to come from the belly of the plane. His breathing caught again. He reached over to splash cool water on his face, and dried it with a paper towel. There was nothing to be done for it, whatever it was, so he rose and opened the door. An attendant sat nearby, leafing through a magazine.

"Um, excuse me, ma'am, but what was that sound just now?"

"Oh, that. Not to worry, sir; hydraulics cycling . . . but the seatbelt sign is on, so please return to your seat?" she said, ending the phrase in an inflection, a habit which annoyed him. It was a *professor* thing, he'd decided long ago. *You're a pain in the ass when you're scared, you know that?* he informed himself, as he picked his way back to his seat.

"All right?" Senga asked, properly, when he returned.

"Mm-hmm. Did you hear that sound?"

"Yes. What was it? Do you know?"

"Hydraulics. The stewardess—I mean, *attendant,* said not to worry." *Aren't they trained to say that?* "Ah, do you have that, ah, nasty tasting stuff?"

She raised her eyebrows at him and reached into her pocket for the small amber bottle. He opened his mouth and she administered several more drops. *Yep, dirty socks is right.*

"It helps. Thanks. And, it's deep water does it. I think. It's happened before, over the Gulf."

She looked intrigued. "Really," she stated; not a question.

He smiled sheepishly. "In Louisiana when somebody freaks, sometimes we say a person put a *gris-gris* on them. Ever heard of that?"

"You mean like a curse?"

"Well, I suppose." He watched her consider it; could see her thinking.

"Gabe. Do you remember ever being nervous around water when you were little?"

The cabin was quiet now. He had no idea of the hour, as they were crossing several time zones. Only a few other passengers were conversing. Senga spoke in a whisper and he strained to hear.

"When I was *what?*" he asked.

"When you were young."

He inhaled, held it, and exhaled. His nerves felt less on edge and the tightness in his chest had released. "My little brother drowned . . . when I was about four."

"Oh, Gabe, I'm so sorry. You've never said."

"Nah. He was supposedly taking a nap . . . crawled out of his crib and went for a walk, just like that."

"Jesus."

"He was only two. Allie wasn't born yet. He had on his holster and play guns. Guess they weighed him down."

"Were you there?"

"My mom and I were out back . . . in the yard. We didn't see him leave the house. There was this irrigation ditch that ran along the fence line. I—I haven't thought about this in a *long, ole* time. I'm sorry, Senga," he said, turning to her, her expression the image of the suffering Madonna in his grade school classroom.

"Gabe—"

"It's all right, *chère;* it was a long time ago," he said. "Weird, I've never put the two together," he added quietly, then sucked in his cheeks. He turned to face her once more. "Guess that's a curse—a little brother dying like that, and seeing him face-down in—" His face twisted in pain, more by an effort to restrain tears. But they came and he brought his fist to his mouth.

The tears belonged to his mother. They were hers.

Senga quickly lifted the center armrest, unfastened her seatbelt and reached for him. He felt her caring arms around his shoulders and she held on as he shook and nearly convulsed with the memory. He'd approached his grieving mother after and offered her similar comfort, young as he was, patting her heaving back with his small, dimpled, dark brown hands.

His heart threatened to burst in his chest now as he struggled to find middle ground between wracking anguish and repression. Senga pulled his head to her chest and managed to hold him until he calmed. She was humming something. The odd thought crossed his mind:

She's riding the bull for you, man.

Sensing a presence at my right shoulder, I turned my head to look. An attendant was standing beside me; a steaming white facecloth dangled from a pair of tongs. He said nothing, but met my eyes with compassion. I reached for the cloth and nodded to the man. It touched me—this simple kindness. Gabe may have nodded off. He lay heavy against me, but then stirred.

"Hey," I said, "Here's a warm cloth for your face. It'll feel good." I moved to wipe his forehead. He sat up, groaned and plucked up the cloth.

"It smells like something . . . what?"

"Um, I detect eucalyptus." I watched him mop his features, then use the cloth on his hands. "Better?"

"Better. Thanks. That . . . was unexpected," he said.

I understood him to mean his show of emotion, not the hot cloth. He sat at a loss of what to do with it, when the attendant appeared with a bowl. I took the cloth and dropped it in, then smiled at him. "Could I possibly have a cup of coffee?"

"We're just brewing some for breakfast. I'll bring you a cup. Cream? Sugar?"

"Both, thanks."

Turning to Gabe the attendant asked if he'd like something.

"Thank you. Just water for me," he added. The man disappeared down the aisle.

After sipping the coffee, I felt the familiar churning of mental faculty and broached the subject of Gabe's writing, as we'd seldom discussed his work.

"What do you want to know, Senga?"

I studied him for a long moment, to judge his condition. *How many layers does he have?* He'd learned to protect himself, I decided. He seemed recovered. I knew *seemed* sometimes misled the gullible. *Well, I'm not. Mostly.*

Having him talk about a passion might ease the distress, I hoped.

"Have you written since you were young? I mean, did you enjoy English in high school?"

"Yep."

Hmmm . . . he's balking. Why?

"Sorry. I don't want to intrude on your privacy around this, Gabe. I just thought—"

"Nah, *chère*, nothing like that. The thing about writing . . . it's just so very *shy*, and if you talk about it too much—well, it runs away and hides. I think it has to do with respect. I can't even *mull* a story unless I'm prepared to put down some words." He paused a few moments, then made a sound. "It's a little like staring at a couple of neighboring stars in the sky, where if you look at one directly you can't see it as well as when you focus beside it. Maybe look at the other, and its neighbor pops into view. Have you noticed that?"

"Yes, I get it. The analogy makes sense, in a *writerly* way. . . But you can say what a story is *about*, can't you?"

"Ha! Only when *I* know—and sometimes that's the harder chore—distilling it. My editor is better at it than I am. He cuts through B.S. But I do try to scribble a word or phrase, or a short description. You know—*ideas.*"

He yawned, covering his mouth, then reached into his shirt pocket for his notebook, where I'd sketched the Indian. He flipped through pages to show me his scraps of inspiration; I smiled and asked to see it. He feigned horror, then handed it to me. His handwriting was practiced and graceful. No rhyme or reason to the entries' order—just random content, with the newest about small towns and a quip about subtlety.

"Well, I hope you'll let me read more of your stories. Sebastian and I enjoyed 'The Carnival Horse.' He read it aloud to me." I handed back the notebook.

"Oh, yeah?" He reached for the window shade and lifted it, but didn't look out. Stirrings of dawn streaked the sky and passengers began to stir themselves. Leaning back, I stretched and almost upset my coffee.

"Whoa, girl, careful!" he said, quickly grabbing my cup.

I looked at him. "I'm glad I know someone who has an all-consuming passion, Gabe. When does the collection come out?"

"Oh, there's a lot to be done before that happens. Edits, proofing, galleys. But Senga, you *have* one . . . your life, as I see it, is nothing if not passionately lived."

I looked at him blankly, not comprehending.

"If you think for one minute that you only started living after meeting up with Sebastian, well, girl, *you done got another think comin'*—as my momma used to say."

I chuckled at his delivery. "I—I wasn't really present to it, Gabe."

"Yeah, you were. Maybe, *differently*. But you had your shit together—if I may be crude."

I wouldn't be swayed and countered. "I don't want to argue the point, but something's changed in the last couple months, and Sebastian *is* the reason."

"Has it occurred to you that he . . . happened . . . as a *result* of something, and isn't the cause?"

A folksy voice came over the intercom to say we'd be landing in Amsterdam in ninety minutes, a bit earlier than expected due to tail winds, and that breakfast would be served shortly. It went on to describe the customs procedure and that attendants would be handing out forms. I heard clattering behind us in one of the galleys.

"Oh, good—airplane food!" I grinned at my friend again. Ignoring his earlier comment, I said, "I don't know why folks complain about it—I think it's great."

"Senga," he said, reaching for my pale hand; his, the color of dark chocolate in the faint morning glow, and just then the cabin flooded with light. The stark outline of my hand resting under his underlined my emotions about him and I perceived the grace of it, the gift and the import, and raising my hand with his, I kissed his recently-scraped knuckles, injured on my account.

"You used my salve, I see . . . Gabe, I am so happy to be on this trip with you. And, your sweet Francesca is a most fortunate woman." Before he could respond, I turned my head aside for a moment, having admitted two heretofore unexamined notions, both tripping a fuse of vulnerability. "Tell me again—the plan when we get to Florence," I said distractedly as I continued to stare up the aisle. A baby's soft cries arose somewhere, followed by another's. People stood, some making their way to the lavatories, others simply for the movement.

"Senga—I thank you, but let's return to what I said. You're ignoring me."

I was. A ring of truth had reverberated around his earlier statement, but I lacked energy for discernment. I was in a near sleep mode, in default, and not entirely capable of a coherent thought process. *Or do I discount my part in this?* I wondered. Then, I heard laughter; again, not in Grannie's soft strains, but bemusement, all the same—from the passenger seated behind me.

"I want to think about what you said, Gabe. . . I need some time," and I squeezed his forearm, then unfastened my seatbelt to rise, telling him I'd better go before the service cart arrived.

The laughing passenger smiled broadly at me as I passed. She had no seat mate.

CHAPTER 52
TASTY DISTRACTION

W hy, you're making some progress, Rufus," the doctor informed him. He couldn't have figured that out for himself? *Guess I pay to hear him say that,* Rufus decided, as he pointed to the cane, hooked over a chair back. The nurse handed it over, then steadied him as he slipped off the examining table. Caro sat in a chair in the corner of the small room. Rufus had told her she could sit in the waiting area, but she'd have none of that.

"I need to hear what he says—so you don't have to remember it!" she teased.

He was to return in two weeks for a follow-up X-ray, to see how the crack on his pelvis was mending; meanwhile, to continue the physical therapy, which he abhorred. He opened his mouth to complain, but held his tongue, knowing he'd be wasting his breath.

They'd left Joey at the ranch with a list of chores: feed, make sure the water tanks were topped off, fill milk bowls for the cats in the barn; to not forget to feed Gus, and to give him a good brushing (the dog had picked up burrs and was caked with mud here and there). Finally, to haul firewood to the house stack. They'd left lunch fixings in the refrigerator for him. "The boy needs to know we trust him," Rufus had told her.

Caroline's old coveralls fit Joey well enough, and a pair of Rufus' gum boots worked if he added another pair of thick socks. The kid paid attention and showed some courtesy, though Rufus wasn't yet sure if it came naturally, or had Gabe put the fear of God into him? He hoped the former. He liked Joey. The kid was game, at least, and hadn't once bitched. *Well, he'd better not!* Rufus amended.

Caroline had asked—no, *ordered* Joey to call his mother, showing him the phone number Senga had provided, and to dial *67 first. The boy understood the reason without it having to be spelled out. He was canny that way. Rufus lamented the circumstances that prompted children to grow too smart too soon for their own good. That wasn't natural, and might only lead to a sour disposition later. But this boy had somehow managed to learn to take the bad with the good while clinging to the good. At least, Rufus hoped so.

Joey had reached his mother on the phone and waited until her sobbing ceased to insist he was fine and in a good place— actually working for a rancher and his wife—Rufus overheard him say. This seemed to allay her fears, but when she asked *where?* Joey told her he didn't want to say yet, as he needed to wait until Dale's "stuff" was over. He told her he loved her and that he was doing all right, so not to worry. Joey told Rufus and Caroline at dinner about her mother meeting the "herb lady" before visiting his brother in the county jail, and that the lady had helped her. His mother had given up drinking, too. "Joined A.A.," he mumbled with disbelief and relief at once. Rufus noted the hard-won wistfulness in the boy's face.

"That Senga—" Caroline had said, "Funny how things work out, ain't it? There . . . you better have another helping of potatoes, Joey." He ate anything and everything she set on the table.

It was lunchtime when they left the clinic. Rufus suggested Alzada for lunch so they could let Earl and Mae know how the boy was doing. Caro agreed. The roadhouse was serving several customers, but Earl coaxed Mae out of the kitchen. She came through the door to where Rufus and Caro were sitting at the bar. Mae wore a black, flour-dusted apron, with a dishcloth pulled through the tie; her hair was tucked under a black and white bandana.

"Nice to see you, Caroline. Been a while . . . how's the kid?"

"He's doing good, Mae. Left him alone for the day with some chores. . . Got those teeth looked at—cleaned, but only four cavities! Gabe did that. . . The kid still hides his grin though. That'll take a while, I suppose. He talks about you and Earl like you was family, you know? Why don't you come for supper on Sunday? Or, whichever night you can."

"Monday night? We're closed then."

"Good! Now, no one knows he's there, so—" She drew a thumb and forefinger across her lips.

Rufus took a deep breath and let it out slowly. He didn't like subterfuge, not one bit, but sometimes . . .

"So, Gabe and that Senga, they got away to Italy?" asked Earl.

"Yep. They get there today. Boy, he was sweating that passport. Arrived in the nick of time," Rufus said and snorted as he took out his cigarette papers and tobacco. "I'd take a Bud, Earl. Caro, you want anything?"

"A beer sounds good. Same, thanks. What's the special today?"

Mae spoke. "We've got chicken-fried steak, garlic-mashed potatoes with green beans, *and*—" she lowered her voice, "*it comes with a slice of pie, just for you.*"

"*Whoo-ee,* Caro—we're getting the treatment!" said Rufus. "You have that Saskatoon berry?" Several bushes grew out front. Tastier than blueberries, he always thought.

"Yeah, I do," she grinned.

"Apple?" asked Caroline.

"Of course. And I'll wrap up a piece for Joey. I'm so glad you dropped in," she said, returning to the kitchen.

Earl surveyed the room to see if anyone needed anything. When satisfied they didn't, he turned his attention to Rufus. "So what's happened with those yahoos that were in here? Heard they were caught."

Rufus wondered if Earl knew Joey was related to one of them.

"They're in county lock-up until the trial, and the Russian woman's waiting around with her little girl—to testify." Rufus took a long drag from his cigarette and blew the smoke up and above their heads. He liked telling this story because it showed the system works. He reached up and took off his hat, perched it on Caro's head, ran both hands through his thick white hair, plucked back the hat and replaced it. "That's better. Gabe told us the wrangler at the Blue Wood visited them at the shelter."

"The brother returned to Russia, I guess," said Caro.

"How old's the little girl?" asked Earl.

"Oh, I don't know . . . you, Caro?"

"Around five, I think. She's going to that pre-school in Sundance, I hear. Somebody's putting out some money for that—it ain't cheap."

"The county?" suggested Earl.

"Nah, wouldn't think so," Rufus replied, "Not their responsibility; maybe some organization, like the food pantry or a church—hell, I don't know. *Could* be the county, I suppose."

"Gabe said those folks who run that guest ranch left for Florida, right before he and Senga left. . ." Caro added. "Everybody's goin' somewhere. . . Hey, Earl! Didja know Rufus here is taking me to see the ocean this summer?" She drank from her bottle of beer.

"No, I didn't, Caroline. Where?"

"Wh—where, old man?" she asked him, as a small burp escaped.

"Oh, I'm thinking that area around Monterey—Big Sur."

"Do you actually want to stick your big toe in the water, Rufus?" asked Earl, "If so, then farther south might do you better."

"Oh, yeah? Guess I think of sunny California as, well, you know, *warm.*"

"Common misconception," Earl said. "Mae and I hung there for a few years. Let me think about this and I'll get back to you. We know some good spots. Still have people there. How long can you stay?"

"Two or three weeks," piped up Caroline, "Our grandson Jake, Gabe and, maybe Joey—if he's still here—will look after the place."

"You driving or flying?"

"Thought we'd fly, then rent a car."

Earl's expression clouded.

"*Wha-at?*" Rufus asked, making it two syllables.

"Hey man, it's fu—freakin' California—'scuse my French, Caroline . . . Traffic is ridiculous. Look, let me look into something and we'll be talking, all right? When we see you on Monday, how 'bout. What time, Caroline?"

"Come around noon—for dinner." When they ate their main meal.

Rufus looked at Earl, then over the old biker's shoulder, into the mirror, to a table of eaters, all of whom sat hunched over their meals, as if it were their last; their forks shoveling the food into their *pie-holes,* and he felt a sad disgust. It only served to bring him lower—in illustration. He so wanted to do this thing for Caro, and now Earl was tossing obstacles into his way.

"We'll figure it out, Earl, and thanks for the warning," he said blankly, then marshaled his eyes to watch Mae bring their lunches, just in time. He needed a tasty distraction.

CHAPTER 53
LA VITA E BELLA

Tuscany

The day dawned clear and bright, with just enough chill of autumn to allow for Francesca's wardrobe staples: dark woolen slacks, a matching Merino shell and one of the wide "pashmina" scarves sold to tourists by the thousands. She owned two which earned the name sans quotes, for being woven from cashmere. Someone had once told her the standard shawl required the hair from three goats. Today she chose the rose-colored one, exquisitely woven with interlacing threads of gold.

Carlo helped arrange her thick, dark hair into a twist, and she carefully applied her mascara and lip color—not too much; Gabe didn't care for it.

"You are a painting, sister," said her brother.

"Yes, as you've mentioned—I could have modeled for Artemisia Gentileschi." She lifted her exquisite eyebrows then smiled, to ease his awkward expression.

"Her heroines grovel at your feet, *cara mia,* as do I," he said and leaned over to plant a kiss on her lightly-scented cheek. "Ahhh, borrowing scent from Mamma, are you?" He leaned in again. "*Santa Maria Novella Zagara*—the newest one. Unisex too, I believe. *Mmmm.*"

"She offered, Carlo. I think I would have given myself away at our leaving, don't you think?" she joked, "But I did consider it, to tell the truth. . . She read my mind. Let us go; are you ready?"

Maria Teresa had chosen to remain home and not accompany them to the airport in Florence. Carlo insisted on driving and took the afternoon off.

"More than ready," he answered, gathering up his jacket. Their mother kissed them on both cheeks at the door. At his usual sunny morning spot beside the door (the cushioned chair of Maria Teresa vacant) *Nonno* asked to inspect her. She twirled for him then bent to kiss his bearded cheek. *This will be a day remembered for kisses,* she thought.

"Enjoy your day, *Nonno,* and tomorrow evening you will meet Gabe and Senga. Maria Teresa is coming, but you already knew this, didn't you?"

He grinned. "You are happy, little one, so I am happy," he said, adjusting his seating and glancing in the direction of Maria Teresa's home. He turned back to her. "Now go! You do not want to get snarled in traffic."

She blew him another kiss as they turned toward Carlo's waiting car.

Erika, Peter and Jytte listened attentively as Sebastian discussed his plans. They had just eaten lunch and he was lulled by the warmth of satiety after a loving, communal meal. Erika had prepared the traditional Danish open-faced sandwich, or *smørrebrød:* buttered dark rye bread, with an assortment of cold cuts, liver *pâté,* smoked salmon, and boiled eggs.

He noticed his daughter catching her husband's eye now and then, as if to ask, *are you hearing this?* His granddaughter remained delightfully ambivalent, but respectful.

Sebastian had attended to his fiduciary obligations around his aunt's estate and was eager for the whole business to be settled. His on-going exhibit on *Flæsketorvet* Square was proceeding well in attracting interest and buyers. It seemed the public, including the queen, had enjoyed his stark images of the natural world. The photographs of Senga would represent a semi-departure; a "new period" was how his publicist proposed to advertise it. Sebastian did not care for the advertising vocabulary and had told him so.

He had completed the necessary steps to acquire a visa to the United States, learning he could stay for up to six months. *Enough time,* he believed, but with mounting concerns around Senga's response. At least until. . . *Until what?* he wondered, then realized he had been living a day-to-day existence, with few concerns or notions for the future. Was this Senga's influence *and* part of her charm? Her facility with living in the present? Or was he trapped in a land of *fé* with her? Was he enchanted?

He chuckled.

"What is so funny?" asked Erika.

"Mm? Oh, nothing. I'm sorry—I was daydreaming."

"Papa, if you want to fly to Florence, or take the express train, *do* it. What is keeping you? Certainly not us!"

"Well . . . I am not one to make these, ah, spur-of-the-moment plans. I suppose I just wanted to hear your—"

"Papa," Jytte spoke up, looking into his face with a pixie's nonchalance and determination, the long bangs of her white-blond hair accenting her blue eyes, "As *I* see it, you *must* go. You have spoken of *nothing* else but this woman since you returned, though you did interrupt her praises to attend my piano recital, and I thank you. You simply must go. . . We grant you permission." Then, Jytte slid off her chair, stepped over to him and kissed his cheek. She turned, waved without a backward glance, and disappeared toward her bedroom.

They sat stunned for several moments, then broke up in laughter, the belly sort.

"From the mouths of babes," quoted Peter.

"Who is the parent here?" Sebastian asked, his mirth finally subsiding. He had not experienced such a fit of hilarity in months and it felt good, *cleansing,* as if all the windows of his soul had been flung open to a brisk wind.

"I can be in Florence tomorrow evening, if I leave today," he told them. "And I'm traveling light, so I'll just walk over. The train leaves at 5:04."

"Actually, I must go to the station today, if you could be ready to leave around 3:00. But why on earth wouldn't you fly instead, Sebastian?"

He smiled and made a low sound of amusement. "I know it sounds daft, but this gives me time to . . . slow down, you see."

His daughter spoke. "I understand perfectly, Papa. Record the journey and you can sell it to a Slow T.V. channel," she teased. The Scandinavian phenomenon had the public viewing eight-hour train rides, persistent knitters, crackling fires, and lazy, all-day sailboat excursions across lakes and fjords.

He smiled at her, shook his head and turned to his son-in-law, "Thank you, Peter. I will gather my things, then." He rose, placing his napkin on the table beside his plate, and leaned down to Erika for a kiss, which she placed on his rough cheek; he hadn't shaved in several days.

"Are you growing a beard, Papa?" she asked, rubbing a hand over tickled lips.

"Not on purpose," he said and paused. "It is only the oblivious artist's usual disregard for corporal concerns." He donned his cap, shrugged into his coat, adjusted his scarf, and sat back down near the door to pull on his footwear.

"Thank you for the wonderful meal, dear ones. I plan to return on the eleventh. I'll call. Not sure of the time yet. No worries."

Peter repeated that he would see him around 3:00, and they wished him a good trip.

Gabe and Senga had breezed through customs in Amsterdam, so their arrival in Florence was simple. They found the luggage area easily, and each had grabbed their bag when they heard a "*Ciao,* cowboy!" Gabe, wearing his hat, wheeled around to see Francesca beaming from a cordoned-off area. Someone accompanied her. *A brother?* The resemblance was there, the man a leaner version.

Gabe grinned, and then turned to Senga, "We're in Italy, *chère.* Sweet Francesca!" he called, but not too loudly. They made their way, and all proceeded until no barrier separated them, and Gabe released his bag to throw his arms around his fiancée. She smelled delicious and he thought he'd never been as happy as in this perfect moment. Stepping back to look at her, his heart filled anew and he embraced her again. After a slight clearing of the throat from the stranger, he released Francesca, who'd kept repeating *Caro mio, caro mio.* Gabe took a deep breath and told her she looked beautiful.

The man beside her extended a hand and Gabe took it. "Carlo Albinoni. I have little English, *Gebb,* but I am happy to meet you." Her brother pronounced his name like Francesca did.

"I am happy to meet *you,* Carlo."

"This is my brother, *Gebb*," said Francesca, "and Carlo, may I introduce Senga Munro, our friend and the granddaughter of Maria Teresa." Senga leaned in to extend her hand to Carlo, then she gave Francesca a hug.

"So good to meet you, Carlo—and Francesca! You look so nice! Are your jeans only for Wyoming?"

"Ha! Well, I wear them sometimes, but this is a special day, no?"

Gabe was sizing up Carlo—the elegant bearing, the polished shoes and perfectly pressed pleated slacks, the steel-gray, wool sport coat and purple scarf tied expertly at his neck. He felt woefully underdressed. *Uh oh,* he thought.

As they made their way to the car, with Senga and Carlo leading, Gabe whispered to Francesca, "Um, I don't think I brought the right clothes—does, ah, your family dress like this all the time or is today special for your brother, too?"

"Ah, *Gebb,* wait until you meet my other brothers. . . You will feel more. . . *come si dice?* Comfortable. . . Carlo likes to dress well. Oh, and he is a gay man. Not that the two always, ah, *relate,* but with him, *sì.*"

Gabe relaxed, then wondered why she hadn't told him about Carlo. *Because it doesn't matter,* he heard.

He and Senga craned their necks this way and that to take it all in—the sporty small cars, the beeps, musical Italian overheard everywhere they turned, the smells as they whipped around the old city—just for a quick reconnaissance, to whet their appetite, thought Gabe. Francesca promised a return for a proper visit.

As it was after lunchtime, and they hadn't eaten since breakfast at the airport in Amsterdam, Francesca asked Carlo to park near the historic square, the *Piazza della Signoria* in the city's center. Their overloaded senses threatened to short-circuit. While he couldn't read Senga's mind, he was fairly sure in this case—her expression was ecstatic.

"My God, I can't believe I'm here," she repeated.

Carlo ushered them to a small *trattoria* on a side street off the *piazza,* whose proprietor he knew well. He ordered for them and Gabe asked to pick up the check, to great offense. *Assolutamente no!* came the reply. Gabe told Francesca he expected to pay sometime. She smiled at him and said, *"May*be." Carlo's friend spared no one his culinary expertise and they began with *antipasti, bruschette* and glasses of *prosecco*. He heard Carlo say something to Francesca, perhaps an appraisal—by her flashing eyes after a wry laugh. They obviously adored one another.

Christmas decorations gave the cobblestone streets an even more festive air, if this were possible, with Senga quipping, "Gilding the fucking lily, isn't it?" to him in a quiet aside.

Ah, it's grand, thought Gabe, as he pulled Francesca close while they walked off the hearty lunch and sparkling wine. They strolled through the outdoor *Loggia,* admiring the magnificent marble sculptures. Then Carlo announced, quite abruptly, that it was time to get on the road, as he hoped to miss the traffic— this translated by Francesca. So they squeezed back into his red Renault Clio, with barely enough space for the luggage, and Carlo made a pass by the *Ponte Vecchio,* per Francesca's request.

"No one believes they are in *Firenze* until they see the bridge," she explained.

Senga, seated in front, turned to smile at Gabe, then reached her hand back to him. He squeezed it and happened to see Carlo watching him from the rear-view mirror, wearing a look of scrutiny. Gabe leaned to Francesca to kiss her forehead. They gazed out the windows to the throngs of tourists (*even in December!* he marveled; *especially in December,* he corrected*).* The sheer number of cars all vying for position, and the smartly dressed pedestrians were decidedly not tourists, he guessed.

They were soon away from the congestion, and motoring through the Tuscan countryside toward Lucca. Shadows grew longer, highlighting the iconic cypresses, vineyards and hilltop structures, revealing the soul of the landscape. He heard Senga sigh, "It's just so *beautiful.*"

Forty-five minutes later, we arrived in Lucca. It took a while to wrap my head around the shorter distances between populations. *Populations.* This sounds like science-fiction. I had landed in a seething cauldron of humanity. Comparisons to Wyoming raised their heads and I stuffed them back into their drawer, not wishing to entertain them—at least not yet, and maybe I wouldn't. *Comparisons are odorous!* misquotes a Shakespeare comic, to best effect.

When the plane touched down in Florence a cheer rose up from the passengers, most of whom were Italian—expressing gratitude for safe deliverance, I suspect. It had been sweet, and child-like. We Americans are *oh-so-sophisticated* and uptight. (Oh dear. Comparison there.)

Carlo dropped us at the inn and told us he would see us in the morning. He insisted on giving Gabe (and me, in parentheses) the traditional two-cheek air-kiss.

Francesca introduced us to her mother's friend, the innkeeper, whose name I promptly forgot in my fog of travel. She was friendly and scurried about, wearing a bright apron and scarf on her head. Her sister, however, was entirely opposite in bearing and stature. Tall and dressed impeccably, she seemed to live at the inn as well, or was perhaps visiting. We were introduced just before she floated down into a chair, tea set waiting. She looked us up and down in obvious appraisal. I'm fairly certain we didn't disappoint her preconceptions.

A small dog, resembling a Yorkshire terrier, lay snug against her thigh, in the upholstered chair.

Gabe and I were both exhausted, and when the innkeeper unlocked the door to my room, I wanted to collapse on the inviting double bed, whose white linens and pillows beckoned, but Francesca proposed we stay awake until our normal bedtime.

What was normal after an eight-hour leap of time?

The windows' shutters swung into the room, rather than out, with the glass panes hinged separately. Muted colors and dark woods, much as how I'd imagined Italian taste, soothed me: butter-cream walls, and burnt umber stain on the exposed wood beams, shutters, headboard, bedside tables; a small round table stood between two sturdy wooden chairs. In the bathroom I discovered a *bidet* and a large, claw-foot bathtub, its spray nozzle and taps situated on the tub's center-back, so *two* could enjoy its charms.

If only . . .

Beside a standing sink, a cabinet offered ample room for my toiletries.

After Gabe and Francesca took some time to themselves in his room, she showed me how to use the *bidet* in mine.

"Senga, look, it is *easy*," she crooned, assuming the position, clothed. Gabe had moseyed, yes, *moseyed* in and stood against the bathroom door, arms crossed, his expression—wistful. Then, he grinned. The quick sex was written all over his face; he looked— *peaceful*.

"*Knock it off*, you, as if *you* know how it works," I barked in jest.

"As a matter of fact, I do. Some houses in Louisiana have them. The *old* ones. And they're coming back. . . You could have one installed in your cabin. Somewhere."

"*Gehh*, Senga, stop," Francesca laughed. She inspected the room herself, making sure all was as it should be. A vase of fresh white mums and a basket of fruit and wrapped *biscotti* brightened the small table. A small coffee maker with several packages, all caffeinated, sat beside a flat-screen television on a shelf between two windows. A small, discreet refrigerator rounded out the amenities. Chilling within were three bottles of water and two cans of a sparkling orange drink. "I brought them. The *San Pellegrino Orange* is my favorite."

I smiled at her and opened one, feeling dehydrated from the travel.

She stepped to a second window and pulled it opened to the late afternoon air. "There! The rarified air of Lucca and your room with a view!" she announced, backing up to allow the window as frame. She'd told us, as we wearily climbed the steep stairs, she'd asked for third floor rooms explicitly, to give us a more distant view.

I think I gasped at the picture before us. Gabe, who'd stepped up beside me, made a sound I can only describe as something you'd hear either during lovemaking or while eating particularly good ribs.

Bluish-gray mountains, the Apuans (we were informed) folded themselves against the farthest horizon. I counted six further outlines, each successively more faint, the nearest being a crooked, lacy procession of dark autumn foliage among intermittent bare trees. Two towers rose majestically; one white, and one Siena brown—a campanile—its bronze bell perfectly visible from our vantage point. I turned to our Italian friend.

"Francesca. *Rarefied* air? *What* have you been reading?"

She giggled.

"I taught her that word," said Gabe, ". . . a *good* word—though in this case, I don't think it works, love."

"And why not?" she demanded.

"Because . . . it signifies *less* dense air, and while I don't see any smog . . . well, how about 'the *redolent* air of Lucca?' I smell half-a-dozen things just standing here—including you!" He grabbed her up and snuggled his face into her neck. She screeched.

"Gabe, you scratch! Stop! You will have *la signora* asking you to leave. . ."

"You're the one yelling," I observed, moving to the door and pulling it closed with a sharp and precise *click!* And then, I heard my cell phone ring. The tone—Sebastian's. *Where* had I put the thing? I rummaged through my pack and pulled it out.

"Hello you, we're here!" I stated expansively.

"How is my mermaid?"

"Is that the riddle?"

"Absolutely. Oh, it is good to hear your voice, Senga. Where are you?"

"In my room—in Lucca. A beautiful room with a view," I said, smiling in Francesca's direction. Each waving, they quietly moved toward the door, and Francesca blew me a kiss, before it clicked shut once again.

"To answer—your mermaid is reconsidering the delights of *terra firma,* and the prospect of sleeping in this *gorgeous* bed—tragically, without her salty sailor." I heard him groan. "This inn is—well, I feel like a pilgrim during the Renaissance. Even with the presence of a television. There, I just threw my scarf over it. All gone!"

He chuckled. "What is the name of the inn? I'll look it up."

"Um, let's see. . . It's called *La Vita è Bella.*" I'd spotted a brochure. "We're near one of the gates."

"*La vita è bella, la vita è amore,* yes. Are you inside the walls or out?"

"Just outside. What does that mean, what you said?"

"Life is beautiful, life is love, my dear—an old Italian adage. . . What else?"

"Oh! It's written under the first phrase; I see it now. So later, we'll go eat inside the old town and walk along the ramparts.

Then, I'll be ready for bed. I am so tired. I'll see my grandmother tomorrow. And what are *you* doing?"

"Oh, this and that. I ate with Erika, Peter and Jytte . . . All is well, but I need to go, my dear. Be mindful, and watch your belongings. Keep your passport in a safe place in your room."

"I remember, but thank you for reminding me. All right then . . . I love you, and I am too weary to riddle—you will have to wait until tomorrow."

"Until tomorrow then, Senga . . . I love you," and he hung up.

I sat on the edge of the bed for several moments between the need for sleep and desire, then stood, crossed to the bathroom and rinsed my face with cold water. I loosed my hair, brushed, then braided it again. On a narrow shelf sat elegantly packaged samples of skin care products, I assumed. Surely placed there by Francesca. I opened a moisturizer (though it could have been hair conditioner), and spread it thinly on my face. It felt soothing and smelled like spring.

I also remembered Caroline had asked me to call when we arrived. I did so, but no one answered. A message, then.

After, I slid the table and chairs to the open window, sat and slowly sipped my *San Pellegrino Orange,* letting my gaze drift where it would. I had seldom, if ever, experienced such a mood as this and I struggled to define it, tempered, as it was by a poignant sense of lack. Something was missing and, as I considered the view and my exquisite little room, I recognized that the *something* was of course, someone. *Sebastian.*

When my drink and reverie ended, I passed the next forty-five minutes unpacking and making myself at home in Tuscany, at least for a fortnight.

Peter lifted his father-in-law's bag and set it on the back seat of his Peugeot. Sebastian was already seated and checking his mobile for messages. Nothing. He clicked on one of Senga's photos not associated with the new collection.

"Do you need to stop anywhere—the bank?" asked Peter.

"No, no. I have what I need, thank you. Why do you need to go to the station?"

"Work related. A person of interest is arriving today at 3:35."

"I see."

Peter glanced over to him. "It shouldn't take long; you could sit in the restaurant."

Sebastian said nothing.

His son-in-law consulted the timetable for the platform number of his man's train. Sebastian chose against the restaurant and followed several steps behind Peter, as per his wishes, until they reached the area just as the train pulled in. Peter knew which train carriage to head for and Sebastian watched, intrigued, as the Interpol agent shed any resemblance to Erika's husband. It involved bearing and focus. "Just stay back. Please," Peter told him.

Earlier, he had told Sebastian he was merely doing surveillance, and that two Danish police were posted near the station exits. He was verifying a suspect's identity.

Train brakes screeched with the halt and doors slid open, to release rivers of humanity. Peter waited, seemingly peering down the far length of the train as Sebastian stepped forward. Out of the corner of his eye, he glimpsed a passenger descending the steps. The man paused to study Peter for a long moment. Sebastian glanced at the passenger, then quickly away. The man was stout and dressed in a puffy black parka. A navy muffler hid much of his face. *So much for identifying anyone,* Sebastian thought; *he resembles most every male here*—apart from the metal briefcase in a gloved hand. Sunlight glinted off the silvery case handle attached to his wrist. Locked, he suspected.

Then it happened.

The man rushed Peter. Pushed off balance, Peter fell off the platform onto adjacent tracks. The man then swung his arm in a wide arc, like an athlete preparing to throw a discus. A corner of the metal case met with Sebastian's left temple and he went down—the unforgiving concrete of the quay, the last thing he remembered.

CHAPTER 54
WHY DIE WHEN SAGE
GROWS IN YOUR GARDEN?

Lucca, Italy

L ast Sunday, when she felt sufficiently recovered from the angina, Maria Teresa had walked to the church, timed to arrive shortly after Mass. Francesca's news of Senga's imminent arrival had spurred her over and above her usual devotions. The interior of the church had felt cool, and the lingering smell of extinguished candles hung in the dim light. *The girl will be here for the feast of the Immaculate Conception,* she'd realized. Incense remained one of Maria Teresa's favorite sense memories from childhood. The interior would be redolent with frankincense for days.

She smiled inwardly, figuratively lighting her own candle, remembering. In the church, she had lit her five tea lights, but had wished to include this man, *Gehb. Do I light another?* Checking her coin purse for the necessary change, she discovered enough, but, "No. No candle number six. Unlucky," she'd muttered aloud, under her breath. "I will count him with yours, little one. . ."

Someone cleared their throat behind her and, glancing over her shoulder, Maria Teresa was met with the judging eyes of the black-and-white-clad religious sister, whose day off from her young charges had not appeared to sweeten her features. To antidote the image, Maria Teresa had given the woman a saccharine-sweet smile.

"Still practicing your heresies, eh, *Signora Barone?*"

Maria Teresa had slowly stood, turned and bowed her head to the painted, medieval statue of the Madonna, and, nodding once to her interrogator, had leaned for her handbag and left, muttering a *Salve Regina.*

Sofia and Nadia greeted Maria Teresa in unison. They waited to be invited into the apartment. Each balanced an empty errand basket over an arm, having arrived to gather Maria Teresa to walk to the *piazza* market together.

"*Buongiorno,* friends. *Come in! Come in!* I need my coat. Chilly today, isn't it?"

"*Sì, sì,* Maria Teresa," said Nadia, "But a beautiful day for your granddaughter. What time is the dinner?"

"Seven-thirty. Francesca wondered if I would like to meet with Agnes, or, Senga—as she is called now—alone, before we go to Albinoni's. I told her yes. Oh, but I am a bundle of nerves! No reason to be." She watched Nadia exchange a glance with Sofia, who turned toward the tiny kitchen and silently set about brewing a pot of tea.

"Let it brew the full seven minutes!" Nadia insisted as Sofia set it on the table, around which *Le Befane* normally sat. Today was no different.

"*Grazie,* Sofia. You are kind. And Nadia—it has been an eventful, few weeks—no?" Maria Teresa said.

"*Sì!*" she replied, then stood to let Bianco in, his white tail swishing back and forth with some irritation.

"Madonna warned us to tend to our chickens," said Maria Teresa. The cryptic statement was met with silent understanding as they sipped their chamomile tea. *Address the distress!* hung in the air. Their stroll to the market, today's remedy.

The housekeeper had given the apartment a good cleaning, which eased her mind. So much tranquility depended on simply seeing, then *doing* what needed to be done—even if it could be accomplished by someone else.

We couldn't have chosen a better guide. Wishing to pace our sightseeing over the fourteen days, Francesca had drawn up a list of favorites and some surprises found off the beaten path, thereby avoiding crowds. Days for rest and reflection were essential, she advised, as she knew we might quickly become saturated and this would lessen our capacity for appreciation.

Francesca, Gabe and I spent yesterday morning wandering the streets of Lucca. Feeling flush, we decided to climb the 230 steps of the *Torre Guinigi*, to be rewarded by the view. Behind the grin permanently pasted on my face, the sight of the oaks growing on top made me weep. I was a walking contradiction of feeling and, while I didn't believe it was culture shock (unless a *surfeit* of culture) I did wonder if something else was at work.

After descending, to the sting of burning calves, we sat at an outdoor café to decide what next. There was no hurry, insisted Francesca. I was glad.

Today I planned to visit *Nonna* in late afternoon, before joining everyone at Francesca's. Gabe and I had met her mother (her father had left for work), and I noticed how solicitous she was of her daughter's fiancé. *Quite* taken. He presented her a bouquet of mixed flowers *and* a box of chocolates, hedging his bets.

Our order arrived. The beautiful Italian waiter expertly balanced our coffees on a tray, with joy. What flair he brought to the simple action of delivering an order! He was acquainted with Francesca, and she introduced us. The server's eyes rounded and he broke into a dazzling smile, set down the tray, wiped a hand on his apron and reached for Gabe's, to pump it several times; then, he whisked up the tray and was off, saying something unintelligible to us English speakers.

"Um, I think Francesca is considered someone *special,* Gabe," I ventured. Maybe *meowed.*

She laughed and waved her hand in dismissal. "*Nooo,* it is Gabe's hat. It is *exciting* to Gio," she explained. "That boy. . . I was his babysitter when we were young. He is sweet."

Gabe made a sound.

I took a sip of my cappuccino, moaned for its restorative qualities and again took out my phone.

"Francesca, I think our Senga has joined the ranks of phone addicts," joked Gabe.

I hadn't heard from Sebastian, which was unusual, and when I tried to reach him it went to voice mail. "I join nothing, but I can't get through to Sebastian. Something's not right . . . is it *broken?*' I whined in frustration, handing it to Gabe, a shadow crossing my mind. He dialed Francesca. The phone worked.

Back at the inn, what I particularly anticipated was a soak in the large bathtub. I set the stopper and turned on the tap, then poured in some of the liquid soap and a squirt of the oil I'd brought. The room soon smelled of scented steam. I placed a chair beside the tub to hold my collection of toiletries—such as they were—and the samples Francesca had provided.

A niggling tug on my heart dampened my pleasure. Gabe had reported no missed calls on my phone. *Where was Sebastian?* The occasional apparition didn't seem to include a constant clairvoyance, for which I was grateful, *but sometimes . . .*

During the course of the bath I dried my hands and checked my messages, in case I'd missed the beep. Nothing. I sent a text: *Where are you?*

I submerged myself for a long moment, remembering my grandparents' claw foot tub and my weekly soak, nearly equal to ice cream at the corner drugstore's fountain in Blowing Rock. Funny, I hadn't remembered this when bathing at Sebastian's, but then, he was distracting me. . .

I distracted myself with the scintillating memory, then turned on the hot tap to reheat the cooling water. Eventually, I climbed out, dried myself, slathered on scented lotion and towel-dried my hair. I spied a hair dryer on the top shelf of the closet and used it—in the interest of time. Normally, I allowed my hair to air-dry, having no other means.

After thirty minutes of trying different combinations, I settled on the long olive skirt and a light turtleneck. As a nod to fashion, I wrapped my scarf around my neck as Francesca had once shown me. Hair dried and braided, I consulted the mirror and wondered how it would be, seeing my *Nonna* for the first time in thirty-eight years. My eyes welled up, for behind that thought followed one of Emily, whose death had cruelly precipitated another—the relationship with my grandmother. *Why?*

No Grannie Cowry would answer me, so I waited, *willing* some other response.

Again, why?

Often, there are no reasons; only responses. Or lack thereof, in our case—*Nonna's* and mine. We had both retreated at the same time, into our own outer-reaches of the universe, on opposite sides of Emily's, and *Nonna's* son—my father's—*memories;* positioned so we couldn't see one another. Our transits, ever eclipsed, by our children.

I didn't cry. I accepted. As she had, evidently.

After smoothing cream on my face, I dabbed on some of the fragrance sample. I would smell of jasmine.

The room feeling stuffy after the steaming bath, I crossed to a window and yanked it open, to be greeted by a tenor's full-throated aria from an Italian opera. *Yes!* Puccini, I suspected. I'd heard the piece many times, but lacked a title. It rose from the floor below me like—*oh God*—the whale in my dream. But the moving voice *sounded* (like a diving whale), *deep calling to deep.*

Vibrating with delight, I leaned out my window to listen. A blue surgical cap (like a surgeon's) emerged from the lower window; next, shoulders and arms, to vigorously shake a large bath mat, the notes rising in glorious crescendo. I was buoyed and comforted by this surprise of music. It ended and there hung a charged interstice of silence, before I helplessly broke into applause. The head of the man jerked and he twisted round to see me, smiling beatifically. Quietly, he said, *"Grazie, signorina,"* bowing, as best he could, given his awkward stance. I recognized him as the owner's son, Guido, who had left us each a *Ferrero Rocher* chocolate truffle on our breakfast plates that morning. Gabe and I decided we *loved* the Italians.

Back indoors, I checked myself in the mirror once more, adjusted the scarf, grabbed my leather jacket from the back of the second chair, and remembered the packet I had brought for *Nonna.* Not at all sure she would welcome the photographs, I could think of nothing else to give her. I included one of my father and her together. As far as I knew, Emily had been her only great-grandchild. Francesca would have known and told me if she had another family. Perhaps *she* was her family.

I was ready. Gabe was taking a nap, *maybe*—if his window was closed—so I didn't disturb him, but passed his room and descended the two flights of steep stairs, my calves screaming with every step. I replaced my room key on its hook in the foyer and stepped outdoors to wait for Francesca. The side yard was lovely with evergreens and colorful shrubs, whose salmon-colored leaves quaked in the late afternoon breeze. The air felt cool and I was glad for the jacket and scarf.

Francesca arrived and we set out.

Our inn, Francesca's home and *Nonna's* apartment building were situated in a near-triangle, save the inn's location (outside the ramparts), requiring a bit of a dog-leg trek, but I welcomed the calf-stretching walk. Plainly, this was the hour most employees left work and pedestrian traffic was dense. I was jostled and heard *Scusi!* at least twice, and hadn't appreciated the quiet environs of the inn. I told Francesca she'd done well.

Ignorant, I asked, "What's the name of that famous aria from one of Puccini's opera's?"

"Senga, that is a *difficult* question," and she laughed. "*Impossible,* even."

"The owner's son was singing it today as he cleaned the room below me. It was outstanding. But I've heard it a *lot,* so you must know which one I mean."

"Sing—or *hum* a few notes. Can you?"

I'd managed about five notes when she recognized it.

"Ah, *sì!* We all know *that* one! We learn it in school." She began to sing it. But I still didn't know what it was called.

"And the title?"

"Ah. *Nessun Dorma,* or, 'None Shall Sleep.' Happy?"

I grinned, thinking of Gabe.

We turned a corner, to come face to face with an old, but elegant, structure.

"Those windows there, do you see? The middle ones?" My guide pointed with her chin. "That is your grandmother's home. See the corner of the curtain?"

I nodded. A tail of white peeked between two window sashes. The three shining windows were magnificent, each sparkling and stately behind their own wrought-iron balconies. Three windows aligned above, and three below. I thought I saw a quick movement behind a curtain.

"Come," said Francesca. "Maria Teresa is anxious," using the word instead of *eager,* the two often mistaken. But in this case, I believed her. So was I.

Glancing about, I noted the small garden beside the sunny entrance to the building. An herb patch, where grew rosemary, oregano and thyme. Most evident was a wild assortment of sage species, their soft green leaves still vibrant in the late autumn sun.

CHAPTER 55
FOR WANT OF A DANE

From her second-story apartment, Maria Teresa watched the two women approach. *Which was which?* She wished her eyesight were better. The taller one looked up and, instantly, she recognized her little Agnes Maria. *Called Senga now,* she remembered. She grunted and moved away from the curtained window named *Gabriele.* Pausing at *Rafael* in the kitchen, she again peered down. Senga was inspecting the herb garden, while Francesca motioned for her to come.

"I come, I come. . ." Maria Teresa called when she heard the knock. She had lost most of her English, but they would find a way, she hoped.

She stole a glance in the gold-leafed, Florentine mirror near the door, and touched her heart with trembling palm. "Madonna, *per piacere.*" Please, she asked, then opened the door.

Her granddaughter's expression had altered little with the years. At forty-seven, she resembled her nine-year-old self. *She was ten when I returned,* she corrected. Speaking with her eyes, she opened wide her arms and the child melted into them, like butter on warm bread. *What child?* Her granddaughter was weeping. Maria Teresa and little Francesca guided Senga to the sofa. After reaching into her bosom for her lace handkerchief, Maria Teresa dabbed her rheumy eyes, then offered it to her granddaughter. *Agnes Maria? Senga?*

"What am I to call you, *bambina?*" she asked in Italian.

Francesca answered for her. "Senga, *Nonna* . . . I must use your bathroom. Excuse me," she added in English, suspecting *Nonna* understood more than she was able to speak.

Her granddaughter composed herself and sat up. Maria Teresa saw her smile and, for a fleeting instant, caught a likeness to her son Andrea. What she needed to see.

"Senga, I no talk the English well, *ma, is good* to see you!" and she lifted her granddaughter's hand from her lap to kiss the knuckles over and over, silent tears falling now.

"*Nonna.* It is good to see *you*," Senga said and turned the gnarled hand to Maria Teresa's knuckles, to return the kiss. They sat, absorbing one another's presences, when the now-grown woman reached into her pocket and withdrew a packet. "These are for you," she said. "Pictures of our Emily, and one of Daddy and you. I hope it's all right."

Maria Teresa frowned, wondering what was meant by the last phrase. How could it not be all right? And, she understood Senga perfectly, she was relieved to note. The packet lay in her lap and she looked at it, then at Senga—who smiled, if sadly.

"Emily. . . Andrea. . ." She reached inside for the photographs.

Francesca returned and asked if she could get everyone a glass of something. She looked at *Nonna,* in question.

"*Sì;* whatever you wish, *cara mia.*"

Several moments later, a tray holding a decanter of port and three, small crystal tumblers waited beside them on the table. Francesca returned to the kitchen for a dish of olives. Maria Teresa gestured for Senga to pour, her pale hand languidly motioning, as though working a spell. *Water to wine, indeed,* she wryly reflected. Francesca raised her glass, followed by her friends, and only said, "*La vita è bella,*" to which Maria Teresa responded, "*La vita è amore.*" She gazed a moment into each woman's eyes, holding their attention, then, with a smile, she took a sip, as did her guests—*No. Not guests; la mia famiglia,* she corrected. My family.

"May I see?" Francesca asked in English, and Senga nodded. Seated beside her, Francesca leaned over and kissed her friend's cheek in solidarity. Maria Teresa noted this and felt a wave of well-being. *So, they are friends,* she thought. Before viewing the first photo, she looked to *Gabriele* and made a prayer. *May I be strong for them.*

The first photo showed Emily at two, hugging a plush Easter bunny. . .

Gabe woke from his nap to a ringing phone. He answered, still groggy. It was Caroline, returning his earlier call, to say all was going well, and for him to enjoy himself and not be checking up on them every couple of hours.

"You're exaggerating, Miss Caroline," he said, "but I'm glad to hear you don't miss me."

She chortled, adding that Rufus was getting along better and was happy with the kid—that Joey was working out. After telling him to say hello to Senga and Francesca, she hung up without saying goodbye, as usual.

He tried to recall his dream, in which a famous Italian opera singer figured, when he heard a knock on his door. "Hang on!" he called and pulled on his jeans.

It was Senga. "Hey," she said. "Well, I just saw my *Nonna.*"

He'd never seen his friend so, so—*what?* "How'd it go? Is— is she *okay?*" he asked as he grabbed a tee shirt.

Senga entered his room, glanced around and sank to the bed. "She's so *frail,* Gabe, and older than. . . *God,* she's so *old!*" She rolled to her side into fetal position.

"Senga. She's in her nineties. Haven't you been around old folk?" Tee shirt in place, he sat down beside her and stroked her back.

"Not since Papa and Grannie, but they weren't this old when they died. So, I haven't, no; not much lately, I guess. It—it was just a shock, for both of us, I think. But Francesca, *bless* her, hauled out the port—which may or may not have helped. Alcohol goes both ways. . . Oh, I'm all right; I just hope *Nonna* is. . ."

She lay quietly for a moment. He continued to stroke her back. She made a sound, indicating comfort, then said, "I'm glad we have a little time before dinner. You ready for it?"

"I am. But I'd like to shower first, so. . ."

"I'm sorry—" She pushed herself up and made to rise, then didn't.

"Nah, *chère,* nothing to be sorry about. We've got an hour. Why don't you go rest your eyes a bit and I'll knock in thirty. . . That give you enough time?"

"Yes. And, thanks."

He watched her slowly stand and leave the room. *She's had a rough month,* he thought, as he stripped again and turned on the bath's taps, anticipating an uncommon experience.

Dinner proved such as well, and Gabe decided he'd never felt as accepted into the proverbial bosom of family as he now was—excluding his own and Strickland's. Francesca was correct in easing his sartorial fears, as her brothers Gianni and Marco dressed down and Gabe actually felt more stylish—never having given the word much thought, save when bull riding, of *all* circumstances. Well, no; Francesca influenced his dress now.

It raised his confidence, if nothing else.

So, he'd worn one of his nicer shirts, pressed jeans and boots, but had left the hat at the inn. His corduroy jacket had sufficed.

Senga's grandmother was altogether surprising. She didn't wear black, as Francesca had once suggested. She wore the color purple; a deep, dark shade, *almost* black—*aubergine,* or eggplant, it was sometimes called; easy, how his sweet Francesca might have mistaken it. Maria Teresa, as she was introduced, wore it like a queen.

He was itching to take out his notebook to record observations, but refrained.

Francesca's grandfather was in love with the woman, but the elderly man saved his charms this evening to engage Gabe, as much as the language barrier would allow. Francesca translated. He felt the eyes of the grandfather upon him often, but the old man would quickly avert his gaze. Francesca's parents spoke English fairly well, and Carlo made an effort. In short, Gabe looked forward to any and all encounters with this new family, and was eager to tell his father about them. He hadn't laughed so much in years, and suspected, neither had Maria Teresa. Her head bobbing back and forth, long teeth flashing, she sat between Senga and *Nonno.* Her eyes glistened with happiness under the string of lights, these stretched from limb to limb above the table.

Gabe caught Francesca's eye during a lull between courses and nodded to the back of the terrace. "What's there?"

She coyly smiled, stood and guided him toward the partially hidden, vine-covered door he'd spied and found curious.

Catcalls followed, but the ruse worked. He needed to hold her—
to ground and corral his emotions.

The trio passed Saturday on the road, visiting hilltop villages,
including Pienza, where Zefferelli had filmed much of his *Romeo
and Juliet*. A harp player entertained them; his umbrella deployed
against the sun. They each dropped a euro into the busker's can.
Gabe kissed Francesca on a narrow side-street named,
impossibly, *Mille Bacci*. A thousand kisses. "Only in Italy,"
muttered Senga, who took a picture of them standing below the
street sign. Kissing.
   They enjoyed a long lunch in Montalcino and, after, strolled
to a grassy area overlooking the valley, to allow for digestion.
Before returning to the car, they drank espressos and sat longer.
Gabe enjoyed watching people, a national sport in Italy. During
this shoulder season, approaching Christmas tide, they were
privy to viewing how the culture actually cooperated. He pulled
out his notebook to take some notes:
   *Stores close for two-three hours from lunchtime on. Siesta. Excellent
idea!*
   No one checks phone while walking, nor carries a coffee cup.
   Townspeople stop to visit with one another; none seem in a hurry.
   A little like Sara's Spring—plus siesta.
   In the larger cities, where tourism contributed more to the
Italian GNP, the old customs might be less feasible. He asked
Francesca about it.
   "No, *caro mio*, here tourists are important too. Everywhere in
Italy. But in the villages and, at this time of year, they are less—
ah—"
   "Disruptive?" suggested Senga, as she snapped another
photo of her friends.
   "*Sì!* But mostly, we don't mind the tourists. Most are happy
to be here, and that is good." She leaned over to kiss Gabe on
the lips, but he pulled her into his lap and, holding her, he
quoted: *"These violent delights have violent ends and in their triumph die,
like fire and powder. Therefore love moderately; long love doth so; Too swift
arrives as tardy as too slow.* Act II, Scene VI."
   Francesca pushed away from him and stood, "You shorten
it, *il mio amore*. I read this, in the English; *I know*."

"Well, it's more to the point," he said, chucking her under her chin as he stood.

Francesca drove them to the vineyard where her brother, Gianni, and his girlfriend worked. Two couples from France joined them for the wine tasting, and all were soon ushered into an ancient, rock-walled room. Gabe figured it measured about twelve-by-twelve feet, with an enormous fireplace and hearth spanning one side, in which burned dry grape vines. Meant for ambience and quick heat, the crackling flames warmed the old stones. An elderly man pitched in another bundle of vines.

Out came the notebook. . .

They introduced themselves to the French guests, after settling into their seats at a massive oak table. Gabe beamed when he saw Gianni at the door, come to help with their tasting. After, Senga bought two bottles of the *Gatto Nero* for Sebastian, one for Francesca's parents and one for her grandmother. *Generous gifts,* Gabe found himself thinking and he also bought one for the Albinonis.

Feeling pleasantly inebriated, he and Senga sat quietly, as Francesca deftly negotiated the winding roadway through the Val d'Orcia. She pointed in the distance to the tiny, Renaissance *Madonna di Vitaleti* chapel, flanked by cypresses. Senga and Gabe both groaned with, again, *what?* he wondered. *Yearning? Appreciation?* He remembered a first encounter with truly high mountains and his desire to be there, *right* there, as if the sight evoked a visceral, physical need.

With understanding and élan, Francesca whipped onto a narrow lane and they shortly pulled up beside the near-apparition. The undulating fields, surrounding the iconic image, shone golden in the slanting sun's rays. The old chapel stood on private property and remained locked against vandals, but they found it quintessentially Tuscan and thanked her for the detour.

Francesca mentioned an upcoming concert at one of the old theaters in Lucca, and might they be interested? An Italian composer was scheduled to play Sunday evening. *Tomorrow.* Neither he nor Senga recognized the musician, but they agreed with enthusiasm, after Francesca hinted that she very much wanted to attend. . .

They wished each other good evening at Senga's door after Gabe carried in her wine. He thought her recovered from her reunion with her grandmother, though he suspected it might prove an ongoing heartache—the distance. He knew his friend as *mostly* sensible and that she'd sort it out. Somehow. Even if it involved herbs and candle light. . .

Now where'd that come from? he asked himself then sighed.

He pulled Francesca close as they walked the few steps to his room, inserted the old-fashioned key, gave it a turn and opened the door to their indoor *bower*—how he thought of it: *romantic to the core,* and he made a sound. They planned to eat a late dinner, preceded by a soak in the tub with a glass of *Campari* on the side, followed by an appetizer.

I didn't think I could endure even muffled sounds of sex this evening—for want of Sebastian—so I sought the small café, or *trattoria,* Guido had recommended. It appeared around the corner from our inn, just inside the old town gate. I ordered a half-carafe of Chianti, sparkling water and a small plate of antipasti, but I picked at it. The bread, however, I devoured.

My phone beeped for a text and I fumbled my way to it in my jacket pocket. It was Muriel back home, asking after me. I typed that I'd seen my grandmother and that things were going well, omitting Sebastian. After tapping goodbye, I set the phone down, urging it to vibrate with something from him.

Glancing at the other diners, I noticed only one consulting his phone, and he was also seated alone. Those dining together engaged in conversation; laughing, speaking with their hands (*not* an exaggeration) and having fun. Two additional solitary diners seemed content to sit, quietly observant and dignified, as they sipped their wine, appearing quite satisfied and self-possessed. *Was this the distinguishing characteristic?*

Fatigue caught up with me and I asked for the check, paid it and walked back to the inn or, *villa,* as I was told. The entrance now shone sweetly festive, lit by a string of fairy lights. My gritty-feeling eyes were drawn above to a single burning candle in the window of what I believed was Gabe's room. In mine a small lamp burned, and the glow lent comfort.

Inside, Guido was busily wrenching decorations from a bin. I greeted him and he returned it, stepping behind the counter for my key.

"Thanks for suggesting the *trattoria,* and . . . you really do have a beautiful voice." He shyly lowered his head, covered in thick, black curls.

"Do you sing for a company?" I ventured, and he admitted he did, ". . . during season, and study the rest of time." *Practices,* I took it to mean—*while changing sheets and sweeping out guest rooms.*

"Ah, *signorina,*" he asked in halting English, "do you wish a *digestivo?*"

"Limoncello?" I asked and nodded wholeheartedly. I could barely keep my eyes open, but it sounded medicinal at this point and *good.*

He returned with the frosty bottle and two, tiny cups on a silver tray; set this on the table; poured us each a tot; and raised his cup, "*Diciamo cin-cin!* We say *cheen-cheen,*" he translated.

"*Cin-cin,*" I toasted and took a sip. The familiar, icy lemon sweetness after-burned with the alcohol, in a flavor-temperature experience I learned to anticipate, after first tasting it at Sebastian's. His Aunt Karen's hospitality still in play, even from the other side. *Association?*

After the unnecessary second one, I felt woozy, but offered to help with the decorations.

It had *seemed* a good idea.

I managed to deck the mantle with what looked to be an heirloom collection of diminutive ceramic—witches. Brooms and all.

So . . . they celebrate Halloween with Christmas here. Instead of putting out Christmas decorations before Halloween, like at home, they combine them. . . And here I began to see, if not double, then certainly, a jostling behind my vision. I steadied myself against the edge of the mantle.

"*Signorina?*" A woman's voice; I heard it as someone speaking through a long underwater pipe. "Guido!" she called. He was there in a moment and helped me to the soft chair, into which I sank. *I should have eaten more at dinner,* I lamented. *O . . . foolish . . . me.* And then, I knew nothing else.

I woke during the night in my bed, clothed, ignorant of how this was accomplished. Head pounding, I gingerly rose on an elbow. On my bedside table stood a glass of water and what appeared to be two aspirins. I swallowed them gratefully and lay back down, not to stir until mid-morning.

CHAPTER 56
ALCHEMY

In the morning, Gabe knocked gently on Senga's door. A second time. He heard something unintelligible.

"You all right, *chère?*"

"I will be," came a croaked reply.

"Guido asked about you. Feel like breakfast? He says he'll fix you something. "

She opened the door. He grinned at her appearance: disheveled hair, wrinkled clothing, a deep frown.

"It'll stick if you don't watch out." He pointed to her forehead.

"You sound like Grannie," she whispered, then asked if a chunk of bread with butter were available. She'd make coffee in her room. "Oh, a small pitcher of steamed milk, too, please," she added, then shut the door without response.

"Yes ma'am," he called through the wood, snickered and turned toward the stairwell.

Gabe and Francesca were seated in the villa's garden when Senga appeared an hour later, refreshed, and looking once again human.

"Hey," she said.

"*Buongiorno*, Senga," said Francesca. "Guido says you helped him last night. It is all so—*bella, sì?*"

"About that . . . what's with witches at Christmas?" she asked.

"Ah, *La Befana*. . . You will ask *Nonna*, as she is one—*they* say. You will like the story, I promise. *And*—she is coming to the concert with us this evening! She is so excited, Senga—like a child. It is wonderful, no?"

"No—*yes*. . . I—I look forward to it," she said as she groped her jacket pockets for something. "I think I left my phone at the café last night. *Damn!* Will they hang on to it?"

She took a deep breath and Gabe looked at her with concern. "Senga, it's all right. I'm sure they will. Let's go now." He reached for her arm and raised her from the bench where they sat.

Gabe was right; the young server remembered Senga, walked to the cash register, opened it and withdrew the phone. He handed it to her with a more-than-necessary grin, and, Gabe thought, a degree of salaciousness. He didn't care for it. Well, this *was* Italy, he reminded himself. He pulled out a ten-euro piece and handed it to the boy, who raised his palms in protest, while backing away.

"I expect he's been compensated," Gabe heard Senga mutter dryly.

"What's that?" he asked, thinking he'd misheard.

They were nearing the medieval city gate, when she stopped. She seemed to be studying the dark rose stones, when she said, "I modeled nude for Sebastian and he sent me three of the images."

"You *what?*" Gabe nearly choked; his voice, an octave higher on the second word.

"Oh, quit. It's nothing I'm ashamed of, Gabe. On the contrary . . . and, he *is* an artist, after all. He's doing a series for a show, but that kid wouldn't know the difference."

Between porn and erotica? Gabe wanted to ask, but he kept his mouth shut. He couldn't wrap his head around it and looked down at Francesca, his lips pulled tight.

"*Gebb,*" she said, "If our Senga is comfortable with this, then you must be too."

"There isn't a message from Sebastian," Senga said, as she tucked the phone into her inside pocket. "It isn't like him . . . and I thought phones locked or something. . ."

"It's a setting, Senga, for how long before it does," explained Gabe. "Want me to reset it?"

Senga shook her head.

Francesca, ever the cruise director, suggested they walk along the ramparts. *To clear the air,* Gabe silently added. After placing a call to her mother, to let her know their plans, Francesca guided them to the tree-lined walk, most devoid of foliage, but stately, in a bare-bones sculptural way. The stroll measured nearly three miles around the oblong enclosure, perfect for a Sunday sauntering.

They spotted the villa where several film adaptations had been set—Henry James' *Portrait of a Lady,* but one; the villa's architecture rivaled those of Florence.

Cyclists whirred past, families ambled with strollers; dogs, children running and—laughter; the very sights, sounds and activities of peace, Gabe realized—*including the freedom to pose for one's lover*—if one wished. He felt a stab of regret for his earlier reaction and reached over to pull Senga into his walking embrace, Francesca on his left.

"Now this is what I call a *real* pleasure," he said, grinning at each in turn.

Early in the evening, Francesca's mother provided antipasti on the terrace. Gabe wouldn't use the word "snack" anywhere near these people or environs. It seemed sacrilegious. He worried for Senga, who was preoccupied with Sebastian's silence. *What's the matter with the man?* Gabe wondered, as he arranged several appetizers on his plate.

They had dressed for the concert. Francesca suggested it might "improve their experience." Gabe interjected heighten? and Francesca frowned, not understanding. He'd done it again—been finicky. He tried not to be, but he also knew she'd prefer the correct idiom.

"You *heighten* my experience of Italy, love." Gazing at her, he felt such pride—he might have burst with it. His sweet Francesca resembled a beauty of the Italian Renaissance, dressed in a long, crushed-velvet skirt in browns and rose; her favorite blouse (and his) and the *pashmina* shawl placed over a shoulder, for later, if needed for warmth.

Senga coughed then quipped she would have worn her furs and gold had she known. *Nonno* heard the joke and grinned, then winked at her, comprehending the gist. Gabe caught this and watched as the old man rose to his feet with the aid of his cane to shuffle indoors. He thought of Rufus.

No one heard the knock or bell, but in a few moments *Nonno* returned to the terrace, accompanied by Maria Teresa.

The old man has a sixth sense about the woman, Gabe sensed.

The addition of a string of pearls and drop earrings transfigured her appearance. On her head, and draped over the shoulders of her coat, lay a black lace mantilla.

"*La bella Maria Teresa Barone,*" announced *Nonno*, to her batting his arm in disapproval.

They turned around and a reverent sigh issued from everyone.

La signora Albinoni invited *Nonna* to come take a plate, but she declined, citing she'd recently eaten; however, she'd take a sip of *prosecco*.

Senga wore her long skirt as well, and had evidently borrowed a blouse from Francesca, else been shopping. Of a silky turquoise that offset the olive knit of her skirt, the shirt fit her perfectly *and* closely. She had wrapped a scarf at her neck upon joining the family and her friends, but Francesca had scurried over and artfully removed the neck wear, to uncover her friend's décolletage. Gabe was startled and inhaled, but didn't know if he should make a remark. Which indicated he shouldn't. He simply smiled at her and nodded once in admiration. When she returned the smile, he knew they were reconciled.

They left for the concert thirty minutes later by car. Maria Teresa, like *Nonno*, would steal a glance at him now and then. They hadn't conversed as yet, other than polite greetings, but he felt questions building, like a summer storm in flatland Louisiana, where you can watch its progress from a distance. He hoped there would be no need for the deluge. . .

At the theater, they found their seats easily, with Francesca leading, then Gabe, Maria Teresa and Senga. He noted only a few vacant places in the hall. Beside Francesca, two seats waited for occupants who never appeared. The lights dimmed and a hush descended. Out of the corner of his eye, Gabe saw Maria Teresa reach for Senga's hand and squeeze it. "*Something comes with this music,*" he heard her whisper to her granddaughter. "*Gabriele—he say to me.*"

"*Gabe?*" Senga whispered and glanced at him. Their eyes met.

"No, *bambina.*" Furtively, Maria Teresa pointed three times toward the ceiling with a knotted index finger.

"Ah," said Senga.

Not comprehending, thought Gabe.

The lights dimmed once more and there followed applause as the pianist walked onto the stage to his shining grand piano. He bowed then sat.

For forty-five minutes he held the audience, sweeping them into a vortex of sound and emotion, perfectly married and bestowed with generosity and grace. *The vivifying charms of music.* Gabe tucked away the impression for later.

At intermission they stood, save Maria Teresa, who sat, seemingly asleep, but then spoke with eyes closed when Francesca called her name. "I only rest my eyes, *cara mia.* No worry. I wait."

The cell phone set to vibrate did so in his shirt pocket and Gabe reached for it. He saw Senga raise her eyebrows in question. He turned away and put a finger to his ear to better hear. After a moment, he returned the phone to his pocket and made to find his place again.

"I sit by Francesca now," he heard Senga's grandmother tell her, and Gabe squeezed into the back of his seat to give the woman room to pass. The lights dimmed a third time, to alert the audience.

"Is this seat taken?"

Gabe heard and smiled. Senga had not heard.

"*Miss?*"

Gabe watched her twist and glance up. The price of admission notwithstanding, he couldn't remember a more satisfying, but confused expression of utter disbelief, delight and consternation. Francesca sat up and squealed—a sound he'd thought reserved for their more intimate moments. Maria Teresa stared, with a look undoubtedly borrowed from her cat—*Bianco, was it?* They all watched the man pull Senga to her feet, appraise her, then kiss her thoroughly—her body gone limp as a rag doll. Appreciative applause from the stage began with the returning performer, to be joined by the audience, some of whom hadn't spotted the reunited lovers. And, when everyone had, cheers followed.

"You look ravishing, my dear," said Sebastian to Senga, his hands cupping her face.

"*He didn't just say that, did he?*" Gabe whispered in an aside to Francesca. "*More like ravished,*" he muttered, as the lovely breasts of Francesca heaved with laughter and mirth. He wanted to bury himself in them.

The applause died and Senga glanced at the delighted faces, then shyly lowered her head and took her seat, Sebastian beside her. Gabe heard her say in a forceful whisper, "*Where* have you *been?* And *what* happened to your *head?*"

"*Shhh,* later," said the Dane as the room grew dark, and Ludovico Einaudi began to play with no preamble. They had provided none better.

Gabe leaned back into his seat, holding Francesca's forearm to his chest. The music floated over them, like unseen spirits. He exchanged a glance with Maria Teresa, who sat sphinx-like. Leaning over, he spoke near her ear:

"This is your granddaughter's, ah, *friend.* His name is Sebastian and he is *simpatico.*" With the last word, she beamed a toothy grin, nodded and faced the stage and music. The back-and-forth dialogue in melody—how Gabe heard it—rose in crescendo, then tumbled, like a mountain brook over stones. *Not unlike plot structure in writing.*

He overheard Sebastian sigh—no, *groan*—and the man say in his softly accented English, "I give this song to you, my dear. From the air I pluck it and place it at your feet. It is yours." The Dane then touched her temple gently with his, bandaged and fearsome in aspect.

Well, no wonder—thought Gabe, then he consulted his program. The piece was called *Nuvole Bianche.*

"White Clouds," translated Francesca quietly, as she laid her head on his shoulder, and they let themselves be transported by the truth of the music, the love in the hall and unexpected beauties of life.

Guido's eyes rounded when I walked into the villa's foyer with Sebastian. *"Buonasera, signorina,"* he said and nodded at the imposing, but gentle man beside me.

"Buonasera, Guido. My friend will be staying with me for a few days," I informed him, and he squinted at *my friend,* then smiled. The bandage *was* disconcerting, if strangely reassuring. I'd told Sebastian he looked like a French revolutionary.

He'd started to tell me what happened, but we were distracted by *Nonna's* leave-taking and my wishing to accompany her to her apartment. Once there, she took a long moment to study my features—as Grannie had once taught me, in learning a plant's inward parts. *Stigma, style, and ovary.*

"This man—you love him?" she asked.

"Yes, *Nonna,* very much."

"He *good* to you?"

"Yes." I heard Caroline's concerns, if not her voice.

"Then you are, how you say . . . *lucky,* yes?"

I nodded.

She paused and seemed to scan the room for something. "Then I say goodnight, *bambina.* You go with man now. He hurt head. Almost die. But why die, when sage . . . it grows in your garden?" she asked, and I inhaled and exhaled, *Indeed . . .*

"May I see you tomorrow, *Nonna?"*

"Why not?" she said and rose on her tip-toes to plant a kiss on my cheek. I leaned down and kissed hers. . .

Sebastian spoke my name, calling me back to him. "I'm here," I said, smiling, and taking my room key from Guido's teasing hand, my lover and I climbed the two steep flights to my room. I felt timid, but shot through with joy at the same time.

Gabe and Francesca were expected at her home for a late supper. I felt hungry for both food and Sebastian. The fruit and biscotti in the basket would suffice, I thought. Then, I wondered when he'd last eaten. "Are you hungry?"

He half-smiled. *Oh, his poor face!* A purple bruise, moving into the mustard stage—peeked from beneath the bandage. It gave him a lopsided look, as though he'd been cut from different patterns and badly combined. "May I see?" I asked.

"Oh, Senga, I am all right. Truly. I was lucky. The corner of the man's briefcase missed the artery by two centimeters. I am convinced I was saved for you. If you'll have me."

I held back tears this time, but paid the price exacted by my heart. . .

After holding me for what seemed hours, but only moments, he drew a bath. Time and perspective had stretched, and myself in it. We lighted candles (a drawer contained a box; *oh, these Italians!*), then slowly sank down into hot water. Not wishing to wet my hair, I clipped it on top of my head and watched Sebastian negotiate his movements with (apologies to Gabe) *heightened* awareness, as though I were seeing his naked body for the first time. Time and distance had indeed warped my perceptions. Shrunk them. *God, he's beautiful!* I heard. *Sinew and substance at once.* We semi-reclined at opposite ends of the long bath tub, facing one another.

His limbs were long and glowed in the candlelight. A quiet strength. I had visited the *Uffizi* Galleries and the *Accademia*, and no marble by Michelangelo moved me as much as these bones, flesh and blood. *Spirit counts for a lot,* I conjectured. My eyes naturally fell to his cock, resting neatly against his groin. Under the water, it appeared interested in its surroundings. He saw me regard him and made a sound, then reached for my right foot and began to rub it, while fastening his eyes on mine. I surrendered to his gaze.

Leaning forward, eyes still locked, he reached for the scented bar of soap in the dish. It smelled sharply of rosemary. Then slowly (so slowly I thought I'd have to escape, for fear of joining the molecules of water on a purely cellular level) his eyes moved to further appraise me with his photographic eye, I believe, every *visible* square inch, and I felt—nay, *was* seen, acknowledged, honored and found *true.* My soft parts burned, despite the water.

The steamy alchemy of love.

A musical phrase from "my" song reverberated through me, the notes all *a-ripple,* like dozens of fingers massaging my body. I hummed what I remembered, as I kneeled before him to wash his back. His soft mouth rooted for my breasts, my belly, my armpits. "How fortunate, to recall a tune like that!" he mumbled between possibilities, and then he washed my back, as I buried my face in the soft wet hair of his belly and chest.

380

I poured oil from the small bottle on the tub-side chair. Reaching into the water, I anointed him, then moved to my hands and knees. Clearing my throat, I spoke over my shoulder.

"I've missed you. I've . . . missed this,"—the words coming breathlessly, and I needed him at that moment. Wits deserted me in favor of pure experience.

"I missed you more," he dared to say and, within two seconds, he found his mark, the reference to archery too obvious and I laughed, then coughed, as he brought his point home, further dulling my wit, but not my senses.

"Oh!" I said, "Oh!" Again, and again, my lover reiterated his having missed me, while I twisted and squirmed to draw him deeper. I moved his hand to touch me where my joy resided while another gallon of water sloshed to the floor. His hand cupped my breast and I yielded to the mounting pressure of his need, and *my* desire.

After, I stepped out to mop the water with a towel, and then quickly climbed back in. The bright overhead light left off, we'd bathed solely by candlelight. I'd almost forgotten his injury.

Almost.

"What happened to Peter, again?"

He groaned. "I will tell you, since you are the curious one, but let's not speak of it anymore, please?"

I nodded and he began.

As I reheated the cooling water, I asked, "So he's all right? Really?"

"Yes, as I said. Peter told me he was able to climb away from the tracks, no worse for wear. He called someone on his cell to apprehend the man at the exit, and he was. I was taken to hospital, where they kept me for some time. When I woke, they told me I was . . ." He looked up from the sudsy, scented water, into my eyes. "They were concerned about a possible—" He paused, ". . . epidural hematoma. I looked up the English because I knew you would require the proper term. But I did, and *do* have a massive headache, my dear, and—" His features contorted.

"It's what happened to Emily, Sebastian, but you knew this."

He nodded, his eyes on mine.

"Why were —" I began, "*What* were you doing so close to this person, pooh? I mean, *really*, why would Peter allow you?"

"I have expected this question . . . and I have no answer—save stupidity. It was certainly not his fault. He ordered me to stay back. But in my arrogance, I thought I could help. So, you see, my dear, your lover is foolish."

I groaned a response, then awkwardly turned in order to lie against him. He felt warm and strong and alive. "I was scared, Sebastian," I admitted, as I held my hand under the tap and poured it out onto my belly. "But you're here, safe. . . Have you called Erika to tell her?"

"Yes, at the airport . . . I wanted to take the train, but flew instead, to make up the time."

"So that was you who called Gabe earlier?"

"Yes, and I'm sorry for the intrigue, but I didn't want to. . . You see, I didn't know if I would arrive actually conscious, not to be dramatic, but there it is."

"Oh, Sebastian. . . You are the least dramatic person I know. The *antithesis* of drama, but possibly the most unnerving. . . I'm cold. Let's get out."

We did and dried one another with the thick white towels (warmed on an electric towel bar!), and I stepped to the basket of fruit and biscotti to choose an orange. I placed the sections on a napkin and unwrapped what I considered *cookies*. These I placed on an exquisitely painted, small tray done in blacks, reds and gold leaf. Then, I opened the small refrigerator and asked him what he'd prefer. "And do you want something for the headache?"

He smiled. "No, not yet; and I have something. Maybe at bedtime."

We pulled back the duvet on the bed and crawled naked between the sheets, positioning the tray beside us. *Nonna's* comment surfaced and I jerked my head toward him. "You almost died, Sebastian," I stated. "*Nonna* told me." I ate a section of orange.

"How—*how* would she know? But I am here, am I not? Almost is relative."

"No, it's 'almost,'" said I, handing him a slice. "Oh!" I remembered and crossed to my jacket from whose pocket I drew a bar of dark chocolate.

"The bit of caffeine in this might help your head . . . here." I broke off a piece and held it to his mouth.

"Ever the healer, my dear," he said, and I fed him two more pieces.

We ate in silence, listening to late evening sounds, audible through the closed windows. After, I gathered up remnants of our hasty meal and returned the tray to the table beside the window. The candles had burned down half their length.

"Senga," he said, extending an arm for me. As if my name was charged with power, I responded to the summons and crawled in beside him, my head below his, re-bandaged now and propped on two pillows, against the salmon-colored, tufted headboard. "The music earlier. . ."

"Extraordinary, wasn't it?" I said.

"I had heard of the composer, but only just. '*Nuvole Bianche.*'"

"I thought his name was Ludovi—"

"Yes," he interrupted, "but the piece, your song . . . "White Clouds" . . . *Nuvole Bianche.* I love it . . . and I *adore* you." He squeezed me against him.

I lay still, infused with a musical composition, as an herb exchanges power with its *menstruum* or solvent, and the erotic merged with the spiritual.

Sebastian turned his length to me. . . We made love in 12/8 time, in a minor key, like tides in flux, and laid bare our souls on one another's island bodies in our mermaid sea of love and we summoned one another's demons to be vanquished then banished and we loved one another well and remembered our hidden joys and hungry places as we returned there to find one another again with labored breathing and musky animal smells and soft sounds of present and distant species, then, in the quiet aftermath, I heard a tiny *mew, mew, mew.*

Had a kitten made her way into our room?

But no; it was my soul, rendered bare and pulsing, a raw and exposed star, peeled to her most hidden aspect, very much a small, silver, quivering orb.

CHAPTER 57
A DELICATE MATTER

Black Hills, Winter Solstice

Sebastian returned to Denmark from Italy, and I didn't see him until solstice evening at his home in Spearfish, where, with his family, we prepared a feast (including my squash soup). They arrived the day before and passed the morning of the twenty-first in the National Forest, seeking the perfect spruce. Later, they searched high and low for Aunt Karen's box of decorations, only to discover them in the lift-top bench in the foyer. She'd preferred old-fashioned candles to electric lights, and everyone but Erika and Sebastian was forbidden to enter the area, where stood the tree, until permitted.

At the appointed time, every light was extinguished in the house, to signify the darkest, longest night of the year. At Sebastian's merry call, we firmly shut our eyes, giving way to darkness, and waited for Erika and her father to lead us from the den. Standing behind me, he covered my eyes with his hands.

"Ready, my dear?"

I nodded. And may have gasped. Before us blazed a splendid apparition of joy. Joe Rafaela had once handed me a quote by the Quaker poet, John Greenleaf Whittier. It sprung to mind: *Nothing before, nothing behind. The steps of faith fall on the seeming void and find the rock beneath.*

Jytte squealed. Peter sighed. Sebastian and Erika grinned. After much praising, we drank *gløg,* a warmed drink made with port and brandy, flavored with spices, slivered almonds and raisins. Jytte was allotted a small amount diluted with hot water. More praise ensued. The faces of everyone radiated wonderment, happiness and love in the candlelight. Candles flickered everywhere, not confined to the tree.

Later, our lovemaking was necessarily subdued, on account of his family's proximity, but it was warm and gentle, as the entire evening had been.

That was only three nights ago. What happened in-between was this: I found a business card in my lover's wallet with a woman's name, followed by, *Doctor of Psychiatry,* printed in French, with a Paris address. I was not snooping. Sebastian had asked me to remove some bills for a Salvation Army donation as he filled the car with gas, and the card was tucked in beside them. When I asked about it he hesitated, and no one recognizes misdirection as well as someone who's employed it, so I questioned him further, teasingly. He was not amused and suggested I was looking for trouble. *Was I?* No. But I was seeking answers.

Who carries a psychiatrist's card? I asked him. "It's a simple question," I pressed. My mother's experience fed irrational fears. So, this was our first disagreement, if it could be called such. . . I sensed Sebastian was stalling for time, and for a reason. *All right,* I thought, so I changed subjects entirely, to offer him that time.

I mentioned, off-hand, the shrine Rob had placed at the spot where Emily was born, that we could go see it, if he liked.

He swerved the car to the curb and lurched to a stop. The driver behind laid on his horn and just missed our left fender. The consequent silence felt as if all oxygen escaped the vehicle. I sat, trembling, and looked at him with concern. "What's the matter?" I demanded, finally.

He seemed in pain, as though anticipating a bursting blood vessel and wishing his suffering to end. And then he spoke, evenly and quietly, "This—*Rob*—did *not*. . ." He stopped. I realized I'd never seen him upset. This was new territory— scorched earth—and my feet were being held to the fire. I remained mute. Sebastian stared from his window for a long moment, then took a breath and quietly asked, "Why do you say he put the shrine there?"

I looked at him through eyes that watered and stung as I realized my mistake, my colossal mistake. *Oh, God.*

"I—I'm sorry, Sebastian. I . . . *You* made it? I . . ."

He stared at me, mute, his furrowed cheeks moving with clamping jaws and I beheld, for the first time, by some means of projection or *sight,* what those eyes had witnessed—the final, fatal knowledge he had penetrated in watching life ebb from my Emily; she'd survived the fall, as he'd held her broken body to him, only to die in his arms, as he waited for my hurried descent from the cliff. He'd protected me from a terrible knowing. I would protect him in return. I nodded my excruciating understanding, as he nodded back to me. We sat, absorbing his truth.

Regarding the present misunderstanding, I had hurt him deeply and there were no words. *How* had I presumed Rob had created the shrine? *His presence, for one, and the song. . .* And how to remedy this? I wondered, as I gazed out my window to last minute Christmas shoppers and rushing traffic. "Forgive me," I feebly repeated, raising my palm to my mouth in consternation, humiliation and remorse.

Sebastian put the Volvo in drive and we slowly pulled away. He began speaking about this woman Danica, to address my utterly forgotten concern. I listened without interrupting; still feeling I'd shattered trust in an unconscious fit of pique. But, I hadn't been alone in it, had I? We'd managed to do this together. Or, was it simply the cost of relating? Sometimes things get broken.

And that's how the light gets in.

I made a sound at Leonard Cohen's lyric and Sebastian looked over to me.

"You laugh?"

"No—I'm sorry—again. . . Something occurred to me that was—apt, I guess. Wha—*what* were you saying?"

He paused. Undoubtedly waiting for my consciousness to clear. "She had been abused, Senga, by several men."

"Mm." I swallowed moaned and turned away. "Could we park for a minute? I need to be looking at you," I said, as I avoided his gaze.

"Agreed. That pub?"

"Yes. Please."

After ordering beers, we passed two hours catching up with our delicate truths, as we held them, seeking and finding one another yet again. I wept when he described the day he created

Emily's birth shrine: his search for the perfect handmade bowl and having it inscribed. Then, imagining my discovery. My not having actually discussed it with Rob eased his mind, I sensed, from a tiny, candle-lit corner of my heart.

He talked of meeting Danica and her mother, and detailed his earlier encounter ten years ago. When he admitted her "strange" interest in him, I bristled; *not so strange,* I quietly countered. I was, at last, able to fully exhale when he reached across the small pub table, to palm my wet cheek with his large rough hand, and utter my name.

"Senga."

EPILOGUE

We may let go of everything but our own hearts. I returned to Starwallow, leaving Sebastian and his family at *Fred*, his home named for the peace I couldn't conjure. Sebastian tried, mildly, to change my mind, citing the living loves among us. He faded to a snowy blur in my rear-view mirror, as he resignedly watched me drive away, into late afternoon snow, to be with my daughter's memory.

His granddaughter Jytte is so like Emily was. Even in age. Coloring, too. Her sweet, but *edgy* humor—all Sebastian's. When we were introduced three days ago, I felt heat rise to my face, and pressure build behind my eyes. I wanted to weep, but didn't. Sebastian never intimated how similar they looked, but he didn't know my Emily when she was . . . as *vibrant* as this child. The eyes; those sparkling, bright blue eyes, and the near-white hair.

We may let go of everything but our own hearts.

I returned to spinning wool, my winter pastime. The Ashford wheel resides opposite the fire this time of year, released from its dark corner in the bedroom. I imagined strands of Emily's long, silky hair being drawn through my fingers and twisting around wooly filaments, creating a twice-strong fiber. More memory than imagination; she and I experimented with using hair from our brushes and that of a neighbor's pet Angora goat. The soothing clatter of the wheel's revolutions worked their magic, as the glory robe enveloped me.

All senses ultimately flow into "a one big one," as Grannie's just-deceased friend had once declared to her in a dream. My own glory robe was necessarily cut from different cloth: I *saw* white hair in my mind's eye, but emotion flooded, overruling sensory input.

Erika is stunning—her father's daughter. Peter? Kinder than kind. He apologized for Sebastian's injury and blames himself.

I reached to stop the wheel, and leaned to the work basket on the floor for more wool. Putting my foot to the treadle again and moving the wheel forward, the kinky tuft turned on itself, a fantastical insect spinning its own cocoon. My thread grew longer, to be twisted onto a spool and, later, double plied.

Thoughts found easy discourse with themselves by the repetitive action. Much as during walks. A looping electric current, discovering a never-ending source of images, observations, judgment and reflection, egged on by the inexorable bounty of a warm fire, bubbled in the cauldron of my mind. . .

I've recorded nothing since leaving for Italy, poor chronicler that I am. I let myself be swept to another universe and permitted nothing to take the place of actual experience, save a few photographs. I made no note of *many* things, including an extraordinary sight in the night sky, during our flight home, between Detroit and Rapid City.

Here, I must.

I hadn't wanted to rouse Gabe, who was dozing, but this wasn't the only reason. The phenomenon was personal. A selfish notion, but there it was. I told him about it on our drive from Rapid City. He was disappointed, but (I believe) could not have spotted it in time, and I may have missed it for gaining his attention. It was a *singularity* (not in the astronomical sense); an, "in the moment," event—as so many are. The image is seared behind my eyelids, with blinding impact, demanding testimony: In the plane, I'd claimed the window seat and had just been served a cup of tea. After a sip, I idly gazed into the night sky, when a star—growing brighter, and *yet* brighter, held me fast. I watched it recede to its original magnitude and *seemingly* disappear altogether.

We may let go of everything but our own hearts.

Gabe wondered if I'd (*merely*) seen a falling star, one perhaps headed straight on, rather than a nova. *Or,* according to recent observation, black holes swallow (*gulp!*) stars, which cause them to burn brightly, in successive bursts, before succumbing to oblivion. *Or,* an *iridium* flare, from a gaseous nebula, was another possibility.

I consulted the Web for mention of a nova on that particular evening, but found nothing to corroborate it. So, "It's a mystery!" Joe's blithe answer for much in life.

As novas are stars that died millennia ago, a wonder, my sighting of the hunter and the two persons below the Leap are supported, in *my* universe. Time is not what we believe it is. Or, even what we *think;* it is more elastic, and moveable, like a *feast;* like Hemingway's Paris—which, in keeping, brings me, finally, to my sojourn in Italy. . .

Journal Entry, Christmas Eve

I mailed postcards nearly every day—to the Stricklands (and Joey), to Muriel, to Marie, to Joe and, to myself. Oh, and one to Charlie Mays at the Sara's Spring Police Department. Sebastian remained with me five nights and insisted on paying for my entire two-week stay. I, in turn, offered to pay for our dinners and brooked no argument. He allowed me three meals for my vanity, he said. Pride, I corrected.

Because of Sebastian and Francesca, Gabe and I enjoyed an incomparable experience.

We ate wild boar at a hilltop restaurant, drank excellent wine (except Sebastian, who abstained, until his headache subsided on the day before he left us). We passed two days in Florence, visiting museums and gardens. We shopped at the old market beside the Duomo and rubbed the bronze boar's worn muzzle, to guarantee a return trip. We ended our visit with a twilight horse-and-buggy tour of the historic city center.

Francesca showed us the American Cemetery near Florence, where hundreds of soldiers lay buried, including many from the "Buffalo Soldiers" regiment. Nonno insisted she take us; Gabe, in particular. From the highway, the memorial is nestled against a green sward of hillside, its high obelisk bearing witness in stone to the somber gravity of the place. The Earth holds these lives—and deaths—dear. We were moved by the significance, intent and effort to immortalize the warriors, but my words sound hollow in light and recollection of so many graves.

Standing several feet from me, I noticed Gabe, holding very still, with his hat in his hand as though in prayer, contemplating a headstone. Sebastian and Francesca conversed a few yards away. Nonchalantly, I started in Gabe's direction, reading the markers as I went, and here, was his very own nova:

Belizaire, Thomas J., PFC

The name stared from white stone, below an etched cross.

"Gabe," I said quietly.

He grunted. "Well, it gave me a turn."

"I expect so."

"My little brother—the one who drowned?—was named Tom. Grave's back home."

"Oh Gabe. Do you think Nonno knew? I mean, about this one?"

"Hard to say with him. I had an Uncle Tom— don't laugh—who was killed in the war. My great uncle. But I never knew much about it. I'll have to ask my daddy. . . In writing, you aren't allowed to come up with this stuff, you know."

"Even 'truth being stranger than'—and all that?" I proposed.

"Well."

"Take a picture of it anyway. In case. Besides, it'll mean something to your dad—the name and all."

He made another sound, put his hat back on and took his phone from his jacket pocket. I spotted a small black pebble on the ground. Basalt? Stooping, I laid my palm on the earth beside it, then placed the stone on the marker. Left of center. It suggested an oddly comforting symmetry. The Yang in the Yin. Gabe gave me a half-smile. Photo made, we joined Sebastian and Francesca, who wanted to see the grave for themselves, when told.

Maybe his little brother's grave figured, but Gabe's demeanor altered that day. He grew introspective and quiet. The next day, he bought a ring for Francesca—a beautifully simple style, with a single ruby. I believe part of my friend's soul remained behind in Italy, in her care. And maybe that of Private Belizaire, First Class.

Erratic Thought, Number? Travel.

Uttered in the imperative case, and heeded, I am called to consider the word daily, and to return home each evening to a lighted candle named Sebastian, or, to a certain juniper tree. I journey between them. The tenacity of fate clings to each of us, ergo, may we explore while we can still pass through time.

My self-imposed, nineteen-year exile in "upper-lower Slovobia," (as Gabe once dubbed our rural geography) ended with Sebastian's arrival, as though someone knocked on my cabin door and I opened to this person, who said, "Please, come with me,"—and I have. As pilgrim. But what *precipitated it?*

I hear something outside . . .

Jingling bells and an eerie procession of candlelight greeted me, as I stepped away from my porch to see who had arrived. Snow had fallen lightly through the evening. I inhabited a snow globe. Jytte appeared first through the flakes, wearing an impossibly wonderful hat, of red wool, with a green tassel and several jingle bells. She was followed by Erika and Peter. Each held a candle, with threatened flame guarded by cupped hand, and none was extinguished by the wet flakes.

Sebastian brought up the rear, holding aloft and ringing a fistful of large, round bells on a leather strap, once part of a harness, I surmised. Their grinning faces broke into song when they saw me. *"Glædelig Yul!"* they cried, followed by *Good King Wenceslaus* sung in Danish.

It was magic. They were magic. *All* was magic.

Once inside, after hugs and kisses, a hasty rearrangement of chairs and being shown the bed for coats and the bathroom for such needs, Sebastian stoked my neglected fire and Peter fetched more split wood from the stack beneath the porch. Jytte wanted to investigate Emily's ever-decorated juniper tree with Erika.

They brought dinner, telling me they couldn't abide (*yes, abide!*) my being alone on this of all nights.

There were gifts—small wrapped packages in brown paper, tied with simple white string and sprigs of evergreen; "For long life," explained Jytte. They had brought their presents, still wrapped, I'd brought from Italy: a Florentine journal for Jytte; stationery for Erika; a wallet for Peter; and, for Sebastian, a handsome *sommelier's* corkscrew. I'd also found him a merino turtleneck, in a shade like his eyes, but decided to wait to present it.

"You're staying, aren't you?" I whispered to him.

"What did the salty, ah, *old* sailor say to the land-locked mermaid on the eve of Christmas?"

"Not with everyone here, Sebastian," I replied with a scowl.

"Precisely, my dear!" he whispered into my ear, then playfully bit the lobe.

"*Ow!*"

"Father, can you not wait until we leave?" teased Erika. Jytte giggled. I smiled.

"Peter," I said, switching subjects, "do you know anything about Larissa's case? You know, the Russian woman who was being kept prisoner?"

Erika gave her husband a quick glance. The covered dishes waited on the table after warming in my oven. I'd placed a stack of plates beside the cutlery.

"Her brother, Sasha, has returned to Petersburg," Peter said, "I'm sorry I can't tell you more. . . The woman, however, is remaining here to testify against her captors. I know this: she is *brave*," and he returned to his wife an equally inscrutable look.

I guessed it a matter of discretionary protocol.

As I lacked an indoor tree, we simply arranged the gifts on a tray, and set them aside until later. Erika had brought yet *more* candles and Jytte began lighting these, placing them high and low. The little room glowed with well-being and something Erika called *hygge*, pronounced "hue-gah." Sebastian had used it once; a difficult word to translate but, he'd tried: "*Cozy, content and convivial. To belong. Oh, and, 'candles, many candles',*" he'd added. And so it seemed. I was reminded, simply, of that which we call *God*.

The phone rang, interrupting our *cozy* party. It was Caroline.

"Merry Christmas, neighbor," I greeted her.

"Not yet, hon," she corrected me, "How're you doing?"

"Right as rain, Caroline. Sebastian and his family are here with me. How're y'all?"

"Oh! Well, how nice! We're good. Joey, Gabe and Rufus are playing cut-throat pinochle, and I'm building a cake for tomorrow. Come over sometime for a piece. It's got apple cider in it, some of your apples and pecans. Oh, and Bourbon. It'll be good."

"I'll bet. Thanks! What time?"

"Oh, any time, hon. And Santa's leaving something here for you—I think."

"Oh, Caroline, you shouldn't have."

"*I* didn't. I said *Santa*," and she hung up.

"Bye, Caroline," I said as I replaced the phone on its cradle.

Sebastian handed me my glass and we toasted one another's health, "*Skål!*" with *Akvavit*, before eating, while Erika reheated a traditional Danish supper of soup, bread and pickled vegetables. Herring as well—the kind soaked in sour cream and sold in small jars. We popped open the *crackers* Jytte handed out and laughed, Sebastian insisting we all don our paper crowns. I mentioned thinking this was an English custom and Peter said, rightfully, "Why should they have all the fun?"

When we finished, I cleared the table with Erika's help, and we washed and dried the few dishes. Peter, Sebastian and Jytte went outdoors to view the sky, mainly to search for sign of my star. There were none visible, on account of clouds and light snowfall. "Pity," said Sebastian. Peter wondered if the star of Bethlehem might have been one going nova over several weeks. "It would account for the Magi's curiosity and perseverance," he added.

Sebastian's son-in-law regarded me as somewhat peculiar, I thought, after learning of my claim—as in the odds being *astronomical*, pun intended. "Think of all that sky, and you happen to look at one coordinate at the same instant it explodes!"

I grinned, "Yes, well, fortune smiles on the prepared, they say." I looked at Sebastian, "And, it *could* have just been, as Gabe wondered, a falling star." My lover pulled me to him, while shaking his head; he kissed my forehead and pronounced it A Miracle, whatever I'd seen.

It's good to be cherished.

We opened gifts and everyone was gracious. From Erika, Peter and Jytte, I received a silk scarf in blues and greens. Sebastian gave me a bottle of scent—Chanel No. 19—adding it was one of his favorites. I secretly hoped it wasn't something his wife had worn, and promptly regretted it. He must have guessed my thought and later told me that Elsa couldn't wear perfume. "Allergic," he said. I'd never worn any, having no disposable income for such, but this fragrance reminded me of something—*someone*—and I wracked my brain to remember. It would come, I knew. Scent and memory share the strongest tie.

Sebastian's family left about nine o'clock in his Volvo, with clear directions back to Spearfish and *Fred*. At their leaving, we hugged and wished one another *god yul,* and Sebastian promised we'd return sometime between one and three o'clock tomorrow, to enjoy a late Christmas dinner with them. Erika insisted her father be there to help in the kitchen, and I couldn't begrudge her feelings. She was showing me magnanimous generosity of spirit.

My best gift was having him stay.

Alone with him and a dangerous number of lighted candles, I suddenly felt shy.

He smiled and said, "I will only be a moment," and went out the door.

I took a deep breath, let it out slowly, and began to return the room to its previous state. When he reappeared, he was carrying a large, a *very* large wrapped item. *A photograph,* I guessed, by its weighty dimensions. Oh, twenty-four by sixty-six inches? Give or take. I sat down in my wing chair and gazed up at him, still awkwardly reticent.

"Happy Christmas, my dear," he said, as he leaned the gift against the wall. It was plainly wrapped in white paper, with brown jute tied in a bow, signifying its purpose.

"Thank you," I said, "*Where* did you hide it?" I wondered if I should rise to fetch his other gift now, or wait. He ignored my question.

"Please. Open it."

We were more than a *little* inebriated. I melted at his dear, quiet insistence, a child-like glee, and began to untie the cord.

The paper fell away and I sucked in my breath. "Oh, Sebastian," I whispered, and then I giggled.

"Do you like it?"

"I *love* it." I reached for his shoulder, to pull his face to mine and I kissed him. He tasted of caraway and a lingering breath of *Akvavit* still tasted hot in his mouth. I watched him prop the photo. It was framed in the modern fashion and matted in soft gray board.

A photograph from that day, weeks ago now.

In it, I am looking over my shoulder (at him), with an expression of coquettish pleasure, while leaning over the side board in his aunt's home. My right hand is poised to wind an antique clock; my right breast, uncovered (as is the rest of me), is partly in shadow. My back is straight, and my buttocks—a sweeping *blur*—from the quick, sassy motion of my having just swayed them. The technical aspects, about which I know little, seemed perfect; lighting, composition, the subject's—*what?*

We may let go of everything but our own hearts.

He watched me study it, then, speaking in a near-whisper, asked: "*And what did the mermaid desire, more than anything in the world?*"

Starwallow

ACKNOWLEDGMENTS

The folks I would heartily thank remain those listed in the first novel of this series. Several bear repeating: To my husband Jeff, for bemused acceptance of my later-blooming interest in writing novels; to my children, AdriAnne and John, for their continued encouragement, and their families, for giving me such joy; to Gabe, the yellow Lab, for comic relief; to those who provided reviews and blurbs, my everlasting thanks: Laura Jones; The Prairies Book Reviewer; Kevin Sweeney; Andrelle Hummel and Morgan Callan Rogers; you all primed the pump, as we say. Thank you for your generous spirits. To long-time friend Linda Spears, for lending her eyes and intellect.

To Candace Christofferson, for once again providing gorgeous art for the cover, thank you; also, for teaching me to read more dramatically at book signings. I am a singer/guitarist and performer, but an abyss yawns between the two genres. I suppose I could put a passage to music and sing it. *Hmmm.*

To the Hulett, Wyoming, Library ladies, Nancy and Echo, who organized the first reading on an icy December day and provided hot soup, deep gratitude for your kindness. To Sabrina Heredia at Antuñez in Spearfish, for a "pub party" and reading, muchas gracias, amiga. To Sue McBride, of The Whistle Stop Bookstore in Douglas, Wyoming, thank you for the book signing and gathering familiar faces from thirty years ago. To Sarah Pridgeon, award-winning reporter of The Sundance Times, for being a delight to work with, and whose editing much improved the story; deep bows of admiration and thanks. All errors herein are mine.

As I mentioned after the first volume, if you were moved and feel inclined, please leave a review wherever possible, and word of mouth, after laughter, remains the best medicine.

"Senga lives!" proclaimed a friend after reading the first novel in the Riven Country Series. It might have proven an apt title for the second book, given her choice to engage once more with life after a prolonged period of grief. Does it work this way? A conscious decision to simply return to the fray? Or, as curious creatures, are we enticed and programmed in the end to find out what happens? At last, an abiding desire to be present? To belong? I believe something like this moved our Senga.

May it touch each of you, my friends, as you navigate an increasingly busy river of obstacles and misery. Our world is beset by a killing virus as I prepare this title for publication. May you and your loved ones be safe and sound.

Lastly, I thank each of you who chose to pick up a novel by an unknown author. I am grateful and humbled by your faith, and I hope you find Senga's story a continuing feast, as have I in the telling.

ABOUT THE AUTHOR

As a child, Renée lived in France and five Southern states, 'migrating' to Wyoming at eighteen to attend the university, where she earned a B.A in French. Having lived in rural Wyoming for over four decades, she remains its "student of place."

Renée and her husband, a retired school superintendent, tend an apple farm, a too-large garden, raise garlic and herbs—medicinal and culinary. Their children are grown and live out-of-state. In 2018, she was awarded the Frank Nelson Doubleday Writing Award by the Wyoming Arts Council. She is indebted to the organization for this, and for their assistance with developmental grants.

Renée sings and play the odd musical performance, and practices family herbalism—which winds its way into her writing, "like possessed vines."

She is currently preparing the third book in *The Riven Country Series* for publication, and drafting a nonfiction narrative called CROFTER, *A Wyoming Homestead Manual and Radical Memoir, Rooted in Place."*

To inquire about booking a speaking engagement, or to purchase inscribed books, please visit the following links:

reneecarrier.wordpress.com
Instagram@reneecarrierauthor
Twitter@reneecarrier12
reneecarrier11@gmail.com

READ ON FOR AN EXERPT FROM

EARTHBOUND
by Renée Carrier

Book Three of *The Riven Country Series*
Available late 2020 or early 2021

OF SINGING STONE

H is mother had always addressed him by his first and last name—the one from her, the other from his father. *Tom Robinson, better take out that trash! Tom Robinson, how was school?* Tom Robinson had worked at the monument for twenty-seven years as chief of maintenance, and had recently found himself daydreaming about extended fishing trips. He knew he needed to work another three years to ensure a decent retirement, so why now? Too early to be going off the rails. . .

The season was gearing up and, already, park visitor numbers were growing. Tour buses pulled in daily with Chinese, Japanese, French, German and American-Association-of-Retired persons. School was still in session, and tour companies took advantage of the shoulder season when students were still in lock-up, TR's acerbic conclusion. TR was what his minions called him, after Teddy Roosevelt, the president who had established the monument in 1906.

Growing up in the area, Tom learned he was handy. He welcomed the fix-or-repair dailiness of his job, when dealing with people didn't interfere. His most difficult challenge at first lay in summoning the patience to explain a chore to a crew; to not say "screw it," and do the thing himself. He liked the winter season best, when he and the animals had the park mostly to themselves. The rangers were dutifully occupied and he had a good working relationship with most of them. The Visitor Center bookstore employed several people, but he rarely saw them, even when repairing a leaky faucet or installing a new counter. He ignored staff in favor of less tame inhabitants.

Devils Tower exuded its force of presence best when frosty air wrapped it in cold; when it punctuated the stillness; when a slight tap to one of its hard surfaces pinged, like a becalmed ship's bell in the fog. The composition of the "igneous intrusion" (one of several geological theories) was porphyry phonolite—the latter term, for sound made by the rock when struck. Singing stone figured in Tom's way of thinking. He didn't remember why this feature impressed him, but it had since he was young. His mother had blithely told him that the rock spoke to him. So, he'd organized his life to seek work in the park, failing to understand that leisure time, in which to listen to what the rock might impart, would be necessarily circumscribed by long hours in service to America's first national monument.

Her gender was calculated. He'd figured that out long ago; not that the rock was female. He'd ascribed the sex to the park, herself. It may have had to do with Mother Nature. If anything, the Tower had a decidedly male bent. Even one of its indigenous names was Elk Penis. How he'd laughed when a ranger told him that one. No; he was married to the park and he cared for her—what his mother had once told him a man did for a wife. What his father had not done.

His mother had lived with him at the Tower until her death last year. He missed her. As head of maintenance, he'd been assigned one of the housing units on the grounds and felt lucky to be able to walk out his door and cross the road to the "shed" every day, where his office was located. It was a large, efficient government building that housed equipment and tools. Tom took pride in keeping it orderly and clean. It was how he liked his personal life as well.

Then came the day in Sara's Spring last fall, when he'd had to step in to keep a woman from foolishly stabbing a man with what looked to be a very large knife. She'd come unstrung at a customer who'd called her "a lover of n—." His mother had taught him never to use the slur for Blacks. As he yanked the woman back, he recalled telling her trash wasn't worth jail time.

The grocery clerk had called the woman a root digger, and he remembered Rufus Strickland mentioning their neighbor. Tom had noticed her from time to time in town over the years. After the incident, he'd called the ranch to see if the woman was all right. Caroline Strickland hadn't seemed too surprised by the behavior.

Senga Munro. . .

Renée Carrier

Also by Renée Carrier

A Singular Notion, published by Pronghorn Press
Essays and Memoir

The Riven Country Series
Braeburn Croft Press

> *The Riven Country of Senga Munro*, Book I
> *Starwallow*, Book II

Starwallow

Renée Carrier

Starwallow

Renée Carrier

Made in the USA
Coppell, TX
05 December 2020